"It is a knowledgeable herbalist I speak of . . ."

He rocked back upon his heels and crossed his arms against his chest. "And who might this herbalist be? I should like to search out the charlatan and tell him what I think of his quackery."

"Quackery?" Isabel spit out the affront. "You're no better than Wooster Farley." She beat a rhythm on her collarbone with her thumb. "Me, Mr. Adair. I'm the charlatan. And it will be a cold day in hell before I turn over the key to *my* building to you!"

Jove titles by C. J. Card

ONE WISH
MY LOVING FAMILIAR

My Loving Familiar

C. J. CARD

JOVE BOOKS, NEW YORK

MAGICAL LOVE is a trademark of Penguin Putnam Inc.

MY LOVING FAMILIAR

A Jove Book / published by arrangement with
the author

PRINTING HISTORY
Jove edition / January 2000

All rights reserved.
Copyright © 2000 by Carol Card Otten.
This book may not be reproduced in whole or in part,
by mimeograph or any other means, without permission.
For information address: The Berkley Publishing Group,
a division of Penguin Putnam Inc.,
375 Hudson Street, New York, New York 10014.

The Penguin Putnam Inc. World Wide Web site address is
http://www.penguinputnam.com

ISBN: 0-515-12728-0

A JOVE BOOK®
Jove Books are published by The Berkley Publishing Group,
a division of Penguin Putnam Inc.,
375 Hudson Street, New York, New York 10014.
JOVE and the "J" design
are trademarks belonging to Penguin Putnam Inc.

PRINTED IN THE UNITED STATES OF AMERICA

10 9 8 7 6 5 4 3 2 1

DIVINE INSPIRATION

*They come to sit on the table by the writer,
keeping his thoughts company, and gazing
at him with intelligent tenderness and magical penetration.
It seems as though cats divine the thought that is
passing from the brain to the pen, and that as they
stretch out a paw, they are trying to seize it on its way.*

—Theophile Gautier (1811–1872)

This book is dedicated to my own divine inspirations:

In loving memory of my sable Burmese,

MOO

and

to my very much alive British Shorthair,

SIMON

Prologue

~

St. Augustine, Florida
1877

"Tell me the legend again, Mama," Isabel Farley begged between tears. "Please!"

Mother and daughter leaned against the joined oak and palm that grew on the property—property that no longer belonged to her mother. The thought made Isabel's twelve-year-old body tremble with anger. Everything, including her, now belonged to her stepfather, Wooster Farley, and had since a year ago when he had married her widowed half Seminole mother, Kalee Gomez.

It wasn't fair that the Gomez land that had belonged to her father's family now belonged to a man who cared nothing about it, or his acquired family. It wasn't fair that she, Isabel Gomez, wasn't allowed to keep her birth name.

She fought back another bout of tears and let the breeze from nearby Matanzas Bay cool her heated skin. The soft current of air scented with a mixture of briny water and sun-baked sand made the Spanish moss sway like an old man's beard. Oblivious to the drama taking place at the base of the tree, a laughing gull cackled as he flew over the treetops, and from a leafy branch above their heads a fat brown squirrel chipped away at a cup-shaped acorn.

"I'll tell you the legend," her mother said, bringing Isabel back to the moment, "but you must promise your *madre* that you will cease your weeping." She trapped a tear with the edge of her work-worn finger before Isabel buried her head in the crook of her arms. "Only crocodiles, my sweet, are allowed such tears."

Kalee ran her hand over her daughter's honey-colored hair. This child was so like her father, the golden-haired Spaniard who hailed from a country across the sea. Pico Gomez had stolen her heart the first day she had laid eyes upon him in the city market, and he had broken her heart when he died a premature death last year. But her pain was nothing compared to that of her daughter's. Kalee hated her second husband, whose cruelty made Isabel shed such heartfelt tears.

The knobby elbows and knees that hid the child's face reminded Kalee of the cypress trees that grew farther south in Florida's swampy interior. When she thought of the swamp where most of her mother's people now lived, a yearning to join them surfaced. She fought the feeling as Isabel raised her head and rubbed a fist across her amber-colored eyes.

"How can you stay with a man who treats you so?" Isabel asked.

"Curb your tongue, daughter. He is your father now and deserves your respect."

Isabel studied her mother's unhappy expression. Determined to whisk away the sadness, she leaned closer and whispered, "I love you, Mama. See, I have stopped crying crocodile tears. Will you not tell your favorite child the legend now?"

"My favorite child indeed!" Her mother laughed. "You are my only child."

The sound of her mother's laughter reminded Isabel of happier times before her papa's death.

Draping her arm around her daughter's shoulders, Kalee leaned her head back against the trunk. "The legend," she said, and began to recite the story that had been passed down from her ancestors. Ancestors who came from tribes such as the Euchee, Yamasee, Timugua, Tequesta, Abalachi, Coca, who lived as the "free people" across the head of the Florida peninsular. It was the English speakers who ignored the free peoples' separate tribal affiliations and called them all Seminoles.

"Some say the legend began at this very tree," Kalee said, pointing upward into the branches where their cat, Grimalkin, sat listening to the tale. "It was where the two lovers met secretly and fell in love."

"And also met their death," Isabel added. She had heard the story so many times that she knew it as well as her mother, but she never tired of hearing her mama retell it.

"They were two people from very different cultures. The girl was an Indian maiden, the man a Spanish soldier."

"Like you and my real *padre*."

"Your *padre* was not a soldier, little one. He was a respected merchant." Her mother brushed Isabel's forehead with a light kiss.

"Like you are a respected healer, Mama."

"I try to be," her mother answered, before continuing with the tale.

"The maiden was the only daughter of a great chief with many sons, and also his last born. It was only natural that she would be the old chief's pride and joy. Not only was the maiden beautiful outside, but she was also beautiful inside. All the young braves in the tribe competed for the maiden's hand, but she had promised herself that she would not take a husband whom she did not love. Because her father adored and indulged her in all things, he believed when his daughter was ready to settle down, she would choose a brave worthy of her love, and his respect.

"Don't forget," Isabel interrupted, "that she was as tall and as sturdy as a lodge pole while all the other squaws of the people were short and squatty and not nearly as lovely."

Her mother smiled. "The maiden was also as graceful as a swaying palm.

"It was on market day when the Indian maiden first met the Spaniard who was fresh off a big canoe from Spain. The soldier was so handsome and built as burly as an oak that the maiden fell immediately in love and decided that he was the one she had been waiting for all her life. The Spaniard, too, was enamored of the maiden, but there was such animosity between the Indians and the whites that a union between them was frowned upon by both peoples."

"So the lovers had to meet secretly," Isabel said. "Not an easy task when she had so many brothers who kept a close watch over her."

"Right," her mama agreed, picking up the story where Isabel left off. "The Spaniard couldn't stand being separated from the maiden any longer, and being an honorable man, he insisted it was time he ask the old chief for his daughter's hand.

"The old chief, who hated all white men, forbade his daughter to marry the Spaniard or to have anything more to do with the soldier. It was time, her father decided, that he pick a suitable brave for his daughter. But until a husband could be found, she was to be kept under close supervision by her many brothers.

"The maiden grieved for her Spaniard, and her grief made her very ill. Her mother, who loved her only daughter very much, feared for her child's health and decided to go against her husband's orders. She would help her daughter and the Spaniard elope. Since her marriage to the chief had been a love match, the wise squaw felt that once the couple were married, her husband of many moons would see how happy they were, and he would accept their marriage. A rendezvous was planned."

"At this very oak," Isabel said.

Kalee nodded her head. "Unbeknownst to the two women, one of the maiden's many brothers was listening outside their tent. The brave waited in the shadows until he saw his mother and sister leave, then he sought out his brothers. The brothers agreed to follow the women, and when the Spaniard appeared, they would kill him, knowing the Spaniard's death would make them revered in their father's eyes."

Isabel snuggled closer into her mother's embrace. "Although this is the sad part, it's the part I like best." She waited for her mother to continue.

"The brothers trailed the two women to this tree where the young couple were to meet. Then they hid in the bushes and waited for the soldier to appear. Many suns had passed since the lovers had last met, and when they saw each other again they stood apart, drinking in the other with their eyes. The pause was the perfect time for the braves to attack. But when the arrows flew, the two lovers also flew into each other's arms. When they embraced, one arrow traveled through the Spaniard's back, piercing his heart, then lodged in the heart of the maiden. The lovers died in each other's arms."

Looking upward into the overhead branches, Isabel said, "That is why this oak and palm grow together from the same root."

Her mother's gaze followed her daughter's. "That is what is said. The oak embraces the trunk of the palm. It is believed that the two trees growing together as they do are a symbol of the young couple's love."

Isabel sighed. "When I grow up, and if I should marry, I want my husband to ask for my hand beneath these two trees that grow as one."

"And if he does," her mother added, "your marriage will be a lasting one filled with much happiness."

"Not like yours with Wooster."

"You must call him Father," her mother cautioned.

"I—"

"An obedient daughter does as she is told." Her mother stood, extending her hand toward Isabel. "Do you want me to finish the story?"

Isabel nodded.

"Then come, little one, we have work to do in the garden. I'll tell you the ending on our way there."

Isabel knew her parent was trying to distract her. Because of the pained expression on her mama's face, Isabel kept her own council on what she would call Wooster Farley.

"Let me finish, Mama," Isabel said instead. "I like this part of the story, too.

"When the couple fell to the ground with their life's blood pooling around them, the braves were fearful. They had not meant to kill their sister. Once their father learned that his only girl child had died from his sons' arrows, they would be banished from their tribe forever. So the braves retrieved their arrows and removed all traces that they had done the deed.

"Before they left, the brothers arranged the bodies side-by-side. They removed an amber crucifix from around the Spaniard's neck, positioning it between the couple on the black cushion of their hair.

"When the old chief learned of the death of his only daughter, he was stricken with remorse and guilt. He believed that if he had sanctioned the marriage between his daughter and the Spaniard, maybe her death could have been avoided. To atone for his guilt, he ordered that the couple be taken to the sacred burial ground where they could spend the after-journey together. It was night when the Indians returned for the two bodies. Instead of finding them as they expected to, they found instead a huge black cat with amber-gold eyes sitting on the very spot where the young couple had died.

"When a thorough search of the area turned up no bodies, the chief ordered that the cat be brought back to the village, where it could live out the length of its days without fearing for its survival. When his sons tried to capture the animal, the regal beast leaped into the sky, never to be seen again."

Isabel pondered the ending before she spoke. "You know what I think, *madre?* I think the velvet darkness of the night sky is the fur of the black cat, and the twinkling gold stars are his eyes."

Isabel glanced at the cat still perched in the tree. "My *padre* said Grimalkin's fur is like that of the leaping cat—the same color as the couple's hair, and that the cat's eyes are the same orange-yellow as the amber crucifix."

"Your *padre* also said that El Gato Grande was magic like Felis, the mystical constellation in the night sky. But we both know that is not true. The only magic that rascally old cat is capable of is disappearing when he is scolded for digging in my herbs."

"Ah, Mama, he is only helping."

"He makes more work for your *madre*."

"But he belonged to my *padre*'s family. That should say something of his worth."

"I know, Isabel. Your mother teases you. I love that cat as much as you do. And for as long as he lives, we shall have a part of your *padre* with us. But you must remember, little one, Grimalkin is getting old. He will not live forever."

"Oh, he will, Mama. My *padre* said he would, and I believe him."

Kalee looked at Isabel, her love for her child overflowing her heart. Since Pico's death, and her marriage to Wooster Farley, her daughter had endured more than her share of unhappiness. What harm could come if her daughter believed the family cat was not only ageless but also magic?

It mattered not to Kalee if that magic came from the Indian yarns passed down by her ancestors, or in the form of a worthless, black cat with amber-colored eyes.

Her Isabel needed a little enchantment to gladden her soul.

One

~

GONE FISHING!

Cooper Adair swabbed his brow. The carefully lettered sign that was attached to the iron gate leading from the street into the walled yard swam before his eyes that were already irritated by his sweat. He blinked, hoping to prevent yet another salty sting before continuing to read.

IF YOU NEED ME, YOU CAN FIND ME ON THE RIVER BESIDE THE TRAIN STATION.

"Great!" Cooper grumbled irritably. "That's just great." He had only left the depot some thirty minutes before.

The day-long trip from Jacksonville had been grueling enough, and it appeared it wasn't to be over soon. In order for Cooper to procure the key to his newly purchased business, he would have to hike back to the ferry landing and seek out the absent Miss Farley.

"And in this bone-melting heat," he complained.

Never, in all of Cooper's twenty-seven years, had he experienced such a climate. Granted, Philadelphia could be hot during the summer months, but the weather in his hometown was rarely saturated with the heavy damp air that almost smothered him the moment he had stepped down from the train in St. Augustine, Florida.

He removed his gray felt derby and eyed with distaste the soiled ring of perspiration around its rim. It was the kind of heat that could liquify your bones, excreting your skeleton from pores along with your sweat. With this thought, he mopped his brow again. It never failed to amaze him the sacrifices one made for the love of the right woman.

Bone weary, Cooper pushed open the gate and stepped inside the walled yard. He dropped his valise, sending up a small cloud of dust. The one suitcase he had brought with him after lugging it from the depot felt as though it were packed with bricks instead of clothing. He shuddered, thinking of the two wool suits stowed inside; both not unlike the one he wore. What was he thinking when he'd packed for this trip south? Most certainly not of his destination in the tropics. The beginnings of a headache stirred behind his eyes, and he squeezed the bridge of his nose. Thank the Lord his trunks were scheduled to arrive at the end of the week, but for now he had more pressing things to worry about. Like finding Miss Isabel Farley and retrieving the key to his building.

Hadn't she received his telegram informing her of the time of his arrival? Apparently not, since the woman wasn't home. It was no wonder that she was almost destitute. When there was a living to be made, a person shouldn't go fishing.

Cooper looked around the enclosed courtyard, the small but quaint cottage with its distinctive Spanish Colonial architecture. Too bad Miss Farley had not been willing to sell the dwelling and the adjoining acre along with the post building, because Cooper would have tried to purchase the whole parcel. In time he would have torn down the tiny house and replaced it with a modern structure more fitting for his soon-to-be bride.

The thought of his fiancée, Marcella, and the impending evening with her family brought Cooper up short. If he intended to have a much-needed bath before he joined Marcella and her parents at their home, he would have to fetch his key posthaste.

This decided, he searched the area for a suitable place to stow his bag. Opting to store it at the base of a huge oak close to the wall, Cooper turned and placed his hat back upon his head before retracing his earlier steps.

Isabel Gomez sat on the grassy bank of the placid blue river, a worn book of poetry open upon her lap.

> "I love thee with a love I seemed to lose
> With my lost saints—I love thee with the breath,
> Smiles, tears, of all my life!—and, if God choose,
> I shall but love thee better after death."

She sighed then flopped backward upon the grass, the book of poems clutched against her bosom. "Oh, Grim," she said, "is such a love possible?"

The big black cat, his eyes glowing like yellow topaz in the bright sunlight, gave her an indifferent look before turning his attention back to the fishing line and cork that floated on the gently flowing current.

Isabel sighed again. "The Brownings were so in love. Would that I should have such a relationship with a man."

Frivolous, romantic fool. Would that you should even know a man who could ever come up to your expectations.

Isabel fingered the copper bracelet encircling her wrist. Even the metal that was sacred to the love goddess Venus had not helped her in attracting a love for herself, but she wore the trinket anyway. She believed in the magic metal. In time she would find her perfect man.

Of course her notions of the perfect man came from between the pages of the dime novels and other books she read so avidly. Other than her real *padre,* whose presence of late had become nothing more than a fading memory, there had been no romantic heroes in her life. Perhaps that was why she entertained such fantasies.

Closing her eyes, Isabel willed away her foolish thoughts. Completely relaxed, she lay mindless, basking in the feel of the sun baking her skin beneath her garments. Most people detested Florida's hot, humid summer months, but Isabel loved them. Where others faded in the heavy heat, she flourished, feeling more alive than in any other season.

When the cork attached to the line bobbed beneath the surface of the water, she tossed the book from her chest and sat up.

"A fish, Grim, we've caught a fish!"

She grabbed the fishing pole and jumped to her feet. Righting her straw hat, she stepped upon the wooden pylons that edged the riverbank near the ferry landing. Grimalkin, catting her every footstep, eyed their possible dinner with hungry interest, meowing loudly beside her ankles.

Isabel gave a hard yank on the bamboo pole. The end bowed as the line went taut.

"It's a big one, Grim!" Isabel called, trying to pull her catch from the water. But as suddenly as the line had tightened it went slack. She yanked the tip of the pole upright. Nothing. Nothing but disappointment.

Her shoulders slumped. "He got away, Grim."

Isabel hastened back to the spot on the bank where she had left the empty creel. By now it should have been filled with fish that she and Grimalkin could enjoy for dinner, but it appeared the fish were faring better than she was. Unless she caught something soon, they would be sharing another meal without fish or fowl. Although Isabel had some cash remaining from the recent sale of her building, she didn't dare spend it foolishly. So instead of buying meat from the local market, she had decided to supplement their supper this evening with fish from the river. Too bad the cold-blooded swimmers had other ideas.

Isabel picked up the can of worms. There was only one worm left. She walked back to the pylons and plopped down.

Grimalkin followed her, and when she began to thread the spineless, flexible body onto the hook, the cat batted at the bait with his paw.

"No," she scolded, gently shoving him away. "This is our last worm and our last chance at catching a fish today."

"Meow," the cat protested, ignoring her reprimand.

Grimalkin swatted at the worm again, and it broke in half, both parts slipping from Isabel's grasp and dropping, wiggling, into her lap. Grimalkin pounced. Isabel grasped one half of the worm as the other half discharged into the river.

"That does it, Mr. Puss. You can kiss your fish dinner goodbye."

As Isabel tossed the remaining half of worm into the water, she noticed a tall man walking toward them. He was blond, his looks reminding her of her *padre,* or what she could remember about him. As the stranger drew nearer, lines from one of Shakespeare's sonnets flitted through her mind:

> "Shall I compare thee to a summer's day?
> Thou art more lovely and more temperate."

Unaware that he was being observed, Cooper felt anything but temperate. The combination of heat and exercise had him baking inside his wool suit. He searched the riverbank, which appeared to be studded with numerous sportsmen, their lines cast into the waters. He wondered how he would distinguish Miss Farley from the others since his broker had handled the whole transaction by mail and he had never met the woman. None of the fishermen appeared to be women.

He knew only two things about her. According to his broker, she was near destitute, and also of Indian descent. Immediately his mind conjured up the image of an olive-skinned woman with black hair and eyes, dressed in buckskins. For the moment those two things weren't much to go on. He thought about calling out her name, but such behavior seemed unbefitting to a gentleman. Besides, in these parts, she might have decided to go by her Indian name. Like the famous

Seminole warrior Osceola, who was also known as William Powell.

"Curse the woman anyway," he mumbled. For the second time in the last hour, Cooper found fault with Miss Farley, who in his opinion should have been home waiting to receive him and to hand over his key instead of idling away precious time fishing. He couldn't imagine a lady enjoying such a sport when he himself couldn't imagine touching the slippery, slimy, smelly aquatic vertebrates.

Having made one pass along the shoreline, he stopped at the foot of the ferry landing. A lad with his back to him sat facing the river. A huge straw hat shielded the boy's face, but nothing could shield the large black cat sitting beside him.

Cats! Cooper shuddered. He couldn't tolerate the animals. Cat and boy seemed to be engaged in a tug of war with the worm the fisherman was spearing onto his hook. Apparently the cat believed the invertebrate was fair game and kept swatting at the defenseless creature. Observing them, Cooper couldn't decide which of the three was the more barbaric; the fisherman, the worm, or the cat. Finally his aversion to felines won out. The animals were nothing but domesticated carnivorous Mammals good for catching rats and mice.

Cooper turned and started back across the bank. Time was running out, and he had none to spare for taking in the local color. Still unable to locate Miss Farley, he was considering what to do next when his hat was snatched from his head. Surprised he whirled around. His derby skipped across the ground as though it had suddenly come to life. Since the day was absent of any breeze, Cooper knew the wind hadn't lifted it. Not until the black cat he had spied earlier began chasing the derby across the grass did it occur to Cooper what had transpired. His hat had been hooked by the fisherman.

The boy jumped to his feet. "Grimalkin, no!" the lad scolded, swinging the tip of his pole high in the air and back over his shoulder, trying to jerk the line free of the derby. "No! You naughty cat. Leave the man's hat alone."

On seeing his derby skipping across the grass, the cat in

hot pursuit, Cooper was determined to retrieve his hat before the beast could sink fangs and claws into the rich felt.

"Scat, cat!" he yelled, waving his hands at the animal. The animal ignored him. Drawing closer, Cooper reached for the hat. His fingers closed over the narrow brim at the same time the lad jerked hard on his fishing pole. Snatched from his hand, the hat flew backward over the fisherman's head and plopped in the water like a hooked fish.

Cooper followed the two to the river's edge.

"Now see what you've done!" the fisherman scolded the cat, who stood between Cooper and the lad. The black feline meowed his loss as the lazy current carried Cooper's derby farther out into the river.

"Sir, I'm so sorry," the lad apologized. He jerked on the line again. Both cork and hook came up empty. "Oops. Lost another one."

The boy giggled behind his hand, and at the girlish gesture, Cooper took a closer look. *The fisherman was no lad.* In a matter of moments, the *he* had turned into a *she*.

During the struggle to reel in Cooper's hat, the lad's—no, he meant lass's—straw hat had fallen off her head and now hung around her neck by a silk cord. Where before Cooper hadn't noticed the boy's, er, the girl's hair, he couldn't help but notice it now. It was the color of honey, and where the sun touched it, the strands turned to gold.

When she had jumped to her feet earlier, wrestling with the pole, she appeared to be nothing more than a gangling boy; but as his gaze skimmed over her, his opinion altered dramatically. The lankiness was gone and concealed beneath her loose-fitting garments was the body of a woman, and a very shapely one at that. And of all things, she was wearing men's clothing; pantaloons held up with red suspenders and a man's baggy shirt. If she had been wearing a breechcloth, Cooper wouldn't have been any more shocked.

He jerked his gaze back to her face. Her expression said she knew exactly where his thoughts had been. He felt his ears turn red. Without the protection of his hat, the sun had already begun to burn his skin. *You're rationalizing, old son. You're blushing because you were caught in the act of ogling.* Even now, when he knew his impertinent staring was improper, Cooper couldn't break eye contact with the woman.

Her eyes held him spellbound. Perhaps it was the bright sun playing tricks on his sight, but he had never seen eyes the color of the stranger's. Like the fossil amber they looked both translucent and semi-opaque. The same honey color as her hair, but in their depths were chips of copper.

"Sir?" she said, breaking the spell. "If you'll tell me your name and address, I'll see that your hat is replaced."

He gaped for several more seconds before he found his voice. "I'm Cooper Adair from—"

"Philadelphia?"

Her finishing his sentence took him by surprise, and for the second time since meeting her, Cooper wondered if she had the uncanny ability to read minds.

"I'm Isabel Gomez," she said, extending her hand toward him.

"Gomez? I'm sorry," he apologized, "but should I know you?"

She laughed then, and the husky sound brushed his skin like a lover's caress. He had never heard a woman laugh with such full-bodied amusement.

"I'm the one who sold you my Trading Post."

She smiled, and he felt hotter. "You're Miss Farley?" he asked, unable to believe his good luck.

"Around these parts most folks know me as Isabel Gomez."

"Then you have two names like the famous chief Osceola." Cooper hoped to impress her with his knowledge of Indian history, but the look she sent him was anything but impressed.

In a matter of seconds her sunny disposition changed. "Did you expect a squaw, Mr. Adair?" Her thick brows arched in question.

"I-I meant—"

"*Farley* was my stepfather's name," she responded, not giving him a chance to explain. "You may call me *Miss* Gomez."

Running his finger beneath his damp collar, Cooper decided that dealing with this *Miss* Gomez would be easier than dealing with the alarmingly attractive one of a few moments before. He cleared his throat. "I've come—"

"For the key," she finished for him, twirling away and bending to gather her fishing gear.

Having never seen a female in britches, Cooper gawked. His Marcella would never do anything so unladylike as to wear men's trousers, or if she did, he couldn't imagine her looking nearly as shapely as Miss Gomez. If the truth were known, he couldn't picture his very proper betrothed's figure, and the thought suddenly struck him as odd. They had been engaged for less than a year.

As for Miss Gomez, her buttocks were as round and firm as ripe melons. The blatant display of her backside made the insufferable heat go up several degrees.

What was the matter with him anyway? His head was clogged with thoughts he shouldn't be having, especially in the presence of another woman, and one he found alarmingly attractive.

"Yes," he said, "I've come for the key." During the interchange, Cooper's gaze became locked in a staring match with her cat. "And I shall need it posthaste." He was eager to part company with the odd pair who had the power to bewitch.

"Posthaste?" She laughed, but her laughter sounded more sarcastic than mirthful. "I'm afraid not, Mr. Adair. Not in this weather. You'll find that we locals move slower during the summer months."

As she gathered up the fishing pole and creel, the huge cat meowed loudly as though he, too, expected to be gathered up.

"You'll have to walk, Grimalkin," Miss Gomez told the feline, "unless you can convince Mr. Adair to carry you."

There was a question in her eyes that mirrored her cat's in color and intensity.

Cooper swallowed. "Carry a cat? Why, I'd never. I don't—"

"Then I assure you our walk home will be a slow one. When Grimalkin gets in one of his belligerent moods, he can move slower than cold molasses."

"But surely if we were to leave him, he could find his way."

She looked at him as though he had asked her to make a sacrifice of her cat.

"I don't allow him to roam, Mr. Adair. Besides, he's very old."

"Old? Well, he's not feeble—or he didn't appear to be when he trounced my hat. I'd say judging from his size, he has a right healthy appetite."

"The British Shorthair is a large and sturdy cat," she responded. "Grimalkin's ancestors are from England, although he came from Spain with my father."

"In my opinion, a cat's a cat no matter what country it hails from."

"You, sir, have a lot to learn. Not only about this climate you've chosen to live in, but also about cats. Grimalkin is a very special animal. The breed has survived many years of superstition and persecution. It's a marvel the species is still around for us to enjoy."

"Superstition and persecution. Words associated with the Salem witch trials. A witch's cat, huh?" Cooper laughed at his quip, but it was apparent that Miss Gomez didn't find his observation clever, because she didn't crack a smile. Instead she gave him a mindful look and thrust the fishing pole and creel into his hands. Bending, she picked up the cat. With the hairy varmint nestled against her shoulder like a newborn babe, she moved away from the riverbank.

"Come along, Mr. Adair," she called over her shoulder. "If it's a hurry you're in, I suggest we be on our way."

Salem witch trials! Cooper puzzled over the alien thought that had popped into his mind. Like an obedient child, he tagged along in Miss Gomez's footsteps. The earthy scent

emanating from inside the creel wasn't one he relished, nor
did he enjoy parading through the streets of his new home
like an urchin carrying a fishing pole. But soon the unpleasantness of the situation was forgotten as he concentrated on
the graceful sway of Miss Gomez's hips as she walked.
Watching her brought to mind the hula he had once seen
performed in Philadelphia by a troupe of Polynesian dancers.
A more seductive dance Cooper had never seen, and the same
could be said for the walk of the woman he followed.

He shook his head, hoping to clear it of such lascivious
thoughts. If he kept thinking as he was, he might be tempted
to goose her with the end of the fishing pole before they
reached their destination.

His gaze locked on the cat's. Round golden eyes stared at
him as though they, too, had read his devious thoughts.
Guilty, Cooper looked away, but only for a second. His gaze
snapped back to the cat. He knew for certain that the heat
had finally addled his brain. Grimalkin, or whatever the cat's
name was, was smiling at him.

Ridiculous! Cats only smiled in fairy tales. *I must be closer
to collapse than I first suspected; lusting over strange women
and imagining a cat can smile.* His mind's deterioration had
him so perturbed that he was unaware that Miss Gomez had
come to a stop in front of him. Until the end of the fishing
pole poked her right in the center of her shapely buttocks,
hitting home with an upward thrust.

She shrieked, jumped, and swung around to face him.

Cooper dropped the pole.

Cursing his soul to hell and back, he prayed his bones
would melt and he would dissolve into the dry sand beneath
his feet.

Two

"Mr. Adair!"

When Isabel swung around, Grimalkin jumped from her arms and scurried past the open gate toward the "love" tree, leaving Isabel to discretely massage her wounded backside. She couldn't believe the audacity of the man.

"I'm—I'm sorry." His face turned the color of a freshly boiled shrimp, and he flung the fishing pole to the ground. "Believe me, ma'am, I'm not in the habit of assaulting young women in broad daylight."

"Ahh," she replied, raising her brows. "Am I to understand that you prefer assaulting them at night?" Not giving him a chance to respond, she turned and moved inside the courtyard, smiling now that he couldn't see her face. His attempt to put things right had come out all wrong, and Isabel was enjoying his discomposure. She still didn't understand the meaning of his earlier remark about Osceola, and until she did she wasn't yet ready to forgive him. "Since you've admitted to being a rogue," she added, "I'll have to remember to keep my doors locked."

"A rogue? Miss Gomez, please." He caught up with her, restricting her movement by grasping her arm. "I assure you that I'm no criminal."

Isabel's eyes fastened on his long fingers where they gripped her arm. When her gaze shifted from his hand to his face, he must have realized the impropriety of his actions. Disbelief spread across his features, and he released his grip as though her arm like the fishing pole had suddenly turned smelting hot.

"Beg your pardon," he mumbled, dropping his hands to his side. He took a deep breath and released it, making his cheeks swell. "I seem to be doing everything wrong but I assure you, Miss Gomez, you have no reason to fear me. I have excellent references both personal and professional that I will be happy to show you once my trunks arrive. My training in pharmaceutical chemistry at the Philadelphia College of Pharmacy should be testimony enough that I am of good character."

Only half listening to him, Isabel stepped through the coquina-arched walkway that ran the length of the house. She grabbed a metal ring of keys that hung on a nail and began working a key off the loop. *Philadelphia College of Pharmacy.* She froze in place and studied the man standing several feet away. Surely she hadn't heard him right. "What did you say?" she asked.

"I said I have excellent references that I'll be happy to show you from—"

"Tell me you don't intend to open a drugstore?"

"Why, yes. Yes I do." As he announced his intent, he stood a little taller. Puffed up like a toad, he was, with all his pride. Isabel sent him a scathing look.

"Is there something wrong, Miss Gomez?" He no longer looked so haughty, but more concerned with her well-being. "You look a little anemic," he announced. "Are you sure you're all right?"

No, she wasn't all right. In truth, she felt wretched and was having difficulty breathing. "You—you can't open a drugstore in my building."

"*Your* building?" His arrogance returned. "I seem to recall that you sold the property to me, so that makes the building mine. The bill of sale is in my valise." He glanced toward the base of the "love" tree. "If you wish, I'll show it to you, but then I'm sure you have your own signed copies. Now if you would be so kind as to hand over the keys, I won't impose upon you any longer."

This was not what she expected at all. "Mr. Jetsen never mentioned you were going to open a drugstore. If he had. . . . I—I assumed you were going to reestablish the trading post."

"Miss Gomez, the days of trading posts are obsolete, especially in a town that's on the verge of major growth. Now that Mr. Henry Flagler has schemes to turn St. Augustine into an American Riviera, there will be a need for more urban businesses to serve the traveling public. When one is so far from home, reliable medical care is of the utmost importance."

"I beg your pardon, Mr. Adair. In case you weren't informed by Mr. Jetsen, St. Augustine already has an established herbalist who comes from a long line of respected healers."

His expression was filled with contempt. "Herbalist? Healers? All poppycock! We're nearing the twentieth century, Miss Gomez. These so-called herbalists you speak of will be replaced by pharmacists as the healers are being replaced by trained doctors." He ran a finger beneath his wilting collar. "I understand the town already has several of the latter, but there are no trained pharmacists in the area."

"But we don't need—"

"These so-called herbalists peddle snake guts from the back of their wagons while claiming their tonics as cure-alls, but the days of panacea medicine are over."

For the second time today Isabel couldn't believe the audacity of the man. "I'm well aware of snake-oil peddlers, Mr. Adair, and I assure you the person I speak of would never resort to duping the public. It is a knowledgeable herbalist I speak of."

He rocked back upon his heels and crossed his arms against his chest. "And who might this herbalist be? I should like to search out the charlatan and tell him what I think of his quackery."

"Quackery?" Isabel spit out the affront. "You're no better than Wooster Farley." She beat a rhythm on her collarbone with her thumb. "Me, Mr. Adair. I'm the charlatan. And it will be a cold day in hell before I turn over the key to *my* building to you. Good day!"

Isabel spun around and stomped toward the door to her house. The moment she opened it, the black cat scooted between Cooper's feet, nearly toppling him to the ground before disappearing inside the cottage on the heels of his irate mistress. The door slammed.

"You can't close me out!" Cooper shouted. "I have a legal and binding contract stating that your building now belongs to me."

He hammered his fist against the wooden panel. When he received no answer, he began pacing, wondering how the situation had gone from bad to worse in less than a heartbeat.

Hell! A cold day in hell indeed. Cooper could tell Miss Gomez a few things about hell. He had experienced it first-hand from the moment he had stepped down from the train in this insufferable heat to discover that Miss Farley-Gomez, or whatever she called herself, wasn't home to present him with *his* key. And now he had this latest atrocity to deal with; an overwrought female who fancied herself a pharmacologist when in truth she probably dabbled in nothing more than crude elixirs.

"Now what?" Cooper stopped his pacing long enough to kick at a clump of crabgrass. What the hell was he going to do? He knew what he would like to do. He would like to wring a certain woman's scrawny neck.

Recalling Miss Gomez's neck, Cooper decided it wasn't actually scrawny, but long and graceful like a swan's. A neck made for kissing.

Kissing! The heat was getting to him. An engaged man didn't entertain thoughts of kissing the neck of any woman other than that of his betrothed. But from the moment when he had first discovered that Miss Gomez was a lass instead of a lad, it was as though the discovery had bewitched him.

Nonsense. Cooper grimaced in disgust. Impossible that he, a rational, no-nonsense man, should entertain such thoughts. Although at the moment he felt jinxed, he was a man of science and didn't believe in hexes. Besides, he had more important things to worry about, like resolving this latest dilemma, and soon.

"And how am I to do that?" he grumbled, searching his mind for an answer. *Take off this hair shirt for a starter.*

If doing penance was his way out of hell, then Cooper had done that today, too. He jerked at the jacket sleeves that gripped his sweaty arms like glue. Now that he thought about it, if given a choice, he would take that cold day in hell Miss Gomez had threatened him with any day over this torturous heat.

After Cooper freed his arms, he wriggled out of his coat and tossed it over a bush. Then he discarded his tie, loosened the buttons of his shirt, and rolled up his sleeves. Not exactly proper dress for a gentleman, but such a climate could bring out the savage in the best of men.

The word *savage* turned his thoughts back to Miss Gomez since the word was synonymous with Indians. Not that she looked anything like an Indian. She was all honey-gold hair and yellow-gold eyes. Even her skin was honey-hued. Would her lips taste like honey as well?

"Damn it all," he swore. He wouldn't be tasting her lips anytime soon. He wouldn't be tasting her lips at all.

But you would like to.

The idea popped into his head unbidden, and Cooper had the strangest feeling that the thought didn't belong to him. But how was that possible? He glanced back over his shoulder to the Gomez dwelling. The door appeared to be locked up tighter than a tomb. On the windowsill beside the entrance, her fat cat dozed, dreaming, Cooper supposed, of whatever predators dreamed of.

"Where was I? Oh, yes. . . . Indians." Miss Gomez's heritage was proof enough that she could be a thief. Her actions certainly supported the validity of the rumor that Indians could not be trusted. He had often heard that if given half a chance, they would steal a person blind. Miss Gomez had no qualms about accepting his money for the purchase of her building, yet she refused to turn over the key. In Cooper's opinion that was the same as stealing, and he was tempted to seek out the law.

A gust of hot air fanned his face. He couldn't believe how much cooler he felt after removing his coat and tie and rolling up his shirtsleeves. Surprisingly, his temper had cooled as well, making him feel more affable. Instead of calling in the law to settle their little dispute, perhaps he could talk some sense into the lady. One of his strong points was his persuasiveness, so he believed he was perfectly capable of handling the situation himself. But first he had to convince Miss Gomez to speak with him.

This decided, Cooper approached the front door again. He paused beneath the covered archway that ran the length of the house, taking note of his surroundings. The air definitely felt cooler beneath the shady pergola. In fact, it was almost pleasant.

A slight breeze stirred the air, and the inner courtyard came alive with sound. For the first time since entering the yard, Cooper noted the strings of shells hanging from driftwood. These wind instruments were responsible for the pleasing, music-like sound. His gaze sought out the various pieces dangling from tree branches and the wooden arches that held up the ancient grapevine. Not only shells made up the orchestra, but also spoons; their bell-like ring adding to the musical performance.

"Enchanting!" He wondered who was responsible for making the wind ornaments. Maybe he could convince that person to allow him to sell the sculptures in his drugstore. If he could, he would advertise them as wind bells to soothe a troubled mind. He would be the first to attest that the bells worked. Already the calming sound made him feel more relaxed.

Only the *clop, clop* of horse hooves against pavement or the distant bark of a neighbor's dog attested to the fact that there was life beyond the shady bower.

Cooper inhaled deeply. The air was redolent with growing things, and he felt as though he had been dropped down in a leafy jungle. Feathery green ferns bordered the brick patio and spilled from randomly placed clay pots. Yes, he thought, looking around the walled-in yard that felt like a world into itself. One could definitely get used to this place that was proving to be so different from Philadelphia.

But first things first. Before Cooper could claim this town as his own, he needed to claim the key to his building. The only way to do that was to confront Miss Gomez again. Not his choice of priority, but an immediate must-do.

Inside the house, Isabel paced in front of the empty fireplace, uncertain who she was more angry with—Cooper Adair or herself. Or perhaps it would be more appropriate if she directed her anger toward Mr. Jetsen, the businessman who had handled the sale of her property. He should have told her of Cooper Adair's plans to open a pharmacy. Such an establishment would be in direct competition with her own business. Struggling as she was to reestablish herself as a respected herbalist, the last thing she needed was a pharmacist a mere stone's throw away.

Unlike Cooper Adair, Isabel hadn't been granted the luxury of a higher education. Everything she knew about herbs and healing she had learned from her mother—teachings that had been passed down from one generation to the next. Granted, the world was becoming more modern, but there was still a need for her ancient cures and potions. She doubted that Mr. Adair would know how to make a love potion, or know the proper ingredients needed for an aphrodisiac. If it hadn't been for the money she earned selling her potions and herbs, she didn't know how she would have survived after Wooster's death last year.

Isabel had accused Mr. Adair of being no different from Wooster Farley, when in truth it had been she who acted more like her late stepfather with her quick show of temper. She might not approve of her neighbor's newfangled drugstore because it would be in direct competition with her old-fashioned business, but at least the old post building would become a respectable establishment again.

Isabel took a deep breath and stopped her pacing. She wasn't pleased that she had allowed her temper to rule her actions. She knew firsthand the effects of a bad temper, and for that reason she had vowed to control her own. Her manner with Mr. Adair had been totally uncalled for.

He had purchased her property in good faith. She was in error by refusing to turn over his key, especially after accepting his money. Money she had needed desperately in order to keep a roof over her head, and to keep her home from being sold to pay back taxes.

Isabel knew establishing herself as a respected herbalist wouldn't be easy, but she had never expected to be in competition with a man with a degree in pharmacology from some fancy college up North. *Dang it all!* If she had known, she wouldn't have sold him her building.

Yet as soon as the notion had formed, she knew the futility of her thought. Without Mr. Adair's money, her mother's garden with all its specially cultivated herbs would have been sold to the highest bidder, leaving Isabel without her mother's legacy. After her mother's death two years earlier, Isabel had worked long and hard to keep the herbs healthy and producing, and she wasn't about to give up now. She certainly couldn't return Mr. Adair's money, so she would have to think of some other way to get rid of him.

While glancing toward the window where Grimalkin dozed, the thought occurred to Isabel that perhaps her old fairy cat could help her. She had never tested Grim's so-called magical powers—powers her *padre* boasted the ancient cat held. Perhaps her pet could make Mr. Adair disappear into thin air.

"Mr. Adair!" *I almost forgot him.* By now, he could be on his way to fetch the law to have her hauled away to the lockup for not having turned over his key. Besides, the least or the most she could do would be to apologize to him for her earlier actions. And for the moment she should try to appear agreeable.

This decided, Isabel sprinted toward the door. Attention from the law was the last thing she wanted. Wooster Farley's dealings with the authorities had been long and eventful, and those exchanges had left her own reputation as fragile as a dandelion in the wind.

With her heart in her throat, and praying that she wasn't too late, Isabel swung open the door. To her surprise, Cooper Adair stood mere inches away facing her, his arm raised, his fist bunched as though he were about to knock. Before he could wipe the startled expression from his face, Isabel waved the ring of keys beneath his aquiline nose.

"The key, Mr. Adair," she said, stepping past him. "I'll show you *your* building now."

He blinked in astonishment. "*My* building?"

"Yes, come along," she said, waiting for him to join her before she moved across the courtyard.

He raised his hand to his throat as though reaching for the knot of his tie, and when he realized it no longer encircled his neck, he dropped his hands to his sides. His lips pursed suspiciously. "I'm glad you've begun to see reason."

"I have," she said, using a cloyingly sweet tone, "and I wish to apologize. You were correct. The building no longer belongs to me." As he approached her, she handed him the key.

"Thank you." He appeared to puzzle over his thoughts before speaking. "Perhaps I should apologize to you as well. I'm sure you're very good at whatever you do with your little herbs."

My little herbs!

His mocking tone irritated her, but she swallowed her annoyance, determined to remain affable. "Yes, I am very good. I have a beautiful garden. When you're settled in, perhaps you would like to see it. After all, we're in the same line of work, aren't we? Making remedies to cure the ills of the body."

Not only did Isabel read dime novels and poetry, but she also read everything she could get her hands on about herbs. Herbalists had been around a lot longer than pharmacists, and she supposed the two studies were related no matter what her new neighbor believed.

Mr. Adair's response was long in coming, and not a particularly enthusiastic one when it did. "Your garden? I-I suppose that would be . . . nice," he said, "but I'll be very busy stocking my store in the next few weeks." He cleared his throat. "I've a big shipment arriving from laboratories up North."

"Of course you have," she replied, with a sinking feeling in her stomach.

Her laboratory was her garden. She made all her own remedies.

It was evident that Mr. Adair wasn't interested in either, but that didn't dissuade Isabel. After all, if she were to somehow send her competition packing, she needed to learn as much as she could about him.

Once again his hand moved to the absent tie. Isabel noted that without it and without his coat, he looked different. With his sleeves rolled up and his collar unbuttoned, he appeared much more human. Isabel preferred this informal version over the earlier stilted one, and as she studied him, she felt a fluttering of her heart beneath her ribs. Because her *padre* had been a blond with fair skin and blue eyes, Isabel had found from a young age that she had a weakness for fair-haired males.

As she deliberated this latest thought, Grimalkin dashed from inside the cottage. His eyes glowing gold, he met her stare briefly before he began weaving a figure eight around her ankles. Isabel shooed him away and began walking toward the post building with Mr. Adair beside her. Halfway across the courtyard her foot connected with the root of the "love" tree, and she stumbled.

Straight into Cooper Adair's arms.

He caught her by the arm and helped to steady her while she regained her footing, but instead of releasing her, he pulled her firmly against him and looked deep into her eyes. Isabel struggled to breathe when common sense told her she should struggle to free herself. But she did nothing.

Never had she been held so intimately by a man. This man was almost a stranger, and an enemy of a sort, yet his embrace felt familiar. If anything, she felt very comfortable in his arms. It was as though she belonged there.

That bumping in her heart returned only to be replaced by the bumping sensation against her legs, which brought her back to the moment. *Grimalkin*. Was this the wily old feline's doings?

Because her *padre* had always told her that Grimalkin was a magic cat, Isabel believed him, but she had never actually seen her pet perform. Yet if this was the cat's idea of casting a spell, he had it all wrong. Didn't he realize that Mr. Adair was her downfall and not her salvation?

This moonstruck affliction must end now.

But instead of stepping from his embrace, she pressed closer. It was enchanting being in Cooper Adair's arms. As Grimalkin continued to weave around hers and Mr. Adair's tangled feet, his purr sounded like that of a cooing pigeon. She knew she should stop him, but at this point she was powerless to do so. She, like her neighbor, had fallen under Grimalkin's spell.

It hurt to breathe, and from what Isabel could tell from Mr. Adair's labored response, he, too, appeared to be afflicted with the same malady. Her head felt light, the private place between her legs felt heavy, and the world outside Cooper Adair's embrace ceased to exist.

She noticed immediately that they were of comparable

heights, her shoulders almost even with his, but there the similarities ended. Where her shoulders were narrow, his were broad; her chest was raised and soft while his was flat and hard.

With a sigh, Isabel leaned closer. Intermingling with his powerfully male scent was the unmistakable fragrance of the herb anise. She sniffed. Yes. He smelled just like licorice and he looked good enough to eat.

They stood so close that she could feel the thunder of his heartbeat. With her gaze she traced the perfect lines of his face. Thick blond brows arched above eyes the same blue-gray color of the horizon where sky and sea meet. Beneath his aquiline nose he had a generous mouth—a mouth mere inches from her own and descending closer. When his lips were so near that his warm breath brushed her cheek, Isabel closed her eyes and pressed closer, the action so natural it might have been the work of destiny. This experience, she realized, had nothing to do with Grimalkin's sorcery, but with her heart's deepest longings.

Was this the man whom Isabel had been waiting for all her life? Had she been waiting for Cooper Adair's kiss?

She relaxed against him, giving herself over to the exquisite pleasure. At first his lips brushed hers tentatively, tasting, before the kiss deepened and his tongue thrust past the seam of her lips, ravishingly.

For Isabel, time stood still. From within the branches of the "love" tree, a catbird sang, and her heart mewed in sync with its *tcheck, tcheck* melody. Mr. Adair ended the kiss and smiled down at her.

Isabel was still caught up in the moment until a voice sounded from the other side of the walled courtyard. "Hello, is anybody home?"

With the intrusion, Grimalkin stopped his weaving. Cooper Adair blinked in astonishment. "Marcella?"

"No, I'm Isabel," she responded lazily, snuggling closer into his embrace.

"Marcella!"

Cooper thrust Isabel aside so suddenly that she nearly stumbled, but this time not into his arms. When the iron gate to the courtyard clanked shut, Grimalkin charged up the tree, and Cooper Adair looked as though he had been caught with his hand in the cookie jar.

As Isabel glared at the intruder, reality returned, and she realized to her chagrin that she had been kissing the enemy.

Three

The fashionably dressed young woman moved from the iron gate toward the front door, then raised her lace-gloved hand to lift the knocker.

"Marcella," Cooper Adair called again, this time moving toward the woman. She turned and on spotting him she smiled with such radiance that Isabel feared her smile might give the man a heat stroke.

"Oh, Cooper, there you are."

The couple exchanged endearing glances, making Isabel stand a little taller and take notice. Although she didn't know the woman, the look that passed between the couple said they were more to each other than mere friends. Narrowing the distance between them, she, too, walked toward the visitor. A man who had just kissed Isabel the way Cooper Adair had couldn't possibly have an interest in another woman. Unless, of course, the woman he had just kissed owned a cat who after all these years had decided to use his magic to stir up trouble. Brushing aside this last thought, she studied the stranger.

Not only was this Marcella person beautiful, but she was also everything that Isabel was not. As a child growing up, Isabel had always towered over her friends, and compared to this lady with her small, voluptuous figure, Isabel felt even more lanky. No raven curls crowned Isabel's head; instead she had hair the color of buff that was straighter than a poker. Where Marcella had a peaches-and-cream complexion, reminiscent of the heroines in Isabel's romantic novels, her own skin held gold undertones. As the woman fluttered toward them in a dress of pale pink lawn, she put Isabel in mind of a gossamer-winged butterfly, and herself in mind of an ugly brown moth.

The butterfly dragged her gaze from Cooper Adair's only long enough to give Isabel a thorough going over. It was apparent when she raised her pert little nose several inches higher that she didn't approve of Isabel or her manly britches.

Her bow lips twisted unpleasantly as she asked Cooper, "Are you acquainted with this creature?"

Creature? The girl's attitude rankled Isabel, and Cooper looked embarrassed.

"Marcella, dear," he said, starting to introduce them, "this is—"

"Silly old me," Marcella said, not allowing him to finish. "This is your hired help, isn't it? I should have known, considering how he—she's dressed."

Cooper grabbed his friend's arm as though he wanted to shake her, but instead he began again. "Marcella, this is—"

"Not the hired help." This time it was Isabel who interrupted him. Usually it wasn't her nature to be spiteful, but Marcella's attitude annoyed her. She was so spoiled the salt wouldn't save her. Isabel wanted to put the spongy-headed girl in her proper place, and now was as good a time as any.

"Tell me, Marshmallow, does Mr. Adair usually kiss the hired help?"

"The name is Marcella," she corrected, "and of course he doesn't kiss the hired help." She looked to Cooper for confirmation, and when none was forthcoming, she turned a frosty glare on Isabel. "Why would you even suggest such a thing?"

For a brief second, Isabel wondered the same thing, but the

words poured from her mouth anyway. "Because only seconds before your arrival, he was kissing me." Isabel looked at Cooper, who appeared both confused and abashed.

"Kissing you?" Marcella's lace gloved hand fluttered against her bosom. "Surely you jest. Cooper would never consort with the hired help. We're betrothed."

The man who had just kissed her as though there was no tomorrow was betrothed to another?

Life really wasn't fair, Isabel decided, but perhaps the twosome deserved each other. Earlier she had thought Cooper Adair as arrogant as a toad when he spoke about his profession. So maybe His Arrogance deserved a spoiled princess. Let them have each other, Isabel thought. She was about to tell Marcella she had lied about the kiss they had shared when Grimalkin jumped down from the tree and begin rubbing against her ankles. Suddenly it seemed important that Isabel keep up this pretense.

The feline left her ankles and grazed Cooper's legs once before turning and repeating the action.

"A cat," Marcella squealed. "Quick, Cooper, shoo him away before he gets that black fur all over my dress." Scooting behind Cooper, she used him to shield herself from any contact with the pesky feline. Her protector didn't appear too pleased that he had to ward off the animal, or more importantly, he didn't look too pleased with Isabel for telling about their kiss. As he glared at her, she smiled innocently.

Before she bent and scooped the cat into her arms, Isabel allowed him free rein with his brushing. There *must* be magic in Grimalkin's dander.

With her head now resting against her pet's, both she and Grimalkin stared straight into Cooper Adair's eyes. Next to her ear, she heard the feline's purr and knew that everything would be fine. Especially when she heard Marcella's next words.

"Tell her, Cooper," she said, "that you will not tolerate such behavior." Now that the cat no longer threatened to dirty her frock, she moved from behind Cooper, threading her arm with his. "We both know you wouldn't kiss such a creature."

When he didn't deny it, she tugged on his arm, her words wavering. "Cooper, you didn't, did you?"

Grimalkin and Isabel stared, waiting for his answer. An answer they both knew would be long in coming.

Cooper felt Marcella beside him, her fingers locked around his arm. Although he knew he should look at her, he felt powerless to do so. Instead his gaze remained glued on Miss Gomez and her cat. Both animal and woman shared the same golden eyes—eyes that held him mesmerized with their depthless intensity. A man could get lost in such eyes.

"Cooper Adair! What's wrong with you?" Marcella demanded.

His thoughts drifted like clouds on a windy day. Although he was aware of Marcella's presence beside him, she seemed miles away. Then her fingers gripped his chin, turning his face toward hers. "Did you?"

"Did I what?" He blinked, trying to recall the proper response to her question, which he had all but forgotten.

"Kiss?" she asked.

Kiss? He had certainly kissed someone, and logic suggested it would have been Marcella. Who else? After all, she was his intended. Cooper searched his brain, reaching for the elusive answer. He studied the woman beside him, who seemed to be hanging on to his every word, although he hadn't answered her. After a moment the embrace materialized in his mind, and he recalled every vivid detail of their passionate kiss, and the memory fired his blood.

Yes. It had been a wonderful experience. Cooper couldn't recall another time during his and Marcella's long courtship when he had enjoyed a kiss so much. He smiled down at her, wanting to pull her back into his embrace and feel her warm body against his once again.

"It was the best kiss I ever had," he answered, feeling playful. "What do you say, sweetie, you want to do it again?" He grinned foolishly, but Marcella didn't look fooled at all. She looked furious as she slammed her fists against his arm and stepped away.

"What's wrong with you?" she asked, "I've never seen you act so—so vulgar."

Vulgar. Me? Cooper realized he had said something wrong, but he didn't know what. He puzzled over her accusation.

"It's true, isn't it? How could you, Cooper Adair? I thought it was I you loved."

"It is you—"

"I—I trusted you. And you—you kissed that—that thing." She sent Isabel a scathing look. "Then you have the gall to claim it was the best kiss you ever had."

"But it was the best kiss we ever shared."

When Marcella looked as though she might burst into tears, Cooper knew he was in trouble. "It was *you* I kissed. Wasn't it?"

Marcella pointed an accusing finger at his neighbor. "It was her," she wailed, "not me." She pushed past Miss Gomez and raced toward the gate. "I—I hate you Cooper Adair," she called. "I never want to see you again."

"Never want to see me? You don't mean that. You're the reason I'm here. It's because of you that I moved to this backwater town."

Cooper looked to Isabel for help, but one glance at her stoic expression told him he would receive no help from that quarter. He rushed after Marcella. "Surely, you don't think?" It was evident she did. "Marcella, I can explain."

Or he thought he could. But then maybe he couldn't. He wasn't certain he understood what had transpired here himself. *I kissed Isabel Gomez?* If he had, why in the devil had he admitted it? More importantly, why had he done it when he had a beautiful fiancée who would soon be his wife? Once they were married—

Married. She had said she never wanted to see him again.

"Damn it all, Marcella. Wait. We have to talk."

She was out the gate before Cooper could reach her. The heavy iron clanked shut, imprisoning him inside. He gripped the iron bars and shook them with such force he thought they might come loose from their hinges. He hoped they would.

"There has to be an explanation," he mumbled. He looked back over his shoulder and saw that Miss Gomez had not moved. She still stood in the same spot, still holding her cat, a bemused smile upon both her face and the cat's.

"Damn it all. Cats can't smile."

Cooper turned back toward the street and propped his head against the iron bars. If he had kissed Isabel Gomez, he sure as hell would have remembered doing it.

You're right—a man doesn't forget kissing a woman like her.

"That's not what I meant, and you know it."

Realizing he had spoken his argument aloud, Cooper clamped his lips shut. *What the hell is happening to me?* It was as though someone other than himself had put the thought into his mind. Earlier today, he had experienced the same type of interference, but such a deed was impossible. Was he hallucinating? After all, he was bordering on exhaustion, which could explain his false notions.

What he needed was a cooling bath and a good night's sleep, but before that was possible, he needed to straighten out this latest crisis. He would go to Marcella and explain. Surely she would understand and forgive him.

Not bothering to look back, he opened the gate and stepped outside. Glancing up and down St. George Street, he saw no sign of his betrothed. She had vanished completely. As Cooper set out for the Kent home, he could only hope that his promising future hadn't vanished along with his angry fiancée.

Isabel watched him go, then started to follow him, but stopped when her gaze caught on the key he must have dropped. She bent and picked it up. She returned to the stoop and placed the key in the keyhole so that he would be sure to find it later. This done, she traced his footsteps to the iron gate.

Opening the gate, she stood just outside until she caught

sight of him striding down the street. Although Isabel had known Cooper Adair for only a few hours, she could still pick out his tall form from those of the other pedestrians moving along on busy St. George Street. She watched him until he rounded a corner, then she returned to the walled garden.

Grimalkin trotted up to her with a fat green lizard hanging from his jaws. "Let that varmint go," she scolded. Grim was always presenting her with presents more preferable to felines. "Lizards are good," she told her pet. "They eat mosquitoes, and heaven knows we have too many of those." She swatted at one of the little blood-sucking insects that landed on her arm.

Seeming to understand, Grim dropped the lizard, but began the chase anew when the reptile darted beneath a fern border. "It's like I said before," Isabel continued. "The hunt is more exciting than the kill."

When she thought about hunting, Isabel wondered how Marcella had captured Cooper Adair. Although he seemed a bit puffed up, he was nothing like his mollycoddled fiancée. But what did Isabel know? Maybe the two deserved each other.

And Isabel did know Marcella's kind. In the last few years St. Augustine had drawn many of the same type of women. These were young ladies whose wealthy parents sent their daughters to the town's two private female academies, or they were the pampered daughters and idle wives of the rich northern men who brought their families to winter in Florida. The visitors came in droves every year, filling up the hotels and guest houses to while away their days in idleness.

Not that Isabel envied those women their lot, because she didn't. She might be poor and constantly struggling to make ends meet, but she would choose her life over theirs any day. At least she had a purpose. Working with her herbs and curatives was the most important thing in her life, and she also valued her independence.

But in the last year she had been lonely. She was of an age

to marry and have children, almost past the age, yet Isabel set high standards for herself. She wouldn't marry just any man. In Wooster Farley she had seen the worst, so it was only natural that she should seek the best. Isabel had decided long ago that when she married it would have to be to a man who was like her *padre,* or what she could remember of him. Cooper Adair certainly resembled her father with his blond good looks, but looks weren't everything.

The man intended to ruin her. Well, maybe that wasn't his intent, but if his drug business was right next door to hers, it certainly wouldn't help her situation.

Isabel stared into space. She was at a loss as to what to do about her neighbor. He had come South to marry Marcella, and it was clear he wouldn't be leaving any time soon, not if the wedding took place. But he wasn't married yet! Maybe Isabel could feed him a potion that would make him fall out of love, and then he would sell the post business and go back North.

"A potion to fall out of love." As far as she knew, there was no such potion.

Walking beneath the arbor, she flicked one of the many shell chimes—her spiritmakers—that dangled from the viney ceiling. The rustling shells reminded her of the tide pulling against the shore. The sound always soothed her, and the shells had another purpose as well. They, like the copper bracelet she always wore, were love charms.

In order to attract a true love, the seeker was advised to wear an amulet, a necklace of seashells. Not only for this reason did Isabel sometimes wear shell jewelry, but she had also made the shell adornments for her home. Under Wooster Farley's reign, her house had witnessed too much unhappiness. Isabel had hung up the shells not long after her stepfather's death, deciding it was time her home enjoyed a little love as well.

Love as well.

"That's it!" Excitement flushed her cheeks. It suddenly occurred to her how she could get rid of Cooper Adair—how she could make him sell the post building and move back North. Since she had no potions that would make Cooper Adair fall out of love with Marcella, she would have to use a potion to make him fall in love. With her. Of course, she wouldn't use a real love potion; instead she would use her womanly wiles.

Recalling his kiss and how pleasant it had been, she decided that wooing him might not be so terrible. Isabel's spirits soared. Through the years she had helped dozens of young ladies cast spells on their young men; therefore, she shouldn't be helpless in casting her own spell. What had she told her friend Dora about her potions? "A potion only helps you send out your own personal vibrations to attract the right partner, but once the spark is ignited, the rest is up to you."

Cooper Adair definitely wasn't the person for Isabel because of the business he was in, but she could certainly use her magic, and Grimalkin's, to make Marcella jealous—jealous enough to send Cooper packing, laboratory stock and all, all the way back to Philadelphia where he came from.

Grimalkin buzzed her ankles when she tried to move. Lifting the big tom in the air, she stared into his golden eyes and in so doing, realization dawned. "You were trying to tell me to keep up the ruse about the kiss I shared with Cooper, weren't you? We have to make Marcella jealous so she'll break the engagement. And you, my old fairy cat, are going to help me."

"Meow."

"Yes, me-now," she said hugging him to her. "The sooner we get started, the sooner we'll be rid of that—that Yankee." Grim's bushy tail swished when she dropped him back on the ground.

As she moved toward the front door, her reflection in the window gave her pause. Dressed in men's clothing as she was, it was no wonder that Marcella had mistaken her for a man and the hired help. How, looking as she did, could she win Cooper away from the beautiful Marcella? Her trusty cat would help her, but Isabel was smart enough to know that such an undertaking would require more than her womanly wiles and her potions.

Although Isabel wore britches only when fishing or working in her garden, she feared the damage was done. Because Cooper had seen her at her worst, he would always think of her as a gangly, unattractive female. Isabel had never had the time or money to spend on her appearance, but if she intended to win Cooper away from Marcella, she would have to make some changes. It was time she began to look and act like a woman.

The acting part wouldn't be that difficult because her *madre* had drummed good manners into her from the day she was born, but how did one become beautiful? After pondering this thought for several moments, Isabel decided that a bath would be a good place to begin. Not just any bath, mind you, but a hot, steamy soaking using her special herbal soaps and creams that would make her smell and feel like a real lady—a lady impossible for Cooper Adair to resist.

The sun had dipped below the treetops when Cooper left the Kents' residence. The evening he had been eagerly anticipating had been anything but pleasant. It had turned out to be yet another troublesome incident to add to a growing list of problems that had confronted him from the moment he stepped down from the train this morning.

When he had arrived at Marcella's, she had refused to see him. Only after her parents' insistence had she granted him an audience, but she had done so resentfully. That he had caused the woman he loved so much unhappiness went against Cooper's nature, and although Marcella had forgiven him, he wasn't yet ready to forgive himself.

The last hour spent on Marcella's porch had been a grueling one, and Cooper admitted there were moments during that hour when he feared there wouldn't be a wedding. It took some time, but finally he convinced her that Miss Gomez had misinterpreted his act of assistance to be more than it was. He had merely assisted the girl when she stumbled into his arms after tripping on the tree root. The kiss he had claimed to enjoy had been more difficult to explain away, but after he had practically groveled at her feet, Marcella had forgiven him. Once again his future appeared bright.

But as Cooper walked home, he still puzzled over that kiss. Not only had he admitted kissing a strange woman whom he had not met until today, but also he had enjoyed doing it, claiming it to be the most enjoyable kiss of his experience. Cooper shook his head in disbelief. The entire day had been an enigma from start to finish, but it was time now to put the whole business behind him and begin again.

Even this evening's dinner had been postponed until to-morrow, and for this Cooper was thankful. Although he hadn't eaten since breakfast, food was the farthest thing from his mind. At this point, all he wanted was a bath and a bed, and with this thought Cooper increased his pace.

Dusk settled like a fuzzy blanket over the quiet town. With it came a soft breeze blowing inland from the bay, bringing the scent of briny water and the sweet fragrance of an uni-dentifiable flower. The gentle wind caressing his skin was a blessed relief after the hot, oppressive day, and Cooper de-cided to slow down and enjoy the evening.

When he reached the gate, the courtyard was dark except for the glow of light that spilled from the windows of the Gomez bungalow. Cooper glanced toward his own building, the two-story clapboard that was nothing more than a dark-ened shadow against the star-studded sky, but to him it rep-resented home. He had invested heavily to purchase the property, but the risk was worth it, because he and Marcella would stake out their future together here.

He was the luckiest man alive. He had a promising future and a lady like Marcella Kent as his fiancée. Cooper still wondered how he had been lucky enough to capture the heart of a woman like Marcella. He had met her at a college dance through a school chum of his. For both he and Marcella it had been love at first sight. After only a few months they had become engaged in spite of their different backgrounds.

Marcella had been born the only child of a rich and successful businessman, while Cooper had been born the oldest and only son to a railroad worker who also had two girls. Cooper's parents had worked, skimped, and saved in order for him to get an education. He loved his family and knew the sacrifices they had made on his behalf. Once his business was established, he intended to pay back that debt along with the money he owed Marcella's father, Jack Kent.

When the Kents had relocated to Florida, they insisted that it would be a sound investment in their daughter's future if Cooper would take the money they offered for a down payment on Isabel Gomez's property. An early wedding present, so to speak, that would allow the young couple to relocate to Florida as well. Cooper hadn't been too keen on accepting the money from his future in-laws, preferring instead to work and save the money needed. But at Marcella's insistence he had finally agreed. He couldn't fault her for wanting to be close to her parents. She had also convinced him that taking the gift would allow them to marry sooner. And like any young man, Cooper was eager to begin his life with the woman he loved.

Still deep in thought, he lifted the iron latch, pushed open the gate, and stepped inside the courtyard. Allowing his eyes to adjust to the walled-in darkness, he closed the gate and began moving toward his building. Cooper was glad that Miss Gomez was nowhere to be seen. He had had more than enough conversation with her for one day.

He passed beneath the tree where the woman had tripped, guarding his footsteps as he went. The only root that he cared to come in contact with was a cheroot. He did have a box of cigars inside his suitcase that he hadn't retrieved from where he had left it earlier. He would collect his baggage after he unlocked the door.

Reaching the stoop, Miss Gomez's cat appeared beside Cooper's ankles. "Scat," he said, hoping to scare the animal away. When the cat moved enough to allow him to step on the concrete slab, Cooper fished in his pocket for the key, the key Miss Gomez had given him earlier.

His hand delved first into one pocket, then the other. Cooper repeated the action, giving himself a thorough frisking.

"Empty!"

He was no better off now than he had been earlier when Miss Gomez had refused to give him his key. He still couldn't get into the accursed building. He still was locked out.

"Meow, meow."

"You—whatever your name is—I don't need your help."

The cat brushed past his ankles several times, his rumbling purr filling the night. Beneath his breath he mumbled, "I'm certainly glad you've got something to purr about."

Because it was too dark to see, Cooper traced the keyhole with his finger, making certain the mysterious key hadn't ended up in the door by chance. Nothing.

"Meowwwww!"

The cat brushed against his trousers several more times.

"Scat, cat," he said, shooing him while he fought to keep his balance. "Go eat a rat—or rat poison would even be better."

As the cat continued to weave around his ankles, Cooper felt guilty for having such a cruel thought. Although he didn't like animals, cats in particular, he shouldn't wish this one a bad end. The cat was only doing what all cats did.

Closing his fingers around the knob, Cooper jiggled it. Why would he even expect the damn thing to open? The way his luck had been running all day, why expect anything?

He jolted the knob again, then thrust his weight against the door. A sharp pain ripped through his shoulder, numbing his arm.

Taking a deep calming breath, he cradled his arm against his chest. Usually he didn't believe in omens, good or bad, but he was beginning to think it would take an act of God to get him inside this building.

Cooper swung around and leaned against the door. He had probably lost the key when Isabel Gomez tripped. Hell! He almost lost everything else then as well; his self-control, his memory, and his fiancée. Cooper glanced at the ground. Without a light, finding that key tonight would be like searching for a needle in a haystack.

His stomach knotted as he worried over what to do. It was too late to rent a room in town; besides, he wasn't familiar with the local hotels. The way he saw it he had two choices. He could ask to borrow a lantern from Miss Gomez to search for the lost key, or he could sleep on the stoop. When a mosquito buzzed his ear, then began feasting on the back of his neck, Cooper slapped it away and made a decision. Although it was against his better judgment to seek out Miss Gomez, after considering his options, he beat a path to her door.

Once beneath the portico, Cooper sucked in a deep breath. Facing a firing squad was preferable to facing his odd neighbor again.

Eccentric! That was exactly how he would describe his neighbor. Cooper reasoned that any woman who dressed like a man and enjoyed fishing instead of spending time earning a living when she was supposed to be near destitute wasn't exactly normal. Adding to the list of her peculiarities, she had refused to turn over property that she had legally sold, and then had made an engaged man kiss her. She was definitely a deviant. That was it, he thought. There was something wrong with her, not him.

Upon realizing this, it was as though a great weight suddenly lifted from his shoulders. Instead of losing his mind as he had begun to suspect he was earlier, he could lay the blame for the day's strangeness on Miss Gomez. This assumption made facing her seem less threatening. As Cooper moved toward her front door, a gust of wind ran beneath the portico, making the many wind instruments come alive with sound.

In addition to the unusual music, he heard a woman singing. The beautiful, simple melody and the plaintive words of the song gave Cooper pause. Instead of knocking and announcing himself immediately, he was drawn from the door to the window. Miss Gomez had a lovely voice, if indeed the singer was she. Curious now, he bent to peer inside.

It took a moment for his eyes to adjust, allowing him to see past the gauzy curtain that was pulled across the opening. Soon the picture formed. The small room that served as a kitchen and parlor was aglow with candlelight that burnished gold the whitewashed walls and ceiling. The wavering flames of the many candles spilled pools of rippling light across the highly polished wooden floor, giving the spartan interior a softer, more dreamlike atmosphere.

Heavy wooden beams supported the low ceiling where dried herbs hung in clusters, their silhouettes shadow-dancing in the wavy muted light. Miss Gomez must love copper, because the room was filled with bowls, plates, and various other implements made from the reddish-brown metal. Even the huge tub she sat submerged in was made from copper.

Submerged in?

The woman was bathing!

Cooper's heart slammed against his ribs. It took a moment before he realized that her damn cat had begun bumping against his legs again, preventing all movement. A gentleman, Cooper reasoned, would not linger, peering in on such a personal scene like some loathsome Peeping Tom. A sane man would run as fast and far as his feet would carry him. But it appeared that Cooper was neither a gentleman nor sane, because his feet remained rooted to the ground.

If Miss Gomez should learn of this latest transgression, he knew she would have him locked up in the slammer. And rightfully so. He was a man not to be trusted. Not only had he goosed her with her fishing pole in bright daylight and kissed her senseless, but now that night had fallen, he had taken to peeping into her window like some depraved pervert.

As he watched transfixed, she stood. With her back to him, she reached for a copper pitcher on the adjacent stand. Holding the pitcher above her head, she poured the rinse water through her hair. The liquid sluiced over her tall, long-legged, not-at-all-gangly, boyish figure that now appeared lean and willowy, gilding her skin golden in the soft light. And Cooper's very manly body reacted.

Oh, my god. I've got to get out of here.

A sense of urgency drove him, but unfortunately the bothersome cat continued to weave around Cooper's ankles, and when he jerked away from the window, his foot trampled the animal's tail.

"Meowrrr!"

The feline's yowl put Cooper in mind of cats in heat—put him in mind of his own wretched condition.

"Grimalkin?" Isabel Gomez called from the opposite side of the sheer curtain. "Get in here now."

Cooper flattened himself against the side of the house, not daring to move for fear of being discovered.

The four-legged piece of fur glanced at him with eyes that glowed like candle flames before he pounced upon the windowsill and disappeared inside the cottage.

"Bad boy," his mistress scolded, "you're not to be out tomcatting."

Cooper felt heat rush through his body as though the rebuke was meant for him.

He allowed several moments to pass before he moved from his hiding place beneath the eaves. As he made his way across the courtyard toward his building, he reclaimed his suitcase, his jacket, and tie. Where he would be spending the night was no longer a concern.

Considering his actions of the last half hour, Cooper knew he deserved to do penance. If his atonement commanded that he sleep on a stone cold slab, then so be it. More righteous men than he had done so and become better men for it.

Four

Isabel stared down at the man sleeping on the concrete stoop, or she supposed he was sleeping, since she couldn't see his face. His head and shoulders were covered with the rumpled, travel-weary jacket that he had worn yesterday when she first met him. Although Cooper's face was not visible, Isabel recognized the rest of him. All six feet plus lay curled on his side with his arms and legs drawn up toward his chest. Even rolled up as he was he was still a sight for sore eyes. A sight that made her blood rush through her veins as dangerously as the currents that flowed beneath the trolley track across Matanzas Bay.

When she recalled their shared kiss, her thoughts went spinning out of control, and she reined them in. The kiss they had shared meant nothing to her. It had been only a means to rid herself of Cooper Adair's presence.

There, she told herself, she was back on track, but why was Cooper Adair sleeping outdoors with the mosquitoes and palmetto bugs? Isabel glanced at the keyhole where last night she had placed the key after discovering it on the ground. The morning sun splashed against its bronze skeleton shape. Apparently Cooper hadn't found the key when he had returned, which would explain why he was sleeping outside on the stoop instead of inside in the upstairs apartment.

Isabel shot a curious look at Grimalkin, who was coiled up
on Cooper's ribs. Usually Grim slept the night at the end of
her bed, not rising until she did. This morning he had been
nowhere in sight. The cat stared at her, his eyes mirroring the
sun's rays as much as the bronze key before his drooping lids
slid shut.

You old fairy cat, what mischief have you been up to now?

Not that Isabel was opposed to his tricks, especially with
regard to Cooper Adair. She intended to use the feline's
magic to help further her cause, but what surprised her was
that she had never known Grimalkin to take to a stranger the
way he had taken to their neighbor. A good sign, Isabel decided, her spirits lifting with the thought.

A breeze fluttered the cloth that covered the basket she
held in her hands, filling the air with the scent of warm
flaky dough. She had been up before daybreak baking biscuits to bring to Cooper this morning. She had also included a jar of her best honey as a peace offering. Now, if
the recipient of her gift would awaken, maybe he would not
only be pleased with her offer of neighborliness, but also
see that the hoyden of yesterday had turned into a
respectable-looking lady. Well, sort of, Isabel corrected.

She might be as clean as a whistle, but she feared her
wardrobe was sorely lacking and she had a plan to remedy
that. Later she would take a trip to the shop run by the Ladies'
Aid Society, where they sold second-hand clothing. But for
now she wore her Sunday best. The navy material was worn
and faded from too much wear. It was time, Isabel decided
to save the garment for working in her garden. A worn dress
would never woo Cooper away from the beautiful Marcella.

"Mr. Adair," she called, nudging Cooper with the toe of
her shoe.

A barely audible groan escaped from beneath the rumpled
coat, making Isabel question the wisdom of disturbing a
sleeping man. Wooster Farley, when awakened from a deep
alcohol-induced sleep, would come up punching, and more

than once Isabel had had to dodge those blows. But even Grimalkin didn't look uneasy. In fact, he looked very relaxed. His eyes were still closed, and he appeared unmindful of the noise beneath him, or of her standing above him.

Did she dare nudge Cooper again? Isabel watched, and when his legs twitched, hope sprang into her heart. He was waking up.

When several more moments passed and he still didn't open his eyes, Isabel decided she would just have to wake him. It was getting late, and from what she had learned about her neighbor yesterday, she knew he wouldn't appreciate being discovered asleep on the stoop. Instead of nudging him, Isabel bent, lifted the edge of the coat, and slowly peeled it away from his torso.

Cooper blinked and was momentarily blinded. Every muscle in his body ached. His ribs, saddled with a hot, unmovable weight, pressed his bruised flesh deeper into the concrete slab.

Concrete slab? Cooper groped for lucidity. He thought to fluff the hard pillow beneath his head, then realized it wasn't a pillow at all. It was his valise. Why the hell was he lying on a concrete slab and using his valise for a pillow?

The sun's glare continued to blind him. Dark spots danced before his eyes. What he thought was nothing more than sunspots slowly changed into the silhouette of a woman, her figure haloed by the rising sun.

"Meow!"

"Marcella?"

He tried to sit, but found his movement hampered by the pressing weight upon his ribs. He sniffed. Biscuits? Surely he was mistaken. The aroma of the bread made his stomach rumble, reminding him that he had not eaten since yesterday morning.

Yesterday morning!

The thought jerked him upright, and the abrupt movement sent the pressing weight from his ribs to the ground.

"Mr. Adair?"

"You!" he accused, glaring at the woman who stood several

feet away. "And your cat." He noticed his jacket lying in a tumbled heap on the ground. The rumpled wool was now the private perch of Miss Gomez's cat, who looked at him through shining iridescent eyes.

"His name's Grimalkin."

"A good and proper name," Cooper sputtered, jumping to his feet. "Because, lady, *grim* is exactly what my life has been since I made the acquaintance of both you and your pesky cat."

"I'm—I'm sorry—"

"Don't be. All I ask is that once I'm granted admittance to my building, our paths will be long in crossing."

"Are you always so grumpy in the morning?"

"Usually no, but then I'm not in the habit of sleeping on a stoop with a suitcase for a pillow and a beast using me like one."

"I wondered why—"

"Why, Miss Gomez? Because I apparently lost my key last night when we—"

Cooper caught himself before he made a reference to the kiss that had not only caused him to lose the key, but also had almost cost him his fiancée. The last thing he wanted was to recall that kiss, or the memory of Miss Gomez naked in her bath. Sleeping on the stoop all night had been the lesser of his discomforts; the stone slab hadn't been the only thing hard. The pain in his body had been so great that he had welcomed the diversion of the mosquitoes that had feasted upon his blood. Even this morning he couldn't block her naked image from his mind.

"It's in the keyhole," he heard Miss Gomez say.

"What?"

"The key," she said. "There it is."

Cooper looked at the lock. Sure enough the key was where she claimed it was. "You put it there," he accused.

"I did. After you left last night I found the key on the ground. You must have dropped it."

"No," he insisted, running his fingers through his hair. "That key wasn't in the door last night."

"I know it was—maybe you overlooked it."

"Trust me, I wouldn't have overlooked it. That door was locked. I have bruises on my shoulder to—"

Cooper caught himself again. He wasn't about to admit that he had resorted to brute force when the door wouldn't open.

"It doesn't matter," she said. "The key is there now, so you can get inside." She stepped closer. "Here, I brought you some fresh biscuits. I thought you might be hungry."

Hungry? Yes.

But it's not food your body craves.

The unbidden thought was so powerful it was as though someone had voiced it aloud. The cat? Cooper's gaze locked on her cat, who stared back at him with his keenly perceptive stare. Impossible! What he needed was to distance himself from this strange pair, and the sooner he did so, the better.

But even that wasn't going to be easy. Both woman and cat blocked his entrance to the building. "If you'll excuse me . . ." His voice trailed off as he studied the woman in front of him.

Gone was the manly garb of yesterday. Today she looked very much like a woman. Of course, her beauty couldn't be compared with Marcella's classic good looks, but Miss Gomez was a strikingly beautiful woman with her exotic appearance.

Her faded blue dress with its fitted bodice emphasized the perfection of her womanly curves, leaving no doubt in Cooper's mind that she was absent of the rigid, stayed corsets that fashion dictated women wear. As a student of anatomy, he believed that such contraptions were injurious to the health. And it appeared that on this one opinion, he and Miss Gomez were in agreement.

Again he was taken in by her eyes. Once he looked into the golden orbs, he had trouble looking away. Cooper had never seen eyes of such an unusual color except for those of her cat.

"The biscuits," she said, her words making him release her gaze. "You do want the bread, don't you?"

"No, thank you. I'm not hungry," he lied.

Disappointment flashed across her perfect features. "I also brought a jar of my orange-blossom honey."

Cooper felt like a cad. Miss Gomez was probably just being neighborly, and the biscuits did smell delicious. He was famished and needed to eat. If he took the biscuits, he could kill two birds with one stone. First, he wouldn't have to go in search of breakfast, and second, he could get rid of Miss Gomez.

"Since you mentioned orange-blossom honey, I think I'll have to accept your gift. I love orange-blossom honey." Cooper forced a smile. "It's right neighborly of you to bring me breakfast." He held out his hands, expecting her to give him the basket.

Until Miss Gomez mentioned orange-blossom honey, Cooper hadn't thought one way or the other about there being different kinds. To him, honey was honey, and it all came from bees.

"Good," she said, plopping down on the stoop. "You and I can enjoy the biscuits together."

He didn't want to appear ungrateful by not joining her on the stoop, but he didn't particularly relish the thought of sitting beside her while eating his breakfast. What if Marcella should happen by and discover him breakfasting with Miss Gomez. Where Marcella was concerned, Cooper was already walking on eggshells.

"Sit," she said, patting the concrete slab beside her and smiling up at him. "If you have questions about the post building, I'll be happy to answer them. I probably know more about it than Mr. Jetson, because the property was in my family since its completion."

Fair enough, Cooper thought. What harm could come from his joining her in a discussion of his building? He might as well eat, too; then he could get right to work. He dropped down beside her and, once seated, he stretched his legs out in front of him. In the next few weeks he would be busy receiving and stocking the shelves of his drugstore and might not have another opportunity to speak with Miss Gomez.

She took a cue from him, stretching her own legs out beside his. Not a very ladylike way for a woman to sit, but then, from what he knew about his neighbor thus far, proper behavior for a lady was the least of her concerns. Cooper tried not to notice the way the material of her skirt, worn thin from many washings, fell over her legs, defining their long shapeliness. He traced their length from her slender feet to the basket now sitting on her lap, and a ripple of desire surged through him.

Disconcerted that she had the power to affect him, Cooper sniffed. She—no, he corrected, the *biscuits* did smell good. He watched her fold back the napkin. Nestled in the butter-stained cloth were the biggest, fluffiest biscuits that Cooper had ever seen. His stomach rumbled, and he salivated. She promptly handed him one of the puffy rolls, then opened her honey pot and spooned on a healthy portion.

"Eat away," she said, smiling.

And eat he did. The flaky biscuit, gooey with honey, tasted as sweet as the famed nectar of the gods. If he were a poet, he might have compared the enclosed courtyard to Eden, and the woman beside him to Eve.

The rising sun beat down on his head and shoulders, its warm fingers massaging away the kinks he had gained from sleeping on concrete for the better part of the night. The verdant lawn was dappled with leaf shadows, and from the nearby trees the many wind instruments stirred by a soft breeze sounded like tinkling fairy music. He breathed in and discovered the air was redolent with the aroma of exotic plants. Close behind them, Grimalkin snoozed. His purr, which seemed to run nonstop, made Cooper appreciate a cat's therapeutic effect on humans.

All in all, the moment felt comfortable, and Cooper stole a glance at Miss Gomez. She appeared to be enjoying herself as much as he was. She leaned back on her hands, her face lifted toward the sun with her eyes closed. His gaze strayed the length of her long, golden throat, settling on her high rounded breasts that were thrust out because of how she sat. Guilty, he jerked his gaze away and crammed the last bite of biscuit into his mouth and swallowed. Yesterday she had teasingly accused him of being a rogue, and since that time he had entertained many unscrupulous thoughts about her, so maybe her accusation was true.

"So tell me," he began, disrupting the tranquil silence. Before he could finish his sentence, his nose began to burn with a tickling itch. He sneezed, so loudly that he scared a bird from a nearby bush.

Beside him, Miss Gomez giggled and picked up the honey pot. "This," she said, "will cure what ails you."

Considering where his eyes had been, Cooper almost choked. As a druggist, he knew that bee pollen was taken for a range of problems, but the one that came immediately to mind was impotence. He felt his face grow warm. Such an ailment had never affected him. When needed, Cooper always performed, and in the company of this woman, impotency was the least of his worries. Since meeting her yesterday, his body and his mind had been in a constant state of arousal.

"This," she said, tapping the jar with one finger, "will help you build up an immunity to the local pollen."

Cooper knew about pollen, and he certainly knew about the male element in fertilization. Since meeting Miss Gomez, he hadn't thought about anything else.

"I know that," he responded more sharply than he intended. Then he chastised himself for jumping to conclusions about her meaning. Cooper couldn't understand why she evoked such a reaction in him, but she did. He corrected his description. *Provoked* would be a better word.

She ignored his sharpness. "Bees love orange-blossom nectar. Although most of the orange growers have moved farther south, there are a few local groves that weren't destroyed completely by the big freeze a few years back. But I imagine—don't you?—that it's a combination of the different flora in the area that makes this honey a good remedy for pollen sufferers. I know I sell a lot of it."

"Indeed" was Cooper's only response.

Hunger drove him to accept another biscuit when she offered it. He took a big bite and chewed.

It was true. His nose did itch, and his eyes did burn. Yesterday they had burned like the devil, but he had contributed the sting to his sweat. Considering his lack of sleep last night, he could be taking a cold. Or all his symptoms could be caused from his own stench. God, he needed a bath. It was at that precise moment that Miss Gomez's cat decided to leave his perch behind them, and as he passed into the yard, he brushed against Cooper's arm. He watched the overstuffed beast disappear up the trunk of a nearby tree.

Until now, he hadn't noticed the odd tree growing in the courtyard. The tree had two trunks, each one a different species of tree, and in Cooper's opinion looked like something that Alice might have encountered during her bizarre adventure into Wonderland.

"Two trunks?" Cooper spoke aloud.

"The 'love' tree," his hostess informed him.

"Love tree?" Cooper hooted. "Now I've heard everything. Next you're going to tell me that those two trunks love each other. Granted, this town by the sea has its enchantments, but anyone with half a brain would recognize that two trunks are merely nature's way of playing tricks on humans. Some bird, or perhaps even the wind, dropped a palm seed in the crook of that old oak, and the seed sprouted into a palm."

"Are you always so realistic?" his companion asked, irritated by his mocking tone. "Legend has it—"

"Legend? Something tells me you believe in fairy tales, too."

"I do believe in—"

The front gate opened and clanked shut, prohibiting further conversation on the subject. Isabel set aside the basket, and she and Cooper stood. He expected to see Marcella rushing across the yard toward him, and wondered how he would ever convince her of the innocence of his having breakfast with Miss Gomez after last night's fiasco.

"Dora?"

It wasn't Marcella. Cooper let out a breath he hadn't realized that he was holding. The visitor, on hearing her name, veered from the path leading to Miss Gomez's house and rushed toward them in a flurry of nervous energy.

"There you are, Ysabel," she said.

Ysabel? It seemed that Miss Gomez had yet another name to add to the growing list. Not only was she known as Isabel Gomez Farley, but now it seemed she was also known as Isabel Ysabel Gomez Farley. The woman was a walking crossword puzzle.

Coming to a rocking halt in front of them, the woman called Dora exclaimed, "The potion worked." She grabbed Miss Gomez's hands, and the two fairly danced with excitement. "Last night Ralph asked me to marry him. Can you believe it?"

Miss Gomez laughed, the same throaty laugh of yesterday that managed to make his insides jiggle with excitement. "But of course I can believe it," she responded, winking. "My potions are very powerful."

Potions? What an old-fashioned term to apply to medicines. Although Cooper believed there was no longer a need for herbalists and their backyard cures, he supposed there were some people who still relied on the herbalists' home remedies. But in his studies at the institute, Cooper had never come across any old or new medication that contained properties that would compel one to propose marriage. Only would-be sorcerers claimed to make love potions—which in Cooper's opinion were both ineffective and nonsensical. And sometimes dangerous. People had been burned at the stake for less. Surely he had misunderstood their conversation.

The two women's excitement ebbed, and the new arrival pinned him with an appraising stare. At the same time Cooper did some appraising of his own, deciding that if anyone needed a magic elixir to win a man's affection, he was staring at her. This Dora was the homeliest woman Cooper had ever encountered; short and buxom with a patch of thinning, limp brown hair and a sallow complexion. Small beady eyes assessed him from beneath droopy lids that held no sign of any lashes, or the lashes were so thin they appeared almost non-existent.

"Dora," Miss Gomez said, "please forgive me. In all the excitement, I've completely forgotten my manners. Allow me to introduce you. This is—"

"Your new beau?" Dora finished for her. The woman jabbed a short, plump elbow into Miss Gomez's ribs and winked with one of her lashless eyes. "Been practicing your own magic, have you?" The woman tittered, revealing a mouth full of big teeth.

Cooper sputtered his denial. "I'm afraid not—"

"I don't do magic," Miss Gomez interrupted, glancing at Cooper before continuing, "and he's not my beau. This is Mr. Adair. He's the man from Philadelphia who purchased my post building. Remember, I told you about him. This is Dora Gay."

With down-home politeness, the woman thrust her hand toward him. "Call me Dora," she said, capturing his hand and almost shaking his arm off. "So you plan to reopen the trading post, do you? That's real nice. I take it you're unmarried and in need of a good woman to take to wife?"

"Mr. Adair won't be reopening the post," Miss Gomez said, her face almost level with his. Her eyes looked even more like amber in the bright sunshine. She smiled at him then, her lush, wide lips revealing teeth as lustrous as the finest of pearls. "And, yes," she continued, her eyes never leaving his, "he's found a good woman to take to wife."

You're looking at her. The thought was so profound that Cooper broke eye contact with her. His gaze snapped to the branches of the "love" tree, where Grimalkin scrutinized him with his golden eyes. The hair prickled on the back of Cooper's neck, and again he felt as though someone or something was tampering with his thought processes.

Impossible. He was overreacting as usual, just as he had been doing for the last twenty-four hours in Miss Isabel Ysabel Gomez Farley's presence. The woman of many names had done nothing to warrant his distrust. She had only spoken the truth. Cooper knew better than anyone that he had found a good woman to take to wife, and that woman was Marcella.

Deciding that he might be talking to a prospective customer, Cooper decided to act like the professional that he was.

"I won't be reopening the post as a trading center," Cooper told Dora. "I'm a pharmacist and I'll be opening St. Augustine's first modern drugstore." His lips curled upward, showering her with his most charming smile. Cooper had been told by many that his pleasing smile would give him the advantage when dealing with people.

"Drugstore?"

Dora's expression turned sullen, making her face even more unattractive, if such a feat was possible. "You intend to compete with our Ysabel?"

Cooper watched as the woman stiffened, seeming to grow several inches taller as she spoke.

"Our Ysabel is a fine herbalist, just like her dear departed mama. Or more to the point, sir, you should know that this town is loyal to its own." She looked at Miss Gomez. "I can understand, dear, that it's easy to be taken in by a handsome face, but aren't you worried about the competition his drugstore will offer?"

Isabel saw the storm brewing behind Cooper's eyes. Considering everything the man had been through in the last twenty-four hours, she supposed he wasn't in the best frame of mind. Although she appreciated her friend's support, she was in no mood to get into another confrontation over the nature of hers and Mr. Adair's businesses. In time Isabel felt very confident that everything would work out for the best.

"There's plenty of business for us both," she lied. She placed a hand on her friend's shoulder and steered her away from Mr. Adair and toward the cottage. "Why don't you come inside? I'll make us a nice cup of herbal tea, and you can tell me all about your wonderful news."

"But surely, Ysabel, you can't mean—"

"Shush," she whispered as they walked away.

"—that man who has the power to ruin you?"

Once out of earshot of Cooper, Isabel said, "Oh, Dora, all men have that power. My mother was a perfect example. But you, dear friend, should know better than most that we women have our ways, now don't we?"

Dora tittered behind her hand. "I guess we do, dear girl."

When Isabel glanced back over her shoulder, she saw a confused and bewildered Cooper Adair entering his building.

Seconds before the door closed, Grimalkin slipped in, too. Undetected, Isabel supposed, when the shaggy ball of fur didn't come flying right back out the door.

Smiling to herself, she opened her own door and escorted Dora inside.

Work your magic, you old fairy cat. I'm depending on you.

Five

Home at last. Cooper pushed open the door, stepped inside, and closed it behind him. He paused just beyond the entrance, the brass key enclosed in his palm. After last night's experience, the key would never be far from his person again, even if it meant he had to wear it on a chain around his neck.

Several moments passed while his eyes grew accustomed to the dimness. Something, its origin unknown, scooted past his ankles, but he never identified what the unspecified thing was because it disappeared as suddenly as he had felt it. Probably a mouse. Not yet ready to deal with rodents, Cooper shifted his attention to the building's interior.

As he stepped deeper into the room, his feet stirred up a cloud of dust. Powdery motes floated on a ray of light that slashed past the window and shutter. His spirits sagged. Although he knew the building had sat empty for almost a year, he hadn't expected such shabbiness. Maybe the place would look better in full light.

Drawing in a deep breath, Cooper stepped to the nearest window and unlocked the shutter. Once the warped wood was released from the rusty center latch, the wooden lattices clattered back against the wall. A missing hinge caused one of the shutters to hang precariously, and his earlier elation on finally claiming his property faded.

The condition of the building was much worse than he expected. From Mr. Jetson's glowing description, Cooper had assumed he'd purchased a well-maintained property, but so far that wasn't the case. The interior smelled rank, mildewy, and in need of a long-overdue airing. As he moved deeper into the room, the flooring beneath his feet felt spongy, suggesting rotten wood or termite infestation. What other problems would he discover hidden in the ancient clapboard structure?

He eyed the furnishings that were part of the purchase. Several chairs were scattered haphazardly across the room, and a cracked mirror hung behind a long cupboard that had probably served as the post's counter. As for needed shelving, the room contained no such luxury. The charred remains still in the fireplace could very well have been his shelves.

Anger swelled inside him. He felt cheated. He had purchased a near derelict building whose former owner had sorely neglected the property. That neglect explained why the property had remained empty, and why it had been sold for a bargain price. The thought occurred to Cooper that if Miss Gomez had been looking to give the building away, she would have been hard pressed to find a taker.

"Damn it all. Now what?" He ran his fingers through his hair. How in the name of Judas was he going to explain *this* to Marcella and her father, especially after having given the Kents such a glowing account of the purchase?

More than curious now, he gave the room another critical sweep with his gaze. He spied the staircase at the back of the room that led to the next level and to the apartment where Cooper planned to live. The same apartment where he and Marcella would live after they were married until he could afford to build her a house. The image of his beloved in all her finery coming down those rickety, dusty stairs was almost laughable. But it wasn't mirth that accompanied him toward the stairwell. Instead it was anger not only with himself, but also with Mr. Jetson and Miss Gomez. The two had suckered him in but good.

And if the downstairs wasn't bad enough, the upstairs wasn't any better. It was actually one long room sectioned off by the arrangement of furniture into a kitchen and keeping room, with the bedroom at the far end.

As he walked through the cavernous space, he decided the furnishings would have made good kindling. He passed by two tufted-back armchairs that looked as though toughs had used them instead of gentlemen. He ran his fingers over the table between the chairs, feeling the many cigar burns that scarred its surface. A parlor lamp, with chimney still intact, sat on the table, but to Cooper the dancing cherubs on the flowery base looked out of place among the shoddy furnishings.

The kitchen area held a wood cookstove, a dilapidated dry sink with a cracked porcelain bowl, and a square table with two mismatched chairs.

As he moved toward the bedroom space, his spirits sank even lower. So much for a good night's sleep. The three-quarter iron bed held a soiled and lumpy mattress with remnants of its mossy stuffing hanging from a hole in the ticking. He supposed some displaced animal had decided to return the moss to the tree where Cooper, too, thought it belonged, or perhaps the rodent had taken up residence inside the mattress.

Not wanting to dwell on such possibilities, Cooper inspected the commode and washstand. A chipped and stained chamber pot sat behind the chest's wooden doors, and he quickly swung away from the disgusting sight and closed the doors.

"This place will never do for Marcella," Cooper said out loud.

Then don't bring her. I'm sure she will hate it.

There it was again. The same sensation he had experienced yesterday. The feeling that someone else's thoughts had infiltrated his mind, yet today he was prone to agree with the intruder. Marcella would hate it here.

Cooper's gaze skirted the wooden dresser with its wishbone mirror, then moved to the window with its shredded curtain. He jerked his gaze back to the dresser, his heart speeding up several beats, thinking the building had come furnished with its own wild animal.

"You! How did you get in here?"

It wasn't a wild animal at all. It was only Miss Gomez's cat who sat perched on the dresser. With his front paws curved beneath his thick chest, and his full round cheeks giving him a chubby, chipmunk appearance, Grimalkin studied Cooper's every move with his round, expressive eyes.

The look the feline sent him was almost unnerving. Again Cooper felt as though the cat had the power to read his thoughts. A ludicrous idea! Grimalkin was nothing more than a dumb animal with claws instead of brains.

"Boarding you isn't part of the agreement," Cooper said. "Scat, cat!" He swished his hands at the animal, hoping to scare him away, but instead of the cat skedaddling as Cooper expected, the animal continued its vigil, seemingly indifferent to his threats.

Cooper pointed at the stairs. "Get out now." The animal didn't budge. "If you won't leave, then I will." He turned on his heels and headed back toward the stairs.

Behind him, he heard Grimalkin hit the floor. Dashing past his feet and coming to a dead stop in front of him, the animal almost tripped him. He crouched in front of Cooper's feet; his pupils narrowed to black slits while his tail swished. When Cooper tried to step around him, Grimalkin repeated his earlier movement, blocking Cooper's exit.

Never one to fully trust cats, Cooper froze. He had heard that you should never allow a strange dog to sense your fear, because that gave him the advantage. Did the same rule apply to cats? Hoping to sound more in control than he felt, Cooper demanded, "What in the name of Judas is wrong with you?"

At any moment he expected Grimalkin to leap on him and begin tearing him to shreds, but instead of attacking, the cat made his usual annoying passes against Cooper's ankles. His fear of the animal abated, only to be replaced by a strange, prickling sensation that walked up and down his spine, making him feel almost light-headed. The room swam in and out of focus, and Cooper gripped the rail, thinking he might tumble down the length of the stairs. He dropped down on the landing, hoping the dizzy spell would pass. When Grimalkin eased up to his side as though he were an invited friend, Cooper felt too woozy to send him on his way, but he did note that the marred steps, too, were in need of repair.

Cooper squeezed the bridge of his nose and closed his eyes. When he looked up again, the whole room had been transformed. Gone was the earlier dank smell. Now it smelled like freshly varnished wood. Lemon-yellow sunshine streamed past the windows, making the wooden floors look like glass. No longer was the furniture shabby and in need of repair; now it appeared to be brand-new.

Then, as suddenly as the picture had formed in his mind, it vanished. His dizziness vanished as well, causing Cooper to question his sanity once again.

"You're just tired," he cautioned, "so tired that now you're hallucinating." As he lifted his arm to blot the perspiration from his brow, he smelled his own body odor. "And in desperate need of a bath."

Water. He realized for the first time that he hadn't seen the well. He recalled the sales agreement had stated that the two properties would share the well jointly. Cooper hadn't noticed a well in the courtyard where he had spent the night, so where the heck was it?

Cooper stood, eager to vent his anger over the condition of the property. He could not wait to tell Miss Gomez that he didn't appreciate having been duped by her and her salesman. He glanced around the room one last time, deciding that after his vision, or whatever it was, the task of setting the place to order didn't seem quite as monumental. It would require him checking into a hotel for a few days, but he could do that even with his limited funds. But for the moment he had more pressing matters that needed his attention.

Displeasure filled him as he looked down at the woman's cat. "You mangy beast, it's time you returned home." With but one thought, Cooper sprinted down the stairs and out the side door.

He moved fast, but Grimalkin moved even faster. Cooper had never seen a cat walk so fast before. As the cat preceded him on their trek across the yard, he questioned who led whom—man or beast? If Cooper had been a betting man, which he wasn't, he would have placed his money on Grimalkin.

Six

Isabel and Dora closed the gate and began the trek down St. George Street together. Dora was on her way home, and Isabel was on her way to the shop run by the Ladies' Aid Society of St. Augustine.

Before today Isabel had never visited the establishment, and she had decided she wouldn't mention her destination to Dora for fear her old friend would believe Isabel was near destitute, and would take it on herself to take up a collection for her.

She wasn't in need of charity, only in need of a new wardrobe. Since her income didn't allow her to go on a spending spree, she decided that second-hand garments would have to do. Besides, she had heard the shop carried clothing in the latest styles, and that most were reasonably priced. If she must compete against the rich and beautiful Marcella for Cooper's favor, she knew she would have to look her best. With that settled in her mind, she decided to spend the next few minutes pumping Dora for any information she could tell her about Marcella.

Dora knew everything about everyone in the community, not only because her father was a schoolteacher and on the

board of commissioners for the town, but also because she
loved to gossip.

Isabel fidgeted, hating that she had resorted to meddling,
but her situation demanded it. If she wanted Cooper Adair to
sell his business and return home, Isabel had to make Marcella so jealous that she would break her engagement with
Cooper. She had to make Marcella believe that her fiancé had
fallen out of love with her, and fallen desperately in love with
Isabel. Under normal circumstances, the chance of that happening would be near to impossible, but Isabel had her trusty
cat to help her.

"Okay, Ysabel," Dora said, surprising her, "ask me what
you want to know."

"Know?"

"We've been friends forever, and I know you're as nosy
as I am. But unlike me, you don't pry. Instead you wait for
me to tell you all the juicy gossip."

"I never do any such—"

"Then you don't wish to know about your handsome neighbor's intended?" Dora's thin brows inched higher on her forehead, and she peered straight ahead, her expression
indifferent. They walked several more feet without either girl
speaking before the suspense became too much for Isabel.

"Tell me," she threatened, "or I'll give your beau a potion
that will turn him into a toad."

"You wouldn't!" Dora exclaimed.

Her expression was so funny that Isabel laughed. "Simple-
ton, of course I wouldn't, or couldn't. As I've told you numerous times, my potions only help a person send out their
own personal vibrations to attract the right partner, but once
the spark is ignited, the rest is up to them. It wasn't magic
that made Ralph propose, it was his love for you."

"You can say what you want," Dora said, "but I know I'm
no beauty, and I still can't believe that Ralph picked me
when—"

"Hush! You are beautiful. Your beauty comes from the
inside out, and that's the best kind. It's lasting."

"Well, then," Dora said, looking pleased, "I guess I'll have to spill my gossipy guts."

"Dora? Gossipy guts?" Isabel was delighted that her quest for information wasn't going to be as difficult as she first expected. "You must understand my interest is purely professional. I want to know all I can about my new neighbor only because we're going to be in direct competition with each other."

"You, my dear friend, aren't the only one with powers," Dora replied, linking arms with Isabel. "You've heard of the power of being a good listener?"

"I've heard of the power of the pen—"

"As you well know, instead of the written word, I'm more interested in the spoken." Dora laughed. "I do so love to gossip, but not maliciously, of course."

"Of course."

"The family's name is Kent. They moved here from Philadelphia about a month ago when their house was finished being built. It's a lovely home, overlooking the bay. And such porches," Dora lauded with a devilish glint in her eyes. "They wrap around the entire house, affording plenty of private space for spooning."

"Spooning?"

"Oh, yes, I forgot. Your interest is purely professional."

Isabel jabbed her in the ribs."

"Anyway, Mr. Kent has been here longer than the women."

"Women?" The way Dora said the word made Isabel believe there was a whole parcel of them. Heaven forbid! "How many women are there?"

"Quintuplets!"

"Five?" Isabel gasped.

It was worse than she suspected. Grimalkin's magic would have to be mighty powerful if it was to help her win Cooper away from a gaggle of Marcellas.

Dora slapped her hand across her mouth to stifle her giggles. "Oh, Ysabel, you are so easily duped. There are only two women. A wife and daughter."

Isabel decided that two could play at this teasing game. "Is the daughter's name Marshmallow?"

"Marshmallow?" Dora's dark gaze landed on Isabel.

This time it was Isabel's turn to giggle.

"Marcella is the correct pronunciation."

"La te da."

Dora slapped Isabel's arm playfully, and they both laughed as they stopped at the street corner to allow several carriages to pass.

"Family's loaded," Dora continued, "probably carpetbaggers."

"Carpetbaggers. Oh, Dora, really. Just because they're from the North doesn't mean they've come South to take advantage of us southerners. Besides, I don't hear any complaints against Mr. Henry Flagler, and he's a northerner. The tourist business is booming, and then the hotel has brought jobs—"

"Jobs," Dora interrupted, "that are mostly filled by career hotel workers who migrate from the northern hotels in the summer to the southern hotels in the winter."

"Not all of the workers," Isabel reminded her. "We were a sleepy little village with a small population until Flagler built his grand hotel. The Ponce de León with its gala opening this past winter put St. Augustine on the map."

Dora shrugged her narrow shoulders. "I suppose you're right, but as far as I'm concerned, the whole lot of them could stay at home. I for one liked the town the way it was before we became a winter destination. Even without this steady improvement to the economy, I'd be as happy as a clam that missed the clambake."

Isabel leaned toward Dora. "I'd chance that nothing could make you unhappy now that there is a wedding in your future."

"I'm not a betting woman, but I'd bet you're right."

Laughing, they began walking again, crossed the street, and nodded at several people they passed before stopping in front of the August Mercantile that displayed all manner of items in their window: dinnerware, flatware, knickknacks, and linens.

"I'll need so many things when I do set up housekeeping," Dora said.

As they stared at the display, Isabel noted their reflections in the big plate-glass window. Her gaze locked on Dora's, and they exchanged reflecting smiles.

Dora reached for Isabel's hand, linked fingers with her, then squeezed. "I'm so happy," she said, "and now that I'm to be married, I want you to find your special someone, too."

Isabel answered wistfully. "I suppose I will someday, but you know how I feel about affairs of the heart. After my mother's bad experience with my stepfather, I'll think long and hard before I give my heart to just any man."

"I know there's someone out there for you. Someone whose kiss will take your breath away like my Ralph's."

Cooper Adair's kiss had certainly done that, but he most assuredly was not the someone for Isabel. But did she dare tell her friend her plan?

Dora looked into her eyes. "You've found someone, haven't you?" she asked. "It's the druggist, Cooper Adair?"

Were her thoughts so transparent? Fearing they must be, she swung away from the window and began walking again.

"I'm right, aren't I? It is him?"

Isabel could feel Dora's knowing gaze, drilling into her profile.

"You can't fool your oldest and dearest friend."

"Don't be ridiculous, Dora. A girl would have to be both deaf and blind not to notice such a well-turned-out man, but need I remind you, he's spoken for."

"And when did that make a difference to you? In all those books you read, don't the women always get their men, engaged or otherwise? It's no wonder that you were dying to know everything I could tell you about the Kents."

"Really now. I wasn't dying to know. I was only asking because we're to be neighbors. Remember? Besides, he could never be my special someone. You said it yourself—he could ruin me."

"But, oh, what a way to be ruined."

"Dora Gay!" Isabel blushed. "You talk as though you were already married and new about such things."

"And you love it."

"I don't—"

"Neighbors, huh!" Dora asked, prohibiting any further comment. She laced her arm though Isabel's and fell into step beside her. "So if it is the druggist, Mr. Adair, then you do have a problem."

Isabel slammed to a stop. She hadn't expected Dora's response. "What do you mean I have a problem? Not that I'm the least bit interested—"

"Marcella Kent is not only rich, but she's also beautiful."

"And of course," Isabel huffily replied, "I'm neither of those things." Her dearest friend's reminder of her shortcomings wasn't exactly what she wanted to hear.

"Rich, no, beautiful, yes," Dora answered, "except when you're wearing those scandalous britches."

"There's nothing wrong with my britches—"

"Scandalous," Dora repeated.

"But practical for working in the garden, or for fishing."

"Marcella Kent would never wear men's britches."

"Marcella Kent would never work in a garden or fish."

"Now, you don't know that. She probably clips roses from her mother's garden and catches fish from her daddy's yacht."

"They own a yacht, too?"

Isabel had seen the fine ladies who accompanied their fathers and sweethearts to the yacht club of St. Augustine. Dora was right, none of those ladies wore britches.

"If it will make you feel any better, no, the Kents don't own a yacht. Yet."

"Yet?" The word came out as a weak peep.

"All I'm saying is that if Mr. Kent fancied owning a boat, he has enough money to buy one. Or anything else," Dora added, "including a husband for his daughter."

"He bought Mr. Adair for Marcella?"

This latest tidbit might muddy the waters, and Isabel only hoped her disappointment didn't show. She had never heard of such an exchange between couples, but she wondered if the intended husband didn't suit, was he returnable?

"Rumor has it this is the second or third man she has been betrothed to."

Isabel relaxed. Dora had answered her question. "Her father bought her two other suitors, and she returned them both?"

"I understand she is very hard to get along with. Spoiled rotten, as my father would say. And extremely jealous."

Jealous! Everything was going to be fine. "Now I understand," Isabel said, "why Marcella thought I was the hired help."

"You've met Marcella Kent?" Dora asked. "You never told me that."

"I never had a chance, but, yes, I met her. Last night. She mistook me for Mr. Adair's hired help." Isabel wasn't about to tell Dora the circumstances under which she and Marcella Kent had met. Some things were best left unsaid. "Can you believe her audacity? But then, if my family had that much money . . ."

"You were wearing those scandalous britches, weren't you?"

"Noooo, of course . . ." Dora shot her an accusing glance. "Yes! I had been fishing earlier. What did you expect? White linen?"

"No, but if you have designs on your neighbor, then it's high time you started looking and acting like a proper lady."

For years Dora had been trying to get her to give up her britches, but Isabel would never have considered it. But after her decision to win Cooper away from Marcella, things had changed. She took a deep, calming breath. "I've been thinking along those lines myself."

Dora's small eyes grew large. "You have? Now I know you're smitten."

"Am not."

"Are, too."

"Not."

"Too."

"Dora, you can be so hardheaded, and now that you're engaged, such a romantic. Need I remind you, since Cooper Adair plans to open a drugstore right next door to my herbal business, it is only natural that I should want to look and act more like a professional in order to compete."

"In order to compete? Ha! You don't fool me, Ysabel Gomez. In order to compete with Marcella Kent, you want to look and act more like a woman."

"Since when have you known me to care about my appearance?"

"Never. And that's why I know what you're up to. All I can say is it's about time." Dora slammed to a halt. "Time! Lordy, lordy, what time is it?"

"I would imagine it's close to noon. Why?"

"Noon? I've got to run. My father forgot his lunch, and I meant to take it to him after I stopped by your house."

"Where is his lunch?"

"Oh, no," Dora groaned. "I must have left it at home. I was in such a hurry to tell you my news that I must have walked right out of the house without it. Now I'll have to hurry home and get it."

"What's your father going to do when you're no longer around to bring him his lunch when he forgets it?"

"I'm certain he'll do just fine. Ralph's house is only a block away, so I'll still be close enough to look after him." She whirled away from Isabel and headed in the direction of her home. Calling over her shoulder, she said, "You and I will finish this conversation later."

I'm sure we will, Isabel thought, resigned. She still wasn't sure if she should let Dora in on her plan. Since her friend loved to gossip, bless her soul, it might be wise if Isabel kept her intentions to herself for a while longer.

Pulling her gaze from Dora's retreating back, she glanced across the street at the Plaza. She could see a few shoppers filing past the fresh produce and meat sold daily at the open City Market, but most of the Plaza's occupants were elderly locals, languishing on benches beneath the native oaks, whiling away the summertime hours.

Several old-timers played checkers regularly in the square, and Isabel could see that one game was already underway. Gathered around the two checker players was the usual crowd of watchers, offering advice or silently looking on.

A feeling of well-being settled over Isabel. During the summer months, the mood was easy in the quaint town—the way she remembered it from her youth. Not many tourists chose to brave the heat to stay in the smaller hotels, but that would all change when the winter season began in January, and the Ponce de León reopened its doors.

Before heading west, she glanced toward the Basilica Cathedral of St. Augustine, noting that repairs to the structure were almost complete. The great fire last year had destroyed the building's wooden roof, causing it to burn and collapse, leaving only the historic structure's coquina walls standing. There were times during that fire when flames had leaped from building to building in the block north of the Plaza—times when Isabel feared that she, like so many others, would lose everything. The memory of that night still made her shudder, and she turned away from the church, eager to leave her thoughts behind.

Because the day was so beautiful, Isabel decided that she would take a roundabout way to the second-hand shop, a route that would carry her past Flagler's now empty hotel. During the season, she stayed away from that part of town, refusing to gawk with the rest of the locals at the rich and famous visitors frequenting the Ponce de León. But off-season was another story. The magnificent building and grounds, though empty, still held the power to enchant.

Isabel likened the setting to those in the many books she read, and tried to imagine what it would be like to stay in such a splendid place, attending one of the many entertainments that took place at the hotel. In her daydreams she would be the belle of the ball, and all the young men in attendance would be vying for her attention. But today her fantasy was different. Instead of dozens of young man vying for her hand, there would be only one—Cooper Adair. And, for a short time, she would go willingly into his arms.

"But first you have to eliminate Marcella Kent from the picture." Realizing she had voiced the thought aloud, Isabel glanced guiltily around her, and after concluding no one had heard her declaration, she continued on her way.

The closer she came to the hotel, the slower she walked. While gliding across shadows cast by the massive structure, she peered up at one of the building's two graceful towers. Built in the Spanish-Renaissance style, the hotel's pearl-gray walls and red tile roof always made Isabel wonder if this was what the castles in her father's country were like.

She rounded the flagpole on the corner, passing three stories of rooms with dormer windows and airy loggias before stopping in front of the arched entrance that led into the inner courtyard.

The gate stood open, and the courtyard appeared empty. Moving deeper into the shaded concrete archway, Isabel stopped. Although the day was hot, the air inside the passageway felt cool.

Her gaze drifted appreciatively over the many shady arbors that hugged the building, the meticulously landscaped garden, and finally came to rest on the fountain of spitting frogs in the courtyard's center. Isabel smiled on seeing the fountain again. All those frogs with water pouring from their mouths made Isabel wonder if they were placed there as a warning to the throngs of young ladies who visited the hotel—a warning that not all frogs turned into handsome princes.

Directly across the courtyard at the main entrance to the castle, voices drifted her way. Since the hotel was closed to visitors during the summer, maintaining only a minimal staff, Isabel opted to move on rather than to be asked to leave. Besides, she didn't need to go inside the great hall to remember how it looked.

Before the hotel's grand opening, she had seen the rotunda, and the magnificence of the room would be forever engraved in her mind: the ceiling decorated with mural paintings, the floors of imported marble, the carved-wood landings and stair rails, and last but not least, the jewel-like windows made by a man named Louis Tiffany. A peek into the interior of that one room was all Isabel had been allowed, but that one peek was enough to last her for a lifetime.

The distant voices became louder, blotting out the sound of the fountain's trickling water. Leaving the passage behind, she stepped back into the bright sunlight and continued around the western side of the hotel until she reached Valencia Street.

It was here that Mr. Flagler had built the Artists' Studios. The building had been built to attract artists to the Ponce de León during the winter season, and already the facility had been filled with well-known painters. Rumor had it that all seven studios on the second floor had their own skylights. *Imagine that!*

Isabel looked at the balcony that ran the length of the building, allowing her very active imagination to imagine what kind of unsolicitous goings-on might have transpired in the bohemian apartments when she heard shouting from one of the upstairs rooms.

A woman argued, using both English and Spanish words. The heated words carried to Isabel over the balcony wall.

"*Amor.* How you could do dis?" the woman questioned. A long mournful sound akin to weeping followed, stopping Isabel in her tracks.

"*Por de Dios!* You have my heart broke." More wailing followed this last expletive before the speaker spit out the next words.

"*Puta,* I no be!" Glass shattered against the wall, and Isabel listened as footfalls sounded loudly across the floor.

"Dese? I show you what I think of your gifts."

More shuffling occurred upstairs, and Isabel decided she had best be on her way. She didn't want to be caught eavesdropping on what she believed was a lover's quarrel, although she was yet to hear any utterance from the man. She heard a loud thump and a noise that sounded like something heavy being dragged across the floor. Eager to be gone, Isabel had taken only a couple of steps when a swirl of material dropped from the heavens, landing on her head and obstructing her vision. As she struggled to remove the blinding fabric, she heard other objects being flung to the ground from overhead.

"Dis Consuela is not no ornery whore!" the woman shouted.

Isabel yanked the heavy, musky-smelling material from her face just as several more pieces flew over the rail, followed by a pair of women's shoes. Isabel froze, clutching the cloth to her chest.

A woman's voice traveled to her ears again. "Dis is Consuela, de great actress. She needs not you or your peasant's gifts."

Studying the garment she held in her hands, Isabel recognized that it was a dress. A corset, along with silk-stripped stockings, a red petticoat, and black lacy drawers sailed past her eyes, landing in colorful clumps at her feet.

When the garments stopped raining down around her, Isabel chanced a look upward. A beautiful dark-haired woman hung over the balcony railing, her silky black hair swaying over an ample bosom barely concealed beneath a shear nightrail.

On seeing Isabel, the woman called, "Hey, you dere, you want Consuela's clothes? You take dem or let dem rot in de street. It makes no matter to me. Consuela has no more need for de horrible man's gifts."

Did she say Cinderella?

After finding her voice, Isabel answered. "Surely, you can't mean to throw away such beautiful things." She bent to gather up pieces of the discarded clothing, believing as she did so that the woman was the next best thing to being Cinderella's fairy godmother. Even she could tell that the garments were of the finest quality and workmanship.

"I have plenty more where dese did not come from. Consuela wants nothing from de lout."

"But you could sell them." Isabel bent to pick up the leather boots. They felt like butter to her touch.

"Plenty more in de trunk, too. Give Consuela your address, and I'll have dem delivered, or I can toss de whole bunch to you now. I've no use for dem, nor do I have lots of time. I'm leaving on de afternoon train widout de lout and his gifts."

"I—I could pay—"

"No. I should pay you for taking dem from my hands. Besides Consuela is plenty rich. I leave dis hellhole behind and return to place I'm 'preciated."

If this woman really meant to give away her clothes, Isabel would be a fool not to take them. Literally the castaway garments were a windfall. Not only had they come to her from the wind, but now she wouldn't have to spend her limited funds on a new wardrobe.

"You want dem or not?" the woman asked impatiently.

"I—I guess, but will they fit?"

The dark-haired beauty eyed her critically from her perch on the balcony. Pushing away from the rail, she threw back her shoulders and stood tall, thrusting out her plump bosom.

"What you dink, señorita? We look about de same size?"

"No, ah, well, maybe."

Not in the habit of comparing bosoms, she felt her face color. But if the truth were revealed, in the bosom department Isabel was well endowed, and she figured she could hold her own against the woman. But their heights were another matter. She couldn't tell if the stranger was short or as tall as she was.

"You take, yes? You can have dem sized." The woman leaned against the balcony again. "Now tell Consuela where you live."

Fearing the woman might change her mind, Isabel quickly spouted off her address. She would take the lady's clothes. If they didn't fit, she could alter them herself or give them to the second-hand store to sell.

Fingering the silky smooth fabric in her hands, her excite
ment grew. She had never touched, must less owned, anything
of such fine quality, and there was more of the same where
these came from. Isabel couldn't believe her good fortune.

"I'll send dem dis afternoon," the woman said. "I only hope
dey bring you better luck wid your man dan I had wid mine."

"Thank—thank you." But already Consuela had disap
peared back inside the apartment, leaving Isabel alone.

As she gathered up the remaining garments strewn across
the ground, using the dress that had blinded her to bundle up
the lot, she couldn't wait to get home and try on her new
wardrobe. The way Isabel saw it, she had nothing to lose and
everything to win by accepting Consuela's castoff clothes.

Her biggest reward would be in seeing Marcella Kent's
jealous reaction when she saw Isabel dressed in all her finery.

Seven

Fortunately for Cooper and Miss Gomez, he hadn't found her at home when he went looking for the location of the well. At the time he had been in a foul temper, but most of that anger had been washed away with his much-needed bath. After learning she was not at home, he had decided to look for lodging before confronting her again.

He had reserved a room at the Magnolia Hotel on the corner of St. George and Hypolita streets that was in close proximity to the store. Not only was the hotel conveniently located, but it was also clean and reasonably priced because it was summer. He had booked the cheapest room available and had decided he would stay in the room for one week only so that he could ready the upstairs apartment for his occupancy. He was on a tight budget and was determined to live within his means.

After his bath and a change into clean clothes, Cooper felt like a new man, better equipped to face his neighbor. Maybe, he decided, he had been too hasty to condemn Miss Gomez because the post building was not what he envisioned.

As the buyer, it was his responsibility to make certain that what he spent money on was worth the price. Although the building was shabbier than he would have liked, it didn't take him long to determine that the post was in a prime location. Shops lined both sides of busy St. George Street, and all manner of traffic traversed the busy thoroughfare. With a lot of hard work, and probably more money than he had budgeted for, he would have the building spruced up and ready to receive stock in no time.

He also needed a new wardrobe. After he purchased some cotton trousers and work shirts, he would do away with his wool things until the climate turned cooler. Now that he lived in the tropics, he could do away with them altogether. But having spent the last twenty-four hours in his scratchy wool trousers and jacket, a prickly red rash covered his skin. The bothersome itch along with several mosquito bites had him scratching like a flea-bitten hound. A soothing talc and cotton clothes would help to keep his hide intact.

Already the day's blistering heat beat down with a vengeance. Dressed as he was, he knew in a few hours he would be ready to shed both skin and clothes. It was no wonder that natives in tropical climates wore loinclothes. For a moment Cooper considered this last thought, wondering what Miss Gomez would think of such a practice. Since she was part Indian, a loincloth might not offend her delicate sensibilities, but Marcella's was another story. He doubted Marcella would be entertained by such foolishness after last night's trouble, but the thought still made him smile.

Reaching the post building, Cooper came to a stop in front of the cypress structure. After checking into the hotel this morning, he had reread the description of the property that Mr. Jetson had sent him. At least now he knew the building wasn't infested with termites, or rotting as he had first suspected this morning. Termites couldn't bore into the rock-hard lumber, and the tree's resistance to decay had given it the name of "wood eternal." Cooper decided the building would probably be standing a lot longer than he would.

He groped inside his pocket for the key. After last night's fiasco, he had secured the key to his pocket-watch chain, and it would not be far from his person again.

Inserting the skeleton key into the lock, the door swung open, spilling sunlight across the wooden floor. Cooper stepped inside. The musty smell still lingered in the air, bringing with it this morning's disappointment, but he swept aside the negative feeling. It was time to get to work, time to put his misgivings aside. In all due respect, his future never looked brighter. Once he opened all the windows and doors to give the place a much-needed airing, he would go in search of the well.

As Cooper moved around the room opening the windows, he heard the iron gate in the courtyard open and shut. Keeping to the shadows, he watched Miss Gomez enter with her arms laden with a bundle of clothes. A pair of women's boots dangled from one hand. His gaze dropped to the hem of her skirt, fully expecting to see her naked feet, but he couldn't tell from where he stood if she wore shoes or not.

Thank God she wasn't wearing those awful britches of yesterday. But then, he recalled, she'd been wearing a dress this morning when she had brought him the basket of biscuits. Now that he was no longer suffering grogginess from having spent the night on the stoop, he recognized the faded navy dress, recalling the garment had seen better days. He supposed the dress was passable and a heck of a lot better than those blasted britches that had outlined her every curve, and then some.

The *then some* that he had seen last night when she was bathing—the *then some* that today had the power to make him sweat even more when he thought about her naked image.

"Damn it all," he said, "I'm an engaged man and shouldn't be entertaining thoughts of another woman, especially a naked one."

Disgusted, Cooper pushed aside his reflections and eyed the bundle of clothes in her arms.

Along with her herb business, did Miss Gomez also take in laundry? Not that he could fault her for being industrious—one did what one had to in order to survive. But if she was a laundress, maybe she would consider doing his clothes once he was settled in. He smiled wickedly. Doing laundry might be her only source of income after he opened his drugstore for business.

He watched her open the cottage door, pass through it, then leave it ajar. Only after she disappeared inside did Cooper turn away from the window.

He took a slow walk around the room's perimeter. If he planned to get this place cleaned up, he would need water and plenty of it. Although, he admitted, with the sunlight spilling past the open windows and the scent of some exotic flower seeping through the openings, the interior already looked and smelled better.

He stopped beside the counter and propped his elbows on the worn wood. Everything was going to work out fine. It might not be much now, but in time this building would house a thriving business. A feeling of well-being washed over him. What more could a man ask for? To his way of thinking, he already had it all. A promising future in the drug business that he loved, and a beautiful woman like Marcella who would soon be his wife. When he thought about the upcoming evening with Marcella and her family, an excited flush warmed his skin. Cooper rubbed his hands together, eager to get started.

The way he saw it, the world was his oyster, and tonight he would be sharing dinner with the pearl.

Isabel, on entering the cottage, shook out the rolled-up clothing and eyed it approvingly. Now that she could really examine her windfall up close, she delighted in the extraordinary clothing. She ran her hand over the saffron-yellow silk dress, the finely tatted lace collar and cuffs. With one finger she traced the row of tiny amber buttons that trailed the entire length of the dress's front opening. Then she picked up the gown, held it to her, and moved toward the long looking glass hanging on the wall.

"Too fine a dress for the likes of me," Isabel told Grimalkin, whose reflection appeared in the mirror beside her. But she could see the color brought out the yellow-gold highlights in her hair and made her eyes, like Grim's, look even more amber.

She rocked from side to side. The dress didn't follow the current fashions worn by the visiting tourists from the north. It looked fuller, flowing away from the waistline instead of clinging like a second skin. If this dress fit her, she could relinquish her corset or bustle, and both possibilities suited Isabel.

She had never cared for either, believing bustled skirts looked as out of proportion as a bale of fodder tied to a pitchfork, although she did own a dress made with tapes that could control the shape and size of a bustle. Because Isabel didn't own a bustled undergarment, the rare times she had worn the dress, she had stuffed it with old dish towels. Even now the memory she had of trying to sit in such a contraption made her balk.

Comfort was Isabel's first priority when it came to clothes, and perhaps the woman named Consuela had felt the same. Actresses and artists were notorious for being eccentric, and this dress certainly didn't fit the conventional mode. Though she could hardly wait until the trunk arrived, eager to examine the rest of Consuela's unwanted garments, work called her. She needed to weed the garden before the troublesome little plants took over the whole plot.

Crossing the room, Isabel spread the dress back over the chair beside the red silk petticoat. She picked up the pair of striped silk stockings; they felt as insubstantial as a cobweb, and she imagined wearing them would be like wearing nothing at all.

After gathering the other items, she placed the corset on the table beside the leather boots, spread the black lacy drawers across the back of a kitchen chair. On a whim, she tossed the stockings into the air and watched as they draped their sheerness over the candle chandelier that hung over the kitchen table. So delighted was she with the finery that Isabel decided that instead of putting the clothes away immediately, she would keep every piece in plain sight so she could enjoy looking at them. After she finished her work, and after her bath, she would try on the wonderful new outfit.

Sometime later when Cooper knocked on Miss Gomez's door that's where the garments were—in plain sight. Since the door opened into the center of the room, he couldn't avoid seeing the haphazardly strewn articles. When no one answered his knock, he leaned against the frame and peered deeper into the room, his gaze taking in the red silk petticoat, the lacy black drawers, and the sheer stockings hanging from the chandelier.

Cooper had grown up in a house with sisters. He knew what women wore beneath their dresses, but the articles of clothing tossed across the chair and table didn't look as though they belonged in such a humble abode. The red silk petticoat, the lacy black drawers, and the silky sheer stockings put him in mind of the few brothels he'd visited in his youth. Not the kind of undergarments worn by a proper young woman, or a woman who wore men's trousers. He was correct in believing that his earlier assumption was true. Miss Gomez did take in laundry.

He knocked on the doorframe again, but instead of the lady of the house answering his summons, her fat cat loped across the floor to greet him. Grimalkin's purr was so loud that it sounded as though his bones were rattling inside his broad chest.

"Scat. It's not you I'm looking for." When the animal moved to stroke his ankles in the usual manner, Cooper tried sidestepping him. "Oh, no, you don't," he said, "I've got enough of your fuzz on my trousers to stuff a mattress." Cooper scuffed his feet. "Now get."

Surprising him, the animal obeyed. He turned tail and trotted back into the center of the cottage, opting to lounge on the amber-colored dress thrown across a chair. Cooper couldn't help but notice once the black furry critter was settled comfortably on the silk fabric that his eyes were the exact same color as the material. The cat continued to stare at him until Cooper was the first to look away. On second thought, he would find someone else to do his laundry. In the last twenty-four hours, he'd seen enough cat hair to last him a lifetime.

Bracing his hand on the doorjamb, he looked inside again. This time he ignored the clothing, noting instead that the facing wall mirrored this one. Identical windows and doors faced each other across the long wide space. The opposite door stood open as well, and for the first time Cooper saw there was another arbor that ran the length of the house, and what looked like another walled-in courtyard beyond that.

"Because it's broad daylight, I assumed I was safe."

Cooper nearly jumped out of his skin. Embarrassed, too, that he'd been caught with his head inside her door, he pushed away from the jamb and swung around to face her. She had on the same straw hat that she had worn when he had mistaken her for a boy.

"Miss Gomez," he acknowledged, then asked, "Safe?"

Her remark puzzled him until he recalled his words of yesterday.

She smiled, friendly like. The reflex to return that smile was so natural that Cooper found himself responding. "Remember, I only assault women at night." His remark brought on her husky warm laugh, a laugh that did strange things to his insides and too contagious not to join in. They laughed together.

"I did knock," he assured her, still smiling. As his declaration drifted into silence, he felt the need to straighten his tie, which he had purposely left behind in his hotel room. Realizing the tie wasn't there, Cooper dropped his hands to his sides. "Only your cat," he continued, "appeared to hear my summons."

"Grimalkin has excellent hearing. He was the one who alerted me that you were here."

"A witch cat—watch cat," Cooper corrected, wondering why his tongue stumbled over the word. He'd noticed in this woman's presence that his tongue did a lot of stumbling. "A watch cat," he repeated. "Now that's a first. Where I come from, we had watchdogs. Does he bite?"

"Oh, no," she assured him. "He prefers using his claws."

"Claws?"

"I'm teasing," she said, laughing again. "Grimalkin is nothing more than a big teddy bear that purrs. Besides, I think he likes you."

Wonderful. "I think I should tell you now that I've never been too fond of cats. My folks never allowed us children to have pets."

"No pets?" Her expression was disbelieving. "How unfortunate for you. Of course, I was an only child, so I guess Grim took the place of the siblings I never had. Even now, he is still a wonderful companion."

Cooper couldn't see anything wonderful about the lady's cat, but he decided enough had been said about the animal.

"How may I help you?" she asked.

She held a small hoe in one hand, so Cooper assumed she'd been working in the garden she had mentioned yesterday. His gaze traveled the tool's length and stopped at the ground where the bottom of her skirt should have been.

Should have been. It was then he noticed her bare calves and feet. She still wore a dress, but from what he could determine without being too obvious with his perusal, she had pulled the skirt's back up between her—her limbs, tucking the hem into her front waistband. Did the woman know no shame? First britches, and now this latest blatant display. Before he could yank his gaze away, he noted her bare calves and feet were caked in mud.

Their gazes collided. Beneath his shirt collar, Cooper's skin burned, the rash tormenting him with a renewed vengeance.

"Water," he croaked. He had meant to say well, but as usual in Miss Gomez's presence, it came out all wrong.

"Yes," she said, her smile widening yet again. "Mud. I'm watering my garden. It's very wet by the well."

Her explanation sounded as though they were discussing

the weather instead of her very exposed limbs. It was apparent that Miss Gomez thought no more about revealing her bare parts than she thought about wearing britches. A most unusual woman.

Cooper waited, expecting her to show him the well's location, then he realized he had never asked to see it. Catching her with her skirt up instead of down had caught him completely off guard.

"I've come," he finally said, "seeking the location of the well."

"But of course you have. I don't know what I was thinking."

Cooper knew what he was thinking, and so did his body. Beneath his shirt and trousers, his skin fairly steamed. He blamed his discomfort on the torturing rash that threatened to eat him alive. He wished it would.

"We have to share," she said, tucking in a stray lock of hair that had escaped from beneath her hat.

He watched the very feminine gesture, the way her breasts rose and fell with the motion.

"Are you opposed to sharing?"

His gaze locked on her very prominent chest. At this point, Cooper wasn't opposed to anything Miss Gomez deemed sharable. Taken aback by his thought, he reminded himself that he was an engaged man. "An affair would be fine," he replied.

She trapped her bottom lip between her teeth as though she was trying to hide a smile, making him feel even more uncomfortable.

"What I meant to say is sharing is fine."

He felt as though he were coming apart at the seams; not only because he appeared so addle-brained in this woman's presence, but also because she had caught him staring—at her chest. And the damnable rash was driving him mad.

No longer able to resist, Cooper scratched his chest. Why worry about good manners when she thought britches and bare limbs were the norm? Besides, scratching felt so damn good. With her looking on, he scratched his arms, his neck, then returned his hands to his chest and gave it a thorough rubbing.

"Do you have a problem, Mr. Adair?"

"No problem," he replied.

"Yes, I can see that you don't." Not waiting for a response, but looking for all the world as though she didn't believe him, she turned. "Come along, then," she said. "I'll show you the well."

For the second time in the last twenty-four hours, Cooper found himself marching behind the woman. He tried not to look at her backside, which was still very recognizable beneath the ridiculous drape of her skirt, or to stare at her shapely show of calves and ankles. But he did. He supposed he could count himself lucky that it was she who carried the hoe instead of him, or maybe, he decided, after the fishing pole incident it was she who was lucky.

They left the shade of the arbor and moved toward the back wall of the property. As they neared the end of the house, Cooper noted for the first time a doorway in the adjoining coquina fence. He hadn't seen it earlier because the huge oak with its mantle of Spanish moss hid the opening.

"It's in here," she said. She looked back over her shoulder to see if he was still trailing her. Satisfied that he was, she continued past the opening.

Still scratching, he followed her through the archway.

"It's a well of good water," his leader told him, "cased with stone and lime." He saw her standing beside the well curb where a wooden bucket sat on the well's wooden cover. "My *padre* built this 'draw well,' and the water is still sweet because of many periodic cleanings."

Cooper came to stand beside her. She lifted the square covering, and a stench reminiscent of rotten eggs hit him full in the face. He grimaced, wondering briefly what dirty smelled like. If he lived in Florida for a lifetime, he would never get used to the sulfur smell.

Miss Gomez picked up the wooden bucket with the rope and lowered it into the well.

"No pulley or windlass?" Cooper asked.

"You're it." She lifted the bucket and stood back to show him its content. "Clear as a mountain stream."

"It sure doesn't smell like a mountain stream."

"You'll get used to it," she said, "but maybe this will help." She bent and pinched off a sprig of leafy green plant that grew at the base of the well. "Mint," she said. "It thrives in cool damp places. That's why I planted it here, and of course it smells heavenly." She stuck the shoot beneath his nose before he had time to take it from her. He inhaled deeply, and the minty scent washed over him like a cool mountain breeze.

When she twirled away from him, the trampled herb sent up a cloud of its peppermint fragrance, and he looked down at her feet again. The ground beneath her feet was saturated from the water, and he could see why her toes and ankles were covered with the rich loamy mud. For a moment Cooper wondered if her bare feet would also smell like mint . . . and taste like it as well.

"And over there," she said, pointing, bringing him back to the moment, "is the one-holer."

The woman did know no shame, Cooper thought. She pointed out the necessary as though it were a tourist attraction.

"My *padre* built that fine stone privy as well. You and I will be sharing it, but I don't expect it to be abused."

Cooper wondered briefly how one abused a privy, but he didn't dare ask.

"Now if you'll follow me," she said, "I'll get you something to cure that itch."

Under other circumstances, Cooper would have denied he suffered such an ailment, but she had already seen him scratching, so what was to deny? Besides, anything the woman might have to relieve this infernal itch, he would gladly take it. Even if it meant sucking down one of her potions.

Eight

Following her deeper into the side yard, Cooper was stunned to see such an orderly and well-maintained garden. It wasn't what he expected from its wild and somewhat adventurous owner. Her garden was set apart from the usual because it blended into the landscape; thus the landscape was the garden, and the two designed as a whole.

He paused on the crushed shell path to look over the entire space. "Miss Gomez," he called, "you have a lovely garden. I never would have suspected such beauty."

Isabel came to a stop and turned to face him. "You really think so?"

They had just passed a circle of the crushed shells where a two-foot-high rock stood in its center. She looked so pleased that her pleasure washed over him like the warm breeze that chose that moment to lift several strands of his hair. As the wind tripped across his shoulders, the walled space came alive with sound. It didn't take Cooper long to locate the familiar wind instruments whose enchanting music filled the air.

"I can't take all the credit," Isabel said. "Most of the plants come from the ones my mother cultivated when she was alive. I did design the layout, though, if you can call it such, and as you can see, I had a difficult time making up my mind

how to design the beds. That is why there are plants planted
in rows as well as in circles, geometrically, and also free-
form."

"But it's enchanting."

"It pleases me that you like it." She clasped her hands
behind her and rocked back and forth on the balls of her feet.
"My mother believed that the atmosphere of the garden had
healing elements just as the earth. I know I always feel better
when I'm out here working, so maybe there's some truth to
her belief."

"Could be," Cooper said. "Right now, I wish it would work
its healing elements on this bothersome rash." Although he
admitted since entering her garden, his skin didn't itch with
the same ferocity as it had earlier.

"Your rash. Here we are talking like good friends, and I
completely forgot my direction." She crooked her finger at
him, then swung around and started moving toward the dwelling. "Come, I have just the thing."

The crook of her finger, and the way she lowered her thick
golden lashes, sent up a warning signal. If he didn't know
better, he would presume she was flirting with him. *Ridiculous!* She had learned last night that he was betrothed and
would soon marry, and he mustn't let her forget it.

"If my stock had already arrived, I wouldn't be putting you
to this trouble. I'm unfamiliar with the town, and since I'm
expected to dine this evening with Marcella and her parents,
I need a prescription that might control this aggravating rash
I've developed."

"I'm sure I have such an ointment in my stash of *little
herbs* that will do the trick."

He began to question his agreement to accept her help as
she led him into her den. But help he needed, so he threw
caution aside and kept right on following her. They passed
several bee skeps, he assumed home to her orange blossom
bees, and then he saw her cat perched on a large clay pot
beside one of the archways. Grimalkin's mesmerizing stare

nearly caused Cooper to trip. The cat, like his mistress, made Cooper jittery.

"Most of the folks in town," she continued, "call me Isabel. I would like you to call me Isabel as well."

Her statement brought him up short. "Isabel?"

"That is my name."

"But yesterday you said—"

"Forget yesterday. After all, we are to be neighbors."

"But it wouldn't be proper—"

"Yes, it will, because I gave you my permission. And I'll call you Cooper."

The way she drawled his name, he could almost imagine those full lips of hers puckering as they had done the night before when they had shared a kiss.

What was the matter with him? He shouldn't be thinking of her lips or that blasted kiss. And he had never intended for her to call him by his given name. It just wasn't done when two people hardly knew each other. And there was Marcella. She wouldn't be pleased to hear such a practice of informality between strangers. But then, she'd probably never hear. He certainly wouldn't tell her. Instead, he would tell Miss Gomez he thought it best to use surnames when addressing each other.

He was about to tell her so when she stopped and turned to face him. "Your friends do call you Cooper, don't they?"

He cleared his throat. "Yes, my friends do—"

"Good. Now that that is settled, you may have a seat right there." She pointed to a wrought-iron chair beside a round table beneath the shaded arbor. "I'll get you something to drink and then I'll get that salve."

"Drink? Miss—Isabel, a drink won't be necessary."

But she had already disappeared inside the bungalow, leaving Cooper alone with his thoughts, and with her cat who had jumped down from his perch to join him. "Don't even think about swiping my ankles, you bundle of tacky fur." The animal sent him a catmatic look that said Cooper shouldn't be so biased before stretching out on the tiled floor. Nearby, a

whirligig fashioned in the shape of a man caught Cooper's
attention. The arms of the wooden figure spun with the wind
as though the fellow was swimming as fast as he could to
save his life. Another warning, Cooper thought, a new reminder that if he was smart, he'd beat a path right out the
gate toward home; but when a man had an itch that he needed
to *stop* scratching, a man did what he had to do.

Once inside the house, Isabel removed her straw hat, hanging
it on a hook by the door, then went to the mirror to check
her appearance.

Her reflection in the long looking glass certainly wasn't
that of a proper lady. She could only imagine what Dora's
response would be on seeing her with her skirt rucked up
between her legs, and her bare feet covered in mud. One word
would describe her friend's reaction—"Scandalous," she mur-
mured.

She finger-combed her hair, then retied it at her nape with
the navy ribbon she had used that morning. Because she
would be sharing tea with Mr.—Cooper, she corrected—
Isabel decided to untuck her skirt. Slippers were an impos-
sibility. Her feet were too dirty to put on hose and shoes.
Besides, her guest wasn't going to be looking at her feet
before this session was over, he would be more interested in
her hands. With her hasty toilette completed, Isabel returned
to the kitchen area of the long room.

Standing beside the icebox, she chipped away several sliv-
ers of ice and put them into two glasses. Picking up the
pitcher of sweet tea she had made earlier, she poured the
liquid over the ice, sliced a lemon into wedges, and placed
one on the rim of each glass. Along with the lemon, she also
added a sprig of fresh mint that she had picked earlier. This
done, she closed the lid to the tin box to make sure the precious hunk of ice she had purchased would keep as long as
possible, and eyed the box appreciatively.

There weren't many things Isabel would willingly give
Wooster Farley credit for, but he was responsible for her own

ership of the icebox. Of course, his motives for purchasing
the modern convenience had been purely selfish. He had liked
his beer cold instead of hot. Long before Wooster's body had
grown cool in his grave, Isabel had salvaged the icebox from
the post building. Except for the box, there hadn't been much
else worth saving. Mostly she stayed away from the building,
preferring to remember it the way it had been when her *padre*
was alive, instead of the way it had been under Wooster's
ownership.

After placing the glasses of tea on a wooden tray along
with a couple of cloth napkins, she stepped back to admire
her efforts. She was quite pleased with herself. They both
could use a little refreshment, and the sweet concoction was
Isabel's favorite, especially on a hot summer day.

Everything was going to be fine. Her plan to send Cooper
Adair packing was already under way now that they were on
a first-name basis. Once he had a thorough shellacking with
her ointment, and his itch disappeared, he would realize what
an accomplished herbalist she was. It had pleased her that he
liked her garden, and she decided that perhaps under different
circumstances they might have become friends. But she
couldn't think about that now. For the moment she needed to
remain focused.

Glancing quickly at the new clothes strewn about the room,
Isabel decided next time she had Cooper over for tea, she
would look a sight better than she did now. But already she
had dallied much too long with her preparations, and as skit-
tish as Cooper was, he might try to escape. Hurrying now,
she picked up the tea tray and headed outside to the loggia.

Her prediction was correct. Cooper wasn't in the chair
where she had left him. He must have returned home. Frus-
trated, Isabel slammed the tray down on the table with such
force, Grimalkin jumped as though one of his nine lives had
been scared out of him. Isabel's disappointment quickly evap-
orated, however, when she saw movement at the end of the
loggia. Recognizing Cooper, she picked up the tea glasses and
moved toward him.

On hearing her approach, he turned and faced her. "Your laboratory?" he asked.

She supposed a person with such a fancy education might call her garden room a laboratory. But to Isabel it was the space set aside for the harvesting of her herbs. It was here beneath the lengthy glass that she dried her harvest, stored it, and lastly made herbs into healing infusions and decoctions. The garden room was her favorite spot indoors, and Isabel spent many pleasant hours among the tools of her trade; listing, labeling, stocking, and studying.

"May I?" Cooper asked.

After having walked the length of the glass enclosure several times, peering in as he paced, he paused outside the entrance. He was eager to enter the intriguing space, but wouldn't dare without her permission.

She approached him, cat in tow, carrying two glasses filled with ice and a light brown liquid. To his disappointment—no, his satisfaction—there was no showy display of her naked ankles and feet. Instead, the skirt that had once hugged the very private space between her limbs flowed loosely from her waist to the floor. She had forgone her Tom Sawyer bonnet, replacing it with a navy ribbon that anchored the hank of honey-colored hair at the nape of her graceful neck. As Cooper met her amber gaze, he felt an odd stirring in his stomach.

"Sweet tea," she said, handing him a glass.

Their fingertips accidentally bumped, and the connection sent a spark shooting to Cooper's nether regions. He blamed his reaction on the cold container in his grasp.

He had never had tea served over ice, sweet or otherwise, but the sight of the frosted tumbler looked so inviting that he was already salivating. He accepted the glass, but instead of tasting the drink, he asked, "Is this the equivalent of those mint juleps that I've been led to believe all southern planters were weaned on?"

She fixed him with a penetrating stare. "Some might call it a julep because it's made from sugar, tea flavoring, and water, but I assure you it doesn't contain one drop of liquor."

Her stance stiffened. "I don't hold to drinking spirits."

"I don't hold to drinking spirits, either," Cooper responded. "In excess, that is."

He brought the glass to his mouth, sipping slowly at first while enjoying the scent of mint and lemon, and the sweet, refreshing coolness against his tongue. The drink was much better than he expected it would be, and he gulped down several swallows before removing the glass from his lips.

"It's good," he said. "In fact, it's very good."

Watching her, and seeing how his slightest compliment made her eyes sparkle, Cooper found he wanted to be heir to that radiance for a few moments longer.

"This is twice today, Miss—Isabel—that you've brought me nourishment. I must admit that your biscuits and honey this morning and this sweet tea this afternoon are the best I've ever had."

"Today," she added, smiling, as he watched the emotions play across her face. "I'd be willing to bet it's probably the only nourishment you've had."

Cooper swallowed the last dregs of the tea and returned the empty glass. The drink hit the spot, making him feel very affable toward his neighbor, and he found himself wanting to tease her.

"That wasn't one of your potions that's going to make me fall desperately in love with . . ." His voice trailed off. Realizing what he was about to say, he searched his brain for another word when his gaze centered on her cat. ". . . Grimalkin," he substituted.

She burst out laughing. "I suppose since you've already admitted you aren't fond of cats that a little love potion might make the transition of having a cat as your neighbor a trifle easier." She winked at him, surprising him again with her daring. "I'll have to consult my spell book for that one, but in the meantime, won't you please come inside?"

She preceded him into the glass-enclosed laboratory, and for the second time in the last hour Cooper felt that a wiser man would have turned tail and run. Instead, he tucked his tail between his legs and followed her yet again.

Later Cooper would wonder if the woman had cast a spell on him, or maybe slipped something more than sugar into his tea, because on entering her work space, he became even more intrigued by the woman, and her competency in the methodological discipline of herbs.

Once inside, Cooper breathed deeply, inhaling the scent of mint, flowers, and musk while watching Isabel place their empty glasses on the high wooden table that took up the center of the long room. This done, she walked to where shelves and cupboards ran the wall's length and began perusing the many containers. He watched her finger several different bottles, and while she looked for the ointment she sought, Cooper took the time to further study the room.

Shelves and cupboards held an array of dried herbs stowed in small amounts in well-sealed jars. All the jars were labeled with the name of the herb inside. More herbs hung from the low rafters, and on the center table several drying racks made from wood and metallic netting held bits and pieces of drying bark and leaves. The counter space below the shelves held a large assortment of books and ledgers.

On the wall adjoining the house, an array of tools hung not unlike those of a farmer: a drawknife, a small hatchet, a broad chisel, a pocketknife, a spade, a machete, and shears. There were also herb gathering containers, including a basket with a handle, a sturdy canvas bag with shoulder straps, and several burlap bags. A mortar and pestle, not unlike the ones Cooper used in his pharmacy, occupied the center table along with a stack of neatly folded cheesecloth. He recognized other household items sitting about the room, and after surveying it as a whole, Cooper admitted she had a well-equipped laboratory.

"Here it is," she said, turning from the shelves to face him again. She held up the bottle so he could see it. "With this," she said, "that pesky itch will disappear in no time."

Cooper eyed the dark brown bottle skeptically, recalling his modern-day opinion on her outdated skills. Who was to say, besides Miss Gomez, if the use of her remedy might not only relieve him of his itch, but also of his skin? With this in mind, he asked, "Would you be so kind as to tell me the salve's ingredients?"

Her golden eyes danced with mischief. "Is it the recipe for my love potion you are after or relief from your itch?"

Cooper knew she was teasing, or he wanted to believe she was. But he sure as the devil didn't wish to fall in love with her cat, who now occupied a stool by the door, watching the whole proceeding as though he had staged it himself. Cooper cleared his throat. "You can understand that as a man of science, it is only fitting that I should question the elixir's ingredients."

She set the dark brown bottle on the table, cocked one hip, and tapped a finger against her lip. "Let me think now," she said. "Oh, yes, the ingredients. I remember now. Lizard lips, frog droppings, and the eyelashes of a snake." She paused for effect. "Oh, and I almost forgot, ground-up fish gizzards for smell."

Her answer was so preposterous that Cooper laughed. "Snakes don't have eyelashes," he said. She was teasing him, and he was enjoying it.

"Florida snakes do."

He shook his head. "That settles it, then. Because I've no desire to smell like fish gizzards, I think I'll pass."

"No guts, no relief," she countered. When she realized what she had said, she burst out laughing. "Oh, my, guts are gizzards." Her merriment was contagious, and soon they both were laughing. After her giggles subsided, she said, "It's called chickweed salve."

"Chickweed salve?" He grinned. "By all means, give me a double dose."

Chickweed salve sounded about as appealing as her earlier description, but what the heck. He had been wishing earlier that he could shed his itchy skin. Maybe her salve would save him the trouble.

"Are you certain?" she asked. Leaning forward, she

reached for a piece of the cheesecloth from the stack on the table. "You can put your shirt anywhere." She pulled a stool from beneath the table's end and patted the seat. "You may sit here while I apply this."

"My shirt?" Disrobing wasn't exactly what Cooper had envisioned when he agreed to accept her help. "You want me to remove my shirt?"

"It's kind of hard to put lotion on your skin through a layer of material."

"But you're a—and I'm a—"

"Yes, there are subtle differences in our anatomy," she said matter-of-factly, "but as students of medicinal cures, I think we are both intelligent enough to look beyond those dissimilarities."

Dissimilarities! He knew about those. He had witnessed firsthand their very subtle differences last night when he watched her bathe.

"But it wouldn't be proper," he croaked. The memory burned his skin with renewed heat, and the itch returned with a vengeance.

"I assure you my interest in your back is strictly professional, but if you're worried someone will find out, I promise I won't tell if you don't."

He thought about reminding her about her bringing the kiss they shared to Marcella's attention, but passed on the thought, figuring there was already too much fuel in his fire.

"Can't you just give me the cursed weed and let me apply it to myself in private?"

"I assume from the way you were scratching earlier that your body is covered with the rash. If that is the case, how will you apply the salve to the area you can't reach?"

Cooper weighed her question. The bothersome rash did cover most of his body, and he knew applying her salve to his back would be near to impossible. Besides, he reasoned, he couldn't show up for dinner with the Kents this evening scratching like a dog with fleas.

She continued to stare at him as he puzzled over this latest dilemma. Who, Cooper wondered, would know she had put medicine on his back? They were alone except for her trusty cat. The animal couldn't tell, and Cooper certainly wouldn't, but could Miss Gomez be trusted to keep their secret?

Trust her.

The thought came unbidden again as though someone other than he had put the idea in his mind. What the heck? The only thing he had to lose was his itch, and at this point he would send his soul to perdition to get rid of it.

Still hesitating, he heard her say, "Look, if it will make you feel better, I'll turn my back while you remove your shirt. Then you may sit on the stool with your back to me. I'll apply the salve, and none will be the wiser."

"Sounds like a good plan to me." He sent her a keep-your-mouth shut look. "But no peeking."

"I assure you I won't peek." she said. "I am a healer of a sort, and your back won't be the first one I've seen." Before she gave him her own back, he didn't miss the smile that turned up the corners of her lips.

After removing his shirttail from his trousers, he worked the buttons from their holes with fingers that felt as round as sausages. There had been a few times in his past when he had disrobed in the presence of a woman, never giving the act a second thought. But then, unlike now, he had been eager to sate his desire, and he never recalled being this nervous.

She stood facing the shelves with battleship solidity while Cooper concentrated on her spine, fearing she would turn around before he was ready. It was good, he decided, that no one other than himself was privy to his thoughts, because at the moment he felt about as experienced as a virgin in a whorehouse.

With the last button undone, the edges of his shirt flapped open, allowing the cooler air to circulate over his bare chest. Next came the cuff links. The same links Marcella had had especially made for him as a gift for last Christmas. They were of solid gold, engraved with a mortar and pestle—the symbol of Cooper's trade. He placed the cuff links beside the original that sat on the table in front of him to assure they wouldn't be misplaced. Cooper wore the cuff links daily not only because most of his shirts required them, but also because they were a reminder of Marcella's love.

After slipping his arms from the sleeves, he lay the shirt across the end of the table. Then he turned and sat down on the stool.

With his back to Isabel, Cooper said, "You may turn around now."

He wouldn't think about how vulnerable he felt knowing that her hands would soon be touching his skin. Instead, he would pretend she was a doctor, a professional, as she had suggested. Cooper stilled himself against the intimacy of her touch while staring helplessly into her cat's amber-colored eyes.

Nine

Staring at the broad expanse of Cooper Adair's naked back, Isabel questioned her sanity. How was she going to apply salve to the muscled planes and remain indifferent to the task?

"Meow, me-wow!"

Grimalkin's cry jerked her thoughts from Cooper to the cat, who was perched on his favorite stool. Because Isabel talked with her pet daily, she had learned to identify his different cat calls. His gaze might be fixed on Cooper, but Isabel knew the cat's remark was meant for her. It seemed that Grim shared her opinion about the Yankee's good looks. The animal's me-*wow* said it all.

Knowing they were in agreement didn't make Isabel's chore any easier. She might be the professional she had claimed to be, but most of her clients, unlike Cooper, were of the same gender. They were ladies who sought her cures and advice for problems pertaining to women. Even among those females, Isabel couldn't recall a time when she had seen as much of them as she was seeing of Cooper Adair right now.

She took a fortifying breath. It was only skin, she reminded herself, but why did the skin have to be attached to a powerful male body? He was a nearly naked man.

The prickly rash covered his entire torso, or the part that wasn't hidden beneath the waistband of his trousers. Yet her trained eye told her that beneath the rash, his skin would feel as velvety smooth as the underside of a sun-warmed leaf.

Mercy! The man was beautifully made, all lean and sinewy. She tried not to look at his wide shoulders and narrow waist as she shook the chickweed salve from the bottle into her palm.

"Neow, neow."

Isabel's eyes gravitated to her cat. *Neow* meant Grimalkin wanted something right now. But what?

"Neow?"

Not now, Grim. Can't you see I'm busy?

"Neow!"

Isabel glanced down at her hand. She had been so busy playing mind games with her cat, she had shaken enough ointment into her palm to rub down a horse. Because returning the balm to the bottle would be near impossible, she set the vial aside and began rubbing her hands together.

"Neow, neow."

Grim, please hush. I'm in a quandary here.

Other than massaging the greasy residue into Cooper's back, Isabel's other choice was to wipe it somewhere else. If she reached for more cheesecloth, Cooper would see her. She didn't want to waste the salve, but more importantly, she didn't want to reveal her clumsy error. It wouldn't do for Cooper to believe her less than efficient, considering his already low opinion of herbalists. The salve would eventually dissolve into his skin, but until it did it would require a lot of time, a lot of rubbing. And more contact than she had bargained for.

"Anything wrong?" he asked, breaking into her thoughts.

"Not a thing," she lied. "It's essential the salve be kneaded until warm before applying to the infected area."

"Like anything needs additional warming in this climate," he grumbled.

If it was heat he was interested in, Isabel could give him

a good accounting. She was so hot she could feel the stains of crimson burning her cheeks, but she was thankful he couldn't see the telltale blotches. Like Cooper, those splotches wouldn't be disappearing anytime soon, so it was best she get control of her emotions. No more lily-livered, moonstruck thoughts. It was time to begin acting like a professional.

Isabel cleared her throat. "You have a bad case of prickly heat," she said, "aggravated by a dozen or more mosquito bites."

"Spare me the diagnosis," he countered. "I'm well acquainted with the malady, but for the moment I'm only interested in the cure."

"I'm interested, too, in restoring you to health."

"Neow, neow."

Restoring him to health was uppermost in Isabel's mind. She eyed Cooper's skin, then her hands before moving them within inches of his back. The amount of salve appeared to have increased. *Impossible.*

"Neow, neow."

"Sounds to me," Cooper said, "as if your cat is as eager to get this over with as I am." He sat like a post, his arms rigid. "Hot enough yet?"

"More than you know."

Isabel worried her bottom lip. He wasn't inquiring about her condition, but by now he must believe that her brain was fried. To take her mind off the puzzling situation, she said the first thing that popped into her mind. "This climate is too hot for wool."

"Wool?"

"Yes, wool. Gentlemen may wear wool in Pennsylvania where you come from, but they don't wear wool in Florida, especially during the summer months."

He snorted. "I wasn't inquiring about fashion, Isabel. I meant, is the salve hot enough to begin?"

His tone put her on the defensive. "I know that," she replied, "but I thought you might like to know for future reference that wool is too warm."

Instead of commenting on her remark, he asked, "How much longer?"

"Oh, it's almost ready."

"Neow, neow."

Not now, Grim. Can't you see the dilemma I'm in?

"Neow, neow."

Isabel ignored her pet and made another great show of rubbing her hands together. She hoped Cooper would hear the action and assume she had everything under control. In truth, being in command was the last thing she felt.

She had used chickweed salve many times, but before today she had never encountered a problem. Could the batch have gotten old? Rubbing her hands together hadn't made the salve vanish. If anything, it seemed to grow in volume. At this rate, it would never dissolve into Cooper's skin.

She glanced at Grimalkin, who watched them both with an all-knowing stare. Surely this couldn't be the cat's doing. No, she corrected, it was her error. Because she had been distracted, she had simply shaken out too large an amount.

"I can't stay here all day," Cooper complained. "Maybe this wasn't such a good idea."

When he looked as though he might turn and face her, Isabel shouted, "It's ready!"

His naked back was one thing, but facing his naked front would be her undoing. Isabel slammed her hands against his shoulders, nearly toppling him from the stool. "Sorry," she apologized meekly.

With first contact, Isabel was more concerned with the spreading of the salve than the way Cooper's skin felt beneath her fingers. Soon his back was thoroughly coated, and she began to massage the cream into his skin.

"Smells good," Cooper said, his broad shoulders lifting, then settling again when he inhaled.

The lemon balm she had added to the salve did smell heavenly. The sweet-scented oil was known to help reduce depression, insomnia, and nervousness. Today she could attest to the latter. Already she had begun to relax.

Lost in the sensation of her hands against his skin, Isabel forgot her earlier discomfort and became completely absorbed in rubbing and kneading. His skin felt just as she imagined it would—like warm velvet.

In her collection of books, Isabel had read about a Swedish man who touted the benefits of body massage. The idea sounded intriguing, and after she had read more on the subject, she thought she would like to try the practice herself.

It was rumored that when Mr. Flagler's second hotel, the Alcazar, opened next year, not only would there be a casino and Turkish baths, but also a whole staff of masseurs.

Isabel had toyed with the idea of seeking employment as a masseur to help subsidize her income until her building was sold. She no longer needed the job now that Cooper had purchased the property, but Isabel was still interested in the Swede's techniques.

As long as she needed to rid herself of the accumulation of salve on her hands, perhaps she could practice a few relaxing strokes on Cooper's back. According to what she had read, the person getting a massage was supposed to lay on his stomach on a table. She doubted Cooper would be open to this suggestion, considering his reaction when she asked him to remove his shirt. So instead of asking him to stretch out, she would simply try a few rubs while he was sitting on the stool.

Although he was more relaxed now than he had been earlier, she supposed the lemon balm had worked on him as well, but she could still feel that his muscles were taut. Since he was properly covered with grease, *a lot of grease,* the rest would be easy. Isabel began a fan stroke with her fingers, working from his waist up. Following that maneuver, she applied circular pressure, gradually covering the whole surface of his back.

Cooper sighed deeply. His sigh convinced her that he was now totally relaxed, and Isabel grew more confident. Not only was her first attempt at massage apparently successful, but she was once again in control of her emotions, proving that she was no longer a foolish female, struck dumb by the sight of a half-clothed male. Next she began the kneading process. After covering the entire surface of his back using this technique, she walked her fingers up his spine and began kneading the muscles in his neck.

"Nice," he responded. He moved his head from side to side, allowing her fingers better access to the area where his neck joined his shoulders.

Encouraged, Isabel continued her slow ministrations.

"Neow, neow," Grim called to her.

Now. Whatever does he mean? Isabel met the cat's gaze briefly, then turned her thoughts back to her task. Soon her fingers were sliding over the top of Cooper's muscled shoulders, dipping lower. A shiver of excitement coursed through her when she began applying little circular pressures at the very edge of his pectorals. Isabel had never touched a man so intimately before.

She felt a curious pull to stand closer, and she leaned into his back. As she had yesterday when she kissed him, Isabel smelled licorice. The spicy fragrance mixed with the lemon balm made her want to crawl into his skin with him. Isabel drew in a deep breath and held it. His hair smelled clean, and she had an overwhelming desire to bury her face in the yellow-gold silkiness.

Cooper closed his eyes. *This is Heaven!* Or as close to bliss as he had been since stepping from the train yesterday morning. He was unsure, however, if his present euphoria was the result of Isabel's skilled fingers or the result of her cat's mesmerizing stare. In order to project his thoughts away from his half-clad state, Cooper had locked gazes with Grimalkin the moment he had taken a seat on the stool. The cat's amber, depthless eyes had held him transfixed when Isabel began massaging the soothing salve into his burning, itching rash. With her gentle ministrations his apprehension vanished, and soon the bothersome itch no longer tormented him.

Cooper floated beyond the realm of his body, drifting as light as a feather on a fluffy cloud, her heat his center. When her nimble fingers slipped over his shoulders, working magical circles over his upper chest, it felt as natural as breathing for him to grab Isabel's hands and pull her closer.

The action brought her soft, pillowy breasts in contact with his back, and he could feel her warm breath ruffling strands of his hair. Her hands explored the front of him, tracing first the breadth of his shoulders, skimming across his nipples before slipping to the triangle of hair growing in the core of his chest. When her fingers threaded through the curly fiber, fire coursed through every nerve in his body.

Cooper sucked in his breath and leaned into her. He turned his face up to hers, then she lowered her head, and their lips met with a passion-filled kiss.

Cooper's heart slammed against his ribs. He began to spin out of control and felt as though he were being pulled deeper and deeper into golden whirlpools of light. Someone whimpered. Was it him? Or was it just the throaty purr of her cat? No, it was the woman. He smiled. She was enjoying the kiss as much as he was. Her lips tasted like mint, coated with sweet tea. But there was nothing cool about what he was feeling. He burned with passion.

Amber eyes, amber eyes, amber eyes? No. Only gold dust, swirling in the vortex of his mind.

"I need you," he moaned.

The sound of his own voice hit him like a cold wave, washing over him with icy foam. Cooper blinked. He could hear the erratic pounding of his heart as he worked to focus his eyes. It was then he realized that only inches away from his nose, a pair of amber, gold-flecked orbs stared back at him.

"Grimalkin?"

"No," she answered in a throaty whisper, "it's Isabel."

"Isabel?"

"Mhmmm."

"Isabel!" Cooper jumped to his feet and swung around to face her.

She smiled at him with a lazy, satisfied expression on her face.

"I—I thought you were Grimalkin," he said.

"Grimalkin? I thought you didn't like cats."

"Cats? What does that have to do with *this?*"

She traced her lips with her tongue. "Are you also in th habit of kissing cats?" Then she giggled.

"I most certainly am not in the habit of kissing—"

Cooper snapped his lips shut. She had baited him the sam way she had baited Marcella yesterday with her remark abou the hired help. He grabbed his shirt from the table and speare his arms through the sleeves.

"Poor you, then," she answered.

"Poor me. Why poor me?"

"You said you weren't in the habit of kissing."

"I'm not in the habit of kissing just any woman."

She folded her arms beneath her breasts, a movement h believed was deliberate, especially when his gaze landed o those cushioned globes before returning to her face. Amuse ment flickered in the depths of her golden eyes.

"I've never been accused of being just any woman," sh challenged.

"No, I don't suppose you have." Cooper moved toward th door. "You know what I think, lady?" he said before exiting "I think you're some kind of a witch."

Isabel moved to the stool where Grimalkin sat, and bega caressing the big cat's head. She watched Cooper until h disappeared around the edge of the house.

"He thinks I'm an enchantress, Grim," she said. "Can yo believe that?"

"Yeow, yeow."

"Yes, yes," she agreed. "Isn't it wonderful?" She gave th cat's ears a thorough rubbing.

Isabel couldn't recall a time when she had felt so warn and fuzzy inside, but then, before today she had never touche a man's nearly naked body. The memory of Cooper's muscle back beneath her fingers sent heat radiating to her core, mak ing her tingle. She continued stroking the feline's head an was soon rewarded with a low, rumbling purr.

"You men are all alike," she teased. "I had Cooper purring almost as loud as you." She paused, looking closely at the cat. "You," she admonished. "No, it can't be." She stopped administering her affections as disappointment assailed her, and realization dawned. "It was you, wasn't it?"

Lifting her hands, Isabel brought them closer to her face and turned them from front to back. The chickweed salve had completely disappeared.

"Grimalkin Gomez, you caused it all. The salve, the kiss, everything."

When Grim didn't bother with a response, Isabel turned away from the stool and hustled back to the table. Grim's magic had made the salve increase, made Cooper kiss her, and, worst of all, made her respond to his kiss.

She began slamming things about as she put the room to order. When everything was in place, Isabel turned and faced the table. If it hadn't been for Grim and his fairy tricks, Cooper would never have kissed her. This realization brought a twinge of disappointment and also a feeling of guilt. It wasn't supposed to be this way. No, she corrected, her mood veering sharply to anger, it couldn't be this way. Feelings for the enemy were not allowed. Feeling anything for Cooper Adair wasn't part of her plan. If she kept up this mooning, she would soon need one of her own antidotes for lovesickness—eating ant eggs with honey.

Isabel slammed her hand down on the table with such force that Grim shot from the stool and out the door. The weight of the blow shook the table and caused the mortar and pestle on its surface to rattle. It was then that Isabel saw the cuff links. Cooper must have left them. She reached to pick up the gold buttons. One glance told her the jewelry was expensive and probably had been made specially for him when she saw they were engraved with a mortar and pestle. She turned them over to examine their reverse side. One of the links was signed, *Love, MK.*

"Marcella Kent," Isabel said. The cuff links must have been a gift to Cooper from Marcella. Isabel's fingers curled around the gold buttons, and she squeezed them into her palm.

It isn't fair, Isabel thought. Marcella Kent was everything that she was not: beautiful, rich, and engaged to Cooper Adair.

After a moment her mouth opened in dismay. "An omen," said she. "Finding the cuff links was an omen." Isabel hugged them to her chest, her earlier envy disappearing.

Marcella Kent might be beautiful and rich, but very soon she would no longer be engaged to Cooper Adair.

From what Isabel had seen of Marcella yesterday, and what Dora had told her this morning, she didn't believe that Marcella would take too kindly to Cooper misplacing her gift.

In fact, Isabel suspected, she would be very displeased when she learned where and how he had misplaced them.

Ten

~

Gathered about the Kents' long dining room table was a group of St. Augustine's finest, or so Cooper supposed. The evening had not turned out to be his idea of a relaxing dinner spent with his future family, nor was it the one he would have chosen if he had been given the choice. Monied guests, decked out in their wealthy finery, and here he sat in his second wool suit feeling as uncomfortable as a porcupine in a balloon factory.

For about the second time since the evening began, Cooper was inclined to think that he didn't fit in with such flowered gentry. The careers of the men present had peaked long ago, while he was still at the bottom of the valley struggling to make it past the first hurdle.

Cooper imagined that most would have figured him fortunate to be here surrounded by so much wealth and success, and perhaps under different circumstances, he, too, would have considered himself lucky. But after everything that had transpired in the last two days, especially the episode last night with Marcella, Cooper needed time alone with his fiancée. Their relationship was about as fragile as eggshells, and Cooper had planned to spend the evening wooing Marcella and entrenching himself again in her good graces.

But things hadn't gone as planned. To make matters worse, he wasn't even allowed to sit beside his beloved. Marcella was seated at the opposite end of the table between two distinguished-looking chaps, while he was seated between two aging dames whose wrists and fingers were so burdened with jewelry that Cooper wondered how they managed to lift their forks. They also had no trouble lifting their wineglasses.

Because both women were as plump as the stuffed bird taking center stage on the sideboard, Cooper supposed yet again that the women's eating habits weren't hampered by all those karats. *Of the gold kind.* His clever thought made him smile, and caught the attention of one of his dinner companions.

"If I'm not mishtaken," the woman slurred, "that is the first time I've seen you smile since we were seated." The woman was the wife of the local banker, and she batted her tarantula eyelashes at him, feigning coyness. "I was beginning to think you weren't pleased with the seating arrangements." Her many chins wobbled, making the diamonds at her neck twinkle.

Cooper couldn't believe how close to right her assumption was. But instead of admitting the truth, he said what was expected of him. "Now, Mrs. Slade, you know that isn't true. I can't recall a time when I've had the pleasure of being seated between two such lovely and entertaining ladies." His remark sounded false to his own ears.

"Probably a gas bubble prompted that smile, Silva," the lady on his left said, belching behind her napkin. "I'd wager this young man doesn't feel as though he has much to smile about, considering he is seated so far from his lady love. Am I right, Mr. Adair?"

Cooper would have denied it, but he wasn't given the chance.

"A gas bubble indeed." The banker's wife emptied her wineglass and signaled the butler to replenish it. "How gauche. And in mixed company, too." Silva nudged him in the shoulder and whispered, "It's the new rich, you know? They know nothing of good manners."

Cooper merely nodded, but in his opinion, both of the old dames could use a lesson in proper behavior. He supposed for the third time that perhaps it was this hellish climate that bred such ill-mannered women. Before meeting these two, Cooper had thought that Miss Gomez was the exception with her outspokenness and unconventional behavior, but now he suspected that such rudeness came with the territory. His own conduct of the last twenty-four hours had been nothing to brag about.

Silva lifted her napkin and fanned the air beneath her nose. "Phew! I'll have to speak to Evelyn about her maids. I swan they must have doused the furniture with lemon oil, so much so that the overpowering scent is ruining this otherwise fine fare."

Cooper felt a moment of guilt, realizing that he was the cause of the woman's distress. It was the chickweed salve she smelled, and rightfully he should have been blamed for the citrus aroma, but his concern was forgotten with the audacious woman's next words.

"But then I suspect, Mr. Adair, you're familiar with the term *new rich,*" she said. "I still can't believe that Jack Kent settled his only daughter on a mere tradesman."

Tradesman! Cooper was no more a tradesman than she was, but if he were to point out this fact to her, he would be sinking to her level of rudeness. Yet Cooper wasn't above defending his Marcella against such churlish remarks, and he would have if the woman hadn't delivered her next punch first.

"It's common knowledge that Jack Kent buys his daughter whatever she wants, but you already know that, don't you?"

Cooper nearly choked on the wine he had just swallowed. Had Jack Kent announced in the local society page that he had loaned his future son-in-law money for the purchase of the post building? God, he hoped not, but otherwise how would this old crow know about the transaction?

Silva leaned closer, propping her flabby elbow on the table. She wheezed, and her breath was so strong with the scent of spirits that it would have flamed if Cooper had lit a match. It was apparent that the banker's wife was in her cups, so he would make an allowance for her rudeness.

"Of course," she said, "that was the other man. The fiancé before you. It would seem the lovely Marcella can be very unpleasant, demanding, but I suppose you already know that, too."

Cooper wondered which of the "you already know thats" she referred to. The other man, or Marcella being demanding? He agreed there were times when Marcella could be demanding, but weren't most women? An image of his mother popped into his head. Lillian Adair had never demanded anything of anyone. She loved her children and her husband unconditionally, and she would go to her grave doing just that.

"I'm assuming Jack Kent settled quite a sum on you as well?" Silva's spidery lashes fluttered like a bat's wings over her bloodshot eyes. "You, my dear boy, are most fortunate to marry money." She took another sip of wine. "Humble beginnings, I'd shay." Her words became more slurred. "Peashants! Dining in such splendor and rubbing shoulders with the elite. A great country, isn't shit?"

White-hot anger shot though Cooper. *Humble beginnings indeed.* He was about to tell the arrogant biddy, drunk or otherwise, what he believed to be true humility when he heard Jack Kent's chair scrape across the wooden floor. All eyes turned to their host.

"Gentlemen," he announced, "shall we retire to the library for a smoke and a glass of port? Most of you haven't had a chance to speak with my future son-in-law," he said, his gaze locking on Cooper's, "but I assure you that when you do, you'll be as impressed with the young man as I am."

There was such pride in the older man's expression that for a moment Cooper forgot his disturbing conversation with the banker's wife. His gaze locked with Marcella's, and the smile she sent him dissolved his anger. The old bat was drunk and apparently not responsible for her loose tongue.

Following their host's example, the other men rose as well. Cooper slid back his chair and proceeded to assist his dinner companions with theirs. A crane would most likely be needed to help steady Silva Slade once she was on her feet, but surprisingly the woman remained upright, using the chair back for support.

"Evelyn will show you ladies to the veranda," Jack Kent said. "We'll join you there later."

Cooper believed that the evening would be more enjoyable after he parted company with Silva Slade, and especially after Marcella's encouraging glance. He was aware that she had been engaged to someone before him, but he was inclined to think that broken engagements weren't uncommon among the wealthy, particularly among women as beautiful as his Marcella. But when they were alone later, Cooper would make a point of learning more about that engagement for no other reason than to put Silva Slade's rumor to rest.

With this thought stowed away for now, Cooper adjourned with the others to Jack Kent's very masculine library.

He stood now beside the empty fireplace with a brandy snifter in one hand and a fine cigar in the other. Unlike his former dinner companions, the gentlemen were amiable, even likable, and so he dismissed his conversation with Mrs. Slade as ludicrous, especially when he considered the inebriated source.

Cooper took a sip of the brandy. It was as smooth as silk going down. As smooth and slick as his host, a man Cooper admired and looked up to.

The room was pleasantly cool with the wall of French doors propped open to allow for the flow of bay breezes. It was a warm softness that caressed Cooper's face, and with the lemony scent of citronella strong in the air to ward off insects, Cooper's thoughts turned to that of another caress—that of a woman with magic fingers. His skin tingled just recalling the feel of her warm hands kneading his back.

"Cooper, is it?" The elderly gentleman approached him

from across the room. "Unusual name," he said.

Grateful for the reprieve from the forbidden territory his mind had been traversing, Cooper turned and acknowledged the gentleman.

"It was my mother's maiden name, sir."

Mr. Elliot was an architect who, like most of the other men in the room, was a transplanted northerner. They were successful businessmen who had come to St. Augustine to amass a fortune, but in the case of those gathered here tonight, most were more interested in adding to their fortune instead of building it.

"So, young man," the gent said, taking a long draw on his cigar, "it's a fine piece of property you've purchased for yourself. St. George Street is one of the busiest thoroughfares in our little town."

"Yes, sir, the building is in a prime location, but I fear it's going to take more work than I anticipated. Pretty rundown on the inside."

Mr. Will, an attorney, said, "I guess it's true what's rumored, then. Wooster Farley not only abused his family, but the building as well." The gray-haired man shook his head sadly. "Wooster Farley wasn't much good for anything but breaking the law, breaking his wife by sending her to an early grave. How bad is the building?"

"Nothing that can't be repaired," Cooper said, but his thoughts weren't on the repairs that needed to be made to the building. He couldn't imagine what kind of man would abuse his family, or that the abuse would cause a woman's premature death. It was no wonder that Isabel wasn't too keen on being called Miss Farley. Considering what he had just learned, Cooper couldn't say he much blamed her.

The attorney puffed on his cigar. "My wife's family wintered here when the Gomezes owned the trading post. She doesn't remember a lot about the family, but she does remember that Mrs. Gomez was part Indian, and very exotic-looking. At that time, Kalee Gomez was reputed to be a respected herbalist and healer around these parts. I imagine that was before the town attracted real doctors."

"Can you believe there are now seven doctors in this town?" someone asked.

"Three of us are in attendance in this room," someone else added.

A gentleman who had been introduced to Cooper as Dr. Reed entered the conversation. "And we still have an herbalist," he said. "The young Gomez woman treats the local women for female disorders, or whatever it is the fairer sex suffers from and won't discuss with us gentlemen doctors."

The men laughed at this remark.

"My wife claims her lotions and creams are wonderful for the complexion."

"I suppose Isabel Gomez has her place in the community," Dr. Reed said. "Maybe she keeps those preoccupied by illness at bay so that we doctors can treat those who are seriously ill."

The smooth brandy suddenly turned abrasive against Cooper's tongue. Being a fair-minded man, he took exception to their blanket dismissal of Miss Gomez's skills. He didn't know how valuable her lotions and creams were, but he could attest to the effectiveness of her chickweed salve. The itchy rash that had covered his shoulders and back, driving him to distraction, no longer tormented him after she applied her cream.

Cooper was convinced that this wasn't the time or place to champion Miss Gomez's expertise, especially when he found Jack Kent's eyes drilling into him as they had from the moment the Gomez name had come up in the conversation.

"So, young man," Dr. Reed said, "this fancy new drugstore you'll be opening will probably take away some of Miss Gomez's business."

"As well as some of ours," someone added.

"I'll be stocking more, sir, than ladies' cosmetics; although I suspect I'll carry a few brands of those as well." He took a long pull on his cigar and watched a smoke ring rise into the air. "My intent, sir, is not to take away from your medical practices. I do hope, though, that there will come a time when you will allow me to fill the prescriptions you don't wish to compound and dispense yourself."

"I've always mixed my own prescriptions," Dr. Reed said. The other doctors agreed.

"And I'm sure you'll continue to do so. But I believe that the future of medicine will call for a central drug supplier, one trained in pharmaceutical science who will have a larger inventory of drugs than most doctors have on hand in their smaller practices."

Everyone in the room seemed to be interested in what Cooper was saying, so he continued.

"An indication of the way this country is headed, due to the Industrial Revolution, is evidenced in the new laboratories of Johnson & Johnson of New Brunswick, New Jersey, and Bristol-Myers Squibb in Clinton, New York. These pharmaceutical houses produce chemicals and ethical drugs for the pharmacist to dispense, primarily by prescription, as well as manufacture over-the-counter specialties and medical sundries."

Mr. Tetote, who had been introduced as a prosperous saloon owner in town, winked at Jack Kent. "I suppose the kind of drunkard I make will be out of fashion. Instead of buying spirits from me, he'll be walking out of your son-in-law's shop carrying medicines labeled bracers and soothing syrup."

Everyone laughed but Cooper.

He knew establishing himself as a pharmacist wouldn't be easy, especially with the preconceived notions about doctoring and medicines. The two always had gone hand in hand: doctors usually mixed their own prescriptions, dispensing them to their patients. Yet he hadn't expected opposition from a saloon owner.

"Saloons will always be in fashion," Cooper countered. "I'm assuming those who frequent my pharmacy won't be seeking prescriptions for social pleasure, but because they are ill and have need of medicine to make them better."

Mr. Tetote's expression soured. "Then you've no plans to

open a bar in your store like the one I read about recently in Atlanta, Georgia."

"I believe it's called a soda fountain," Cooper corrected, "and yes, sir, a fountain is part of my plan. A lot of the drugstores in big cities are opening fountains. As for Dr. Pemberton in Atlanta, he makes a drink he calls Coca-Cola with an extract from the leaves of the cocoa shrub, and promotes it as a tonic."

Mr. Tetote harumphed. "Because of state prohibition laws in Georgia, I'd say. The man substituted syrup instead of wine in his popular beverage, and now it has become all the rage. In my opinion, it is still spirits described as bracers and soothing syrups."

"Not if it contains no wine," Cooper reminded. "I understand Dr. Pemberton's Coca-Cola is reported to be an aid to digestion, and also to impart energy to the respiratory organs."

Jack Kent shot Cooper a warning glance. "I don't know about you, gentlemen, but this stuff"—he lifted his whiskey glass so that everyone could see it—"is all I need. It makes me feel a hell of a lot better."

Everyone laughed, and all agreed. Except Cooper. He didn't see the humor in his future father-in-law's remark. He had expected Jack to defend his profession, not openly ridicule it, but then perhaps he had been too outspoken. Jack's warning glare said as much.

"Now, gentlemen," their host said, "I think we've spent enough time away from the ladies. Shall we join them on the veranda?"

When the men had drained their glasses and stubbed out their smokes, they began to move through the French doors to the porch. Cooper moved along with them, eager to join Marcella again. The evening was still young, and after everyone departed, he hoped they could have some time alone together.

"Cooper," Jack Kent called. "Before you go, I'd like a word with you."

Suddenly Cooper felt as though he were back in short pants, ordered by his teacher to stay inside for misbehaving while the others filed outdoors. Now, as then, everyone knew he was being reprimanded for his misconduct, and he wasn't too keen at being singled out.

Once they were alone, he watched Jack grind his stogy in an ashtray before he spoke. "Son," he began, "I know you're new to hobnobbing, but take the word of someone who knows. You don't want to make enemies of the men who are here tonight."

"Excuse me?" Cooper met Jack's black-eyed stare. "I'm not certain I understand. I did nothing but state my opinions and defend my profession. I'm proud, sir, of what I've accomplished, and I feel very strongly about it."

"Simon Tetote is not a man to anger. Granted, he's gruff around the edges, but he could buy and sell this town if he had a notion to do so. Your remark about saloons was uncalled for."

"And his remark about—"

"A man in his position can damn well say what he pleases."

"I was brought up to believe that a man can say what he pleases no matter what his position."

"Impertinent pup, aren't you?"

The look Jack sent him could have frozen a sunbeam, but then as suddenly as it appeared, it disappeared. He moved to stand beside Cooper and draped an arm across his shoulders. "You're young, you're bright, and you have Jack Kent behind you one hundred percent, but you weren't exactly reared in the embrace of high society."

"I never claimed—"

"I'd suggest you learn to skate around issues when dealing with influential men. Just tell them, son, when they ask you anything of importance that you're all right on that, too. It's a good answer for any hard question."

Cooper held up his hands. "Hold on a minute—that's fine for politicians, but not for me."

"That could change, you know. The men here tonight could help you in that direction."

"I'm sorry, sir, I've no interest in politics."

"Oh, yes, I almost forgot." He eyed Cooper with distaste. "Next time you're invited to dinner, I suggest you dress for the occasion."

Cooper's temper was at a flash point. "I wasn't aware, sir, that you were hosting a—"

"You're marrying my daughter, son, and we always dress for dinner in this house." He slapped Cooper hard on the back, making his teeth rattle.

Tempering his anger, Cooper asked, "Is that all? I was hoping to spend a little time with Marcella—"

"One other thing," Jack said, as though Cooper had not spoken. "That incident last night with the Gomez woman upset Marcella very much. She hardly slept at all. I'm sure it was nothing but a big misunderstanding, just as you said, but don't get too friendly with the woman."

"I had no plans—"

"Good! I don't like to see my daughter unhappy. Shall we join my guests?" Jack moved toward the French doors, motioning for Cooper to follow him. Laughter and soft conversation drifted toward them on the warm air. When Jack got to the doors, he stopped and turned to face Cooper again.

"Oh, yes, there is one other thing. Let's hold off awhile on that soda fountain. Tetote wasn't pleased with the idea. Let's give him some time to get used to the notion."

"I'm sorry, I can't do—"

Jack Kent began walking again, then stopped. "Before I forget. The cleaners and the carpenters will arrive at your place tomorrow morning at seven o'clock sharp. You'll be there, I assume?"

"Cleaners and carpenters? But—"

"We'll talk again later." He checked his pocket watch. "Now I must get back to my guests."

Cooper watched as Jack Kent disappeared out the door and

from sight. He paused, listening, as his voice joined with those of his guests.

"Your home is lovely, Jack," said an unidentifiable male. "I do believe you bought the best view of the bay this town has to offer."

"Only the best for my girls," was Jack's reply. Congenial laughter followed his remark.

Cooper hung back, standing inside the library with the intent to bring his anger under control. On hearing the man's words, it made him question if perhaps the older man had made a poor choice this time. If he thought to purchase Cooper for his daughter, he was going to be more disappointed than he already appeared to be, if their recent conversation was any clue.

In the past, his dealings with Marcella's father had been strictly personal, except for when Cooper had agreed to take a loan from him to use toward the purchase of the post building. It was to Cooper's father's credit that the deal had been drawn up legally by the Adair family lawyer instead of Cooper accepting Jack Kent's money as a gift. Maybe his father had more business savvy than Cooper suspected, or maybe his father was a better judge of character than his son.

He had as much as surmised that Kent was a ruthless businessman. That same ruthlessness had made Kent a very wealthy man, and Kent Import/Export was fast becoming a recognizable name throughout the world. Because Cooper had been busy with college and then his apprenticeship, his contact with Marcella's father had been minimal, and then usually on a personal basis. He had seen the side of the man he had shown to his family—the side that had convinced Cooper that Jack Kent was an honorable and just man.

Until tonight Cooper hadn't experienced the man's arrogance, and he wasn't so sure he liked what he saw. Jack Kent's money might have helped him purchase the post building, but he hadn't bought Cooper in the deal. Yet it made him wonder if there might be some truth to Silva Slade's rumor.

A fine kettle of fish. If it weren't for Marcella, Cooper would say his good night and leave. It was doubtful that his presence would be missed, and right now he needed time to himself to reflect on what he and Jack had discussed.

No, he corrected. He hadn't discussed anything. Nor had he been given the chance to. It was Jack who had done all the talking, right down to how Cooper should dress. Didn't the man know that his trunks hadn't yet arrived?

"Cooper, are you in here?" Marcella's soft voice called from just beyond the entrance before she actually appeared in the door. "Daddy sent me to fetch you," she said, lacing her fingers with his when he extended his hand. "Come, our guests are leaving. We must say goodbye."

Saying good night to Jack Kent's guests wasn't a high priority on Cooper's list. On seeing Marcella standing in the doorway in her buttercup yellow dress, framed by the muted glow of the many lamps and candles, his heart flipped inside his chest. She was so beautiful that she took his breath away.

What Cooper really wanted to do was to pull her into his arms and kiss her. Kiss her in the same way he had twice kissed Isabel Gomez. He wanted to forget his conversation with her father and pretend that it had never taken place.

When he didn't follow immediately, Marcella gazed at him, surprised. "Are you feeling okay?" she asked. "Are you ill?"

"Just tired," he answered wearily. "It's been a long and tiring day."

"Oh," she said, her disappointment evident. "I was hoping after everyone left that you and I could sit a spell on the porch. It's been so long since the two of us have had a chance to talk."

"Talk?" Cooper wiggled his brows like a villain.

"Yes, talk, Cooper Adair." She cut her gaze away from him teasingly. "If you're nice, I might allow you one small kiss."

She looked so much like the old Marcella, the one he had come to know and love in Philadelphia, that hope blossomed anew in his heart, chasing away his earlier disappointment.

Maybe, Cooper thought, he had been making mountains out of molehills because he was so darn tired. The concrete slab he had spent last night on didn't make for a good night's sleep.

He pulled her toward him. His intent was to kiss her. "I'm never too tired to talk with you," he said. "In fact, I can only think of one other thing I'd rather do."

She leaned into him, and the scent of violets, her scent, made his pulse beat faster. When his lips were about to brush hers, he heard Evelyn Kent call.

"Marcella? Cooper?"

Marcella jumped from his embrace as though she had been stung. "I almost forgot myself," she said.

"Forget yourself," he whispered.

"Come on, goose." She tugged on his hand. "We mustn't keep Daddy waiting. He is a stickler for formality."

Cooper knew where he would like to stick Jack Kent's formality, but he didn't believe for a moment that Kent's devoted daughter would be in agreement. Moreover, what were a few more minutes of formality when he would soon have the opportunity to finish the kiss he had started when the two of them were alone?

It was Marcella he would marry, not Jack Kent. Once Marcella was his wife, her father would have no more control over her or him. With this thought foremost in his mind, Cooper followed dutifully along behind her.

Eleven

The last of the guests departed, and Cooper stood with the Kents on the long veranda feeling uncomfortably out of place. It was the first time in the last year that his rosy future didn't appear so rosy. His discontent stemmed from his earlier conversation with Marcella's father. Try as he might, Cooper couldn't dismiss Jack's patronizing manner from his mind.

"Now," the older man said, rubbing his hands together and turning to face his wife, who stood beside Marcella and Cooper. "Evey, it was a fine evening was it not? Just as I promised, this relocation will be fine. Already we have influential friends to pass the time with, and you, my dear, look the picture of health this evening." He pecked his wife affectionately on the cheek, making her blush.

Evelyn Kent sent her husband a timorous smile. It was her health that had prompted the family's move south. The older woman had been suffering with consumption for years. Before tonight, Cooper had assumed her frailty was the reason for her timidity, but now he wasn't so sure. Evelyn would be a perfect candidate for intimidation from a domineering man like Jack Kent.

"And now, my dear, I suspect these two young folks would enjoy some time alone." Jack encircled his wife with his arm and shifted his attention to Marcella. "Am I correct in thinking that my princess is tired of her father's company?"

"Oh, Daddy. You know I never tire of your company. I had hoped we could all sit awhile on the porch and relax. It's such a lovely evening."

Cooper wanted to stuff a handkerchief in Marcella's mouth. Sitting a spell with her parents, especially her father, was the last thing he felt like doing.

Jack's robust laughter cut through the peaceful darkness, startling a fluttering moth from a nearby lamp and blotting out the sound of the departing horse and carriage.

"I'm sure young Cooper would much prefer your company to mine." His black gaze cut to Cooper's. "Am I right, young man?"

"You know I always enjoy talking with both you and Mrs. Kent." Cooper directed his remark to Marcella's mother, not trusting himself to respond civilly to Jack.

"Say good night, Evey," Jack said. His tone turned businesslike. "I'm sure you won't stay too long."

Cooper felt as though he had been issued an ultimatum.

Jack kissed his daughter's cheek, then ushered his wife toward the door. Looking at Cooper as they passed, he said, "You won't forget your seven o'clock appointment in the morning with the carpenters."

"Of course not."

"Good. I'll see you sometime tomorrow."

"That won't be—"

"Good night. We'll talk more then."

Cooper stiffened. Why had he not seen this side of the man before now? It was as though with the move south Jack had turned into a different person than the one he had known in Philadelphia. Or perhaps Cooper had only imagined he knew him. . . .

Marcella's words cut into his drifting thoughts. "Isn't it wonderful that Daddy hired carpenters to help with the renovation of our property?"

Our property. It was the first time Marcella had made the

reference jointly, and for a moment Cooper wondered if she was referring to herself and her father, or to herself and him. When had he developed such a suspicious nature?

"I wasn't planning on renovating—I had planned to make do with what was there."

But what was there, he admitted to himself, wasn't at all what Cooper had expected. He had understood that there were shelves for stocking merchandise, but this morning's visit had proved that wasn't so. Most of the shelving appeared to have been used for firewood, but he was handy with tools. He had thought to build several shelves to replace the missing ones. Doing the work himself would have saved money, but it seemed the decision had been taken from his hands.

"Daddy had Mr. Jetson show him around the building before you got here. After seeing it, he decided to employ carpenters. Isn't that just like Daddy to be so thoughtful?"

Thoughtful, or damn right presumptuous!

Marcella led him to the porch swing at the opposite end of the veranda. She was a vision of loveliness as he gazed down into her upturned face. They took a seat in the porch swing, and she settled comfortably in the crook of his arm, her head resting against his shoulder. With a lazy, slow movement, he set the swing into motion with his feet.

When he didn't answer her question immediately, she pressed him. "Wasn't it thoughtful of Daddy?"

"Very," he whispered into the puff of black curls on the top of her head.

The moon that was almost full reflected a silvery ribbon across the calm water of the bay. Coupled with the lemony scent of the burning citronella candles was the ambrosial scent of jasmine. The waxy white flowers covered the fence separating the Kents' yard from their neighbor's, the petals' star shapes imitating the twinkling ones overhead. All that was needed to make the setting even more perfect was the sound of Isabel's many chimes filling the night with their fairy bell sounds.

A stray curl of Marcella's hair tickled his nose. He inhaled deeply to ward off a sneeze. The fragrance of violets washed over him—Marcella's scent, powdery sweet and pure. Nothing like Isabel, who smelled as earthy as the woman she was.

Isabel. He shouldn't be thinking about her when he held Marcella. He drew in another deep breath, hoping to anchor his thoughts on the woman in his arms. Maybe there was truth to the rumor about violets. It was said that taking too many whiffs of the violets' dizzying aroma would make young girls risk "losing their heads." He was not a young girl, but he definitely seemed to be in the throes of unreasonable thinking by permitting Isabel Gomez into his reflections while holding his betrothed.

He shifted his weight, leaning against the swing's creaking chain. Marcella snuggled against his chest. He dropped his arm from around her shoulders and encircled her with both his arms. With her arms resting on his, her hands absently fingered the cuffs of his shirt. She turned her face up to his, inviting him to kiss her. His face descended toward hers, and he was about to brush her lips with his mouth when she jerked away and sat upright.

"Your cuff links." She looked first to the cuff of his sleeve then to his face. "These aren't mine," she said. "You're not wearing my gift."

At the moment cuffs weren't exactly his top priority. Rather than discussing cuffs, Cooper was more interested in smacking her lips. It had been weeks since he last saw Marcella, weeks since he had last held her close. Those weeks had seemed like months, and considering all that had transpired in the last two days, he needed to kiss *this* woman.

Marcella scooted across the swing, breaking contact. "You promised when I gave you my betrothal gift that you would never be without them."

It was difficult to wear the absent jewelry when they sat on Isabel Gomez's table, but of course he couldn't tell Marcella that. Just as he couldn't have gone back to collect the buttons from Miss Gomez the moment he had discovered them missing.

"I—they—" he stammered, groping for a reasonable explanation. "I was in a hurry when I dressed for dinner. I didn't wish to be late."

Marcella jumped up from the swing and began to pace. "But you had no difficulty finding those. Surely you could have put on the ones I gave you just as easily."

"I must have thought I did."

"Thought you did? You treat my gift with such little regard." She glared at him. "You're acting strange, Cooper. First the incident last night with that loathsome woman. Now this." She moved to the porch rail and stared out at the bay.

He left the swing to join her.

"Marcella, please. You know how much I cherish your gift. It was an honest mistake. These last two days haven't been easy. I've never really recovered from the tiresome train trip from Philadelphia. I suppose I'm more tired than I realized."

She crossed her arms, her spine stiff. "Well, this move hasn't been easy for me, either. In case you haven't noticed, this—this town is not exactly Philadelphia."

She implied it was his fault that she had moved here when in truth it had been her idea. No, he corrected, it had been her father's. When Cooper had made the decision to relocate to Florida, he had thought it a good idea. At that time the adventure seemed like a golden opportunity. But after his conversation with Jack Kent in the library, Cooper had begun to question if he had acted too hastily. But this conversation wasn't about decisions.

"Unless you've forgotten," he said, "I moved to Florida for you. You're the one who wanted to follow your parents here. We knew it would be different from—"

"No," she accused, "it's you who is different. You kissed that—that horrible creature and now you refuse to wear the gift I had made especially for you."

"Marcella, you're being ridiculous. They are just cuff buttons, and I'm not refusing to wear them. I just overlooked putting on the right ones because I dressed so hurriedly this evening."

He moved to stand behind her and placed his hands on her shoulders. "Don't be this way," he said. "We haven't seen each other for weeks. You're my reason for being here. Don't you know by now that I only want to make you happy?"

For a moment she remained tense, then she relaxed against him. "I—I know. It's just that I'm having a difficult time understanding why you kissed that woman."

I still don't understand that myself! "I explained that last night. She misinterpreted my actions. It was nothing more than a misunderstanding. It is you I love."

She turned to face him. "I—I know that, or I think I know that," she said, leaning into him. "But from now on, you stay away from that woman." Her expression softened, and she fluttered her lashes at him. "Now that we've settled that, you may kiss me."

"There's nothing I'd rather do." He leaned toward her and bent his head down to hers. Their lips were within inches of touching, and his whole being was attuned to the woman he held in his arms.

"Marcella." Jack Kent's voice boomed from within the house. "It's time you come inside."

She jumped away from Cooper as though she'd been shot. "I'll be right there, Daddy."

"Marcella, please," Cooper pleaded. "Stay a moment longer."

"You know I can't do that." She grabbed his hand and moved toward the front door. "We don't want to make Daddy angry, now do we?"

"No," Cooper answered. He followed along behind her and stopped when she paused inside the door. It was pointless to argue now.

Marcella smiled and pecked him on the cheek. "I'll see you tomorrow," she whispered, "if time permits." She vanished into the interior of the house.

Cooper stood alone on the veranda. "We sure as heck don't want to make Jack Kent mad," he muttered, "but what about me?"

Their reunion was not supposed to have been this way. The longer he stood there, the angrier he got. "And what did she mean, if time permits?"

Disgusted, Cooper loped down the steps. When he reached the gate, he banged it shut behind him.

Consuela's footman delivered the actress's trunk not long after Cooper departed. During the interim, Isabel had weeded her garden and watered her plants. Her chores done, she was eager to examine the contents of the trunk.

She took a hasty sponge bath that removed the grime she had accumulated from her garden—grime that had turned the water in the washbowl gray; unfortunately, the bath had not succeeded in washing away the scent of the chickweed salve that would forever remind her of Cooper Adair. Isabel kneeled beside the large packing case, unfastened the clasps, and lifted the lid. Grimalkin lay in the middle of the saffron yellow dress spread out on the table so he could better supervise her, as was his usual practice.

From the trunk's interior, the scent of musk floated outward, and Isabel wrinkled her nose. Musk wasn't a scent that she particularly liked with its heavy, penetrating odor, especially after she learned the substance came from a sack beneath the abdomen of a male musk deer. This insight, like the scent itself, repelled her, and she was all for giving the garments a good airing once she had gone through them. No one would ever accuse her of smelling like an Asian buck.

Besides, there were too many other light, pleasantly scented florals that were so much more pleasing to the olfactory glands, her favorite being gardenias whose deep and heady scent reminded her of torrid, moist earth. There was an ancient bush that thrived in the filtered sunlight of her side yard, and she wasn't even sure of its origin, but she loved the plant and used the blossoms to make her bath and body oils.

As she dug through the trunk's contents, she was treated to a visual flower garden of colors: magenta, electric blue, plum, green, and last but not least, scarlet. She eyed the red petticoat thrown over the chair that she had brought home earlier. The reds matched, and she decided that the crimson undergarment must go with the crimson dress. Not that Isabel could imagine wearing such a vivid color—it was much too violent for her tastes.

Evidently Consuela had packed her trunk in anger. The garments were tossed about haphazardly, forming a mountain of material unlike any Isabel had seen. Most of the fabrics she couldn't identify, but some she could put a name to: poplin, linen, and batiste.

The contents was a caldron of color, a visual potpourri. After removing all the clothing, she found on the bottom of the trunk a stack of rainbow-colored ribbons and three ladies magazines: *Godey's Lady's Book*, a *Harper's Bazaar*, and one she wasn't familiar with called *Dress*. Since Isabel never allowed herself the luxury of spending money on magazines, she picked up the books, sat back, and clasped them to her chest, almost as excited about the magazines as she was about the clothes.

Consuela was truly her fairy godmother, or that was how Isabel had begun to think of the woman. It was then Isabel noticed that something had fallen into her lap. It was a penned note that had escaped from between the pages of one of the monthlies. Picking up the note, she began to read, visualizing the dark stranger who had given her such a generous and needed gift.

> *Señorita,*
>
> Wear my clothes and make your armor weep, but remember the louts are put in this world for only one purpose and that is to pleasure us women the only way a man can. Take Consuela's advice. Don't confuse this passion for love. If you do, long after the passion has died, the flame will consume you.

"This Consuela sounds like a girl after my own heart," she told Grim. "Or as if she stepped from the pages of one of my romance novels."

Consuela had meant well with her advice, but little did the woman realize Isabel wasn't in need of any such warnings. She had learned from her mother's experience that most men were louts, and this passion Consuela spoke of wouldn't put an excessive strain on Isabel. She would welcome and use the woman's clothes to help her lure Cooper Adair in, but she would never be consumed by passion for the man.

The phrase about pleasing a woman the only way a man could puzzled Isabel, but after considerable debate, she decided the fiery-natured woman referred to kissing. In that sense, Cooper had pleased her twice, but after learning of Grimalkin's involvement, Isabel had decided the thrill she had felt when she and Cooper had kissed had been nothing more than the feline's magic. That was an issue she meant to discuss with her pet.

There were six dresses inside the trunk, two more petticoats, a pair of dance slippers, and three camisoles. There was also a pair of what looked like men's trousers, but were too much like bloomers for a man's taste, and one very sheer nightrail. So sheer that a ghost could have worn it and not been any less transparent. In fact, it put Isabel in mind of the one Consuela had worn this morning when she saw the lady hanging over the porch rail.

Isabel stood and reached for the bundle of dresses and carried them to the full-length mirror where she dropped the pile on the floor. Then she began picking up each dress, holding them against her front.

"Which one should I try on first?" she asked Grimalkin. She turned from left to right as the cat left his perch atop the table and plopped in the middle of the colorful heap on the floor.

When Grim looked as though he was about to sharpen his nails on the nubby fabric of one dress, Isabel toed him off the pile with her foot. "Don't even think it, you old mouser," she scolded. "These clothes are going to help rid us of the Yankee."

"Meowwww, meowwww," he cried.

"I didn't hurt you, you old reprobate," she responded. "I merely bruised your dignity."

Grimalkin turned his fat backside to her as though he meant to leave, but his retreat was short-lived. Soon he backtracked to her side. He brushed her ankles several times, pausing in his swipes only long enough to wrap his fat tail around one leg as though embracing it, before he settled comfortably on the floor beneath the wall mirror.

"That's much better," she said. "If you plan on sleeping at the end of my bed, you will not do it smelling like a musk deer." She picked up another dress from the pile and held it to her. "I don't know if I've the stomach to try on these things. Perhaps I should wait until they air out."

"Neow, neow."

At the feline sound, Isabel cocked her head toward the cat. "The last time you uttered those cat nuances you got me in all kinds of trouble. But since we're alone, I don't reckon I'm in any danger of getting swept away by a rogue's kiss. I'm assuming your eagerness comes from wanting to see your mistress in something other than her scandalous britches."

"Yeow, yeow."

"Patience, please." She slipped the plum-colored frock over her head. "You and Dora are trying to make me into something I'm not."

When she could see again, she stuck her arms in the sleeves, shimmied the skirt down over her hips, and began buttoning the dress's front. As she stared at her reflection in the mirror, she noted that the fuller cut of the dress allowed the fabric to skim her bosom instead of girding it as did so many of the tight bodices in fashion today. Since Consuela had appeared as well-endowed as Isabel in the bosom department, maybe that explained why her dresses fit Isabel. But it was more than that.

The design of the dress was different from the other dresses Isabel owned, the biggest difference being that it flowed from the bust to the floor, putting her in mind of a bell. She moved her arms back and forth, scrunched up her shoulders, then straightened again. It was a perfect fit, designed, she decided, to be looser and lighter, while allowing the wearer to be free from boning and bustle.

Once the buttons were fastened up to the collar, Isabel stepped back. "So, my furry friend, what do you think?"

"Me-wow, me-wow."

Isabel gaped. This was the second time today she had heard Grim give his cat approval about something as human as good looks.

Laughing, she asked, "That good, huh? Wait until you see me in the others. You'll be roaring instead of purring."

She tried on the other dresses, including her favorite, the saffron yellow that was shaped like a flowing robe. Finally there was none but the red one to try on. The red gown, with its high empire waist and full flowing skirt, put her in mind of the dresses ladies wore during Napoleonic times. And unlike the other gowns whose necklines were somewhat modest, the crimson dress was cut indecently low, and she suspected it would reveal more of her than she cared to show.

She held the red up to her, eyed it skeptically, and was about to toss it aside when she heard her cat.

"Neow, neow."

"I will never wear that dress," Isabel insisted. "It is simply not me. Besides, it's too fancy. More like a party dress."

"Neow, neow."

"The others, yes, but this one no."

Isabel was delighted that all the other gowns fit, and she had concluded they weren't too different from the contemporary styles, though they were made looser for uncorseted waists. Of course, the fabrics were finer than anything she ever imagined wearing, but probably no finer than the dresses worn by Marcella Kent.

"Neow, neow."

"Really, Grim, there are times when you can be such a nuisance." She held the crimson dress out in front of her then looked back at her cat. "I'd never have the nerve to wear this. And if Dora saw me in it, she would certainly say it was scandalous. While we're on the subject of outrageous behavior, there is a matter that you and I need to discuss. And now is as good a time as any."

"Neow, neow."

"Yes, now."

As if to give emphasis to her words, she turned her back to the cat. "Oh, my," Isabel said, glancing around the interior. "How did it get dark so soon? I had better light a lamp, or we'll be tripping over ourselves and breaking our necks."

Isabel moved to the table and turned up the wick of an oil lamp, stuck a long match to it, then went about the room lighting several candles.

"Neow, neow."

"Can't you see I'm busy? That silly dress will wait for another night."

"Neow, neow."

"Oh, all right I'll try it on, but only because you are hounding me, or catting me, or whatever you cats call pursuing something relentlessly. I call it nagging."

She walked over to where she had left the dress lying in a crimson heap on the floor. She snatched up the silk, stepped into the dress, and tugged it up over her legs and hips.

"While I have your attention, you stubborn wizard cat, I want it known that you are not, under any circumstances, to cast your spells on me."

Grimalkin's golden stare met hers without flinching. In the gathering dusk, his eyes reminded her of the golden flames of the candles she had just lit, flickering in the slight breeze that sifted through the open doors and windows.

"Don't get me wrong," she said. "It's not that I don't appreciate your magic, because I do, but you of all people—I mean cats," she corrected, "must realize that Cooper Adair and I don't suit."

She stuck her arms in the short sleeves of the dress and tugged the top up over her breasts. There were no buttons but only gathered caps for sleeves and barely enough material in the dress's bodice to properly cover her front and back.

"Not that I won't be the first to admit that Cooper Adair is quite comely looking." She moved to stand in front of the mirror and began tugging at the bodice. "He reminds me a lot of my *padre* with his blond good looks, but need I remind you, Grim, he's out to ruin us with his fancy pharmacy store."

Isabel's gaze met her reflection in the mirror. "Oh, my," she said as she took in her image. The crimson material of the gown was diaphanous, flowing loosely from beneath her bust. Yet it still suggested that she had subtle curves beneath the filmy fabric. "More than scandalous," Isabel said, awed by her own reflection. "It's downright sinful."

But she couldn't help but smile dreamily at her reflection. She lifted her arms and piled her hair on her head. "Do you understand what I'm saying, Grim?" she asked, turning her head from side to side.

"Yeow."

"No more of your fairy tricks on me."

"Me-wow, me-wow."

"You'll behave, then, you silly enamored cat?"

"Neow."

"Yes, now. And in the future."

Twelve

The caterwauling jerked Isabel awake. Through the mosquito netting that draped her bed, she stared groggily about the moonlit room, groping for the source of the sound, and also for alertness.

"Grim," she called, looking for the blob of black fur she expected to see at the end of the bed. Noting the cat's absence, Isabel snapped upright.

The howling sound rent the night again. Stumbling to her feet, she made her way to the balcony that faced the inner courtyard off her upstairs bedroom. The double doors that opened onto small balconies on each side of the room were propped open to allow for the flow of air, and also would allow a marauding cat to escape if he had a mind to.

Judging from the sounds emanating from the "love" tree, Isabel knew the old rascal was out for plunder.

Usually Grim settled in for the night when Isabel did, sleeping at her feet until morning. Last night he had abandoned her for Cooper Adair, and tonight she had been abandoned yet again, but this time Isabel had been replaced by another female, or perhaps several of them.

Leaning over the iron rail of the balcony, Isabel called, "Get in here now, you rusty old tom."

The hissing and howling that followed her order didn't sound as though Grim was suffering deterioration from either inactivity or neglect. "Males," Isabel declared. "No matter what the species, they are all alike."

She peered into the branches, trying to make out the number of uninvited guests. Even with the moon riding high in the sky, it was impossible to see beyond the canopy of leaves that shielded the mating dance from her view.

"Grim," she called again, "you are too old for such carrying on. Come inside now."

"Neowwwwwwwww, neowwwwwwwww!"

"Yes, now!" she cried. "Don't make me come after you."

Her plea landed on deaf ears. Abandoning her position on the balcony, Isabel sprinted toward the stairs and froze in her tracks. When she had retired for the night, she had donned Consuela's nightgown, the one Isabel had claimed was so sheer that a ghost would have felt comfortable in it. She didn't know about a ghost, but the gossamer fabric felt like silky cobwebs against her skin, and after looking at herself in the mirror, she had decided the garment revealed as much of her person as a cobweb would.

Yet Isabel loved it. The gown made her feel beautiful. It was sleeveless with a tucked yoke, and lace frill down the front, trimmed with baby ribbons. She supposed no decent woman would wear such a garment, but then she had seen Consuela with it on, and to Isabel, if a stranger lavished someone whom she didn't know with a gift of such beautiful clothes, that person was kind and generous.

Besides, who would see her? None but the other feline fatales congregating in her tree. There had been no sign of life in the post building next door, so she had determined Cooper Adair had taken a room at a hotel. Feeling perfectly safe from discovery, Isabel was soon standing at the tree's base with a pail of water, looking up into the branches for her recalcitrant cat.

● ● ●

A feral wailing invaded Cooper's dreams. In his dream he was in a strange room lying on a lumpy mattress, with the soft buzz of mosquitoes swarming around his head. The smell of straw, or something reminiscent of mown grass, filled his nostrils. Beyond the open windows he could hear the mewing squall of a dozen cats. Try as he might to close out the annoying sound, it would not go away.

He blinked and opened his eyes to stare at the strange ceiling. The room was lit by the high moon's pearly glow that softened the sharp angles of the barren interior.

"Meowwooo!"

"Damn it all!" Cooper grumbled, rolling to a sitting position on the rough ticking and swinging his long legs over the edge of the bed. "I must have fallen asleep."

He ran his fingers through his disheveled hair before groping for his pocket watch. Unfortunately it was impossible to read the face in the dim light, so he returned the watch to his pocket. Cradling his head in his hands and propping his elbows on his knees, Cooper worked at blinking away the drowsiness.

"Neowwwwwwww, neowwwwwwww!"

The mewing again. Cats? He hadn't been dreaming when he had first heard the noise. It was their caterwauling that had awakened him.

Beyond the open window he heard another quarrelsome screech. It seemed the tom outside was having more success with his lady than Cooper had enjoyed with Marcella.

Sleep, for a few short hours anyway, had brought him forgetfulness, but as soon as he awakened, reality had returned, bringing with it his disappointment in the evening. After leaving the Kents' home, and knowing he wouldn't sleep even if he returned to the hotel, Cooper had stopped by the post building. He recalled walking up the stairs and sitting down on the edge of the bed, but after that he remembered nothing. He must have slept until the noise awakened him. Cooper stood and walked toward the window, and peered down on the tranquil scene below.

Outside, the moon bathed the narrow yard in satin light. Nothing moved in the still June night except several branches of the huge old tree that grew on the property. The one that was part oak and part palm. What had Isabel called it? The "love" tree. Well, it appeared to be living up to its name tonight if the cats climbing among its branches were doing what he suspected they were.

Cooper inhaled deeply, recognizing again the ambrosial scent of jasmine mixed with the sweet, warm, nectarous fragrance of the honeysuckle vines. The soft peacefulness of the summer night made Cooper want to believe his decision to leave Philadelphia and move to Florida had been the right one.

He was jerked from his thoughts by the throaty growls rumbling outward from within the thick canopy of leaves. Almost peaceful, he corrected. Movement inside the tree branches made the foliage tremble and shimmer in the bright night. Another high-pitched snarl rent the otherwise quiet darkness.

"Come here, Grim."

Isabel held out her offering of food to coax Grim down from the tree. His size might make him appear as fierce as a Tung warrior, but beneath all that fur and fluff, he was nothing but a pussycat, and Isabel could tell he was frightened. Not only of the two roaming toms in the branches above their heads, but also of the bawling female that had attracted the Romeo cats to the "love" tree.

Grim was a private cat—preferring the company of humans to that of other felines—and the "love" tree was his own special perch. He was above sharing it with the other four-legged intruders.

"Me-owt, me-owt."

"They'll be leaving soon enough," Isabel promised, beginning her ascent up the tree.

She had reached the crook where the two trees joined, and she paused to catch her breath. Tree climbing had been much easier in her youth, but then she hadn't been wearing a night-gown that floated around her legs like a wind-filled kite, or carrying a pail of water she planned to use to give the tres-passers a good dousing.

Four pairs of eyes peered at her from various heights in the branches. But for the moment she was only concerned with the yellow-orange ones.

"Come to Mama," she crooned, holding the fishy treat to-ward Grim.

Instead of jumping into her arms, exercising the behavior Isabel expected from her faithful pet, Grim pawed farther out on the limb. His bravado caused another chorus of hisses and growls from the attending feline audience.

"Come here, Grim!"

Refusing to do his servant's bidding, the aristocratic cat moved farther out on his perch. His voice became arrogant, imperious when he joined in song with the other disorderly marauders.

Her voice hoarse with frustration, Isabel ordered, "Why don't you just do your magic, Grim, and make them disap-pear? Then we can all get some sleep."

Another round of howls and branch-shaking occurred, proving to Isabel that sorcery wasn't on Grim's agenda. If she planned to rescue her pet, she would have to be the wizard with all the skill.

But her long nightgown wasn't cooperating. Instead it was proving to be hazardous. The diaphanous material kept catch-ing on twigs and rough bark as she moved higher up the trunk.

"Thank God for small blessings," she praised, reaching the fat, smooth limb that Grim had chosen as his own. Straddling it as she would a horse, and with her long bare legs hanging, Isabel steadied the water pail on the flat part of the limb before inching closer to Grim's roost.

Instead of curiosity killing the cat, it was curiosity that drew Cooper down the stairs and into the yard, but that didn't mean that killing wasn't on his mind.

Another feline chorus hallelujahed from within the tree's branches. "What a ruckus," he grumbled.

How he planned to get rid of the revelers, Cooper didn't know, but he had armed himself with a broken chair leg just in case his presence wasn't enough to scare the animals away. He only hoped they were above attacking humans. His trepidation grew as he neared the trunk of the tree, doubling his dislike for cats.

Cooper had never seen the need for domesticating animals, especially cats, and this night's activities was proof enough that a cat couldn't be tamed. They were wild, willful, independent creatures that during the best of times he could find fault with, and after this woolly gang had disrupted his much-needed sleep, Cooper wanted to make trophies out of all their hides.

How to achieve the latter was beyond him, but he marched to the tree, ready to do battle any way he could. Soon the whiskered outlaws would receive their just deserts, and with a little luck he would be able to get back to grab a few more hours of sleep before the sun came up.

Within the dark branches several feet above his head, a streak of white caught the moonlight. For a moment Cooper had doubts as to why he chose to confront the strays when what he saw held no resemblance to a cat. A splinter of apprehension coursed though him as his mind recalled Isabel saying there was a legend about the tree. He wanted to kick himself for not listening when he spotted in the branches above his head a pale blur of billowy, floating material with no visible arms or legs. An apparition? Was the tree haunted?

No, his skeptical self answered. He didn't believe in ghosts, but whatever it was, it resembled a thick cloud of smoke that trembled eerily in the high limbs. His pulse beat erratically on seeing the threatening sight.

"Eee . . . ieh!"

The long, loud piercing cry made the hairs on Cooper's neck tingle. If it was a cat, it was not like any he'd ever encountered. The need for self-preservation took over, and he was about to make a dash for the building when he was suddenly drenched from above.

Blood! Temporarily blinded, Cooper blinked, struggling to regain his sight after his thorough dousing. Several moments passed before he regained his wits enough to realize that it was water, not blood, that had soaked him, when all hell broke loose.

To Cooper, standing beneath the tree, it was as though some giant hand had reached down from the heavens and shook the branches. He dodged the fleeing cats that dropped to the ground like ripened fruit and scattered across the yard. A familiar, black, four-legged critter with eyes resembling burning coals streaked past him so fast he felt its movement slice the air.

There was more motion above his head. Cooper knew he had not scared those cats from the tree, and whatever had done the job was still there, whatever it might be. No, he reasoned. He was being foolish. Just as the water had not been blood, what he had seen earlier was no phantom. It was nothing more than the moonlight reflecting off the coat of a large white cat.

Clutching his fingers tighter around the chair leg, he glanced upward into the still-trembling branches, determined that he would not be felled by an overactive imagination or a cat. "What the devil . . . ?" he swore when a tin pail fell from the branches, almost hitting his head.

Cooper had heard of cats attacking when cornered, but he knew that if this was a cat, it was no ordinary one and that maybe he should leave. But he wasn't given a chance, for the wild, billowing fiend flew from the branches, hitting his chest with such force that he stumbled. Still trying to get out of its way, Cooper shot backward, his weapon sailed from his grip, and he fell flat on his back.

At first he thought he was under attack by the granddaddy of all cats. Fingernails clawed at his eyes. His attacker gasped and kicked viciously until the fight went out of him. No longer under assault, Cooper chanced a look at what now straddled him, pinning him to the ground.

It was neither cat nor apparition.

The caterwauling continued on the opposite side of the wall. Inside Cooper's chest, his heart beat a thundering tattoo against his ribs as the woman, barely clothed in a gauzy excuse for a nightdress, slumped on top of him. Her hot thighs were clamped against his hips, and her breasts rested snugly against his ribs.

"Isabel?" he croaked.

"Cooper?"

"You weren't supposed to be in that tree."

"You weren't supposed to be here at all."

"You're hot."

"You're wet."

"We should get up."

"I fell."

"I suspected as much." He could feel her trembling against him.

Cooper was trembling as well, but it wasn't from fright. He realized he didn't want to get up. It felt so right, lying on the grass with her sprawled on top of him. Their bodies fit together perfectly like two pieces of a whole. His hands, by their own volition, began gently stroking her back.

"We've got to quit meeting like this," Isabel said with a quivering sigh. "But I'm so glad you were there to catch me."

Then she laughed, that low throaty laugh with its deep huskiness that had the power to curl his toes.

His arms tightened around her. "You made a fine landing."

In the moonlight her golden eyes smoldered with amber sparks. Cooper ran his fingers through the skein of her honey-gold hair that draped around their faces like a moon-gilded mantle.

He wanted to kiss her, to reassure her she was fine. Anchoring his hands on each side of her face, he started to do just that when his sudden concern for her outweighed his desire.

"What were you doing in the tree? You might have been—" He stopped, not wanting to think of such a consequence, especially when she felt so alive and warm in his arms.

She snuggled closer. He felt her nipples bud into hard nubs beneath the filmy nightrail. She was so close that Cooper could feel her heartbeat. She looked deep into his eyes and licked her lips in open invitation.

In that moment Cooper knew. She wanted him as much as he wanted her. When she spoke, her voice sounded low and sexy.

"I was trying to rescue"—She looked into his eyes, blinked, then stiffened—"Grim." Casting a furtive glance around the yard and then up at the tree, she called, "Grimalkin, are you up to your old tricks?"

To Cooper's disappointment, the whereabouts of her cat suddenly became more important to the luscious female in his arms than her own whereabouts. As far as he was concerned, her position on top of him suited Cooper just fine. He could stay this way forever, but sadly, all good things come to an end. The indelicacy of her position finally registered, because she looked at him with a horrified expression before jerking from his embrace and jumping to her feet.

With the separation of their bodies, Cooper was hit not only by cooler air, but also by cold reality. "Damn it all," he mumbled, sitting up. He had done it again, engaged in illicit behavior with Isabel Gomez when he was betrothed to Marcella.

Isabel twirled in a circle as she continued searching the yard for her cat. "Grimalkin, how could you do this to me," she called, "especially after our talk?"

Cooper's short lived guilt disappeared like smoke when her twirling action afforded him a view of all her voluptuous curves—front, back, and sides—through the sheerness of her nightrail. Red-hot heat exploded in his loins. Even now, when he knew it was wrong, the woman still had the power to bewitch him.

"You shouldn't be outside dressed like that," he chided, groping for his sanity. "It's—it's indecent."

Isabel ceased her searching to look down at herself. She gasped and began gathering the fullness of the garment into large wads and holding them against her front. Her shoulders stiffened, and she glared at him.

"It's not decent that you should have noticed," she replied sarcastically, "which brings me to another point. What are you doing trespassing in my yard in the middle of the night?"

"Our yard," he corrected.

She didn't answer him immediately, but swung away from him, as feisty as the devil, and stomped toward his building. "I'll show you your yard."

It wasn't property lines that held Cooper's interest as he followed along behind her. Instead it was her lush backside where the sheer garment, bunched as it was against her front, skimmed her near-naked curves from the top of her shoulders, down the long length of her shapely legs, to above her trim ankles.

Stopping, she pointed down at a line of rocks on the ground. "Your yard," she said, swinging to face him. "You, sir, purchased the post building, the use of my well and my privy, but not my property."

Disappointed that she had stolen his view of her backside, Cooper puzzled, wondering if her "privy parts" went with the property purchase. In the last two days it seemed that he had been doing a hell of a lot of trespassing on those.

"When the deed was done—drawn," she continued, "it allowed you five feet of land on this side of the building and nothing more." She pointed to the narrow strip of grass between the post building and the line of rocks. "Your *property*," she said. "And you're not to abuse it."

She had used that same threat earlier. Cooper couldn't help himself. He chuckled. "Just as I'm not to abuse the privy?" he asked.

If looks could have killed, he would have been struck down in his prime. Yet he wondered if she knew how attractive she looked, standing in the moonlight like some half-clad moon goddess with steam rising from her head.

She moved to pass him. "Now I must find my cat."

"He's right there," Cooper said, pointing at the "love" tree.

"Where?"

"There."

She glanced at the tree. Grim sat in the crook where the two trees joined. "He wasn't there earlier because I looked."

Joined. The trees were joined at the crotch. Now where did that thought come from? He corrected himself: Joined at the junction of points, where both palm and oak grew together. With the image a strong and vivid desire coursed though Cooper. A picture of him and Isabel joining in the same way flashed inside his head, causing a tightening coil in his groin. What was it about this woman that made him think such savage thoughts?

When she moved to the tree to collect her cat, he was awarded another view of her backside. What was there about this particular woman that kept him fuddled with longing? She dropped her bunched-up skirt, and the filmy material floated sensuously down around her ankles, putting him in mind again of his supposed apparition.

He laughed, unsure now if it was his nervousness that caused the emotion or the ridiculousness of his earlier assumption.

Holding the cat in her arms, she faced him, her gaze questioning.

"When I first spotted you in the tree," he explained, "I thought you were an apparition."

Her look said she thought he had lost his mind. "Really now," she said. "When last we met, you accused me of being a witch."

He ignored her reference, not wanting to remember the reasons for his accusations.

"I mistook you for an apparition because of your flowing white gown, and because you were in the tree—"

"For one who doesn't believe in legends and fairy tales, you certainly have a keen imagination."

The old tom purred in her arms. She dipped her head to Grimalkin's and muttered a phrase that sounded like "my loving familiar."

Cooper couldn't see anything remotely familiar about cat and mistress, but who was he to question their resemblance? He didn't look anything like his siblings, either, but that wasn't what she meant. What *had* she meant? Dazed and exasperated, he wondered why he had thought of the comparison—he wasn't comparing humans. He shook his head to clear it.

He could tell her a few things about familiar. If anything, he was more familiar with Miss Gomez's body than her annoying cat was. Or more intimate, but then he reconsidered this last thought. Numerous times since meeting the woman, he had seen that fuzz ball snuggled against her bosom as he was now, wearing that same satisfied, cheshire-cat expression.

You wish you were here, don't you?

Cooper started. There it was again, the feeling that someone's thoughts other than his own had been projected into his mind. *Impossible!* he scoffed.

"It's time to say good night," Isabel said, pulling him from his dazed state. The way the moon reflected from the two pairs of golden eyes gave Cooper pause. If nothing else made them familiar, they did have similar-looking eyes—eyes that were both disturbing and exciting.

She smiled at him, and her smile warmed him across the distance. Then she turned and started across the yard toward her house.

"Siren," he whispered to her retreating back.

As countless men before him who had been lured to their deaths by one such as she, Cooper, too, felt that he was about to crash on the rocks, bringing his world tumbling down around him.

No! He would not allow such a fate to befall him. He loved Marcella. Granted there were a few things they needed to work out, but those things were minor. Stiffening his resolve, Cooper turned away.

He wouldn't—no, couldn't—allow himself to be lured from his future plans by such an irresistible distraction as Isabel Gomez.

Thirteen

Isabel closed the door behind her and leaned against the frame. Cradling Grim like a babe against her breasts, she looked down into his eyes. "Was that your doing, you old traitor cat? Were you responsible for what nearly took place between Cooper and me?"

The cat responded by purring louder and placing a midnight-colored paw against her heart. Although Isabel suspected the kiss she had longed for, and almost allowed Cooper to have when she lay sprawled atop him, had been Grim's doing, she wasn't so sure now. "If you were responsible, how can I win this battle to be rid of our neighbor?" She stroked Grim's broad head, rubbing the area just above his eyes. "We must get rid of him, Grim. If we don't, we both could lose our happy home."

Hugging the cat to her bosom, she rested her head against his. "If only I knew it was your magic and not myself who prompted such a reaction."

The big cat, having had enough affection for one night, probably from both a female cat and his mistress, struggled to get down. Isabel conceded, and watched when the animal trotted out the back door to the loggia where the stairs climbed to her bedroom. When he rounded the doorjamb and disappeared, she assumed he was on his way to bed.

Bed! That was where Isabel longed to be, but before she could return to her dreams, she had to deal with reality.

Her mind played back over the evening, from the moment she fell from the tree into Cooper's arms. She had fallen after she had doused the cats with water, after the cats had abandoned the tree, Grim along with them. So, she rationalized, during that time, Grim had been nowhere in sight, or she hadn't noticed him, but then she had been preoccupied with other matters. Mainly the feel of Cooper's hard body under her soft one.

Her pet could have been hiding beneath a nearby shrub, searching for one of the nine lives he had almost lost when she scared the cats away. Or he could have been meddling, working one of his spells. If that were the case, it would explain why she had been as brazen as a hussy, flouting propriety by covering Cooper Adair's body with her own while inviting him to kiss her.

Isabel groaned. What if her actions weren't prompted by Grimalkin's magic tricks? What if she had acted that way because she wanted Cooper to kiss her? The more she thought of the latter possibility, the more confused she became.

When he had held her, her whole being had been filled with desire. She had enjoyed his embrace and the feel of his hands caressing her back. Even now the memory made her nipples harden and become as sensitive to the sheer cloth covering them as they had been when she was pressed intimately against Cooper's broad chest. Her legs felt trembly, and yearning flamed in her most intimate place.

Disgusted with the way her thoughts were headed, Isabel flopped down on a chair beside the table and rested her head on her arms. "This can't be happening to me," she bemoaned. As much as she wanted to expel the strange sensations that were torturing her body, she couldn't. "You old fairy cat," she called, glancing at the ceiling where her bedroom would be, "are you still up to your mischief?"

Grim's magic was strong, but was it so powerful that he could project it through wooden beams?

There was only one thing for her to do. She had to make her own magic, and she would begin by removing her copper bracelet. She wore the amulet to attract a lover and enhance her sexuality. If what she was experiencing wasn't Grim's doing or the bracelet's, and was instead her heart's desire, she must cast some serious spells of her own.

Isabel glanced at the clock on the mantel. The hour on the face read a little past two. Soon it would be morning. Before she could sleep any more this night, she had work to do. Isabel jumped up from the table and headed for her garden room.

Once inside, she lit a candle and moved toward the shelf containing her books. She found the one entitled *Spellcraft,* the title labeled in her mama's neat penmanship, and pulled it from the others.

Isabel couldn't glance through the book without thinking of her deceased parent. Although Kalee Gomez had not been a full-blooded Indian, she had been raised by her mother's tribe, where love magic was a common practice. The potions and spells listed inside the time-worn pages had been passed down from generation to generation. Isabel opened the book and began to thumb through the pages.

The book was filled with many different spells. Most of them were used to help someone attract a desirable partner, not repel one. She searched the pages carefully. There were numerous spells for attracting a lover, returning a lover, bringing back an unfaithful lover, inducing love between a married couple, a spell of desire, and also a spell for attracting a wealthy husband.

If Isabel had known the profession of the man who was going to purchase her building before she sold it, maybe she would have used the last of the spells on herself. But the memory of her stepfather was too fresh. Wooster Farley had married her mama for her property, and Isabel hated to think she would sink as low by marrying a man only for his wealth.

Returning her thoughts to the pages she browsed put her in a real quandary. Was the attraction she felt for Cooper caused by Grimalkin or by her heart's secret longing for romance? At the moment Isabel couldn't tolerate interference from either.

Her plan was to make Marcella jealous so she would break her betrothal to Cooper, thus causing him to sell his business and return to Philadelphia. Isabel hadn't derived the plan with any romantic illusions. Cooper couldn't become enamored with her, and she most certainly couldn't become enamored with Cooper.

"Damn and blast that cat," she grumbled. His hide wouldn't be worth filler if she learned that he was the cause of her latest dilemma.

She stopped turning the pages and read the heading *To Reverse Any Love Spell.* Relief filled her. "This one may work," she said aloud before continuing to read.

The spell was to be carried out on a night of a waning moon, but Isabel didn't have time to wait two or three days. Tonight the moon was almost full, but she would begin her spell regardless and repeat the ritual nightly until the moon waned. By doing so she hoped she could keep Grim's magic at bay. If indeed her sly cat made her behave like a wanton hussy earlier. She rationalized that it could be nothing else.

She read farther for a list of items needed to cast her spell. A white votive candle was required, and she would have to write Cooper's and her name on its side. Then she must anoint the candle with myrrh oil before lighting and recite the chant listed in her book.

"Simple enough," Isabel said.

Already she felt better, and she went to fetch her ritual tools she kept stowed in a hamper on a top shelf. After retrieving the basket, she carried it back to her worktable and opened the lid. Inside were her tools—tools her mama had used for her rituals and had passed on to Isabel—plus a few items of her own; like the corn husk doll wrapped in a swath of Indian fabric that her mama had made for her when Isabel was a child. The doll represented Isabel's sacred goddess, Mother Earth. She had named the figure ME, and she still referred to it by that name.

There was also incense she had made herself from pine wood shavings mixed with cinnamon, orange rind, and vanilla. When she opened the basket's lid earlier, the pleasant scent wafted upward, surrounding her, putting her in the proper mood to cast her spell. Next she removed the ritual knife from its white cotton pouch, as well as the jar of salt water and the earthenware chalice.

Isabel had a ready supply of the other things she would need to cast her spell, because, like her friend Dora, many young women in the community came to her requesting help in matters of the heart. Isabel was probably the only one who needed help discouraging a suitor's affections, but then the other ladies didn't have to contend with the interference of a magic cat.

After scratching Cooper's name and her own into the wax surface of the white candle with her ritual knife, Isabel was ready to begin. She picked up the hamper and left the room for the garden, where she carried out her rituals. She had marked the sacred area in the shape of a pentagram with rocks at each of the five points representing the four basic elements of earth, air, fire, and water, and a fifth element of the self/ spirit. It was at the center of the pentagram where all things worked in perfect harmony. Here she had placed a knee-high rock that she used for her magic altar.

She walked around the rocks, placing colored candles on each elemental point; red for fire, blue for water, green for earth, and yellow for air, and the goddess ME on the self/ spirit point. She lay the white candle with hers and Cooper's names scratched in its surface on the center stone altar.

As for her ritual clothing, Isabel chose to wear nothing. She stepped from the filmy gown, draping it over the nearby whirligig. Freeing herself from the pretense of materially based images made her feel closer and more in tune to nature. She reached for the jar of salt water that represented Earth and Sea, poured a small amount into the earthenware chalice, then moved about the sacred place, sprinkling the water around to cleanse the area. This done, she moved around the points and lit the four element candles before returning to the center altar. After anointing the white candle with oil that sat on the rock's surface, Isabel lit it, raised her hands heavenward, and began to recite:

> "I burn this candle as a token
> of the spell that binds our love.
> Let this magic now be broken
> by the power of the gods above."

A short while later, after Cooper had returned to the building, he had a nature call. The way he saw it, he had one choice after inspecting the chipped chamber pot in the upstairs apartment. He would have to trek across the yard to the necessary.

The jaunt wasn't one he relished, but a person did what he had to. If he wanted to look for positives with regard to the required trip, there was no snow on the ground, and the Gomez bungalow appeared to be peacefully dark, making Cooper believe the residents had retired for the remainder of the night.

During his trek, he chastised himself for not having returned to the hotel after leaving the Kents' home. If he had, the incident between him and Isabel would never have occurred, and he wouldn't now be carrying around this guilt. Try as he might, Cooper couldn't get the woman out of his mind. In the last two days her body had become as familiar to him as his own, and much more familiar than Marcella's had ever been. Granted, his fiancée was not a lady given to forbidden liaisons in the middle of the night, but something told him that Isabel didn't usually dally in such activities, either. Cooper suspected Isabel was an innocent like Marcella, but she didn't wear that innocence like a shield.

Above his head, a soft breeze stirred the branches of the

"love" tree while making the wind bells placed throughout the yard chime softly as he moved toward the back gate. Since the bloodthirsty mosquitos weren't drilling his veins, Cooper imagined the breeze had blown all the cannibals back to the swamps. There weren't many good remarks he could make about this hellish climate, but he admitted that nights like this one were pleasantly habitable. The wind blowing off the bay made the air cooler and chased away all the bugs.

As he reached the gate, he uttered a prayer of thanks that Isabel and her cat were long into their dreams, and he wouldn't be subjected to seeing them again this night. His constitution couldn't handle another episode like the last. He decided when he finished his business at the privy, he would head back to the hotel.

A large clump of Spanish moss had blown from the overhead branches, tangling its threadlike masses over the gate and making his entrance near impossible. As he tore away the threads, he wondered if it were the three goddesses of human nature cautioning him to run to another fate. Cooper dismissed the thought as ridiculous, but he couldn't help but question the enchantment of this place of swaying moss, fairy bells, and a forbidden woman. The moss freed, he pushed open the gate and stepped inside the inner walled yard.

Without the assistance of candle or lamp, the moon was the only source of light. Cooper recognized the location of the well by the horrible stench that put him in mind of rotten eggs, and after discerning its location, he knew the concrete privy wouldn't be too far away. Facing the back wall of the garden, he saw it. Like a sentinel standing guard in the pale darkness, the structure stood out in white relief against the opaque night.

His lips curled upward in a smile when he recalled Isabel's orders about not abusing the privy. Cooper still wondered how such a feat would be accomplished, but he had to admit he had used many such conveniences and found them not nearly as clean as this one.

When he had finished his business, Cooper exited the struc-

ture and started back toward the gate. It was then he saw the
fiery wave of light that reflected against the tree trunks of
several trees and the surrounding walls of Isabel's garden.

His first thought was that Isabel was still up, or perhaps
had left a lamp burning. He moved closer to the edge of the
building to better assess the situation. If the rest of the house
hadn't been dark, the light might not have concerned him. A
person couldn't be too careful with regard to fire, because a
swiftly moving blaze could destroy a whole town.

Was it possible a fire burned that she wasn't aware of?
Concern propelled him deeper into the center of the herb garden. He retraced his steps of earlier today, seeking the oyster
shell path that would lead him toward Isabel's laboratory. He
was about to step around a large hedge when he saw her, and
what he saw took his breath away.

In a glowing circle of candlelight, Isabel stood as naked as
the day she was born, her arms upraised. The soft breeze
filtering through the trees made the flames shimmer against
her naked body. In the soft golden glow of the candles her
skin looked as smooth as a lotus petal. Her body was thin
and willowy with a slender waist that flared enticingly into
rounded hips. She had full, high-perched breasts with tawny
nipples, and a "v" of tawny hair at the apex of her thighs.

When before the sight of her near nakedness in the filmy
gown had rendered him motionless, the sight of her completely bare had the opposite effect. Cooper struggled with
his desire and a need to run to her, to claim the pagan goddess
for his own. Wearing nothing but candlelight and moon-
beams, Isabel Gomez was the most beautiful woman Cooper
had ever seen.

With the delicate stirring of the wind, the wind bells whispered in accompaniment to the drama taking place in the garden. The crushed oyster paths looked like polished pearl in
the moonlight, and the rock in the circle's center put Cooper
in mind of the ancient upright stones of Stonehenge on the
English plains. Legend had it that the ancient circle was the
place where druids carried out their worship.

Druids? Sorcerers? "Witchcraft!"

Realizing he had spoken aloud, Cooper didn't dare breathe, or move, for fear that Isabel would detect his hiding place behind the shrub. When she didn't cast an eye in his direction, he relaxed somewhat, or as much as one could relax when one believed one was observing a witch practicing her craft. Not that he was an expert on witches. He dismissed most accounts of witchcraft as nothing more than mass hysteria of an uneducated people, but what other explanation would explain such strange behavior?

And hadn't he thought her strange from the first moment they met? She was a self-proclaimed herbalist who kept company with a black cat, and there was the question of the kiss they shared, along with other numerous unusual incidents. Had the woman bewitched him, or had he simply fallen beneath her spell because of her charm instead of some magical power?

He ran his fingers through his hair. It wasn't possible, he argued. Witches didn't really exist. Yet when his gaze slid back to the naked woman with her arms raised in supplication, he almost stopped breathing as the reality of what he saw flogged him in the chest.

Trying to make sense of the bizarre situation, Cooper continued watching her. It was the sound of her husky voice that traveled to him above the mystical ringing of the bells that made him believe she wasn't alone. She was speaking to someone, but who? His gaze made a quick inventory of the yard to discover that her always-present cat was nowhere in sight, yet she was definitely in conversation with someone. Cooper strained his ears, trying to hear what she said, but all he heard was the monotonous rhythmic sound of her voice.

Chanting. Was she in the throes of some kind of spell? His deduction made perfect sense, and would also explain her reason for being in the garden at this time of night, completely naked, with her arms elevated toward the sky.

No, Cooper wouldn't accept this conclusion. He considered himself an educated man who didn't believe in witches and hobgoblins. There must be a more likely explanation for her late-night activities. After considerable deliberation, he came up with a better reason.

She enjoyed air bathing. Hadn't he heard that in some parts of the world air bathing had become all the rage? Yes, he decided, this particular activity made more sense, and was in keeping with her unconventional behavior—a pattern of behavior that made her so damnably fascinating. A woman who wore men's britches and enjoyed the sport of fishing would probably enjoy outdoor nudity as well. He certainly was enjoying it. So much so that seeing her thus was almost Cooper's undoing.

"Meow, meowwwwww!"

The familiar bumping against his ankles brought Cooper back to the present. Grimalkin. Her odious cat was about to reveal Cooper's hiding place, and the fear of being discovered put him in a panic. Not that he believed for a moment that Isabel was a real witch, but he wasn't prepared to face a witch's wrath in case his assumption was wrong. Or if she was indeed air bathing, he didn't think she would take too kindly to being observed by a man. What woman would?

"Meow, meow."

The cat made several more passes around Cooper's legs, then stopped beside his ankles and wrapped his fluffy black tail around one of Cooper's legs. Comrades, his gesture suggested. Soon the old tom was purring like a New York pigeon, the low-pitched droning blotting out the other sounds of the night. It was then Cooper realized that the breeze had died, and the mystical bells no longer chimed.

Isabel stopped her chanting and focused her attention on the spot where Cooper hid.

"Grimalkin," she called, "is that you hiding in the bushes?"

No, Cooper answered inside his head, *it's your perverted neighbor.*

At the moment, if anyone needed a little draught of magic, it was Cooper. Since he couldn't disappear, he tried willing her cat away. *Scat, cat. Run for your life!* Cooper swore. If the bothersome animal didn't leave his leg soon and Isabel discovered him, he would personally murder the animal come morning.

"Grim? I thought you had retired for the night." When the cat didn't move but remained stuck to Cooper's ankles like a burr, Isabel did. She picked up the white candle from her altar-stone and began moving toward them.

Cooper's tension rose a few more notches. He glared at the cat. *If all this ankle-rubbing you've been doing since we've met means you have an affection for me, would you please go to your mistress now?*

"Neow, neow."

Yes, now, damn it.

Grimalkin looked up at him. In the candlelight that Isabel carried like a torch, the cat's eyes glowed orange.

To Cooper's amazement, and his knee-wobbling relief, Grimalkin jumped from behind the bush that shielded them, directly in front of Isabel's feet, prohibiting her any further movement.

"Meow, meow."

"It *was* you, you old trickster," she crooned. "I thought you were upstairs asleep." She glanced again at the shrub, studying it for several more moments. "You don't have some female stashed away in that bush, do you?" Grimalkin made his usual passes against her naked calves. His loving ministrations made Isabel lower the candle and bend to stroke her pet's head before standing upright again.

Cooper hid a thick swallow in his throat, trying not to ogle, but up close, Isabel's body was perfection. This was no ugly old crone who faced him. She was a goddess, and he felt as lowly as a worm.

It was then Cooper decided he couldn't be faulted for his ungentlemanly behavior if he didn't glance below her shoulders. He would do this, he decided, after having one last look. His gaze traveled up and down her length, setting each womanly nuance to memory. After having looked his fill, Cooper's mouth felt as dry as cotton, and he didn't dare dwell on how the other parts of his anatomy felt.

"I suppose, little one," Isabel said to her cat, "that it's time we get to bed." She blew out the candle and bent over to scratch behind Grimalkin's ears. She turned and walked back to the circle of candlelight while Grimalkin chose to remain where he was. Both man and beast watched the woman before the cat cast a speculative glance in Cooper's direction.

Please, Cooper silently pleaded, *don't give my hiding place away.*

After all the candles but one had been extinguished, Isabel bent and picked up the filmy nightrail that hung like a hazy cloud over the whirligig.

"Come on, Grim," she said, walking toward the house, "you've caroused enough for one night. It's time you and I get to sleep."

She picked up the remaining candle and moved toward the house. "Now, Grim," she ordered.

"Neow, neow."

"Yes, now."

The big old tom cast another look in Cooper's direction, and Cooper swore he said, "You owe me one." Impossible. Then the feline scooted up the stairs on the heels of his mistress.

Several moments passed before Cooper allowed himself to relax. When he did, he swallowed large gulps of air, hoping to steady his suddenly erratic breathing. It seemed to him that he had been holding his breath for an eternity. Not only was he having trouble breathing, but he also feared his legs might collapse when he tried to move.

He might as well stay a few moments longer. He didn't dare leave his hiding place until he was certain that all activity above the stairs had ceased. After a moment the night was as quiet as a tomb. The mosquitoes must have realized that the wind no longer held them at bay, because they came back out in force. For all that Cooper cared, the cannibals could eat him alive, because he had no plans to slap them away and chance Isabel discovering he had been lurking in the shadows.

A good ten minutes had passed before Cooper crept toward the gate that he had left open. Sleep, that elusive state he so badly needed but as of late seemed to be just beyond his reach, still beckoned him. Yes, he could use some sleep himself.

Don't forget you owe me.

The phrase popped into Cooper's mind so vividly he thought someone had spoken it. He searched the shadows for the black cat to make certain the animal hadn't escaped his mistress yet again. When his search revealed nothing but black shadows, he reasoned the cat was curled up beside Isabel and was fast asleep.

One thing Cooper had learned from his experience this evening was that he no longer envied the cat's familiarity with his mistress. After having viewed Isabel's lovely nude body, Cooper knew there was no way in hell that he could curl up beside her in bed and get any sleep.

Fourteen

When Cooper had returned to the post building last night, he had made a quick departure for the hotel, where he had grabbed a few fitful hours of sleep before rising again this morning at six. After a hasty bath and shave, he had grabbed a rushed breakfast in the hotel dining room, that consisted of grits and cheese biscuits, before returning to the post building. Cooper arrived at seven o'clock sharp, and the carpenter boss arrived shortly thereafter.

As the foreign substance called grits settled in the pit of his stomach like a sandbag, he tried to think what he wanted to tell the workman other than to depart, leaving the work to him along with his money, but of course Cooper did neither. It appeared that Jack Kent had already given the workers instructions on what to do inside the building, but Cooper would be damned if he would allow the man to dictate how to set up his own pharmacy whether he was Marcella's father or not. And he would have his soda fountain.

The two talked for a while, and Cooper gave him his idea. Because the actual carpenters hadn't arrived with the boss, he had assured the foreman who had another early appointment that he would instruct the men when they arrived.

Since they were late, Cooper went about the room opening

the windows, then went outside to use the interval to inspect the outside of the building. Since he, not Jack Kent, would be paying for the carpenters, Cooper had decided he might as well put his money to good use. Having learned last night at Marcella's home that the structure was made from cypress, he doubted that any of the outside boards would need replacing, but he wanted to inspect them anyway.

When he stepped out on the side stoop, Cooper saw the bundle wrapped in brown paper and tied with a string sitting on the concrete. Now who left this? He dropped down on the slab, and with his legs stretched out in front of him—legs that were still encased in wool trousers—Cooper set the bundle on his lap and proceeded to open it.

"Clothes?"

He fingered a pair of denim pants and a plaid work shirt. From the faded, washed-out color he could tell the items weren't new but freshly laundered, because they smelled like summer sunshine. The scent reminded Cooper of his mother, and a strong wave of homesickness hit him in the gut to add insult to the sandbag of grits. He brushed aside the longing when a small brown bottle labeled chickweed salve rolled off his lap and into the grass identifying who his mysterious donor was. Isabel.

The thought itself conjured up the woman—the same woman he had sworn this morning to put out of his mind. A note lay inside; he opened it and read:

Cooper,

These items belonged to my stepfather, and since I have no need of them, and you appeared to need something other than wool to rid yourself of that rash, I thought you might put them to use. Don't know if they'll fit or not, but to my recollection the two of you look to be of the same build and orneriness.

Isabel

Cooper couldn't help himself. He laughed, cutting a glance toward the house across the way. "Ornery?"

He had been called a lot of names in his life, but *ornery* wasn't one of them. Some people thought him stubborn, and Cooper wouldn't deny it. Perhaps he was ornery, too. Isabel probably considered him difficult because they had been in direct opposition to each other regarding their professions, yet it seemed she didn't hold a grudge. In truth, she had been more than kind; first administering her ointment that had all but cured his bothersome rash, and second, this gift of clothing that she believed would also further improve his condition.

She might not be so neighborly if she learned the true depth of his deceit. But Cooper had no plans to tell her of his late-night activities. Some things were best left unsaid and also forgotten.

From now on he would avoid the woman like the plague and concentrate instead on his and Marcella's future. He would accept Isabel's gifts. If the clothes fit, they would save him a trip to a local store, leaving him free to begin work immediately. While the carpenters worked downstairs, Cooper would work upstairs, putting the rooms in order so he could move into the apartment tonight.

He stood and completed a walk around the exterior of the building. His walk confirmed that the structure appeared in sound condition, containing no rotten or bug-infested wood. A feeling of pride swept over him as he stood back and surveyed his building. The cypress planks had aged to a silver-gray color, which gave the building a weathered look. Cooper liked it and decided he would not whitewash the exterior.

After returning inside, he saw the workmen had not yet arrived. This would give him time to try on the clothes. In the privacy of the upstairs apartment, Cooper slipped off his wool trousers and white shirt. When he removed his shirt, he was reminded again of the absent cuff links. As much as he dreaded another encounter with Isabel, he would have to seek her out to collect the missing buttons. Marcella's reaction last night to the missing links was proof enough that if Cooper saw her today, she would be looking for them.

If she happened by now, he had a plausible excuse. The plaid work shirt had its own buttons, but instead of buttoning the sleeves, he rolled them up to his elbows. He was surprised that both shirt and pants fit. It seemed that Wooster Farley had been close to Cooper's height, although the trousers and shirt were larger than he would have purchased for himself. Rather than tuck the shirt into the waistband, he left the shirt-tail out to compensate.

Now that he was dressed for work, he needed some cleaning tools. The foreman had dropped off lumber along with a few household implements. Until Cooper could purchase his own broom, mop, and bucket, he would ask to borrow the carpenters'. Setting up housekeeping was posing more problems and expenses than Cooper had anticipated, yet he figured if he kept a check on his spending, he could still stay within his budget.

As he ran down the stairs, he was hailed by one of the two workers who had arrived in his absence.

"Mr. Kent," the man called, "could we talk with you a moment?" The worker motioned him over to the counter where the two men stood.

As Cooper approached the men, he extended his hand. "The name is Adair," he corrected. "Cooper Adair."

"Sorry," the man apologized. "Since it was Mr. Kent who ordered the work, I just thought you was he." Both men shook Cooper's hand. "I'm Deke, and this here's Skor."

"It's nice to meet you both, and it was a natural assumption that you would think I was Mr. Kent." Cooper pushed aside his resentment of Jack Kent for not informing the carpenters who they would be working for, and said, "I'm betrothed to Mr. Kent's daughter, but this will be my pharmacy."

He looked down onto the countertop at a rough sketch someone had made of shelves. It was a drawing of what he had told the foreman he wanted earlier. The man must have been in touch with his men and informed them of the changes. That could explain why the workmen were late.

"How may I help you?" Cooper asked.

"Just wanted make sure we're in agreement on what it is you want since it's different than what Mr. Kent had ordered."

These two were the carpenters who would actually build the shelves. Although Cooper didn't agree with what Jack had ordered, he didn't wish to put him in a bad light with these men so he tried to explain the changes to everyone's satisfaction.

"My soon-to-be father-in-law thought he was doing me a favor by ordering what he thought I needed. It's hard for him to understand that it's a pharmacy I'm opening and not an emporium. He meant well, but he isn't aware of my needs."

Cooper eyed the sketched plans, satisfied to see that the foreman had understood his instructions. The post building wasn't large, but it was a perfect size for his needs. While he was in college, and then during his apprenticeship, Cooper had studied drugstore plans in numerous books. He not only looked at stores in this country, but also in England and Europe. Having worked in a pharmacy, he knew what layout worked best for him and had long ago decided what his pharmacy would be like when he someday owned his own. These men seemed capable of making some of his dreams a reality.

"Can you do what I asked?"

"Sure can," Deke said. "I like your ideas better than t'others. When I visited Jacksonville awhile back, I happened in a 'pothcary in that city. I think I know jest what you want, especially with this here sketch that Jake made." As an afterthought, he added, "Jake's the foreman. Me and Skor here, we're master carpenters. We can build you some fine cabinets, even get you the glass you requested, but the glass will take a bit longer than the t'other. And of course the few shelves won't be no problem, or the soda fountain." Deke stepped back and eyed the wooden counter.

"This here counter ain't secured to the floor, so we can move it closer to the front of the room. A little sanding and polishing and it'll be as good as new. Might even be able to scrape up a marble top if'n you've a mind to have one."

Cooper rubbed a hand through his hair. "Oh, I'd like to

have one, but I don't know if the cost of such a fine surface is within my budget."

"Mr. Kent told Jake that money weren't no factor."

"Well, Mr. Kent won't be paying for this, so money is a factor." Then, thinking he sounded harsher than he intended, Cooper corrected himself. "You understand that I appreciate Mr. Kent's gesture, but I prefer paying my own way."

Deke smiled, revealing a gold tooth. "I can understand that, young man, and I admire you for it. Me and Skor, we know lots of suppliers about town. Done a lot of work on Mr. Flagler's hotel, so we have a few connections with them fellows. We just might be able to get you a fine piece of marble at half the cost."

"Would you now?"

Deke winked at him. " 'Course, I'll let you know the cost before we make a decision."

"Sounds like a good plan to me."

"Good, then. We'll be starting, if there ain't nothing else."

"Could I borrow your broom and mop? There's cleaning to be done upstairs before I can move in."

"Help yourself, Mr. Adair," Deke said.

"Please, call me Cooper. I don't go in much for formality."

"Sounds like a good plan to me." He winked. "Me and Skor don't go in for formality, neither."

"Then I'll be leaving you men to your work."

"We'll do a fine job for you."

Cooper turned and headed to where the pail sat on the floor beside the broom and mop that were propped against the wall. As long as he was going to the well to fetch water, he would also approach Isabel for his missing cuff buttons.

On his way across the courtyard, Cooper thought about his conversations with the carpenter. A piece of marble for his soda fountain was more than he expected to have so soon. Of course, there was always the chance that Deke would be unable to purchase the slab for a reasonable sum, but already Cooper allowed his mind to run free, envisioning the fountain and what an asset it would be to his pharmacy. When his business began to prosper, as he knew it would, he would purchase high round stools to run the length of the counter.

Jack Kent wouldn't be pleased once he learned Cooper had gone ahead with the fountain, knowing full well the older man was opposed to it. Cooper had decided this morning it was best the man learned in advance of the wedding that he hadn't bought Cooper with the money he had lent him for the purchase of the post. There was no doubt in Cooper's mind that he could handle Jack, but he wasn't so certain about Marcella, who could be difficult at the best of times. Because Cooper had vowed long ago that he would never be manipulated by the woman he loved, it was best Marcella learn that same lesson.

If it came to a fray with his soon-to-be new family, Cooper was prepared to do battle, but would facing Isabel after last night be as easy? At least she wasn't aware of his last folly. Unless Grimalkin, the sneaky pest that he was, had informed his mistress that Cooper had watched her air bathe from behind the cover of a bush.

Ridiculous! Animals couldn't communicate with humans no matter how devious or intelligent they appeared. "Damn it all," Cooper swore, knocking on the open door, "did the woman never stay at home?"

After peering through the window and seeing no activity, he wondered if she might be in her garden or her laboratory. If so, did he dare seek her out within her temple walls?

"Madness, old son," he cautioned. "Temple walls!"

Cooper wanted to believe Isabel had been doing nothing more than air bathing, odd as the practice seemed, but the idea that she could have been practicing some sort of sorcery still niggled at his mind.

He fell still for a moment, disgusted with his thoughts. He was wasting precious time and energy on ridiculous possibilities when he had more important things to do. The woman's late-night activities weren't his business. If she wanted to practice witchcraft, so be it, and he was more than happy to leave her to her sorcery—after he got back his cuff buttons.

When he knocked a third time and received no answer, Cooper swung away from the door. He would check the garden, knowing he could better face Isabel than Marcella's wrath if she should learn where her betrothal gift had spent the night. Heaven forbid she should learn where and what he'd been doing.

The gate stood open, and Cooper passed through it. The moss streamer that he had carelessly tossed aside last night had been removed and was nowhere in sight. Once inside the walled garden, he made his way to the shell pathway that lead to the south entrance of the house and to Isabel's laboratory. As Cooper neared the rock altar where Isabel had stood just a few hours before, he stopped. He would never pass this spot without recalling the image of Isabel and how she looked in all her naked splendor.

He scanned the area and saw that all evidence that anything unusual had transpired there was gone, making Cooper wonder if he had imagined it all. There was no evidence of candles, no puddles of dripped wax, no human sacrifices. It was exactly as it appeared; a flat-topped rock that had probably been chosen as an adornment for her garden and not unlike the whirligig, the bee skeps, or the wind bells.

"Isabel?" he called, peering into the glass wall of the laboratory. The room was empty.

He went to the door of the house that mirrored the one on the opposite side, which also stood open. "Isabel?" The house, too, was empty. Nobody was at home.

So much for retrieving his cuff links. Cooper retraced his steps, hoping as he did so that Marcella's comment last night would indeed prove to be a factor in keeping his fiancée away today.

What had she said? "Tomorrow, if time permits."

Cooper sent a little prayer heavenward that time would be on his side, or enough time to allow him to collect his links from Isabel once she returned home.

●　　●　　●

Marcella, along with her very best friend, Edwina Wolf, strolled south along the seawall that bordered Bay Street. Even in the summer months when the town was relatively empty of winter tourists, it was still a popular place to be, and to be seen.

Promenaders strolled in the morning hours before lunch— before the humid heat of the afternoon would send them home, seeking refuge inside houses with pulled shades and drawn heavy drapes. Or if they were lucky enough, as Marcella and Edwina were, their daddies' fortunes allowed them to live in houses afforded with the best of the bay breezes, along with colored servants whose only job was to keep the paddle fans mounted on the high ceilings moving. These fans circulated the humid air above daybeds where the ladies of the household reclined each afternoon without fail; to pass the time in repose, reading ladies' monthlies, sipping cool drinks, or to daydream.

Because it was morning, Marcella and Edwina were still out, enjoying their daily stroll. Today they planned to take lunch at a bay front restaurant across from the Bath House before they returned to their respective homes.

"Men's trousers," Marcella said from beneath a frothy pink parasol that was the same pink shade of her dress. "And a man's shirt that my daddy wouldn't be caught in on his worst of days."

"Scandalous," Edwina answered. The redhead who had more freckles than sense, in Marcella's opinion, also carried a frothy parasol that matched her dress, but her ensemble was all in blue.

"Scandalous," Marcella agreed. She mouthed the word silently a second time enjoying the feel of it against her tongue. Not only did the word's meaning conjure up all kinds of wicked behavior, but also it made Marcella recall a time when she had strayed from the conventional—a time she had been ordered to forget.

Several society matrons passed, and the two girls stopped to exchange the customary greetings before continuing on their way. It helped to have an influential friend like Edwina whose father was a prominent land developer. The Wolfs had been living in St. Augustine for over a year and knew all the right people as well as those who were not so right.

Marcella's intent this morning was to pick Edwina's brain for information on one of the latter. She wanted to learn everything she could about Cooper's neighbor, that horrid creature, Isabel Gomez. Marcella didn't take kindly to being made a fool of, especially by a female whom she considered to be below her station. She thought nothing about destroying those who threatened her well-being. Once Marcella made up her mind that something, or someone, belonged to her, she would keep it until *she* tired of it. For the moment, Cooper Adair belonged to her. Hadn't her daddy as much as said so?

As the twosome strolled, Marcella thought she might die from the already oppressive heat. She eyed the quaintness of the town with distaste. To her there was nothing attractive about the many sailboats floating motionless on the placid water of the bay, their idleness reminding her there wasn't a breath of fresh air stirring. The wide grassy promenade that was studded with palms and abutted the seawall held no beauty for a girl born and bred in a big city. As far as Marcella was concerned, the tourists and local rustics could have the narrow streets and old coquina houses built by Spaniards centuries before. After arriving here, in this place that she felt rested at the end of civilization, she had prayed the Spanish would come and reclaim all of Florida so that she and her family could return home to Philadelphia.

Marcella knew her father's decision to move to this little southern burg had been partly due to her mother's declining health, but sometimes Marcella believed Evelyn Kent feigned her illness in order to steal her husband's affections away from her only daughter. The other reason for them settling here, she wouldn't dwell on, but she could still hate it. The only thing that kept her halfway sane was the promise of the upcoming winter season when Mr. Flagler's hotel, the Ponce

De León, would reopen its doors, and people from all over the United States would come to town.

But now the town was as dull as the muddy tidal pools dotting Mantanzas Bay. Marcella longed to return to Philadelphia and the social life she had enjoyed there. Perhaps if they had stayed, she could have made a match with a man who had more money than her own dear Cooper—a man who could have kept her in the same style that she had been kept in since the day of her birth some twenty-five years before.

None but her parents knew Marcella's true age, which was more than the twenty years she claimed. Not even Cooper was aware of the discrepancy in her age, among other things. Although she was a girl considered past her prime, she hadn't reached this unmarried state due to lack of suitors. Marcella prided herself on her many offers; twice she had been betrothed to others. Unfortunately the swains hadn't measured up to her dear daddy's expectations, or to hers, and after discovering their shortcomings, Jack Kent and she had sent the swines packing.

"Some say she's a witch," Edwina said, breaking into her friend's thoughts.

Her words brought Marcella back to the present. "Bitch! Oh, I knew that immediately," Marcella replied, turning her eyes heavenward. "Such a shrew I've never encountered."

Edwina stopped and tugged on her friend's arm. "You're not listening to me."

"That creature had the audacity to claim that my Cooper and she had kissed." When Edwina removed her hand from Marcella's arm, Marcella brushed at her crumpled sleeve. "Of course, Cooper explained what had really happened. The woman stumbled, and when he had moved to assist her, she had fallen right into his arms and began taking untold liberties with his person."

It wasn't exactly Cooper's account that Marcella relayed, but she liked her version better. It stroked her ego that had been bruised by the female's audacity. That she would even suggest such a thing . . .

Suddenly she was pulled from her reverie by Edwina's lack of movement. They were no longer strolling. Dumbstruck, she blinked and looked around her. "Are we there yet?" she asked. Realizing they hadn't arrived at the restaurant, she cut her gaze back to her friend.

"Witch," Edwina repeated, a spark of mischief in her blue eyes, "not bitch."

Marcella gawked. Surely she hadn't heard Edwina correctly.

"It's rumored," her friend continued, "that Isabel Gomez is a witch, but then we both know that's not true."

"A witch? But she doesn't look like a witch."

"And just how many witches do you know?"

Marcella puzzled over this last question. "None," she finally admitted. "She looked different, but she didn't resemble an old crone."

Edwina giggled. "A lot you know about witches." She started moving again, and Marcella fell immediately into step beside her. "There lies the difficult part," Edwina whispered. "Witches may look like you and me, but they also have the uncanny ability to change their appearances. Just as they steal personal objects from people to use in their spell casting, and of course, they also have familiars."

"Familiars? I've never heard of that malady."

"Dunce. It's no illness they suffer. It's their propensity for shape-shifting, the witch image with that of their familiar."

A chill crept up Marcella's spine. "Familiar meaning what?"

"A black cat, I would presume." Edwina raised a perfectly arched copper brow.

Marcella sucked in a loud, unladylike breath. "Isabel Gomez has a black cat," she said, her voice trembling. "The nasty thing rubbed against my frock and would have put fuzz all over me if I hadn't jumped behind Cooper."

"Now that you mention it, I've heard of her black cat," Edwina added. "My mother claims that animal to be the most beautiful cat she has ever seen. She tells me it is huge, with a shiny black coat and orange eyes that glow in the dark."

Marcella shivered. "How can she stand such a beast?"

Edwina adopted an air of haughtiness. "Cats make wonderful companions, and as you well know, my mother loves her cat, Beans." She lifted her chin, daring Marcella to challenge her mother's feelings for the family pet.

Marcella was smart enough to realize she trod on eggshells. She kept her thoughts on the subject to herself, waiting, knowing Edwina had more to say on the subject of Isabel Gomez. Marcella didn't wish to make Edwina angry and chance having her not finish telling her all she knew about the woman. Soon her diplomacy was rewarded.

Continuing, Edwina said, "My mother buys lotions from Miss Gomez. I understand she's quite a good herbalist, so good that many ladies in town buy her lotions and remedies. She makes all her concoctions from the many herbs she grows herself. A quaint garden, I understand, just as her home is quaint."

Appalled, Marcella gulped. "Your mother buys lotions from a witch?"

It was then that Edwina burst into laughter. "Marcella, you're such a goose. We may be living in this small town on the backside of nowhere, but I assure you witches went out of style with the Salem Witch Trials."

They paused again. "There's the restaurant," Edwina offered, pointing at a building across the street. "I can't wait to have oysters on the half shell."

Food was the last thing on Marcella's mind. "How can you think about food? And how can you be so certain that she is not a witch?" she asked.

Now that the idea had been planted in her mind, the notion gave her pause. If the Gomez woman really was a witch, that would explain why Cooper had kissed her.

"I assure you the only thing unusual about Isabel Gomez is her exotic looks, but that is probably because she is part Indian. Her deceased mother, who also had Indian blood, once was a respected herbalist and healer in this area. You know what they say—'Like mother, like daughter.' "

"Indian?" Marcella felt the color drain from her face. "Indians scalp people."

"Marcella Kent, how you do carry on. We're not living in the Wild West. It makes me wonder where your head has been, other than in the clouds, if you still believe in witches with black cats, and Indians who go around taking people's scalps."

Marcella glared at her friend. "I assure you that I'm just as in tune with the times as you are."

"Well, I certainly hope so. I agree with you that Miss Gomez may appear unconventional in her dress and manner, but such actions do not a witch make."

"But it was you who claimed she was a witch."

"Lordy, Marcella, I was teasing you. Now can we please proceed to the restaurant? I reserved a table, so we won't have to wait."

Eating was the last thing Marcella felt like doing, especially disgusting oysters. It mattered not to her how the oysters were prepared; she hated the gritty, fishy-tasting mollusks that had become quite popular. Although the soft-bodied invertebrates repelled her, Marcella still managed to down a few because it was the "in" thing to do, but now, after her conversation with Edwina, she didn't have the stomach for them.

Leaving the promenade, they walked to the edge of Bay Street. Once they were safely across the thoroughfare that was filled with morning traffic, they entered the restaurant.

It was a charming little eatery with a shaded courtyard that ran the building's length. Inside the shade-dappled space there were tables set up for dining that were fast filling up with the early luncheon crowd made up mostly of fashionably dressed ladies. The host showed Edwina and Marcella to their table beneath the vine-covered arbor and left them with their menus.

After removing her lace gloves, Marcella glanced at the menu that contained a collection of Spanish, French, English, and American dishes. None of the offerings appealed to her pallet, but when the waiter returned with their lemonades, she ordered a shrimp salad, forgoing the ever popular oysters. Unlike Edwina, who ordered a dozen of the snotty-looking critters still attached to their half shells, and a bowl of the Gopher Stew.

Like the town itself, even the food sounded—and was—uncivilized. In Marcella's opinion, a gopher was no better than a rat, and who in their right mind would eat a rodent? Her friend Edwina supposedly, making her question the redhead's mental health, especially when Marcella considered her recent tale of witches and Indians. The notion made Marcella's stomach feel quivery, yet the source of the queasiness was still a muddle in her mind. Was it the sorcery her friend had spoke of, or was it the promise of watching her eat rat?

"Hello, Miss Wolf," said an elderly lady who chanced by their table and stopped. "Taking in the breezes, I see." The matron eyed Marcella through her monocle. "This is a lovely day for a stroll, is it not? And a fine day for a delicious lunch."

"Mistress Patty," Edwina said. "How nice it is to see you. I wasn't aware you had returned from your sojourn."

"I returned only yesterday," the matron responded.

"I don't believe you've met my friend. Allow me to introduce you. This is Marcella Kent, newly arrived to our city."

"Marcella Kent, is it?"

"Mistress Patty." Marcella exchanged the called-for pleasantries. "It's so nice to make your acquaintance."

"Your father is Jack Kent, is he not? Import/Export, I believe. He built that fine house on the bay."

"Yes, ma'am. My mother and I arrived a few weeks ago, and I'm sorry to say, we haven't had a chance to meet everyone in town, but I hope that will change once we are settled." Marcella cast a pleasant look toward Edwina. "Edwina's friendship has been a blessing. She has made my transition to St. Augustine a most pleasant one."

"Leave it to Edwina to do the right thing. I take it," she

said to Edwina, "that you've told your new friend about our Fourth of July fête."

"I've mentioned it, but we haven't actually discussed the details. I planned to tell her more today."

"Is that so?" The woman gave Marcella a thorough going over with her monocle. "A pretty little thing, you are. I feel certain most of the eligible young men about town will welcome your lovely addition. Am I right, Edwina?

Edwina answered, smugly, "Marcella is betrothed."

"I should have known," she replied, looking from one girl to the other. "That explains why you've taken the lass under your wing. Maybe she can give you some pointers on how to snare a mate."

Edwina's face turned sullen.

"So who is the lucky fellow?" the matron asked. "Is he any one of note?"

Not giving Marcella a chance to respond, Edwina answered, "He is to be the town's new pharmacist."

Mistress Patty's brows arched in disapproval. "A mere tradesman?"

Marcella wasn't certain which of her company angered her most, Edwina or Mistress Patty. But not one to take insults lying down, she responded. "By choice, not chance. Medicine is a hobby for my fiancée. He comes from a very prominent family in Philadelphia. We both come from there."

"His name?"

"Cooper Adair," Marcella answered. Her breath felt tight in her chest. The last thing she wanted bandied about in her new town was Cooper's humble background.

"I know several prominent families from Philadelphia, but Adair isn't one of them." The matron looked thoughtful. "I shall write my dear friend who still resides in the city. Perhaps she knows of the family. But no matter. I'm sure you and your young man will enjoy our little fête, and I'll look forward to meeting him."

"He will look forward to meeting you as well," Marcella countered.

The matron excused herself. Marcella watched her make her way across the outdoor dining room to join a group of women at a table at the far end of the courtyard.

Edwina's eyes met Marcella's over the rim of her upturned glass. "She's a meddling old tabby, so you don't need to bother yourself about her."

With her usual bluntness, Marcella responded, "I don't usually bother myself about inconsequential people."

"Touché," Edwina responded, smiling. "Are you feeling all right? You look a bit flushed."

Marcella took a cool swallow of lemonade. "It's the heat. I'm not yet use to this humidity."

"It does affect one that way," she consoled. "But in time, you'll get used to it."

Their meals were served, and Marcella only picked at the shrimp salad while Edwina devoured all twelve oysters before wolfing down her rat stew.

"The Fourth of July party will be your first big social," Edwina went on to tell her between bites. "It's held every year on the ramparts of Fort Marion. There will be dancing, food, and a wonderful display of fireworks."

Not really caring who would be attending, but feeling the need to make polite conversation anyway, Marcella asked. "Who is invited to this fête?"

"Why, the whole town, of course. It is an annual event."

"The whole town? Then it's not a society affair?"

"Oh, it's society all right," Edwina assured her. "Everyone, and I do mean *everyone* comes. I'm sure you'll find it most interesting. I know I do."

Interesting? Hardly. "I can't wait," Marcella answered, making the proper reply.

When in truth, she couldn't wait for this particular outing to end. Not only had Edwina begun to bore her, but also Marcella had begun to suspect that maybe Edwina was not such a good friend. A truth that really didn't bother her;

friends other than beaus had never held much interest for Marcella.

For the moment, she wanted only to run to her father for counsel, but first, she must warn Cooper, by telling him that his next-door neighbor was a witch.

Fifteen

"So," Dora said, "that is Marcella Kent."

"In the flesh," Isabel responded. "Or I should say in a lovely pink gown." She grabbed Dora's arm and steered her inside the entrance of a neighboring building. "I don't want Marcella to see me."

Dora and Isabel were coming from the City Market and were walking along Bay Street when Marcella and her friend exited the bay-front restaurant.

"The last time I encountered Miss Kent she was wearing pink," Isabel said. "Pink must be her favorite color."

"You know what they say: Beware of women in pink."

Isabel shot her friend a questioning look. "Why?"

"Oh, I don't know, it just sounded mysterious." Both girls laughed as they continued to watch the twosome. "That's Edwina Wolf she is with," Dora informed her. "I understand she has befriended Marcella, but only because she is betrothed. Miss Wolf makes no alliances with girls who might be a threat to her own unmarried state."

Isabel and Dora waited inside the recessed opening for the two women to pass. A few moments later, when only Edwina strolled by alone, without a glance in their direction, Isabel chanced a look around the corner of the doorway.

"Marcella is heading in the opposite direction." Isabel linked her arm with Dora's and pulled her back onto the walkway. "A variable pink tornado the way she is darting down the street."

"She'll be suffering a heat stroke if she keeps up that pace in this weather." The girls giggled companionably. "If she faints and falls on this street, that pretty pink dress she is wearing won't be so pretty."

Isabel sighed. "She would be beautiful if she wore horse dung."

"If she falls, that's exactly what she'll be wearing." The idea made them both laugh. When their laughter subsided, Dora continued. "I'll bet this basket of apples I'm carrying, if Marcella Kent were to bump into you, she wouldn't recognize you. I've never seen you look so pretty, and I'm viciously jealous of that dress."

"Dora, for heaven's sake. You don't have a vicious bone in your body, but I'm glad you like my outfit." Isabel stepped in front of her. Holding her arms out, she twirled in a circle. Several people passing gave the two females a wide berth, making the girls laugh more. "I have my fairy godmother to thank for my good fortune."

"I wish she would fly by me. Now that I'm to be married, I'd love to have a new trousseau."

Grabbing Dora's hand, Isabel came to a dead stop. "That's it," she said, practically jerking Dora off her feet. "I've been scrambling my brain trying to think of something I could give you as a betrothal gift, and now I know what it will be. I don't know why I didn't think of it before now."

"Don't be silly. You have no money. I don't expect you to give me anything. Your friendship is all that matters, and of course, having you stand up with Ralph and me." She winked at Isabel. "Although, I wouldn't be opposed to a small gift of that sweet-smelling lotion that I just adore."

"The lotion is yours. And so is the dress I'm going to give you."

"Don't be ridiculous. I'm not taking any dress from you."

"Hush! I want none of your useless arguments because I've made up mind. I'm going to give you one of Consuela's dresses as an engagement present."

"Have you lost your mind? If the other dresses are as fine as the one you're wearing, I'd look as out of place with it on as a cabbage in a pumpkin patch. Besides, look at me. We aren't exactly made from the same mold."

"No, I'm tall and you're short. But all the dresses are cut fuller than normal just as this one is." Isabel was wearing her favorite of the dresses, the saffron yellow. "Since we're both handy with a needle, we can adjust it to make it fit."

"I couldn't take one of those dresses. It wouldn't seem right when you need clothes more than I do."

"Don't be ridiculous. Granted my wardrobe isn't anything to brag about, but you know it will take me a lifetime to wear so many dresses. And I certainly won't be wearing them to work in my garden. Like this one, they are much too fine for everyday wear."

Dora appeared to be wavering. "Maybe I could pay you—"

"Don't insult me. You know I won't take your money, but I do so want to give you one of those gowns. I'll even let you pick out the one you want." With a springy bounce, she stopped. "It can be your wedding dress."

"My wedding dress?" Dora pressed her lips together in thought. "I do need something special to get married in. I'd always thought I'd wear Mother's dress, but she was so small, and there is no way that I could ever fit into her wedding dress."

"Your mother was a lovely, petite woman," Isabel reminded her. "You're a lovely, slightly bigger one. It's like you pointed out earlier, we're not all cut from the same mold."

A grin overtook her expression. "Yeah," she said, "I'm a lovely bigger one all right."

"Yes, a lovely bigger one," Isabel assured her. "And you will make a lovely bride in one of Consuela's dresses."

"Do you really think so?" Dora asked. "Will I really make a lovely bride?"

"I know so." She threaded her arm through Dora's, attempting to hurry them along. "I can't wait for you to see those dresses, you won't believe their quality. I can't wait to help you pick out one of them for yourself."

"Drats!" Dora said, stopping. "My father's lunch." She held up the parcel she carried along with the basket of apples. "I forgot again. I'm supposed to drop his sandwich by his office."

"That man would starve without you, Dora. Can't he take his lunch with him in the morning?"

"He can, and would. I'm the one who insists I bring it to him. I love my father very much."

"And you should. He's a fine man." Isabel withdrew her arm from Dora's. "I'll tell you what. You take your father his lunch, and I'll meet you at my house when you're finished."

Dora hesitated. "Are you sure you wish to give me one of your dresses?"

"I'm positive. Since Consuela shared her beautiful gowns with me, it's only fitting that I should share them with my best friend. Now you run along. When you've finished your errand, come to my house. I'll see you then."

The two parted; Dora heading back in the direction they had come, and Isabel continuing north along Bay Street. It was a lovely day for a stroll, especially since she felt so lovely in her new saffron yellow dress.

Isabel had taken special care with her appearance before leaving home this morning. She had been eager to see if she could pass for a proper lady. If the gents she had encountered on her way to meet Dora at the City Market were any indication, Isabel knew she had passed. There was definitely admiration in their glances. But it was Dora's praise that had convinced her of the transformation. Her friend wouldn't lie. Besides, Dora was an authority on fashion. Unlike Isabel, she had always cared about such things.

Until now, Isabel couldn't be bothered.

Now she would need to use all her feminine charms in order to convince Marcella Kent that the *creature* was indeed a threat. Isabel had to make Marcella believe that Cooper Adair was interested in her as a woman while making sure that her own emotions didn't get in the way as they had last night.

While convincing Marcella, Isabel still had Grim to contend with. She couldn't allow that cat to interfere by using his magic tricks, if he was bent on sending out the wrong signals. Isabel still wasn't convinced that the desire she had felt for Cooper last night was due to Grimalkin's magic, or due to herself. She was depending on her love spell to resist the latter.

She left Bay Street, taking a side street that would carry her home. As she neared her street, she heard hammering and sawing coming from the interior of Cooper's building. The sounds convinced her that he was determined to open his pharmacy, and soon. If Isabel intended to force him from this town, she would have to work fast.

On seeing a flash of pink in front of the post, she recognized Marcella. "So that was where she was going in such a hurry."

When several carriages passed, Isabel took the opportunity to steal across the street unseen. At the gate she slipped inside the yard.

It was the perfect time, she decided, to return Cooper's cuff links. It was as good a time as any for Marcella Kent to learn just how formidable a foe Isabel Gomez was.

"Cooper? Why are you dressed like that?" Marcella's expression was horrified as she took in his attire.

"I'm working, Marcella. This is how people dress who are doing physical labor."

"But Daddy, he—he works." She looked at his clothes again. "He doesn't wear clothes like that. You—you don't look like a gentleman."

Cooper grabbed her arm to steer her away from the front doors of the building. Her arrival had caused a stir among the workmen, and, being a man, Cooper could well understand.

Marcella was a beauty. She was petite, but with shapely, rounded curves. Her face a perfect oval with an exquisitely dainty nose and a rose-petal mouth. With her thick, dark hair, she presented a picture that would make any man sit up and take notice. He had, so why should he expect Deke and Skor to act any differently?

Yet it wasn't their reaction that bothered him, it was Marcella's. In her present agitated state, Cooper feared she might say something discourteous in front of the workers, and even he wouldn't tolerate that.

"The clothes are clean," he said, lifting a sleeve for her to smell the sunshine fragrance. She drew back, acting as though he had asked her to kiss a snake.

"My God, Marcella. They're only clothes."

"They're disgusting. And I don't wish to look at you dressed as such."

Cooper threw up his hands. "What is the *such* I'm dressed as?"

"A—a commoner."

"A commoner." If her statement hadn't been so serious, he would have burst out laughing, but why was she acting like this? Marcella's actions today, coupled with those of her father last night, was an annoyance Cooper didn't want to deal with. Angry himself, he responded, "What you see is what you get."

The way she looked at him sent a chill walking up his spine, and also made him regret his comment.

To someone like Marcella, he probably did look like a commoner—a common laborer. Yet he still couldn't understand why his appearance had her so upset. She knew his background; knew his father was a labor supervisor for the railroad. Cooper's family hadn't been rich, but they had lived comfortably. Even without wealth, his parents had helped to put him through college and then pharmacy school. Unlike the Kents, Cooper believed that it wasn't a man's position or how he dressed that made him important. It was his character.

But to someone like Marcella who had grown up a rich man's daughter and been protected from the baser side of life, seeing her fiancé dressed as he was could possibly offend her delicate sensibilities. Heck, her father's yardman probably wore better clothes than the ones he had on.

"Look, hon," he said, trying to placate her, "I don't want to argue. I'm wearing these clothes because I'm trying to put the apartment upstairs in order. The sooner I do that, the sooner I can move in."

She cast a disbelieving glance at the weathered cypress structure. "You plan to live here?"

So much for placating, he thought. "Where did you think I'd live, at the Ponce De León?"

"You can't," she responded. "It's only open during the winter season."

"Marcella, I couldn't afford—"

"Why, there you are," the husky female voice said, "I've been looking all over for you."

Cooper didn't need to turn around to know who had spoken. He would recognize Isabel Gomez's voice in a black dungeon filled with strangers; but without hearing her speak, he still would have known her identity because of the look on Marcella's face.

"Miss Gomez," he said, slowly turning toward her, but he wasn't prepared for the extraordinary beauty who stood several feet away. "You look so different with—" He slammed his lips shut. Surely he hadn't been about to say what he thought he was. *With your clothes on.* Surely not.

One glance at her ever-present cat who posed near her hemline reminded Cooper he wasn't the only male present who was party to his thoughts.

He jerked his gaze back to Isabel, whose full lips turned up at the corners in an enchanting smile. Cocking one brow, she sent him a look that suggested they shared some clandestine secret, making his skin burn beneath his collar. He supposed they probably did, considering everything that had transpired between them, but couldn't the woman see that he was with Marcella?

"The clothes fit?" Her golden eyes slid over him from the edge of the shirt's worn collar, down his length, to the frayed hems of the trousers. "I'm so glad," she said. "I could only guess at the size."

"I'm big," he croaked, thankful that the loose-fitting shirt concealed that part of his anatomy. "They fit fine. I thank you."

She held him spellbound, this new Isabel. She was no longer a hoyden, but a lovely and captivating woman. Her yellow-gold gown skimmed her very feminine curves—the same curves Cooper had seen naked only last night. Today those same curves weren't nude, but they weren't caged in restricting stays, either.

If her dress and bearing weren't enough of a distraction, he also had her new hairstyle to consider. On most women, the hair pulled back from her face and secured with black jet combs wouldn't have been attractive. Yet the style's severity only emphasized Isabel's beauty with her high, exotic cheekbones, the yellow-orange color of her eyes, and the flush of sunset on her golden skin.

Something tugged on his arm. Cooper glanced in the direction of the bothersome interruption.

"Marcella," he said, much louder than he intended. "You remember Miss Gomez?"

Marcella appeared to be as dumbstruck by the vision of Isabel as Cooper was, because she didn't respond. Instead she clutched his arm so tightly that he thought the blood might stop flowing through his limb.

"Miss Kent," Isabel said, "how nice to see you again." When Marcella didn't return her greeting, Isabel smiled and transferred her gaze back to Cooper's, continuing. "I assume your rash has completely vanished. The salve worked, I take it?"

"Completely—yes." He felt like a wooden dummy.

"Well, then, I shan't keep you any longer. I must hurry ome. I have a friend coming by." She moved as though she eant to take her leave, but then she stopped. "Oh, yes, I lmost forgot," she said, smiling. "My reason for seeking you ut."

She held out her hand and turned her palm upright. The un's rays filtering past the leafy branches caught on the gold uttons resting in her open palm.

Beside him, he heard Marcella gasp.

"You left these yesterday," Isabel said. "I thought you ight be wondering where they were. A betrothal gift, I be-eve?" Her gaze slid to Marcella's. "I know how much these ean to you."

Like a zombie, Cooper held out his hand. When she ropped the cuff buttons into his palm, her fingers acciden-lly brushed his skin. It felt like a burn, making him jerk his and away.

Isabel must have realized the effect her touch had had, ecause she laughed softly. "Now if you two will excuse me. ll be on my way." She turned and glided away.

A queen, Cooper thought, couldn't have made a more regal xit, and for reasons unbeknown to him, he suddenly wanted bow in allegiance. But the feeling didn't last long.

"How could you, Cooper Adair? You left my buttons with at—that woman. And just why did you remove my cuff uttons in that horrible woman's presence?"

"I can explain—"

"Sure you can. Just as you explained away her kiss." Mar-ella's voice grew harsher, louder.

Several people who passed the building hurried along at a ster pace.

"I suppose you're going to tell me that she tripped again, d that my cuff links flew into her hands." Marcella began pace. "No, not into her hands." She stopped pacing. "They mped across the yard and landed inside her house."

"If you'll allow me, I can—"

"Allow you? I want to know what liberties you allowe her."

"Marcella, a lady shouldn't speak of such things." Coope grabbed her arm and sent her a warning look. "The worker will hear you." He glanced over his shoulder. "This is th place or the time for this discussion—"

"How did she know about a rash?" Her voice increased i volume. "You never told me you had a rash. And why ar you wearing her clothes? More important, how did she kno' your size? I'm betrothed to you and I don't know your size.

"Maybe she guessed." Her argument was getting ridict lous. "Maybe she's more intuitive. Damn it, Marcella, ho' do I know?"

"Watch your language, young man." Jack Kent had com upon them unnoticed. "You'll not talk to my daughter tha way, especially on a public street."

"Oh, Daddy. It's that—that horrible—"

Marcella threw herself into Jack Kent's arms. "There nov darling," he said soothingly, "everything's gonna be fine. Marcella never finished her sentence; instead all the fight wer out of her. She wept against her father's lapels.

The sight of his future wife seeking comfort from her fathe instead of from him made Cooper want to shake both of then

"I think, Mr. Kent," he said, stepping closer, "this is be tween Marcella and me."

"I think not," the man replied with a voice honed of stee "It appears you've upset her enough for one day."

"We need to talk—"

He sent Cooper a look that had silenced many a ma "Come along, Marcella. My carriage is parked around th corner."

"Sir, if you don't mind—"

"I mind. Very much so. But before I tell you just how muc I mind, I'm taking my daughter home." He wrapped his ar around Marcella's shoulders and began steering her awa from the building.

Cooper started to go after them but stopped. What was th

use of it? Right now Jack was guarding his daughter like a bodyguard, and in the mood Cooper was in, he might be forced to come to fisticuffs with the older man.

"A fistfight." Incredible. He couldn't believe he would resort to violence to settle a score—with a man who would soon be his father-in-law.

"Damn it all to hell," Cooper swore.

Swinging away from the Kents, he slammed his fist against the wall. As soon as he did, he regretted it. Pain numbed his fingers and wrist, then shot up his arm.

Jumping back from the building, Cooper shook his injured hand until the feeling slowly came back.

"It's this town," he grumbled. "This godforsaken town has brought out the worst in all of us."

She wasn't supposed to feel like this. She was supposed to feel elated. When Isabel had delivered her final shot by presenting Cooper with his cuff links, she had felt victorious, but only for a moment. Once she had made her way inside the yard and closed the gate behind her, she could hear Marcella's angry voice carrying to her on the wind, and she began to feel lower than skum on a pond.

If she had been smart, she would have walked straight into her house, closed the door, and forgotten the little drama, but just as vengeance wasn't Isabel's strong suit, neither was walking away from a good argument. It didn't matter that she wasn't directly involved in the argument.

So instead of putting the needed distance between her, Cooper, and Marcella, Isabel pretended an interest in pinching off dead hibiscus blossoms that grew the length of the outer wall. As she worked her way down the hedge, the closer she came to the post building, the better she could hear everything transpiring on the wall's opposite side. Not only could she hear, but she suspected that everyone who passed could do so, not to mention the men working inside the building. The construction sounds issuing from the interior didn't sound as industrious as they had before the fray had begun.

Isabel's first reaction on hearing the heated argument wa "Yes, yes!" Her plan to make Marcella jealous was working Yet as the battle continued, and she heard the girl's shrewis tongue, Isabel wanted to run to Cooper's defense. Why wasn' he standing up to Marcella instead of placating her? As Isabe continued to listen, she wondered how a man as nice as Coo per had gotten mixed up with such a shrew.

Go home, the voice inside her head warned, but instead o heeding the advice, Isabel remained. She continued to pinc the scarlet blossoms from the green branches that looked lik bleeding hearts where they rested against the ground.

Then she heard another man's voice. The man's interfer ence and response told her he was Marcella's father. Sigh unseen, Isabel disliked the man; his arrogance reminding he of Wooster Farley. She had known enough of excessively unpleasantly self-important men to last her a lifetime, and fo a moment she pitied the women of the Kent household. Bu surely a man as rich as a king wouldn't raise a hand agains the ladies in his kingdom. Yet there was no doubt in Isabel' mind that such a man would have no qualms about raising hand to protect those ladies if threatened. From Cooper. An from her.

She heard a sharp blow against the front of the building and she thought that the two angry men had come to blows Several moments passed after the explosive sound before sh heard Cooper's remark about "this godforsaken town."

At that moment her heart went out to the man. In spite o the fact that Cooper Adair was a pharmacist whose busines might eventually ruin her own, Isabel liked him.

In fact, she liked him too darn much.

The iron gate clanked shut. She saw Dora.

"I'm here," Isabel called, leaving the hedge behind her.

It was apparent that Dora had heard some of the argumen

"I've been pinching back blossoms," Isabel told her.

"I can see that."

Isabel knew exactly what her friend saw. She saw righ through her.

Sixteen

Once they were inside the cottage, Dora asked, "Why the long face?"

"I don't have a long face," Isabel insisted.

"You can't lie to me. I know you too well. I also know you were eavesdropping on your neighbor."

"Me?" Isabel made a beeline for the icebox to pour them both a glass of tea. "Now why would I be caring what my neighbor does?" She reached for two glasses, carefully avoiding eye contact. "He is betrothed. What goes on between him and his fiancée is of no concern to me."

"Is that so? Why then did their tiff appear to upset you as much as it upset Mr. Adair?"

"I don't know what you're talking about."

"You know, Ysabel. Just as I know what I saw. Not only did their argument upset you, but also you were so engrossed in their conversation that you didn't realize I had opened the gate, or that I stood there for several moments before I announced myself."

"As I said, I was pinching off dead blossoms."

Dora pinned her with her gaze. "Ysabel, you were never very good at disguising your emotions. Now tell me why their argument upset you so much."

"You should know," Isabel snapped. "I haven't forgotten how Wooster Farley loved to argue, even if you have."

As soon as the words were out, Isabel regretted them. "I'm sorry, Dora," she said. "You didn't deserve that."

Dora shrugged her shoulders and said nothing.

"Oh, very well," Isabel said, and began pouring the tea into two glasses. "I'll tell you."

She finished slicing a lemon and squeezed it into the liquid. Dora came to stand beside her, and Isabel handed her a glass. "You probably won't like what I have to say, but don't forget I warned you. Let me get the dresses. I hung them outdoors to give them a good airing."

Several moments later Isabel returned with the gowns draped across her arms. Grimalkin entered the room on her heels.

On seeing the cat, Dora said, "I was wondering where that scoundrel was."

Grimalkin stopped to stretch before strolling to the front window and jumping up on the sill. After a moment he sat down, folded his front paws beneath him, and turned his golden gaze on the two women.

"He is not going to watch me undress, is he?" Dora asked.

Isabel's eyes widened. "He is a cat for heaven's sake. He is not interested in your womanly secrets."

"I don't care that he's a cat. Those eyes see more than you give them credit for seeing."

"Dora, you're being ridiculous. I would think you would be more interested in these," Isabel said, shaking the armload of dresses, "than in what my cat doesn't see."

The cat not completely forgotten, Dora turned her attention on the rainbow of color in Isabel's arms. "Oh, my," she said. "I've never seen such vivid shades. And the material . . ." Her voice trailed off as she moved closer to Isabel and began to stroke the fabrics. "They're even lovelier than you said."

"Only nature can rival such colors." Isabel walked around the chairs, spreading the dresses over their high backs. When she was finished, she stepped back. "Choose."

"Ysabel, how can I? They're all so—so different." Dora began walking around the dresses, fingering lace rushing here and beaded buttons there. When she came to the scarlet gown, she stopped. "This is it, I've found it."

"Red? Surely you can't mean to wear red on your wedding day."

Besides, as much as Isabel hated to admit it, she really didn't wish to part with the scarlet dress. Although she knew she would never have an occasion to wear such a frock, there was something about its color that appealed to her. Last night she had told Grim it was much too violent a color, but today when she looked at the scarlet hue, it evoked passion. An emotion Isabel had been feeling a lot of since Cooper Adair had come into her life.

"Not for my wedding dress, silly," Dora said. "For you. To wear to the Fourth of July fête. It's only a couple of weeks away."

"Me? Wear that? Surely you jest."

"I'm not teasing. It's a lovely shade of red, and you most certainly can wear it. In case you've forgotten, red, white, and blue are the colors of the nation's flag. And it is a celebration dance, our country's birthday. I've seen both men and women wear stars and stripes to the gala, and I've also seen women wearing red."

"Yes, but the material. It's as sheer as a butterfly's wing."

Dora picked up the red petticoat. "I assume that's what this is for. Now that we've settled what you'll be wearing to that event, which one of these lovely creations should I choose as a wedding dress? It's a shame such beauty will be wasted on me."

Isabel propped her hands on her hips. "Dora Gay, you stop belittling yourself. Any of these gowns will look lovely on you, so it's just a matter of choice. The color, the fit, or whatever."

"Speaking of whatever, I'm dying to know the whatever you promised to tell me when you returned from getting the dresses."

Dora had a memory like an elephant, and Isabel had hoped her friend would forget their earlier conversation when she saw the dresses, but it didn't look as though she would be allowed a reprieve. Now that it was time to tell her, Isabel wasn't so certain that Dora would appreciate that Isabel intended to break up a romance. Especially for such a selfish reason as to send Cooper Adair north where he had come from.

"Are you going to tell me," Dora interrupted, "or am I going to have to beat it out of you?"

"Beat it out of me?" Isabel's hand flew to her mouth as she suppressed a smile. "When did you become so violent?"

"When I saw that look on your face when you didn't know I had been watching you. I had hoped never to see you look so unhappy again."

"You're being ridiculous."

"No. I'm being your friend. Remember, we've shared a lot. First your mother's death, then Wooster's; although I know his passing didn't make you sad."

Isabel didn't want to think of either of those times. They were both bad, each in their own way. She wished for her mother's sake that her stepfather could have been a different kind of man, but he hadn't been, so it was best to put the unhappy memory behind her.

"I suppose in a way it is my own death that made me look so unhappy."

Dora's black eyes grew round. "Your death?"

"Not literally," Isabel assured her, "but the death of my herbal business if Cooper Adair opens up that fancy new pharmacy of his."

"Didn't I say as much the first time I met him?" Dora crossed her arms over her bosom.

"Yes, you did, but it wasn't until later when I thought about your words that I saw him as a real threat." She walked to the window where Grim lay snoozing, and began stroking his back.

"I know times are changing. Folks who visit or relocate

here will seek Cooper's newfangled cures over my old-fashioned ones. Just as doctors educated in universities have already replaced healers like my mother. Did you know that we have seven doctors in this town and seven dentists? My fear is that once Cooper Adair opens his doors for business, I'll have to close mine."

"You will not," Dora said, coming up behind her. She, too, began to stroke Grimalkin's coat. "The old-timers will always come to you, especially the women. None of those new saw-bones care a hoot about a woman's needs. In their opinion, childbearing is something women should endure without complaint."

They exchanged knowing looks before Isabel continued. "My intent is not to set myself up as a qualified doctor, or even give medical advice. That's what trained physicians do, although I think some of my cures are as good as theirs. But Cooper Adair will stock items in his drugstore such as lotions, salves, and tinctures that he orders from big factories up North. How can I compete with that?"

"Your stuff is better, and those who have sought out your advice will continue to do so. Trust me on this." She smoothed back her hair. "Somehow, I don't think this is everything that's bothering you. You aren't smitten with the man, are you?"

"Of course not."

"Then tell me the rest."

Isabel sucked in a breath, then let it out in a rush. "You do know me too well." She turned away from the window and looked Dora in the eyes. "My only recourse, considering my circumstances, is to get rid of Cooper Adair."

"You're going to kill him?" Dora's eyes widened with false innocence.

"I swan, Dora Gay, and you said you knew me?"

"Just kidding, but I am interested in how you're going to make him disappear."

"Aren't you interested in *why* I'm going to make him disappear?"

"You've more or less told me the why, now please tell me the how."

"I'm going to make Marcella Kent believe that Cooper Adair is enamored with me."

"I've a better idea. Why don't you make Cooper Adair fall passionately in love with you, and then the two of you can sail off into the sunset?"

Isabel stepped away. Because her friend knew her so well, she feared Dora would see from the guilty look on her face how close she had come to falling passionately into Cooper's arms. Three times to be exact.

"That kind of passion," Isabel said, "only happens in the books I read. Besides, if he falls passionately in love with me, he won't leave, and my business will still suffer."

"But think of the sweet agony." Dora's face brightened with the thought.

"Be serious, Dora. The only way Cooper Adair will leave this town is if Marcella Kent breaks their engagement. He has as much as admitted that he doesn't like it here. You said yourself that Marcella was very jealous and that she had been engaged several times before."

"I am being serious," Dora added. "And I still like my idea better than yours."

Ignoring this remark, Isabel continued. "Besides, I believe after what I've seen of Marcella Kent, Cooper Adair deserves someone nicer than she."

"And you're that someone."

"Dora. You're not listening to me."

Dora held up her hands in surrender. "I'm listening—I'm listening."

It was quiet inside the house. Outside a whisper of a breeze stirred one of the many wind bells. It was Dora who spoke first.

"According to your plan, the argument between Mr. Adair and Marcella should have prompted your smile, but instead you were frowning. I'm missing something here, Ysabel."

"No, I wasn't smiling," Isabel said. "Because it was me who incited their argument."

"You? How?"

Isabel took a deep breath and sighed. "The other day I offered to give Cooper a salve for a heat rash that he developed when he arrived in Florida. The man's been wearing wool in this ninety-degree weather. He left his cuff links on my worktable—cuff links that were a betrothal gift from Marcella."

Isabel moved back to the window and pretended interest in something outside. She couldn't bear to look at Dora for fear of what she might see in her face. "I—I deliberately kept them with the intention of returning the links to him in front of Marcella, because I knew it would make her angry with him."

Isabel's shoulders sagged. "And it did," she said. "That is why they were arguing. And that is why I felt so horrible. Being cruel is a lot more difficult than being kind."

When Dora said nothing, Isabel stood a little straighter. With her ears tuned toward the slightest sound of disgust, she stood, listening, waiting for Dora to respond. Finally, after several moments had passed and Dora still hadn't commented, Isabel couldn't stand the suspense a moment longer. She swung to face her.

Dora was grinning like a cow chewing cud. "Did you swap slobbers?"

A rush of heat washed up her neck, burning her ears. "Of course not."

"Just where was Mr. Adair's rash?"

"Where a rash usually is." Isabel's face grew warmer.

"Beneath his sleeve cuffs?"

"Exactly," Isabel answered, wondering why she hadn't thought of such an explanation. It would have saved her a great deal of embarrassment in the telling.

The look Dora sent her clearly stated that she didn't for a minute believe Cooper Adair's rash was confined to his wrists.

Avoiding her gaze, Isabel walked back toward the dresses. "Now shall we pick out your dress?"

"I've already picked it out."

The tight knot within her slowly loosened. It was apparent Dora didn't think she was such a horrible person that she had to run from the room. As far as Isabel was concerned, enough had been said on the matter. It was time to put her confession behind her and help Dora find the right dress.

"Which dress?"

"I like the green one."

Isabel moved to the chair where the green dress lay. Picking it up and holding it away from her, she looked it over again and smiled. "A perfect choice. It will look wonderful with your coloring."

Dora ran her hands reverently over the silk fabric. "I've always loved green, and it will be a perfect color for an October wedding. But do you think it will fit?"

"If it doesn't, we'll make it fit," Isabel assured her. "As you said, the color will be perfect for an October wedding. Now it's time for you to strip."

Dora glanced at Grimalkin, whose eyes shot open at the mention of the word *strip*. "Couldn't you blindfold that animal?"

"Cats stare. It's their nature, but he isn't ogling you. If it will make you feel more comfortable, you can go upstairs and change in my room."

"I know I'm being silly." She glanced at Grimalkin again, who was indeed staring, then turned her attention back to Isabel. "What difference does it make? It's probably nothing he hasn't seen before, only a lot more of it."

Soon Dora had the dress on, and Isabel led her to the mirror. "It's a little snug, but we knew it might be. And of course it's way too long, but I believe once we've finished our alterations, it will be perfect."

Dora drew in a deep breath as she fastened the large upholstered buttons that ran up the center front. "Very snug," she said.

The dress was made in the princess style in three different shades of moss green fabric: corded silk, plain silk, and velvet. It had an ecru lace collar with a falling jabot of lace, and lace undersleeves.

Isabel stood behind Dora and, mimicking Consuela's Spanish accent, said, "What you dink, señorita?"

Dora giggled, then pivoted in a slow circle while Isabel followed her, turning the skirt. After her revolution was complete, she stopped and faced the mirror again. "I just might make a pretty bride after all, but only because of your gift of this dress."

"Not my gift, but Consuela's."

Grimalkin left his window seat and came to stand beside the females. "Me-wow, me-wow."

Dora's mouth dropped open. "You told me he did nothing but stare."

"On occasion he pays compliments." She laughed, and winked at Dora in the mirror. "That's why I keep him around."

Once Dora had changed back into her clothes, the two of them sat at the table and enjoyed another glass of tea.

"You must wear that red dress to the Fourth of July festivities," Dora said.

Isabel's glance slid to the dress, then back again to Dora's. "It's too fancy for the likes of me."

"It's a party dress, and you're going to a party. You know everyone dresses up, usually in patriotic colors. You'll be the belle of the ball in that dress."

"Yes, and who will look at me? I don't even have an escort. Not that I want one, but I'd look out of place in such a smock."

"You'll attend with Ralph and me. You know he is in charge of the fireworks again this year. With that red dress on, you'll have every man at the dance vying for your attention. You'll be the hottest firecracker there."

"Firecracker!" Isabel rolled her eyes. "I like this dress." She smoothed a crease from her skirt.

"I like that dress, too, but I like the red one better."

"Dora, why are you being so persistent?"

"Are you the same girl who told me earlier that she wanted to make Marcella Kent jealous?"

"Yes, but I also told you how awful I felt after doing it."

"I admit you were bold to give him back his cuff links in front of his betrothed, and I can understand why you felt badly afterward. But if you wear that red dress to the party, and Mr. Adair sees you in it, I guarantee you won't have to do or say anything to get his attention. All you'll have to do is stand there, dance a few dances with the men who ask you, and flirt a little."

"I don't know how to flirt."

"With that dress on, you'll know. Cooper Adair will notice you, and so will Marcella Kent."

"When did you become such an authority? Only a day or so ago you were claiming my potion was what made Ralph propose."

"A mature woman's intuition."

"Oh," Isabel said, raising her brows. "Now that you're engaged, you've become worldly wise."

"Something like that." Dora drained her glass and set it back on the table. "Now I'm going to help you make Marcella Kent jealous. Don't forget, I know a lot of people in this town—let me correct that, I know *about* a lot of people in this town. It won't take me long to find out about those other beaus I heard she dropped."

"Then you don't think me despicable?"

Dora pushed back from the table and stood. "How could I even think such a thing? You're my friend, and I love you. But I still think you should make Cooper Adair fall madly in love with you."

"Dora, I've already explained—"

"I know, I know, and now I must be going. I'm supposed to meet Ralph at the livery and walk home from work with him."

Isabel stood.

Picking up the red dress, Dora held the gown against Isabel's front. "Trust me. If you wear this to the party, Cooper Adair will be leaving town on the next day's train."

"Silly. He'll have to sell his building first," Isabel said.

"I have a feeling that won't be necessary." Dora moved toward the door.

"Won't be necessary? That's the whole intent of this scheme. To get rid of Cooper Adair."

Dora appeared to mull over her thoughts. "I meant to say he won't be leaving immediately. He'll have to sell first."

Isabel walked Dora to the gate. "I feel so much better now that you know of my scheme. With your help, I know I can succeed in getting rid of my competition."

As Dora stepped out into the street and started toward the livery, she squeezed Isabel's hand.

"Believe me, love, I have no doubt whatsoever that we won't succeed in eliminating your competition."

Seventeen

~

Marcella threw herself on the tester bed covered with a spread of frilly pink ruffles. After several unsuccessful attempts at beating the stuffing from the feather pillows, she flopped on her back, exhausted, and stared up at the pink roses strewn across the canopy above her head.

Pink was Marcella's favorite color and had been from the moment she was big enough to identify with the color. Her mother had dressed her in shades of pink from the moment she was born, all through her childhood, until the choice of color had become Marcella's own. More than half her wardrobe was made from fabrics of the coveted color, or at least with a touch of it.

Even the decorations for her suite of rooms—the wall coverings, the upholstery, the drapes, and the rugs—were all made in fabrics of rose and pink. When she and Cooper were married, he would move into these same rooms her father had built especially for her. Here among the roses, ribbons, and bows, Cooper would pay homage to her body for the rest of their lives. On their wedding night he would take her here among the pink furnishings, and she would wear one of her sheerest pink nightgowns that was packed away in her cedar chest, waiting for the day when the two of them would become husband and wife.

Husband and wife.

The thought brought on another bout of anger. Marcella rubbed her hand across her eyes, not surprised when it came away with no evidence of her weeping. No matter how hard she tried, or how much she wanted to cry, tears never flowed from Marcella's eyes. Instead of the usual salty excretions, her emotions were fueled with boiling temper and other angry outbursts.

Disgusted, she picked up a china bowl from the nightstand. Like every other appointment in the room, the bowl, too, was pink, covered with huge cabbage roses. Marcella threw it against the door. The same door, a few minutes later, that her father opened, his big feet crushing the already shattered petal pieces deeper into the wooden floor. Once inside the room, Jack Kent closed the door behind him, then proceeded to the bed. In his big hands he carried a small tea tray with a pink teapot and a matching pink cup.

"Now, now," he crooned, "it's time you and your daddy had a little talk."

Marcella made another great show of rubbing her eyes and sniffing back tears before she flopped on her stomach and buried her face in the bruised pillows.

Jack placed the tray on the bedside table, sat down beside her on the bed, and began rubbing her back.

Marcella liked the way the bed dipped with her father's weight, reminding her of when she was a little girl and believed her father could do anything. Through the layers of the mussed material of her dress, Marcella soaked up the heat of her father's strong, comforting presence.

Wretched girl, that Edwina, Marcella thought. Like everything else in this despicable town, her very best friend wasn't turning out to be the best. Edwina had lied about Isabel Gomez, first claiming that she was a witch, then claiming that she wasn't. But one look at the female Marcella had seen for the second time this afternoon was all the proof she needed. Isabel Gomez was a witch.

What else could explain such a transformation? When she first met the Gomez woman, she had appeared in the form of an unsightly lad; the second time in the form of an enticing woman.

Marcella cried louder. Her fit of weeping elicited another affectionate stroke of her father's hands.

"You go ahead and cry," Jack crooned. "I'll be right here beside you, and when you feel like it, we'll talk."

Marcella shook her shoulders as though her body were torn by heart-wrenching sobs. Then, burrowing her face deeper into the pillow, she wailed loudly. Her action was rewarded by her father's response.

"Cooper Adair will pay dearly," he mumbled, "for hurting my little girl."

Next she wept softly against the pillow, her mind replaying the scene with Cooper. In vivid detail Marcella recalled the moment when Isabel had sauntered over to where she and Cooper stood. The very witch who had cast a spell on Marcella's fiancé.

No, the woman hadn't sauntered up to them, she had floated. Yes, floated was a better description. Right before Marcella's eyes, she had done exactly what Edwina said witches do. She appeared as an enchantress, bringing with her that wretched black cat—her familiar. Using her magical powers, she had stolen Cooper's cuff links, Marcella's betrothal gift to him, to use in her spell casting.

"That's my girl," her daddy soothed when she no longer wailed. "You've cried enough for now. It's time you drink your tea like a good little girl and tell your daddy what upset you."

Marcella faked a few hiccups. After the pretended spasms had subsided, she sat up, palmed her eyes with her hands, before turning her face to her parent.

"Here you go, lovey," Jack Kent said. "Allow Daddy to fluff your pillows." Once they were plumped, Marcella collapsed dramatically against them. "Here's that tea I promised you. With just a drop of poppy."

She sniffed. "You're too good to me, Daddy."

Marcella sipped the tea. The warm brew calmed her anger, and soon the juice of the poppy would allow her to escape into blissful sleep.

"Now, then," Jack said as he watched her drink her tea. "Are you ready to tell me why Cooper Adair was cursing at you on a public street?"

Already the laudanum had begun to make her relax. The catastrophe didn't seem quite as serious as before. She knew that she and Cooper had argued, but try as she might, Marcella couldn't recall the reason.

"Was it that woman again?"

Her daddy's question broke into her now euphoric mood. But knowing her parent expected an answer, she said, "Yes, it was the witch."

Jack laughed, his eyes adoring as he searched her face. "I think you mean bitch," he said.

"Whatever." Marcella sighed. She sunk deeper into the pillows. "Love him."

"You think you do, Marcella, yet sometimes I wonder if we made a mistake. Cooper Adair isn't as malleable as I thought he would be."

"He's all male, Daddy. I assure you of that." Marcella sighed again. She took her father's hand in hers and began tracing his fingers with one of hers.

"What are you implying, daughter?" Jack asked. "Not what your words suggest, I hope." He sat up straighter on the bed. "You've already made one such mistake, Marcella, allowing a man to become too familiar with you before wedlock. Another mistake won't do."

"Oh, Daddy, you worry too much."

Marcella sat up and began pulling the pins from her hair. Instead of placing them on the nightstand, she pinged them across the room. When the last pin was removed, she raked her fingers through her curls and flopped back on the pillow.

"You bought him for me, Daddy," she said. "Cooper belongs to me."

"That's what you said about the last man I bought you, a man who was of our same class. But once he found out about your little indiscretion, he returned the damaged goods and then proceeded to warn away everyone else who might have been interested in marrying you."

The lines from Henry Longfellow's poem popped into Marcella's head. Although poetry wasn't her strong suit, these words were indicative of herself. She recited the lines:

> "And when she was good
> She was very, very good,
> but when she was bad she was horrid."

Marcella giggled.

"Don't be gauche, daughter," Jack warned. "Maybe if you hadn't been so good at what you did you wouldn't be in such a predicament now."

She didn't like her father's tone. "Cooper belongs to me," she said defiantly. "The witch can't have him."

"Who would want him?" Jack stood and walked to the window. "I can't believe I agreed to such a scheme. Allowing my daughter to marry a mere tradesman."

Through a warm haze, Marcella watched her father. He stood by the window, looking out at the bay.

"I've convinced everyone we know that we moved here for the climate and your mother's failing health."

"I know, Daddy."

"This is our last chance to silence the gossipmongers. Once you're married, the rumors will stop and will soon be forgotten. By then you'll be a respectable married woman, and we will have whipped Cooper into the role of a subservient husband. In time, he will take his place in Kent Import/Export and give up this damnable notion of running a shop."

" 'And when she was good,' " Marcella repeated, " 'she was very, very good. . . .' " She wished her father would leave. She didn't feel like talking anymore. "I'll be good, Daddy, I promise. I won't disappoint you again."

"The marriage will take place as planned, Marcella. There will be no fourth chance."

He returned to the bed and kissed his daughter on the forehead. "You sleep now. If I had a choice, I'd send that young man to the opposite side of the continent, but I have to think of you." Jack propped his weight on his hands and leaned forward. "The sooner you and Cooper are married, the better. Once you two are wed, we'll be rid of that Gomez woman's meddling. I'll speak with Cooper this afternoon."

Snuggled in the pillow, Marcella watched her father close the door. Her lids floated shut, and soon she was drifting on a fluffy white wedding cake.

"And when she was bad, she was horrid. . . . "

Cooper returned inside, not bothering to glance at the two men who suddenly appeared as busy as bees making honey after Jack Kent rescued his daughter from her fiancé.

Embarrassed, he stalked up the stairs, grabbed the broom he had dropped earlier, after Deke had interrupted his sweeping to tell him that there was a lady out front wishing to speak with him. On receiving the summons, Cooper's first thought had been that Isabel had come to return the cuff links, and he was filled with both anticipation and dread; eager to have Marcella's gift returned to him, but not eager to see the bearer of the gift. Isabel Gomez evoked feelings that a man in his position had no right to feel.

With his tail dragging, Cooper had descended the stairs. Disappointment hit him square in the chest when the flutter of pink outside the open front doors alerted him to the identity of his caller. Forcing a smile he didn't feel, and hoping he looked the part of a man in love, Cooper moved across the room. One glance at Marcella's frantic pacing, and Cooper's smile faded. Her impromptu visit wouldn't be a pleasant one.

After that, everything blurred together. He recalled that Marcella was appalled at how he was dressed, and then she was appalled that he wouldn't be living in the Ponce De León Hotel, although it wasn't open for guests. He had tried to calm her and might have succeeded if Isabel hadn't appeared on the scene. One look at his neighbor had stunned Marcella to silence.

Not that Cooper could blame her, because he had been a little stunned himself. In the short time that he had known Isabel, he had seen her in various stages of undress, and in his opinion, she had looked beautiful in each stage. Yet today with the yellow-gold dress that was a near match to her unusual orange-gold eyes, her beauty had almost whooshed the air from his lungs. Recalling the first time they met, the transformation from lad to lass had been unsettling to the say the least, but her transformation from chrysalis to butterfly was almost Cooper's undoing.

The brush of the broom against the floor brought him out of his reverie. Cooper stopped sweeping and propped his hands on the tip of the broom. This fixation with Isabel Gomez had to stop. Such behavior was totally unacceptable. Yet until he fully understood it—this attraction to a woman he hardly knew—he couldn't deal with the problems between Marcella and him. Problems he had never been aware that they had until they moved to this town.

Lately, the few times he and Marcella had been together Cooper became more aware of how little he knew of the woman he had pledged to marry. Maybe he had never known her. Maybe he had been so drawn to the pretty packaging that he hadn't bothered to find out what was inside that parcel. He wouldn't be the first person who was disappointed with the contents of a gift.

Yet if his beloved wasn't the person he first thought her to be, how would he deal with it, or more importantly, how would he explain this to Marcella and her father? Perhaps the two of them just needed more time—to settle into this new town and to get to know each other better. Although he and Marcella had never actually set a wedding date, having known each other for six months, Cooper knew that both she and her father expected the couple to wed before the year's end.

Suddenly it was important to Cooper to have more time. He wasn't about to rush into a marriage now and find in a year or so that he had made a mistake. Taking marriage vows was serious business and would affect the rest of his and Marcella's life. Feeling as he did, the only logical thing to do was push for a longer engagement. He could use the excuse of wanting to establish his business first to make certain he could comfortably support his wife.

He glanced around the room's shabby interior. If Marcella didn't want him living in this rundown building alone, she sure as the devil wouldn't want to live here with him. Yet he had no money that would allow them to live elsewhere. He had purchased the building not only because of its location, but also because the apartment upstairs would serve as his and Marcella's home until he could afford better.

Cooper admitted the rooms weren't much, but with a little paint, some curtains, and a few women's gewgaws, the place could become a home. Not a house like the one that Marcella was used to, but still a comfortable abode.

If after the rooms were fixed up and the idea of living here still appalled her, then they would definitely have to postpone the wedding. She would have to be content to wait until he could afford better because he wouldn't take another cent from her father. If Marcella planned to become his wife, she needed to learn right away that he would be making the decisions, not Jack Kent. In the meantime, he needed to focus on getting to know Marcella better, and then to find a way to exorcise Isabel Gomez from his mind.

"Cooper," Deke called again from the bottom of the stairs. "You've got another visitor."

"Another visitor." At this rate his "at home" would never allow him the time needed to clean these rooms so that he could move into them tonight.

But his spirits lifted when he thought that his visitor might be Isabel. Maybe she had realized that she had caused the argument between him and Marcella and she had come to apologize. If so, Cooper would act as though it were nothing while enjoying seeing the beauty grovel.

Smiling, he called, "I'll be down in a moment."

"That won't be necessary," he heard Jack Kent say. "I'll come up."

"Damn it all."

Jack Kent was the last person Cooper wanted to see. Without further hesitation, he shouted down the stairs, "That won't be necessary! I'll be down." Cooper would be damned if he would allow the man to dictate to him in his own home.

Tossing the broom aside, he descended the stairs before the older man put his foot on the first step. Cooper stopped several feet above him on the staircase and met his stare. "Jack," he said, "how may I help you?"

"Is there a place we can talk in private?"

Deke cleared his throat. "Mr. Adair," he called, "Skor and me, we was just gonna take a break. Need a little liquid to wet our whistles. We'll be back in half an hour."

"Sure, you two go ahead. You deserve a break. You've been working hard all day."

Cooper glanced around the room, noting the men's progress. Already the downstairs was beginning to look more like what he had envisioned. The counter now sat closer to the front doors, and the shelving had begun to take shape on the walls. He wondered what Jack would say when he learned Cooper hadn't used his plans. The older man wouldn't be pleased, but then Cooper knew the purpose of his visit wasn't prompted by his interest in the pharmacy.

He could only wonder what kind of punishment Kent had in store for him for upsetting Marcella. Forty lashes with a wet noodle?

Well, Cooper wouldn't take his punishment lying down. There was no time like the present for him to air some of his own dissatisfaction. Jack might have come here to spout more rules, but when he left, he would have heard a few of Cooper's as well.

Purposely Cooper walked to the front of the room where

the counter now sat, and leaned against it. Jack followed him. They exchanged no words until Jack made certain that the men were no longer in hearing distance and the two of them were alone.

"You made changes," said Jack, glancing around the room.

It was more than obvious with the revised penciled sketch lying on the counter between them. "Yes, sir, I did," Cooper responded. "I appreciate your ideas, but they were a little elaborate for my needs. I apprenticed in a pharmacy in Philadelphia and I know what I want."

"Like this soda fountain." Jack lifted his gaze from the sketch where the words soda fountain were written in black letters across the revised drawings. "Just like I suppose you also want my daughter."

"Yes, sir," he answered.

A month ago Cooper could have answered yes to both of those questions without hesitating, but he felt a little more hesitant now, especially with reference to the latter. He thought he still wanted to marry Marcella, but he also wanted more time.

"Tetote probably won't be happy, but then, maybe I misunderstood the man. You did assure him that you wouldn't be selling spirits. Have your fountain, you can always take it out later."

Cooper didn't respond. The audacity of the man still amazed him, but for the moment, it seemed as though Jack was placating him; telling him he could have his fountain for now, but if it didn't work, he could take it out later. Did the man believe him to be stupid?

"As you are probably well aware of," Jack continued, "I didn't come here to discuss your little shop of curatives."

His words brought to mind his own reference a few days ago when he had made a similar remark to Isabel about her herb business. What had he said? "I'm sure you're very good at whatever you do with your little herbs"? Had his remark to her sounded as mocking as Jack's did to him? Cooper hadn't meant to be scornful. Or had he? Maybe then, but not anymore.

Jack said, "I've come to talk about the wedding."

Kent's statement surprised him, and Cooper leveled his gaze on the older man. "What about it?"

"I think we should go ahead with the wedding. I see no need to wait the usual year. Very few people in this town are aware that the two of you have only known each other for a short period. The sooner you and Marcella are married, the sooner we can move ahead."

Cooper's mouth felt as dry as cotton. He shook his head and tried to think of an appropriate response. Jumping into this marriage wasn't exactly in line with the ideas he had been bouncing around in his head before Jack arrived.

"No offense meant, Jack, but don't you think this is something that Marcella and I should discuss before you and I take it into our hands to move ahead?"

A flash of anger sparked deep in the older man's eyes, but it disappeared as quickly as it had come. "Things are done differently in our circle. Usually a marriage is about the joining of money. We both know that isn't so in this case."

The money thing again.

"Maybe I'm old-fashioned. Maybe I believe in a courtship," Cooper countered. "Man meets woman, he courts her, they fall in love and become engaged, he courts her for the appropriate amount of time, then in a year, or sometimes two years, they marry. Marcella and I have only known each other for six months—"

"Six months is plenty of time."

"Maybe under normal circumstances. But as you can see," he said, glancing around the room, "things here aren't exactly normal.

"As you said yourself, we're new to this town. You've been here for a little over a month, and Marcella and her mother less than that. Me? I haven't even been here long enough to get my feet wet. It's my opinion that we can all use a little time to settle in."

"I'm not saying you should marry her tomorrow, but a September wedding isn't too unreasonable. What say you? Are you in agreement?"

The last thing Cooper wanted was to imply he wasn't in agreement, but he wasn't. He cared deeply for Marcella, but he wasn't about to be railroaded into something he had doubts about. Like marrying a woman he wasn't certain he knew. And this discussion didn't feel right. Instead of discussing his and Marcella's future with her father, Cooper felt he should be discussing it with Marcella. It also bothered him that Jack was in such a hurry for this marriage to take place. Now was as good a time as any for Jack to understand Cooper's standpoint.

"September is less than three months away," Cooper told him. "I've a lot to do, getting my business established. I had hoped to have the apartment upstairs finished, ready for our occupancy once we were married. I don't think—"

Jack scoffed, his tone jeering. "Surely you don't expect my daughter to live in a flat above a shop?" His loathing gaze raked the interior.

"Where else would I expect her to live?" Cooper asked. "I seem to recall when Marcella and I first began this discussion of my purchasing this particular building, we agreed that the apartment upstairs would be a place for us to live until I could build or purchase something better."

Cooper and Marcella had discussed the apartment, but that discussion seemed so long ago and far away that it was almost as though they had never had it. Her reaction this afternoon, when he had mentioned he would be living here, was a good indication that she didn't recall that discussion, or maybe she had purposely forgotten it.

"The house I built here," Jack said, "was designed with the idea that after you and Marcella married you would have your own suite of rooms. It's a big house, much too big for only Evey and me. I planned all along for the two of you to live with us. Marcella decorated the suite of rooms with that in mind. I'll have her show it to you the next time you're over."

Cooper held up his hands. "Hold on a minute. I never agreed to move into your house, and why Marcella would think I would is beyond my comprehension."

"It can be a temporary arrangement, then. I'll give you the money to build your own house. That way you'll only have to live there until your house is finished."

"No, sir. I won't be taking any more money from you. I appreciate everything you've done for Marcella and me, but I won't continually take your handouts."

The look Jack shot him was filled with arrogance. "They were not handouts in the true sense of the word, but I'm not too damn certain I can see the difference."

"Of course not," Cooper replied coldly. "You gave them to us because you love your daughter. And I can appreciate that."

The last thing Cooper wanted was for this conversation to turn into an argument. He didn't want to say things in anger that he might regret later.

"Look, Jack, I appreciate your generosity, but a man has to draw the line somewhere. If he doesn't, then he's no man at all."

As they glared at each other in silence, the air in the room fairly crackled.

Jack was the first to speak. "Not only are you an impertinent pup, you are too damn proud." Kent walked to the doors as though he meant to leave, but he paused on the threshold.

"I'm not certain what went on this afternoon between you and my daughter, because Marcella was too overwrought to relate the incident to me. Yet I've no doubt that it had something to do with your neighbor, which brings us to another point." His demeanor became that of a brigadier general's. "Understand me, young man. I'll not tolerate any sordid behavior between you and that woman. In the future, I suggest you avoid Isabel Gomez completely. If you don't, you and that woman will rue the day you defied my wishes."

Cooper's temper was at a flash point. To keep from exploding, he took several deep breaths. When he felt in control, he said, "While we're on the subject of orders, maybe you should hear me out. I care for Marcella and want a future with her, but you should know, and I'll tell her the same thing, I'm not a puppet on a string. I will not dance to your will."

Jack laughed. "Maybe not a puppet, but a pup, Cooper. I'm an old dog, and a mean one if my whelp is threatened. Believe me when I say when push comes to shove, bigger men than you dance. Especially men who have a lot to lose. Now if you'll excuse me, I must be going."

He started to leave, then stopped. "I'll give you a few days to think about what we've discussed. Since Marcella is temporarily indisposed, she'll send a note when she is ready to receive you. Until then. Good day."

Bastard. For the second time today, the man had provoked Cooper enough to make him want to ram his fist into the wall, or preferably into the older man's face.

He wasn't a man who enjoyed conflict, physical or otherwise, and that was why his anger surprised him. Cooper ran his fingers through his hair and turned back toward the stairs. It wouldn't be wise to confront Jack Kent now. He needed to cool off first. He was about to jog up the stairs, then stopped and swung back toward the entrance.

It was then he saw her, standing outside the storefront windows. She wasn't alone. Isabel Gomez stood in conversation with Jack Kent. Cooper started toward them, but Jack had already turned and walked away, leaving her to stare after him.

What a fine mess he had made of things. Because of him, Isabel had fallen under Jack Kent's fire. Cooper wanted to rush immediately to her defense, but decided that would be the worst thing he could do. He would wait and give Jack time to disappear before he approached her.

Watching her, she didn't appear to be too upset. In fact, she looked more composed than he felt. She still wore the same dress she had worn earlier, and she still looked as beautiful to him as she had then. In her arms she held a huge bouquet of white flowers. Still watching Jack, she dipped her head and buried her nose in the bouquet's center. After a moment she turned and headed in the opposite direction from the way that Jack had gone.

Wait a minute, Cooper cautioned himself. Did Jack even know who Isabel Gomez was? When Cooper saw the two of them talking together, he assumed that Jack was carrying out his threat, or at least warning her away. There was only one way to find out if the older man had threatened her.

Cooper would follow her and ask.

Eighteen

Isabel watched the distinguished gentleman who had stepped from the post building just as she was about to pass. The man, having almost collided with her, had apologized profusely, then lingered a moment to comment on the beauty of her gardenia bouquet. He was an elderly man with graying temples and had inhaled the flower's sweet fragrance before bidding her a good day and continuing down the street.

"What a pleasant man," she said, watching his retreat. There was something to be said for a man who appreciated the beauty of flowers.

Once Cooper's pharmacy opened, many such wealthy gentlemen and their ladies would frequent his fine establishment. The stranger, she suspected, had probably heard the rumor of the fancy new pharmacy that would soon open in town and had come to take a look. Again she wondered how her own business would fare against such competition. The likes of the man who had just left her wouldn't buy her herbs and curatives, but he would have no qualms about buying Cooper's.

Inside the building, it was seemingly quiet. The workmen must have quit for the day. How strange it would be, she thought, to have another business operating within the walls

that her *padre* had built with his own hands so many years
ago.

Isabel sniffed the air; the scent of wood shavings and saw-
dust tickled her nose. To Isabel the fragrance of newly hewn
wood with its clean, lumbery smell had always held the promise of new beginnings. But this new undertaking of Cooper
Adair's was causing her more difficulties than she anticipated.

Try as she might, Isabel couldn't push the altercation between Cooper and the Kents from her mind, knowing that she
was partly responsible. Even after alerting Dora to her perfidy
her guilt had not lessened. When she saw Cooper again, what
would she say to him? Not wishing to hasten that encounter,
she turned back in the direction she had been going when the
nice man bumped into her, and continued on her way.

Evening was fast approaching, and she wanted to deliver
her flowers before dark to the cemetery where her parents
were buried. The delicate blooms of the gardenias didn't last
long once they were picked, and she wanted to share their
beauty with her mother before it faded. Kalee Gomez, like
Isabel, loved the sweet-smelling flowers.

As she neared the City Gate at the north end of St. George
Street, she admired the structure that at one time had sealed
the colony against its enemies. Built as part of the city's de-
fenses, the gate of coquina blocks now remained eternally
open to welcome all who chose to pass through. Isabel smiled
as she scanned the sign attached to the rock. All who passed
through could do so as long as they didn't drive or ride
through the gates faster than a walk. If they did, they would
be fined ten dollars.

Being fined wasn't a worry for Isabel. She was on foot and
moved along at a snail's pace, trying not to spill any of the
water from inside the container that held her bouquet. After
passing the gates, she paused and looked toward the silvery
line of blue water beyond the Castillo de San Marcos, the old
Spanish fortification that was now called Fort Marion. The
greens ran right up to the castle's mote and served as a golf
course for tourists and locals alike. In a few weeks the Fourth

of July celebration with fireworks would take place on the greens with the dance held on the ramparts.

"Right," she said. "I can just see me tripping around the dance floor in my fireball-colored gown." She laughed at the nonsensical picture her mind conjured up, before continuing on her way.

She crossed the street and headed toward the public burying ground. Most of the residents of the cemetery had the Yellow Fever epidemic of 1821 to thank for their final resting place. Because of that epidemic, the grounds had been set aside to inter the dead, and many of St. Augustine's residents had been buried here in the ensuing years.

The iron gates were left open during daylight hours, and Isabel passed through them. On entering the hallowed grounds, the usual calm settled over her. She moved under the ancient oaks whose armlike limbs were draped with robes of Spanish moss.

In the middle of the cemetery, she found the tiny Gomez plot where her mother and father slept side by side. She stood there several moments, clutching against her bosom the cool, damp water container filled with flowers, and offering up a silent prayer for her beloved family. As she buried her nose in the sweet, torrid fragrance of the waxy blossoms, tears stung her lids.

"Isabel?"

She jumped, and water sloshed from the container and spilled against her front. Turning, she saw Cooper Adair. He still wore the work clothes she had left for him this morning, and she thought he looked as handsome in the worn garments as he had in his suit of fine wool. But why was he here?

Not knowing what else to do, Isabel glanced toward the graves, then back at him. "My mother and father," she said.

"I assumed as much when I saw you enter the gates. If you prefer being alone, I'll leave you."

"I'm not alone," she answered. "Not here, anyway."

He looked uncomfortable.

"If you wish to stay. . . ." Her voice trailed off. Of course he could stay. This sacred spot was not hers alone. "This is the public burying grounds."

She looked back at the two graves. Considering his remark about her preferring to be alone, Isabel never felt alone when she visited the cemetery where her parents were buried. It was here she came when she felt the need to escape the living. Like today, she thought.

Maybe her need to seek refuge here today had been more than wanting to bring her parents flowers. Maybe it was due partly to him. In the beginning when she had devised her plan to break up his and Marcella's betrothal, Isabel had believed it was a just one. But she wasn't so certain anymore.

"Can we share a seat?" he asked. He pointed to the low rock that was the height and size of a bench that sat not far away from her parents' graves. There were several such rocks throughout the tiny graveyard. Although Isabel had no idea how they came to be here, she thought of them as meditation rocks, and had on more than one occasion used this particular one for just that.

Cooper remained standing until she took a seat on the stone bench, then he sat down beside her. A closer inspection of her face revealed the glisten of tears in her unusual eyes that looked more brown than gold beneath the deep green of the thick foliage. Cooper's first thought on seeing her tears was that Jack Kent had threatened her, and he felt his temper rise.

"What did he say?" he demanded.

Isabel still held the flowers, the container resting on her lap. "Say? Who?" she asked, puzzled.

"Why, Jack Kent of course."

A twist of pain creased her perfect features when Cooper mentioned Marcella's father's name.

"I—I don't know Jack Kent."

"But I saw him speaking to you. Outside the post building. He didn't threaten you, did he?"

"Threaten me?" Her face registered comprehension. "The man who smelled the flowers? He was Jack Kent?"

"Yes," he answered, resentfulness swelling inside him

"Mr. Kent is not too happy with me at the moment, and I think he holds you responsible."

"Me?"

A rush of color tinted her cheeks, and she dipped her head toward the bouquet. With her face resting among the many blossoms, her flawless skin rivaled the creamy smoothness of the flower's petals.

After a moment she raised her head, swallowed, and looked him straight in the eyes. "I suppose Marcella told him about the cuff links. It was thoughtless of me to return them to you when I did. I guess I didn't think."

Her face turned a deeper shade of red.

"Marcella has a tendency to exaggerate," Cooper responded. "Don't worry, I can handle her." Or he used to think he could; now he wasn't so sure. "But I wouldn't wish Jack Kent's wrath on anyone."

Her shoulders straightened. "Don't worry about me," she answered soberly. "I've had plenty of experience handling men whose actions are motivated by anger." Then, as though realizing she might have said too much, she clamped her lips shut and stared ahead at the two graves.

Suddenly Cooper wanted to know about Wooster Farley, to know if what those men at the Kents' house had said was true. It was important to Cooper that he hear it from Isabel instead of men who spoke in idle gossip.

"I heard about your stepfather, Wooster Farley. If what I heard is true, then I can understand why you didn't appreciate me calling you Miss Farley when we first met. It would also explain why he's not buried there." He nodded his head in the direction of the two graves.

"Buried here? Never." She jumped up from the bench and moved to stand between the two graves. "And if you think I'm cruel," she said, glaring, "I don't care. I have no interest in where the devil is buried."

"Then there was truth to those rumors."

She cut him an icy stare but didn't respond. Instead, she dropped down on her knees between the two graves. After settling the container and tidying the flowers as she wanted them, she stood again. Facing him, she twirled one white blossom between her finger and thumb, watching the motion much like a child watched a toy windmill.

Cooper waited.

"Wooster Farley was a no-good son of a bitch." She lifted her gaze to his as though to gauge his reaction.

If she thought he was going to be shocked by her bluntness, he wasn't. After all, with a woman who wore men's britches in daylight and air bathed buck naked at night, a less venomous response would have been false. This wasn't some frail, hot-house flower who faced him, but a woman who had been as troublesome as a weed from the first moment they met. He believed he knew enough about Isabel Gomez to know that if she didn't like something she said so.

"He married my *madre* so he could steal her property. Maybe you're unaware that women don't have many rights when it comes to owning property, especially women who are part Indian. To make a long story short, for nearly ten years we lived under that man's rule, my mother enduring all kinds of hell at his hands, so that I might grow up and some-day rightfully claim the property that belonged to my father. It wasn't a death blow from his fists that killed her, but the degradation and humiliation she endured all those years she suffered his insults that ate away her spirit like some putrid growth."

"Did he physically abuse her? Or you?"

Isabel dropped her hands to her side. He saw her fists clench. "In the early years, he beat her, but he didn't touch me, although I sensed a number of times he wanted to. I've never understood why he didn't, but it seemed my mother held some threat over him that kept him at bay. And by then whiskey had become his god. You've heard of men worshiping gold? Wooster Farley worshiped whiskey. Fitting, wasn't it, that it was his god that struck him down?"

"And deserving."

His interjection sounded like an amen to his own ears, and

must have sounded that way to Isabel as well. She smiled at him, a slight angelic smile that lit up her face and warmed his insides.

"I've never understood brute mentality of any kind, and I certainly don't believe that a man should raise a hand to strike a woman. Heck, I can't even recall my father raising a hand to punish me."

"Your father?" Isabel said. "Tell me about your family." She left the graves, coming back to stand in front of him.

Cooper saw the big wet circle on her bosom where water from the flower container had sloshed. The sight stirred a long buried memory of his mother when he had seen her dress stained in much the same way. It was after his baby sisters were born, but her bodice had been stained with the overflow of milk. The forgotten memory made him wonder how Isabel would look, suckling a babe against her magnificent breasts.

He realized he was staring, and quickly looked away. He leaned forward on the bench. Clasping his hands together between his knees, he studied his fingers.

"Not much to tell about my family," he said, "except that we were very close. We weren't rich by a long shot, but we lived comfortably. And there was plenty of love to go around."

Isabel sat down beside him again. "There are greater riches than gold," she said.

"True. I always thought I understood that until lately. My father works for the railroad in Philadelphia. He works long hours, but he takes pride in his work. Both of my parents skrimped and saved so they could help put me, the only son, through college and pharmacy school. I hope someday I'll be able to repay them by helping to make their life a little easier in their old age."

"A noble pursuit," Isabel responded. "And I think you will do just that because you want to."

She moved her hand as though to clasp his, but realized the impropriety of such an action and let her hand fall back into her lap. "And your sisters?" she asked.

"They're both married with children of their own. All of them still live in Philadelphia."

"And you? You still wish you lived in Philadelphia with them?"

He glanced sideways at her, knowing that she wished he still lived there.

"I'm not certain what I wish for anymore. I'm glad to have the opportunity to own my own pharmacy, but I'm beginning to wonder if this town is ready for me and my new ideas."

"Ready for you?" Isabel leaned forward as though she meant to capture his gaze. "Of course they're ready for you. Whatever do you mean?"

Cooper stared straight ahead. "The other night at Marcella's home, I met a few local physicians and a saloon owner. None of the gentlemen seemed too impressed with a pharmacist they thought might pose a threat to their own businesses."

He heard her swallow hard. "I don't see how you could pose a threat to their businesses," she said, disbelieving, "especially that of a saloon owner."

Isabel had already admitted the first day they met that his business would threaten hers. But in spite of that threat, she was still willing to allow him the benefit of the doubt.

"Doctors have always filled their own prescriptions," he continued, "and many will continue to do so, especially in rural areas. The saloon owner feared my soda fountain would take customers away from his bar."

Her shoulders stiffened. "You'll not be selling spirits?"

After what Isabel had told him about Wooster Farley, he could well understand her aversion to spirits, and why she wouldn't want whiskey sold anywhere near her home.

"No spirits," he assured her. "The new drink Coca-Cola is made with syrup, not wine."

Her golden eyes grew large. "I've read of the coca shrub, but I never heard of Coca-Cola."

"It's a new tonic and an aid for digestion. A man from Atlanta came up with the formula a few years back. A number of pharmacies in big cities are putting in soda fountains and starting to sell the drink."

"My, my. Sounds fascinating to me. Some fancy, syrupy drink, used as a tonic for digestion."

"Mr. Pemberton also claims the drink imparts energy to organs of respiration as well."

"Imagine that," she said, her cheeks flushed with excitement. "I can't wait to sample—"

When she stopped speaking in midsentence, Cooper looked at her. Her lips were clamped as tightly shut as a terrier's. "I'll be happy to give you a taste," he told her. "My stock should begin to arrive any day now."

"I don't think I'd like it," she said, jumping up from the bench.

"Sure you would." He tilted his head sideways and squinted at her. "I'm sure you'll like it. Everyone does."

"I gotta go," she said, glancing toward the gate.

"Well, I'll go, too." Cooper stood. "We'll walk back together."

"That won't be necessary."

What the devil had come over the woman? Cooper wondered. For a while there, she had been hanging on his every word, showing an interest in his work unlike any Marcella had ever shown. He liked talking with Isabel, sharing a part of himself he had never shared with Marcella.

The thought of his fiancée brought him back to his problem, the reason he had set out to follow Isabel in the first place.

When she moved toward the gates, Cooper reached out and clasped her arm. "Isabel, wait," he said. "If you won't allow me to walk you home, will you please hear me out?"

Nearby the sound of a cricket's *thurr, thurr,* intruded in the cathedral-like silence. Again, as so many times since meeting this woman, Cooper was captivated by her beauty. His heartbeat quickened.

A flash of sunlight from the slowly sinking sun cast a gilded halo around her honey-colored hair. Specks of gold fire danced in the depths of her eyes, and Cooper wanted to pull her into his arms and lose himself in her presence. Above their heads the moss swayed gracefully on the breeze. Floating on that same breeze came the sound of a woman's chippy laughter that shattered the intensity of the moment.

Isabel looked at Cooper's fingers where they gripped her arm, then lifted her gaze to his. Instead of releasing her as he knew he should, he held on and stepped closer. He was so close he could smell the gardenia still clutched in the hand that rested against her heart.

"Tell me what you have to say," she said, "then I must go."

He didn't know how to tell her that he was worried about her, or feared that Jack Kent or even Marcella might cause her harm if she interfered with their plans. Not that he believed Kent's threats would result in violence, but there were ways to hurt a person other than by using force. Isabel had said as much herself about her own mother's destruction.

"Jack Kent wants this marriage between his daughter and me to take place. He's pushing for a September wedding. I don't know why the sudden rush unless Marcella is feeling threatened by your presence." As he spoke, he gently stroked her arm with his thumb. "When he left me this afternoon, he as much as told me to stay away from you. That is why, when I saw you two talking, I assumed he was issuing an ultimatum."

When he finished speaking, their gazes met and held. Her eyes searched his face as though trying to reach into his soul.

"And you, Cooper Adair. What exactly do you want?"

Her question froze them in a stunned tableau until he found the strength to release her arm. He would have answered, but she didn't give him a chance. Instead, she lunged away from him, her footsteps thundering against the sandy path as she fled the cemetery.

In her eagerness to escape him, she dropped the flower she held. Cooper bent and picked it up. The petals were delicately bruised where she had held them, crushed against her bosom

Bruised, but still perfection. Not unlike Isabel.

He searched his heart for an answer to Isabel's question. What *did* he want? Perhaps he no longer knew. Cooper thought he wanted to marry Marcella, but shouldn't a man in love know beyond a doubt the answer to that question when it was put to him?

He knew what he didn't want. He didn't want Isabel to be caught in the crossfire between him and the Kents, knowing that things might easily get dirty if he failed to comply with Jack Kent's wishes.

For now, he would keep his distance from Isabel Gomez. But that didn't mean he wouldn't fight to protect her.

Nineteen

~

Isabel cried all the way home. Why she was crying, she didn't know. Between heart-wrenching gulps that felt as though the organ itself was being ripped from her chest, and with the repeated swipes against her sleeve with a nose that suddenly gushed like Ponce De León's Fountain of Youth, she knew there must be a reason. When she finally closed the gate behind her and headed upstairs to her room, the sleeve of her saffron yellow dress was as wet as the unsightly stain of water across her breasts. The same stain Cooper had noticed and stared at without a blink of an eye even when she knew he was staring.

Once inside her room, Isabel yanked off the gown and tossed it to the floor along with her shoes. With nothing on but her camisole and bloomers, she fought her way through the fall of netting draping the bed and dived onto the fluffy mattress. The cool white linens felt like a balm against her overheated skin. She buried her face in the sunshine-sweet fragrance of the pillows, allowing her emotions to flow freely. Not that they hadn't been doing so for the last ten minutes.

Grimalkin jumped up on the bed and lay on the pillows beside her tear-stained face. It was as though the cat sensed her sadness when he stretched out one furry paw and placed it affectionately against her throat. Then he began his low, rumbly purr that filled up the filmy space like the mumbling of some confessional priest. His golden gaze touched hers with such tenderness and understanding that the tight band of emotion that had constricted her breathing since leaving Cooper behind in the graveyard loosened somewhat.

She sighed heavily. "Oh, Grim," she said. "What a mess I've made of things."

Turning over on her back, she stared at the ceiling. The canopy above her head blurred when a deluge of tears swelled behind her lids and overflowed. After the gush of salty water, the canopy came into focus again.

Isabel didn't weep often. There had been a time, after she had buried her *madre,* that she had lived daily with the watery emotion. Finally the ache of her loss had settled like a heavy rock inside her chest, and eventually even that weight had lightened. Afterward there had been no room inside her for foolish tears. The way Isabel saw it, when a person lost everything that was dear to her, there wasn't much left to cry about. Yet here she was today, and for reasons she didn't understand, she was blubbering like some brokenhearted fool.

"I'll feel better soon," she said, wiping away another watery flux.

On the pillow beside her head, Grim snuggled closer. "Neow, neow," he said.

"In a minute," Isabel assured him.

She turned her face and buried it in the silkiness of his fur, wondering what had happened to the other Isabel who used to dwell inside her skin. The other Isabel knew what she wanted and would do anything in order to achieve that end.

This stranger living inside her was wavering between being "damned if she did, and damned if she didn't," if what Cooper had said was true. Jack Kent was determined to have the marriage between his daughter and Cooper take place, and

Isabel was determined that it wouldn't. She had never intended to bring undue wrath on Cooper, or herself, however, by making Marcella jealous. She just wanted him to disappear into the night, leaving her to continue doing what she had always done: to grow her herbs and to sell her remedies.

But something had happened. Something she hadn't planned on. Isabel had started to care. She was certain now that the sensations she had felt in Cooper's arms the other night were not Grim's doings, but those of her own treasonous heart and body. Even a treasonous heart had loyalties if it cared deeply for someone, and that was why it had hurt her so much when her meddling in his affairs had brought on Marcella's and Jack Kent's anger.

"Poor Cooper," she moaned, "why can't anything be simple?" Sitting up on the bed, Isabel inched backward and leaned against the headboard. "So what am I going to do now?"

Grim appeared happy that his mistress had somewhat recovered from her bout of melancholy, and playfully swatted at a dangling ribbon on her camisole.

Isabel's thoughts drifted. Loving Cooper just wouldn't do. It was bad enough that he was slowly overtaking her every thought. She couldn't allow him to marry that woman and remain here. To do so would ruin her in more ways than one.

"I suppose," she said, searching for a solution in case he didn't leave, "I could get a job as a masseuse at the Ponce when the hotel reopens." The idea no longer appealed to her as it once had, however. The massage she had given Cooper with the chickweed salve had made her realize that touching a stranger's body in such an intimate way would be impossible.

"Or I could marry someone else," she said. "If I had a husband to provide for us, we could stay on in our home indefinitely."

Her last remark captured Grim's attention, because he quit

swatting at the dangling ribbon and looked at her with his big head tilted at an angle. "Ne-oh, ne-oh."

"No? Then what do you suggest I do?"

Annoyed, Isabel jumped up from the bed and traipsed toward the balcony. The cat followed her, and when she stopped to lean against the iron rail, he rubbed against her legs.

The sun had dipped below the horizon, and diffused light blanketed the trees and shrubs. Soon the yard would merge into one indistinct inky shape. Isabel glanced across the courtyard toward the post building, wondering if Cooper had returned, but saw no light inside the darkened windows that proved he had. Unless he, like her, hadn't bothered to light a lamp.

For a long moment she stood staring, her mind replaying the scene in the cemetery. She had enjoyed their conversation, learning about his family and hearing the plans he had for his pharmacy. Their conversation had convinced her that a man like Cooper Adair didn't belong with a woman like Marcella Kent.

Isabel's heart told her she couldn't allow the marriage to take place, not only for her sake, but also for his. If he couldn't see the consequence of such a match, Isabel could. He had come from a family whose members loved and cared for each other. Such an upbringing hadn't prepared him for the unhappiness that would come from such a mismatched union. For Cooper to marry into a family that controlled him would eventually destroy him just as her mother had been destroyed by Wooster.

Jack Kent might believe he could frighten her away with threats, but she wasn't afraid of the Jack Kents of the world. She had lived with Wooster Farley too long to run and hide.

Isabel would continue with her plan. She would flirt, she would beguile, and do everything possible to break off Cooper's engagement. She would save Cooper from a fate she considered worse than death—the tragic end that came from marrying the wrong person.

● ● ●

For Cooper, the week had moved along eventfully. The carpenters finished the shelving, Deke did obtain the piece of marble for Cooper's fountain, and daily the supplies he had ordered before leaving Philadelphia began to arrive by train. Having served his apprenticeship in a very modern establishment, Cooper knew how he wanted to stock his pharmacy, and slowly his drugstore was beginning to take shape.

He had seen Marcella only once since the afternoon she had visited his shop. Her father had said on his visit that she was under the weather and would send a note around when she wished to see him. The note had come, asking him to join the family for Sunday dinner, and surprisingly the afternoon had passed quite pleasantly. Marcella had been more like the girl Cooper remembered from Philadelphia, and he had been blessedly thankful that Jack had left them to their own devices, giving Cooper a chance to spend some time alone with Marcella.

The early wedding date was not mentioned by either Marcella or Jack, and the omission of the topic suited Cooper. He had made up his mind prior to his visit that he wouldn't be pushed into an earlier wedding date. There were other factors that needed considering, and one of those was his feelings for Isabel.

After their conversation in the cemetery, Cooper had done a lot of thinking about her. He hadn't seen her to talk with her again, and he suspected she had taken his advice that they stay away from each other. It was best that she keep her distance, but that didn't stop Cooper from wanting to be with her.

He still watched for her. After their talk, he had moved into the apartment upstairs. If Jack were to try some form of skulduggery, Cooper wanted to be close enough to protect her. That same evening he had seen Isabel on her balcony, looking across the yard toward the post. Although it was dusk, he saw she had shed her dress and wore nothing but her camisole and bloomers. Even across the distance of the yard, his body had reacted to the sight of her, confirming in Cooper's mind that a man couldn't have an obsession for one woman and consider marrying another woman.

Throughout the last few days, he had caught glimpses of her going about her chores. It was apparent Isabel enjoyed working. He watched her when she dug in the yard, when she went to the well for water, and wherever he saw her, she always seemed to be administering to something: her plants the many women he saw coming and going, or her ever faithful cat. The more he watched her, the more he wanted to get to know her better, and the more he realized that such a possibility was hopeless.

If he couldn't be near Isabel, at least he had the companionship of her cat. Many times when Cooper was busy stocking his shelves, he would be jerked from his concentration by a feeling that he was being watched. He would turn to find Grimalkin perched on an empty chair, or shelf or windowsill, his golden gaze drilling into Cooper's back

For a man who had always scorned cats, it seemed strange that a cat had become his most accepted companion. Since the night Grimalkin had saved his skin by not revealing Cooper's hiding place in the bushes, the two of them had reached a comfortable truce. There were times in the past week when he had actually carried on a conversation with the furry feline one-sided as it was.

Cooper looked up from what he was doing to see the object of his growing affection jump up on the flat newel post at the bottom of the stairs. Comfortably settled, the cat gazed incuriously at nothing.

"So, sphinx," Cooper said, "how is your mistress faring?"

Although Grimalkin had the head and body of a cat, Cooper sometimes suspected he had the mind of a man.

"Keep a close watch on her, will you? If she needs me, roar."

"Neow, neow?"

"No, not now. When she needs me."

Cooper turned his back on the cat and looked toward the front of the store, where he saw several women strolling. On seeing them, and hoping they would come inside, he moved to where Grimalkin perched and placed him down on the floor.

"Off with you, you ol' fuzzbudget," he said, knowing it wouldn't help his business for any prospective customers to believe he didn't run a clean establishment.

The ladies paused and stared at the colored water show globes he had placed in both windows. They talked among themselves for a few minutes, then continued on their way.

Although he hadn't officially opened for business, his doors were open, and he had made a few small sales. Cooper was eager to show a profit so he could apply for a loan from the local bank to pay back the money he owed Jack Kent.

He knew when he went into business for himself that it would take time for him to get established. But his indebtedness to Jack weighed heavily on his mind. Cooper didn't like the strings attached to Jack's loan, and every day he liked them less. The sooner he could settle the debt, the better he would feel. Even if he and Marcella eventually married, he didn't want to owe her father money.

The realization of what he had just told himself hit him like a cold drink of water. When had he started thinking in terms of *if* he and Marcella married instead of *when?*

"Mr. Adair," a woman said from the side door. "I've come to try your Coca-Cola."

Cooper swung to face the speaker. He recognized her immediately because a person didn't forget someone as homely as Miss Gay. She stepped through the entrance, and his gaze went beyond her to her companion. He knew the moment he

saw Isabel when the *if* and *when* had begun. It began when
he first met Isabel Gomez.

"Isabel." Then, recalling that they were supposed to avoid
each other, he said, "You're not supposed—"

"We've come to try Mr. Pemberton's cola," she said, not
allowing him to finish. "I've been telling Dora about the new
drink, and we both can't wait to try it."

"Do you think that's a good idea?" His gaze lingered on
her lovely face where a hint of a teasing smile turned up her
lips.

"Why, of course it is," she responded, "unless the drink is
made with wine instead of syrup as you claimed."

"I assure you I don't sell spirits."

He smiled. It pleased him that she remembered their discussion about the popular drink.

Today Isabel wore an electric blue dress that put Cooper
in mind of the colored liquid in several of the show globes
in his front window. He, like other druggists, used colored
liquids in bottles to impress his customers, but Isabel in her
vibrant blue dress was doing some impressing of her own.

He liked the style of her clothes. Heck, if he wasn't such
a coward, he would admit that he even liked her in britches,
or in nothing at all.

But as to the style, Cooper had glanced through enough
women's magazines while deciding what he would stock in
his store to recognize the design. It was inspired by fashion
reformers—those who claimed that women's clothes were un-
healthy, uncomfortable, or just plain ugly. Alternative dresses
were what they had been dubbed, and the looser style suited
Isabel.

This one, like the gold one she had worn the last time he
talked with her, skimmed her bountiful curves. A ruff of ivory
lace encircled her neck and the cuffs of the loose-fitting
sleeves. Raisin-sized jet buttons marched in two rows up the
dress's front, from neckline to hemline.

Her glorious honey-gold hair was pulled back from her
face, secured with a black velvet ribbon at her nape. Her

eyes were round with wonder as she contemplated the interior of his store. But it was Dora who commented on the changes.

"Why, Mr. Adair," she exclaimed, "I do believe you've accomplished miracles in this old building."

"Slowly but surely," he responded.

Cooper was proud of the way the interior was shaping up, and he decided to expound on its success.

"I chose this building because of its layout," he said, glancing at Isabel, whose expression had turned wary.

As much as she might regret selling the post to him, it was time she got used to the idea. Cooper hadn't come all this way to give up and go back. He was determined to succeed. Besides, his finances didn't allow for failure.

"The room's rectangular shape allowed me to place the soda fountain near the entrance. Eventually I'll purchase stools and tables for my customers."

Cooper pointed toward the side walls. "Those showcases will display tobacco, medical accessories, and toiletries. If you'll notice the shelves behind the cases, you'll see I've already stocked them with bottles and packages of proprietaries."

He allowed them to look their fill, then he faced the back of the room. "That's my prescription counter with the medicines I'll use in compounding." All three of them moved toward the counter.

"Such pretty bottles," Dora said, "all matched and orderly."

"I picked out the matching bottles myself as well as the gilt-edged labels." Winking at Isabel, who quickly looked elsewhere, Cooper continued. "I also like things neat and organized. Like your laboratory, Isabel."

If she heard his remark, she ignored it.

Cooper moved behind the prescription counter and pulled out several drawers. "Isabel," he said, motioning her over, "you'll appreciate these. These drawers are for storing herbs and packaged drugs."

"Nice," she mumbled, then quickly turned away.

He glanced at Dora, who appeared indifferent as well. After a moment he cleared his throat. "I don't figure I'll need a stove in this climate, but if it does turn cold, there is always the fireplace."

Dora moved closer to Isabel, and he saw her squeeze her arm. "My, my, Ysabel, would you look at all those advertisements?" She pronounced it *ad-vert-is-ments*. "Never knew there were so many products."

"When I've finished stocking the shelves," Cooper said, "I'll hang those posters on the walls." He brushed his hands over the front of his white shirt, then moved toward the front of the store. "Now that we've finished my little tour, I'll get you that drink you came for."

As he reached the soda fountain, he ran his hand affectionately over the marble top. "I'm proud of this piece of marble that Deke, the carpenter, procured for me. Because he sold it to me for such a fair price, I promised him, and the other members of his family, a free cola every day for the next year."

When the ladies laughed, Cooper wondered what he had said that was so funny.

"I hope you realized when you made that promise," Dora said, "what a big family Deke Jacob has." She cut her glance toward Isabel. "His wife, Mattie, just gave birth to her tenth."

Cooper felt color creep from his white starched collar. So what if he would be out twelve glasses of cola a day that over a year's time would amount to four thousand, six hundred and twenty drinks.

"No matter," he said, "this piece of marble is well worth the price."

He moved behind the counter. Lined against the back wall were several glass decanters filled with different kinds of syrup. After dispensing soda water into two glasses along with the syrup, he handed each lady a glass.

Soft drinks were called soft to distinguish them from alcoholic, or hard, beverages. They were made from soda water, flavorings, and sugar. Besides the cola syrup, Cooper had other syrups he could mix to make the effervescent drinks.

While the women drank, Cooper watched Isabel. He could tell the bubbles from the carbonated liquid tickled her nose. She looked at him above the glass's rim. Their eyes met and held, and Cooper felt a flutter of excitement inside his stomach as though he not her had swallowed the bubbly soda. After draining her glass, she licked her lips. "It's good, but I think I prefer my sweet tea."

"I like it," Dora said, smacking her lips. She finished off her own drink and looked at Isabel. "I can't wait for Ralph to try this."

The women returned their glasses to the counter, and Dora asked, "How much we owe you?"

"The drinks are on me," he said.

"If you keep giving away your products," Dora said, "you'll have to close up shop for sure and move back to Philadelphia. Especially when Deke Jacob's large brood collects their year's worth of free drinks."

"You ladies let me worry about that," Cooper said.

"Won't you please let us pay you?" Isabel asked. "We didn't come in here for a free drink."

"I know that." Cooper removed their empty glasses from the marble top and placed them in a pan of water beneath the counter. "We'll just say that I'm paying you back, Isabel. Now we're even."

"Even?" Dora looked from one to the other.

"Yes. Isabel brought me some of her delicious biscuits and homemade honey, and she shared a glass of that sweet tea she prefers." He sent Isabel a private look. "And of course I can't forget the chickweed salve or the gift of the clothes."

While he recited the list of things Isabel had shared with

him, he felt Miss Gay's eyes watching them both.

Dora cocked one thin brow and looked in Isabel's direction. "Right neighborly of you," she said. "All things considered, I think it only fitting that we accept Mr. Adair's hospitality. Besides, if he keeps giving away his profit he will soon be closing his doors and leaving." She sent Isabel a wide smile.

Isabel's cheeks colored, and she clamped her hand around Dora's arm. "I think we've taken up enough of Cooper—Mr. Adair's time, don't you, Dora?"

He watched as Isabel steered—no, pulled—her friend toward the side entrance. Before the two exited, Dora slammed to a stop. "I suppose, Mr. Adair, you'll be attending the Fourth of July celebration?"

"I suppose—"

"With your betrothed, I take it?"

"Probably—"

"I'm certain it will turn out to be a very enlightening afternoon." She glanced at Isabel and shook free of her hold. "My Ralph is in charge of shooting off the fireworks. By the way, everyone wears patriotic colors for the festivities. Ysabel is wearing red."

As far as Cooper could tell, Isabel was already wearing red. Her face was the color of an overripe apple. "That's nice," he replied, but he was uncertain why he was the recipient of this last bit of information.

He followed along behind the two women, looking over the head of the much shorter one. Without stopping, Isabel darted into the yard, making Cooper question why she had left in such a hurry, and without bidding him farewell.

"I guess we'll see you then," Dora said, exiting after her friend, and following along behind her. Midway across the yard, Dora stopped, turned, and shouted, "Thank you for the drink, Mr. Adair! You just keep right on giving away free stuff, and you'll be out of business in no time."

"I'll do that," he called back.

As he watched Isabel disappear inside her house, something clicked in Cooper's head. If he didn't know better, he would believe that behind Miss Gay's words lay an ulterior motive.

Twenty

The day of the Fourth of July celebration dawned with crystal clarity. It was as though the day itself had dressed for the festivities with the sun the color of a fireball, the white clouds the color of spun sugar candy, and the sky a brilliant shade of blue. True to Dora Gay's words, most of the celebrants were also decked out in patriotic colors of red, white, and blue.

The festivities began with a parade of yachts and all other manner of floatable vessels, whose bows and sterns were decorated with ribbons, banners, and flags. The sea craft glided in succession across the blue-green waters of Mantanzas Bay, whose surface was marked only by ruffles of irregular patterns made by a cat's-paw breeze. Gathered along the seawall, the townspeople looked on while an Army band on permanent duty at the St. Francis Barracks played John Philip Sousa's "The Stars and Stripes Forever," along with a medley of other marching tunes.

It was bloody hot in the shade and boiling hot in the sunshine, as was typical for Florida in the middle of summer, and appropriate for the annual Fourth of July celebration.

The town folk didn't dare complain about the heat because there had been a few times in the past when the yearly event had been visited by stormy weather, canceling the festivities altogether. Even the stifling, sizzling heat was preferable to a gullywasher rain.

Cooper stood among the revelers next to Marcella, her parents, and a gathering of their mutual friends. Many he recognized from his first dinner at the Kents' home, and the smattering of those he didn't recognize, he wasn't so certain he wanted to know as the day dragged on.

It was clear that those gathered around him considered themselves superior to the others. Not only did they look down their less-than-aristocratic noses at the surrounding mob, but they also did it from beneath a candy-striped canopy erected specifically for the chosen few.

Despite the covering, where those beneath it believed they had an inherent right to be, Cooper would have preferred to be elsewhere. Away from the heat of the suffocating canopy, and away from the smothering crush of too many bodies. But when he had suggested his preference to Marcella, she had looked at him as though he had asked her to remove her clothing, instead of herself.

So much for his longed-for breath of fresh air. Miserable, he remained crowded in among the others, whose feet tapped and hands clapped in rhythm with the music, and wished like hell that he could be somewhere else. Miserably hot and thirsty, he found himself longing for a drink of that loathsome, rotten-egg-smelling water while he purposely searched the crowd.

Finding a certain red dress would be near impossible. Undaunted, he searched anyway, his gaze sweeping the length of colorful, bobbing parasols and straw bowlers that curved along the seawall like a Chinese dragon kite.

Searching . . . searching for his obsession. Searching . . . searching for a woman who burned like a feverish sun in his mind.

Isabel stood beside Dora and Ralph at the end of the Yacht Club pier. She was thankful that she had friends in high places who afforded her such a delightful view not only of the many boats that glided past the end of the pier, but also of the spectators gathered along the seawall.

Because Ralph was in charge of the fireworks, he and his guests had been invited to review the parade from this choice spot, along with the other volunteers on the Fourth of July planning committee. It had been thoughtful of Ralph and Dora to include her, but because the three had been friends since childhood, it was natural that they should attend the festivities together. Ralph was almost as good a friend as Dora, and nothing could have made Isabel happier than when her two very best friends decided to tie the matrimonial knot.

On the bank she could see the military band. The musicians' polished instruments were as shiny as gold doubloons where the sun's rays touched them before tossing them heavenward again. The bay's surface sparkled like twinkling diamonds, and colors as vivid as any Jacob's coat adorned the crowd gathered along the seawall, adding to the overall colorful view. And the smell, Isabel thought, was heaven itself; the air was scented with the breath of the briny sea and the whole pigs that roasted in pits on shore.

Isabel didn't have to wonder where Cooper would be standing. He, along with the other town elite, would be gathered beneath the candy-striped awning. She could only imagine the heat radiating from that barred shelter, and was thankful again that she wasn't that rich. Yet she hated to think of Cooper having to endure such torture all for the sake of status.

Not that Isabel thought for a moment that he was standing among the others because he felt it was his place. The more she learned about the man, the more she believed that position wasn't something Cooper aspired to. No. Today he would be sweltering beneath the canvas canopy because it was expected of him to do so. And Isabel believed that duty was as much an intrinsic part of Cooper's makeup as was his breathing.

He believed in upholding his responsibilities. It was his responsibility to see that his parents' lives would be easier, his responsibility to protect her from the Kents by ignoring her, his responsibility to his betrothed, and lastly, his responsibility to succeed.

But Isabel had responsibilities, too. This evening when the dancing began, she would put on the show of her life in order to drive a rift between Cooper and Marcella. In her siren red dress, she would become the enchantress whose sweet song would lure Cooper away from his death, instead of to it, and by so doing, she would suffer the fate of having her own heart shatter into a million pieces.

Cooper must leave St. Augustine. It was the only way that either of them could survive. She couldn't allow him to marry a woman as shallow as Marcella Kent who would unquestionably lead him to his destruction. If he stayed, not only would he be destroyed, but Isabel would be destroyed as well. Her business couldn't compete with his modern drugstore with the wooden showcases, special drawers, fancy labeled bottles, fine marble-top soda fountain, and the very ambience of the place. But the most difficult task she would face this night would be to resist the pull of the man who was fast becoming her Lorelei.

"Ysabel—Ysabel?"

Dora's voice pulled Isabel out of her musings. She blinked, seeking out her friend in the crowd. As Dora and Ralph approached her, they fairly glowed with the love they felt for each other. Isabel was happy for them, but also a little envious.

Today the happy couple was dressed alike. Ralph, with his bald head and bulbous nose, wore a red, white, and blue striped shirt with his navy trousers, and Dora wore a red-white-and-blue-striped bodice with her navy skirt. Dora had made both Ralph's shirt and her bodice. On their heads they wore matching straw bowlers trimmed with festive ribbons.

When they reached her, they stopped. "Silly me," Dora said. "I'd forgotten you were wearing that huge hat." She tapped her forehead as though to jog her memory. "I don't know where my head is today."

"In the clouds," Isabel told her friend. "I saw it float by just a moment ago."

Ralph laughed. "It's called love," he said, beaming. "If you don't mind, hon, I'm going to leave you with Isabel. Me and a few other fellows are going over to the livery to start loading up the wagon with the fireworks." He pecked his intended affectionately on the cheek. "I'll see you ladies at dinner."

They watched Ralph join the crowd, then disappear into the throng of others rushing to exit the pier.

Everyone would now move to the greens that skirted Fort Marion to take part in the planned activities. There would be games of horseshoe, potato races, sack races, apple bobbing, and more until it was time for everyone to share the gut-splitting, potluck picnic served on the grounds. Soon after supper the dancing would begin, and once the sun set, there would be a fireworks display over the water.

"I have to admit," Dora said when they finally joined the exiting crowd, "you look lovelier than ever. It's that dress. The style and color suit you perfectly, and I even like your hat."

Isabel blushed, feeling uneasy with the compliment. "You mean you like my fishing hat?" she said, teasing. "The one I wear with my scandalous britches?"

"The scandalous britches that you *used* to wear," Dora reminded her. "You did say you were giving them up."

"Temporarily."

"Ysabel." She clamped her lips shut and sent her a disbelieving look. "Not temporarily," she reminded, "and I'm still amazed at the transformation of that old hat. I never knew you were such an accomplished miller."

Isabel hooted. "Grinding grain is not one of my strong suits, unless maybe I can grind some sense back into your head."

"Oops! I meant milliner. I am kinda witless lately. It's just that I'm so excited about everything. Ralph, the wedding, today, tonight . . ."

The two women moved toward the seawall at a worm's
pace, waiting for the crowd to thin.

"Sometimes it's scary," Dora continued, "how perfect my
life is. I keep looking over my shoulder, thinking something
dreadful is going to happen to ruin it all."

"Dora Gay, I don't want to hear such talk. Nothing is going
to happen."

She shrugged her shoulders. "I suppose I know I'm being
silly and selfish. We should be concentrating on getting rid
of your problem instead of me worrying about a problem I
don't have."

The two stopped when they approached the narrow walk
way that led to shore and the promenade beyond.

"You're going to blow Mr. Adair's socks off when he sees
you in that dress."

"Well, then, I hope he washed his feet."

Dora threw back her head and laughed. "I can't imagine a
man who looks like Cooper Adair having smelly feet."

Isabel chuckled. "In this heat, more than feet will be smell
ing."

"It is hot enough to melt candles. I knew I should have
brought my parasol, but the darn thing is such a bother."

"I agree," Isabel said. "That's why I decorated this old hat
It keeps the sun from cooking my brains, and I carry it on
my head instead of in my hand."

"Mind if I get under it with you?"

"What is it they say? Two heads are better than one."

It was some thirty or forty minutes later when the two of
them finally made it to the fort greens. The tables for the food
had been placed beneath a copse of trees close to the water
Numerous booths that dotted the field were selling lemonade
tea, and water. Already people were lined up, seeking drink
to quench their thirst.

Dora led Isabel toward the tables. "Earlier Ralph spread
my blanket over there beneath that palm. It might be cooler
if we set a spell and allow the lines to thin before we attempt
to get something to drink."

"You're a girl after my own heart."

After fording the field, they collapsed on the blanket, happy
sit after their long trek in the heat.

Dora peeled off her soiled gloves and tossed them on the
blanket. "In this hundred-degree heat, wearing gloves is ri-
culous. You were smart to leave yours at home."

"I don't own any," Isabel replied, "except my gardening
loves, and I don't think they would have gone well with this
ess."

She inched back against the tree trunk and stretched her
gs out in front of her. Not wearing stays definitely had its
dvantages. Poor Dora. She wasn't so lucky. Her friend sat
ross from her as rigid as a birdcage, with her legs curled
deways.

She squinted at the sun. "I can't see anyone taking part in
e games in this heat."

"I can't see why you tortured yourself by lacing on a corset
this heat," Isabel said. "If you don't swoon before this
ternoon is over, I'll eat my hat."

"Then you'll be as uncomfortable as I am. Besides, unlike
ou, I'm used to wearing stays. They aren't so tight that I
n't breath."

Isabel nodded her head. "There's a lot to be said for Con-
ela's taste in clothes. Never again will I subject myself to
at instrument of torture or any dress that requires it."

"May I remind you, you don't need such an instrument.
nlike me, you're tall and thin."

"There's your father." Isabel raised her hand and waved at
r. Gay.

"Shucks. I just remembered I promised to help him orga-
ze the potato race." Dora rolled to her feet. "You want to
lp?"

"Are you mad? No, I don't want to help. I prefer sitting
ght here, listening to the wind rustle the palm fronds over
y head, enjoying the festivities as an observer instead of a
rticipant."

"What wind?" Dora looked at the fronds overhead as she

donned her gloves. "Duty calls. I must go and assist hir
Will you be all right alone?"

"Land sakes, Dora. You're not my hostess. I'll be fine. C
help your father. He looks as if he can use some help."

"Well, then. I'll see you later."

Isabel watched her friend scurry across the greens to whe
a group of children and adults were gathered. Mr. Gay sto
in the center of the gathering, holding up spoons and potatoe
Allowing her gaze to wander, she saw another assembly
people lining up for the sack race.

Farther down, a game of horseshoes was underway. T
clink-clink sound that the shoes made when they hit the me
stake echoed above the other noise. Horseshoes appeared
be the favorite among the male attendees. They must ha
placed a few wagers, she thought as she heard the applau
and booing as each participant threw his shoes.

She leaned back against the smooth bark of the tall cabba;
palm and closed her eyes, listening as the fronds above h
head clacked like so many hens scratching in the grass. The
was a wind in spite of what Dora thought. With the wind t
aroma of the roasting pigs increased, making Isabel's stoma
rumble with hunger. Ignoring the rumble, she relaxed ev
more, the roar of noise slowly fading to a distant hum, a
she dozed.

That was how Cooper found her, propped against a pal
her eyes closed, or what he could see of them, beneath h
floppy-brimmed straw hat. There was something vaguely f
miliar about the headpiece, but he felt if he had seen the h
before, he would have remembered it.

The straw was stained a berry red, he supposed in keepi
with her red dress. A red, white, and blue band circled t
crown, and a similar band secured it beneath her chin. /
ostrich feather and a dozen or so miniature flags, no bigg
than his hand, decorated the straw surface. A suitable hat f
today's celebration, as was the lady who wore it.

He stole a quick glance at her bare arms and long grace
neck. The neckline of the dress showed an alarming amou

f cleavage, but alarming, he assumed, complemented today's
elebration with bells and firecrackers. When it came to this
woman, however, Cooper didn't need any reminders to alert
im to the danger she imposed.

"There you are," Marcella said, coming from the far side
f the tree. "I thought you were getting us drinks, and here
ou—" She stopped in midsentence when her gaze landed on
sabel, whose eyes had just popped open on hearing voices
lose to her.

For a moment she looked disoriented, and touched the brim
f her hat. "I—I must have fallen asleep."

Marcella's dark brown gaze traveled from the tips of Isa-
el's shoes that stuck up like painted desert rocks beneath her
ed skirt, skimmed across her lap, stopping on the low neck-
ne of her gown. She turned an angry gaze on Cooper before
winging away from him and stalking back in the direction
he had come.

"You're in trouble," Isabel said, tilting her head back so
hat she could see him better.

Torn, he squirmed. He knew what he wanted to do. He
anted to linger and talk with Isabel instead of hurrying after
Marcella, but his concern for Isabel's safety won out. If he
new Marcella, she had probably set a course straight for her
ather in order to reveal Cooper's whereabouts. He wanted to
aylay her before she reached Jack.

"Excuse me," he said, and trotted after his betrothed like
n obedient dog.

"Damn it all, Marcella, wait." For the first time today, Coo-
er was thankful for the milling crowd, because it hampered
er escape. His fingers clamped around her arm, jerking her
a stop. "Please—"

"She's a witch," Marcella accused.

"A witch?"

Had she also seen Isabel air bathing? Of course she hadn't.
ven if she had, it didn't mean anything except that Isabel
njoyed air bathing.

"Don't be ridiculous, Marcella. You shouldn't make such an accusation—"

"She's bewitched you."

"Bewitched me?" He tried to calm her. "You're the only one who has me bewitched. It's you who holds me spellbound."

For a moment Cooper thought he had quelled her concern. She appeared to relax, and no longer made a beeline to where her father stood among his peers.

"I have it on good notice," she continued, "that Isabel Gomez is a witch. Edwina told me as much."

"Maybe you misunderstood her."

"I most certainly did not." Marcella stood a little taller and looked him straight in the eye. "She deals in potions, does she not?"

"I deal in potions. Are you going to accuse me of being a warlock?"

"Of course not. But I know you. And don't try to turn the tables." She started to move away, then stopped. "Think about it, Cooper. She cast a spell on you from the first moment you met her. First the kiss, then she stole the cuff links I gave you. And she does have a black cat." Her eyes grew round, her expression serious. "You know a cat is a witch's famil-family."

Cooper couldn't deny two parts of her scenario—the spell and the cat. She had his cuff links because he had left them in her garden room, but he didn't think Marcella would be interested in hearing the real how and why of that. But he had to put an end to her nonsense.

"She also has a broom, Marcella. I've seen her sweeping with it."

"Don't be droll."

"Droll is the last thing I'm trying to be. I just want you to realize that everything you have accused her of can be justified with logic. I already explained about the kiss and the cuff links. As far as her cat, the animal is a pet and is the only family she has. Lots of people own pets."

"She's wearing that red-devil dress. You know witches are in cahoots with the devil."

Cooper lifted the straw bowler Marcella had insisted he wear and slammed it back on his head. "Look around you, my love. Half the women here today are wearing red."

Marcella hesitated. "But it looks different on her."

Cooper couldn't be more in agreement, but he could see Marcella was yielding. "Please," he said, "can't we put this conversation behind us? Walk with me to the concession stand, and we'll get a drink together."

"Daddy will wonder where I am."

To hell with Daddy. "Marcella. I'm dying of thirst and I'm going to get a drink. Either you come with me or go back to where I left you, and I'll join you there in a moment."

"I'm going back," she said, turning and walking away. "No matter what you say, I still believe that woman has cast a spell on you."

He watched her until she disappeared into the crowd, then he, too, turned and walked away. But in the opposite direction.

The potluck supper included entrees of roasted pig, fish, shrimp, frog legs, and oysters fresh from the sea with platters of hush puppies, eggplant espoñole, collard greens, avocado salad, fresh sliced tomatoes, spanish rice, cheese grits, and various other items for fillers. To the delight of all the diners, the desserts consisted of guava pie, jellied grapefruit with pecans, pecan pie, pecan puffs, persimmon pudding, crystallized kumquats, spice cake, spanish custard, and spanish flan, all to be washed down with strong chicory coffee. After sharing the gastronomic feast, it was time to begin the more serious exercise of dancing.

Those who weren't too tired, or too full from dinner, made the trek across the mote bridge into the fort, and then climbed the coquina stairs that led to the designated dance area on the ramparts of Fort Marion.

The stone fortification, built from shellstone quarried on

nearby Anastasia Island in the year 1695 with its impenetrable walls, had protected early St. Augustians from attack by their enemies. Tonight the thick, solid walls of the Castillio protected its occupants from yet another fate—collapsing after they had gorged themselves on the huge feast.

A warm wind that had begun blowing earlier in the afternoon became more pleasant and cooler in the evening. Once the sun began to set, people with sunburned faces and limbs and sweat-dampened clothes began to cool as well, and soon the dancing began in earnest.

When Isabel, Dora, and Ralph finally reached the ramparts, Isabel wasn't certain she had the energy to dance if someone should ask her. Yet she had come here with a purpose, her mission to make Marcella angry enough to break off her engagement with Cooper.

With this thought foremost in Isabel's mind, she searched the ramparts for Cooper's party. Spotting them, she straightened her shoulders, thrust out her bosom, held her head, minus her hat, a little higher, and tried to appear as though she was having the time of her life. In truth, she wished she were home in bed curled up beside Grimalkin.

Isabel had decided earlier that making Marcella jealous wouldn't be too difficult. All Cooper needed to do was cross Isabel's path, and Marcella would go off in a tiff just as she had done this afternoon. What was so comical about the earlier episode was that she and Cooper hadn't uttered a word to each other, yet Marcella had immediately assumed the worst.

Why? Was it Marcella's fear of losing the man she loved to another, or did she resent another's success? Isabel suspected the latter, and she pitied the stupid girl. To have a man like Cooper Adair love her as he appeared to love Marcella was to Isabel a rare and special gift. Cooper was a sensitive, good, and devoted man, and in Isabel's experience with men there weren't many of that type around.

A small number of musicians had gathered under one of the fort's four turrets, and would supply this evening's music.

Already a tune floated above the surrounding walls, luring dancers onto the floor. Because of the men stationed at the St. Francis Barracks in town, there were always plenty of young men looking for dancing partners at functions such as this one. Isabel soon found herself whirling around the ramparts along with the other dancers.

She and her partner glided toward the town's elite who stood apart from the others in attendance. Spotting Cooper, her heart clobbered her ribs, almost making her miss a step. Cooper and Marcella stood in conversation with the distinguished man Isabel now recognized to be Jack Kent. Nearing the trio, Isabel tossed her head, fluttered her eyes at her partner, gave him a beauteous smile, then laughed as though he had just made her privy to some wonderfully funny story.

Her action afforded her the desired response not only from her partner, but also from the icy blue gaze that Cooper sent her way, along with an irritating look from Marcella. Cooper sipped from the drink he held in his hand. Although he appeared to be listening to the conversation taking place around him, Isabel knew his concentration was focused on her. The power she felt with that look was as heady as the finest wine.

"Where have you been all my life?" the gentleman whose name was Roderick Duval asked. "I've never seen you at these functions before."

"My name's Consuela," she said.

Isabel suspected he had probably seen her at other functions, but he wouldn't have noticed her. Dressed tonight in Consuela's beautiful gown, Isabel had been transformed into someone even she didn't recognize. It was only fitting that she should assume her benefactor's name for one night.

Isabel had never learned the art of flirting, but she had read many books about heroines who did. Tonight she would pretend that she was one of those fictional characters, and act out the role of an exciting, elusive, and mysterious female. After tonight, she most likely never would encounter this man again, but she would do her best to make certain that he would remember the enchantress he had danced with in the red ball gown.

Fingers clasped, she twirled away from him, then twirled expertly back into his arms. The movement made her gown swirl out like a trumpet-shaped morning glory, then close to cling to her hips and legs like the retiring blossom it became with nightfall.

"You're enchanting," her partner said, "and I want to know more about you."

Her prince had dark good looks, and in his uniform he cut a handsome figure, but his handsomeness failed in comparison to Cooper's.

"I can't figure out why I don't know you," he rambled on. "I thought I knew most of the young belles in town."

They swirled by Cooper and his party again, and this time not only did Isabel capture and hold Cooper's attention, but also the attention of Marcella's father. It wasn't admiration she saw in the depths of Jack Kent's gaze, but derision.

Her partner claimed her for several more dances, and soon Cooper led Marcella onto the floor. They made an impressive couple; him tall, her short, his blond good looks beside her darker beauty.

Even Roderick noticed the petite brunette dressed in the pale pink ensemble with embroidered miniature roses scattered over the gown's length. Even as petite as Marcella was, she still managed to look down her nose at the two of them.

Bending slightly toward his partner to hear what she said, Isabel thought Cooper had never looked more handsome. He looked the part of a gentleman planter in his dark trousers, white shirt, and a silk vest tailored from the same fabric as Marcella's dress. The matching fabrics stated to everyone present that the two of them were a couple.

As they passed beneath glowing lanterns, Marcella's cuff links winked from Cooper's cuffs. When Isabel saw them flashing, it was like a warning light going off inside her head, leaving no doubt that the man in Marcella's arms was as securely in place as those blasted buttons in his sleeves. Not for long. . . .

She was about to maneuver closer to catch the couple's attention when a flash of blazing light lit the sky, scattering smoke and crystal white stars across the velvet canvas. The fireworks display had begun.

Isabel had been so busy dancing and playing the part of a coquette, she hadn't even noticed how dark it had become, or that Ralph and Dora had left the ramparts.

Dora had told her earlier that she would accompany Ralph to the launching sight. The designated area was on a clear patch of ground close to the water's edge and a safe distance away from the fort's walls. Isabel moved along with the others to the wall bordering the bay, and Roderick Duval accompanied her. They stood shoulder to shoulder among the other spectators, gazing in wonder as the brilliant exhibition lit up the sky.

From Isabel's high vantage point and in the glow of lights placed near the launching area, she saw several men, one of whom would be Ralph, running back and forth to the different launchers. She searched for Dora amongst the gathered onlookers who stood on the grass behind the roped off area, but she couldn't see her friend. Dora had asked Isabel to accompany her to the area, and she would have if she had known the couple were leaving.

Another radiant burst of light blazed across the sky. A shower of yellow, blue, green, and red stars floated like confetti before the sparks burned out. But before the stars disintegrated completely into nothingness, another shinning burst of light lit up the heavens, sending more fountains and stars trailing toward the earth. Each burst of light was followed by another, and another, and then another.

With each launch of the rockets, the audience joined the *boom, boom, varoom,* with an accompaniment of their own. In chorus, they *ooohed*, then *ahhhed* each display separately as the show rapidly built toward the grand finale.

Excitement rose in Isabel's throat and cheeks. It was such

a beautiful night aglow with light and sound. The air was heavy with the smell of sulphur and the taint of singed casings that held the powders of the explosives. Tomorrow the ground below would be littered with the empty casings; only a reminder of today's birthday celebration.

A short distance away Isabel looked down on a group of children gathered on the greens with their parents, waving sparklers. Was it only yesterday that she had done the same thing? The children danced and hopped like a dozen darting fireflys, enjoying their own show as much as the one overhead.

Another burst of color filled the sky, turning the surface of the bay into a yellow, blue, red, and green rainbow before the sparks sizzled out, leaving the water as slick and black as onyx. Another burst sparked the sky, and as Isabel watched it slowly fade, she turned to look across the heads of the crowd, and saw Cooper. His eyes were on her, and the look he sent her was as potent as a kiss. The noisy activity around her dulled from a roar to a buzzing silence no louder than the drone of a bee. In that moment, it was as though the two of them stood alone on the ramparts, their gazes locked, their thoughts centered on each other.

A rush of warmth flushed her cheeks. Time stood still before someone nudged him, probably Marcella, and he dragged his gaze from hers. Isabel stared at the back of his head, her heart growing heavy in her chest. She swallowed. Smothering a sob, she turned again to face the water, and watched the drizzle of stars through shimmering, blinding tears.

It was dark. Excitement grew as the crowd waited for the last big boom. Soon the spectacular explosion rent the air, and the band began to play "The Star-Spangled Banner." Hats were lifted from heads, hands covered hearts, and people joined words with the music. As the last notes trilled to silence, a flash of light on the ground near the rocket launchers followed by a giant boom made those watching believe it was all part of the ending.

Until the smoke cleared, revealing a man writhing on the ground.

From behind the roped-off area, a woman screamed. She pushed forward and began running toward the crowd, clawing her way past the people gathering around the downed man.

Horrified, Isabel watched along with the others.

"Oh, my God. It's Ralph!"

Twenty-one

~

Isabel wasn't certain how long it took her to fight her way through the crowd, down the stairs, and to the roped-off area where people flooded beyond the marked boundaries. It seemed like an eternity. The soft whisperings floating around her barely penetrated into the stunned void of her brain.

I have to get to Dora.

"Nothing much anyone can do for a fellow with such serious burns," someone whispered.

Poor Dora.

"Best if they just take him to the hospital and make the poor fellow as comfortable as possible."

Poor Ralph.

"It's only a matter of time."

In the circle of people Isabel heard a woman's heartbreaking keening. The sound pierced clear to her soul.

Dora, Dora, I'm so sorry.

"And to think he just got engaged."

"A real shame, I'd say."

"Please, please, let me pass," Isabel said. When the curious onlookers tightened their ranks, Isabel began elbowing through them. "She's my friend. She needs me."

It was Mr. Gay who heard her and offered assistance. "Let

her pass," he said. "She's a friend of my daughter's."

When Isabel entered the circle, she saw another small gathering of people standing around the man and woman in the center. Someone had positioned several lanterns near the fringe of the circle, and the yellow glow from the high burning wicks cast eerie shadows across the man's burned hands and face.

Poor, poor, Ralph.

Mr. Gay ushered Isabel to stand beside Dora, who kneeled next to Ralph. "Dora," she said, placing her hand on her friend's shoulder.

Dora didn't respond, but kept up her pitiful moaning. Ralph lay sprawled on his back, motionless. He was either unconscious or in shock, or maybe a combination of the two. Isabel's experienced eye told her that he had suffered several second- and possibly third-degree burns on both his hands and face, and that the burns needed immediate attention. No one seemed to be doing anything.

"Dora," she said again, shaking her friend's shoulder lightly. "It's Isabel." She dropped down on her knees beside her friend to take a closer look at Ralph's injuries.

"Ysabel?" Dora blinked. "Oh, thank God you're here. He—" She shot a look at the small gathering of people and pointed at Dr. Reed. "He won't do anything. He says the burns are too bad." Tears rolled from Dora's eyes. "I—I don't believe him."

Isabel glanced where Dora pointed. There were so many doctors in town that she didn't know them all. Ralph might be beyond the doctor's help, but he could at least make the patient more comfortable.

"Take off your petticoat, Dora."

"My petticoat?"

"It's white where mine is red, and I assume it's reasonably clean."

Dora's eyes pleaded. "Can you help him, Ysabel?"

"Dora, dear, I'm not saying I can help him, but I can darn

well ease his pain. Do you know if there is any reasonably clean water around here?"

For a moment Dora concentrated. "Yes," she said, "over there beside the base of the fort." She pointed. "Someone supplied ice and drinks for the workers."

"I'll need that water," Isabel said, "and I'll need your petticoat."

Soon the bucket of ice water was by her side. After the bucket was brought to her, and Dora had shed her petticoat, Isabel tore the material into squares and strips, doused the pieces in the icy water, rung them out, and then began wrapping Ralph's hands in the material. Next she draped the strips over his face.

"See here, young woman. Who are you to attend this man?" Isabel recognized the man who spoke to be the supposed doctor.

"It's Isabel Gomez," someone said. "She's some kind of healer."

"I'm no healer," she assured the man. "I'm an herbalist. My mother, Kalee Gomez, was a healer, though, and I saw her once attend a man with burns. She said wrapping the wounds in cold water-soaked bandages would ease the burn's sting until further treatment could be administered."

"She ain't nothing but a quack." The remark came from someone at the back of the circle.

"No further treatment needed," the doctor insisted. "Best to leave him. This man is beyond feeling pain."

"He's alive, is he not?" She glared at the pompous man. "And how do you know he's beyond feeling pain?"

"I'm a doctor, that's how. Besides, the man's in shock."

Dora, who had been listening to the exchange, swung toward the doctor like a mother hen protecting her chicks. "Ysabel's right. How do you know what my Ralph is feeling?" She turned toward Isabel. "I don't know why I didn't think of it before. You can treat him. Go home and get your salves, or whatever. The one for burns."

"Dora, love, I don't think . . . My salves are for minor

burns. Not burns as serious as Ralph's. You realize his eyes could be burned as well—"

"Using your salve is better than not doing anything. You said as much yourself."

"Excuse me, please allow me to pass." Isabel recognized the voice immediately as Cooper's. She saw him step into the circle, Marcella not far behind him. He moved to where Ralph lay in a semiconsciousness state.

He looked at Isabel. "Bad?"

She nodded her head. Cooper looked toward the doctor. "Can't you do anything?"

"No, he can't do anything," Dora said, jumping to her feet once again. "Ysabel is taking care of him. She's the one who wrapped his wounds, and she's going home now to get her medical supplies."

Cooper looked at Isabel for affirmation. She nodded her head again.

Marcella called from the sidelines. "Come away from that woman now, Cooper." When several people glanced at her, she looked uncertain. "I—I need to leave. I—I feel faint."

Isabel turned toward Cooper, and spoke in a whisper. "I do have a salve for burns. What about you? Anything on your shelves that might help him?"

Cooper shook his head. "Not all my compounds have arrived. I can think of a few things that might help him, though, like a tepid bath with sulphate of iron. It would give him some relief from his pain, but your wet bandages are probably doing the same thing. Besides, it's best we don't move him immediately until we know more."

Marcella interrupted again. "Cooper, I'm feeling very lightheaded. I-I think I'm going to—"

"Damn it all," Cooper responded, "where's your father when you need him? Someone please hold up that woman so we don't have two people requiring medical assistance."

"Cooper? What's wrong with you? You know where Daddy is." Marcella sounded like a belligerent child. "He took Mother home."

Isabel saw Roderick Duval, who must have followed her down from the ramparts, move to stand by Marcella's side. Gratefully Marcella clutched his proffered arm and sagged against him.

"I've heard of another treatment," Cooper said, "alum mixed with egg whites and lard. But I know I've not received any alum yet." He thought a few moments. "But one of your salves is probably just as good. Maybe better. You run home and get your things. I'll stay with the patient."

Cooper watched as Isabel hurried off, a bundle of efficiency, into the dark. He turned back to the patient.

"See here, young man." The elderly doctor squinted at him. "Oh, it's young Cooper. I didn't recognize you in this light. I'm Dr. Reed. Remember, we met at Jack Kent's house a few weeks back. You're marrying Kent's beautiful daughter, aren't you?"

The man rocked back on his heels. He didn't look like any doctor Cooper had known. He looked more like a pompous fool.

The man spoke again. "I don't think you need to concern yourself with this bit of unpleasantness." He dipped his head to where Ralph lay on the ground, Dora kneeling beside him.

"Dr. Reed, Dr. Reed," Marcella called from where she hung on Roderick Duval's arm. "It's me. Marcella. Jack Kent's beau—daughter. I told Cooper he shouldn't concern himself with this, but of course he wouldn't listen. It's that Gomez woman. She's cast a spell on him."

A man in the crowd snickered. "If she's talking about that gal in the red dress, I could fall under her spell meself."

"Oh, I'm sooooo dizzy," Marcella said, swaying slightly. She drooped against Duval's arm again.

Scatterbrained is a more apt description. "I'm needed here, Marcella," Cooper said. "And if we're lucky, maybe Miss Gomez's salve will help this poor fellow. It's certainly better than not doing anything."

Miss Gay lifted her head and attempted a smile. "I trust

Ysabel. She knows her herbs. Her creams and salves are wonderful."

Cooper could tell the woman was beside herself with grief. "I'm sure you're right, Miss Gay. In fact, I know you are. I had a terrible rash, and the salve she used on my back and shoulders made it completely disappear. It stopped itching in no time."

Marcella heard the comment and looked shocked. "Used? Just how did she use it?" Her gaze drilled into Cooper's. "You said she gave you the salve—you never said she—"

"I'm back," Isabel called, approaching the circle. On her arm she carried a basket. The crowd of onlookers parted, allowing her to pass.

"Eek! She's brought her black cat." Marcella jumped behind Roderick when Grimalkin sashayed into the circle, following on the heels of his mistress. "I knew it! Isabel Gomez is a witch. If we're not careful, she'll cast a spell on all of us."

"A spell?" There were rumblings among the crowd.

Marcella appeared satisfied when people around her shifted uneasily on their feet. "Yes, spells. Love spells. Warts. We'll all grow—grow warts!"

"Warts?" The speaker chuckled. It was the same man who had spoken earlier. He hiccupped. "The way she looks, she can make things grow, but it sure ain't warts."

"Gentlemen," a voice in authority broke in. "There are ladies present here. In case you've forgotten, this is a very grave situation and not a time for lewd remarks."

"Sorry."

Lately Cooper had begun to think that Marcella didn't have the sense to come in out of the rain. It was best he return to her side. She appeared fast approaching one of her bouts of hysterics. He wanted to choke her for claiming that Isabel was a witch. In this crowd where emotions were running high, and a few people had had more than their share of holiday whiskey, who knew what her accusations might stir up.

Isabel watched Cooper return to stand by Marcella. Her

heart sank when he claimed his rightful place beside her, and when she heard his words.

"Thank you, sir," he said, "for attending my fiancée." He waved Roderick aside. "I'll take over now."

Isabel was a fool to believe that she and Cooper could be anything but enemies. The look they had exchanged on the ramparts during the fireworks display had meant nothing. Nor had his earlier show of confidence in her medical efficiency.

For a moment she had begun to believe that the two of them could work side by side as professionals. That certainly wasn't going to happen, just as he wouldn't be giving up Marcella either. Or Marcella wouldn't be giving him up. Isabel had misjudged the whole situation.

But at the moment she had more important things to attend to. Her true friends needed her. She dropped to her knees beside Dora and her father and began to slowly peel away the dampened cloths on Ralph's hands. She would leave the bandages covering his face for last.

At home, after checking her supplies and her cure book, she had determined that an aloe gel was the best thing she had for the use of burns. She had made the gel from juice extracted from the aloe vera plant, then mixed it with seaweed. She had also picked off several pieces from the aloe plant growing in her garden room and had brought them along with her as well.

What she hadn't meant to bring with her when she returned was Grimalkin. She thought for certain that she had closed him up in the garden room before she left, but here he was already causing a disturbance.

No, she corrected herself, it was Marcella with her petty selfishness. A witch indeed! *Were I a witch, I'd draw on that power now to help my friends.*

"Neow, neow."

She ignored her pet and began to gently massage the aloe gel into Ralph's hands.

Everyone watched. Beside her, Grimalkin's purr seemed to

take center stage over the muted whisperings floating among the onlookers.

Really, Grim. How can you purr at a time like this? The cat made several body passes against her shoulder. The salve seemed to grow hot on her fingers—healing, soothing warmth flowed through her fingers—as she gently massaged first one of Ralph's hands, then the other.

"Neow, neow."

"Hush," Isabel warned, nudging the bothersome cat away.

Grimalkin remained undaunted. He stayed by her side and continued to purr.

Very carefully Isabel began removing the dampened bandages covering Ralph's face. As she carefully pulled away the cloth, he flinched. Please God, she prayed silently, let this salve at least dull his pain. Once the strips were removed, Isabel examined the burns, thinking they didn't appear quite as serious as she remembered. Oh, they were serious skin lesions, but hopefully not life threatening.

Isabel dipped her fingers back into the aloe gel. It felt like warm oil to the touch. She glanced suspiciously at the container before rubbing her digits together.

"Neow, neow."

Grim, can't you see I'm busy? This is serious stuff I'm handling here. Please leave me to it.

"Neow, neow." Isabel froze. She cast a suspicious glance at the feline, and realization dawned. If there were any magical cures being dispensed, they weren't hers. They were Grim's.

Yes, now!

Isabel would agree to anything to rid herself of her bothersome pet. Very gently she began to smooth the gel onto Ralph's face.

He jerked. Moaned. Blinked. "Isabel? Dora?"

Like wildfire, a murmur spread over the crowd. Several people caught their breath, disbelief marking their faces as they stared down at the injured man.

"Dora, honey?" Ralph said. "What—what happened?"

"Ralph?"

He blinked again and glanced around at the group who had inched closer. On seeing Grimalkin, not far from his face, his orange-gold eyes glowing as bright as any Fourth of July sparkler, Ralph smiled.

"Hi, old puss. I haven't seen you in a long time." With a shaky hand, he stroked Grimalkin's head while the cat purred. "How you been, old boy?" Then his gaze locked on his hands. He flipped them from front to back. They appeared blotchy, but the redness seemed to fade as he examined them. "These suckers hurt like the devil a moment ago. I must have been dreaming."

"Ralph," Dora said. "Oh, Ralph, you are going to be okay." She bent over and kissed him full on the lips. Then she looked at Isabel, her face glowing, her eyes brimming with tears. "I knew you could help him, Ysabel. I just knew you could."

Even to Isabel, Ralph's burns now appeared minor. Not anything like they had when she first had examined him. His skin was still blotchy and red, and marked with a scattering of blisters. She would send him home with the aloe gel, which should keep his skin from scarring.

"Amazing," Dr. Reed said, bending closer to get a better look at the patient. "What's in that salve, young woman?"

From the sidelines there was a rustle of movement. Marcella pushed away from Cooper and stepped closer to the center of the circle. She pointed a finger at Isabel. "It's her," she said. "She's a witch. First she cast a spell on my fiancée, and now she has cast a spell on that poor, injured man. We all saw his wounds. It was you, Dr. Reed, who claimed the man was near dead. Now look at him."

"Come on, Marcella," Cooper said, stepping to her side. "I'll see you home."

When he tried to lead her away, she screeched, "A witch, the devil's spawn."

The crowd moved backward.

"Witch!" Cooper glared at Marcella. "Isabel is no more a witch than you are. She is just a woman who plays at being a doctor, and this time she got lucky. That man had no serious burns. It was an honest mistake. The light here is poor. Look around you."

The dim light reflecting from the nearby lamps cast wavy shadows. Legs, arms, and torsos looked more like trees where they were shadowed against the ground.

"He's no more near death," Cooper said, "than you or I."

But Marcella wasn't to be thwarted. "Even now," she accused, "you remain under her spell. You're defending her. I tell you, she's a witch. Why else would she steal my betrothal gift to you?"

"Marcella, you're upset. I explained what happened with those links. I'm wearing your gift now." He lifted up one arm and showed the cuff buttons to the crowd. Then he looked at Marcella. "It's you I plan to marry, not her."

"Meow, meow."

Grimalkin made a beeline for Marcella's ankles.

"Meow, meow."

He made one brush by her skirts, and then another. Roderick Duval, who stood on one side of Marcella, looked down at Grimalkin when the cat made a few passes against his ankles as well.

"Meow, meow."

Cooper sidestepped the animal, and Marcella shrieked, jumping behind Roderick. Her position seemed to satisfy the cat because he began weaving around the couple's ankles.

Isabel, watching her pet's sudden strange behavior, began to suspect the old fairy cat was up to his no-good tricks.

"Come here, Grimalkin." The cat ignored her. He purred louder.

"Sounds like a dern pigeon," someone remarked.

Cooper clamped his fingers around Marcella's arm. "I'm taking you home," he said. He gently pulled her from behind Roderick's back.

The wind picked up. Skirts, hats, hair lifted in the sudden breeze. With the approach of the wind, the fight seemed to go out of Marcella. She blinked several times and looked from Roderick to Cooper then back to Roderick again. A dazed expression clouded her face. Then she did the strangest thing. She batted her long black lashes at Roderick and smiled dreamily into his eyes.

Sighing, she said, "Roderick."

"Marcella," he replied. His response sounded as breathless as hers.

Isabel, along with the others, watched the strange exchange. Roderick Duval's expression was that of a lovesick swain, Marcella's that of a lovesick female. Cooper Adair looked angry enough to chew nails.

"Come," he demanded. "I'm taking you home now. We've had enough ostentatious displays for one night." When he said this, he glared at Isabel.

Grimalkin made several more passes around Marcella's and Roderick's legs. Before they could move, Cooper had to push the feline away with his foot.

"No," Marcella insisted.

"No?" the crowd cried in unison, looking first at Marcella then to Cooper, then back to Marcella again.

"I don't want you to walk me home," she continued. Shaking free of Cooper's hold, she laced her fingers through Roderick Duval's arm. The young man's hand covered hers protectively. "Roderick will walk me home."

She looked up adoringly into his face. He, being several heads taller than the diminutive woman, looked down adoringly into her face. "I'll be happy to walk you home. From now on, I'll walk beside you. Anywhere you wish to go."

Arm in arm, the couple left the scene.

"Damndest thing I ever saw," a man in the crowd said. "Thought she was betrothed to that other fellow."

"I've never seen anything quiet so romantic." This remark came from a woman.

"Strangest night I've ever experienced." Someone else agreed with the speaker.

Across the crowd Isabel's eyes locked with Cooper's. Her

breath caught in her throat, and her knees felt weak as he sent her a look that mimicked her own.

It was Dora who broke the silence. Her eyes locked on Isabel when she made her little speech. "I guess you'll be leaving us soon, Mr. Adair, seeing as how your betrothed has taken up with another."

"Leaving? No, I don't think so." The corner of his lips turned up in the smile that Isabel had grown to love. "My future is here," he said.

Dora looked from one to the other. "Yes, I expect it is, but now if you two will excuse us, I need to get my man home."

Mr. Gay helped Ralph to stand on his somewhat shaky legs.

"A witch? Now if that don't beat all." The stranger's words drifted on the breeze as he moved within a group away from them.

After Ralph was on his feet, Isabel watched Dora fling her arms around his neck and hug him. She turned, saying, "Ysabel, it was you who saved my Ralph. How can I ever repay you?"

"Don't be silly. It was someone wiser than I am who saved him. I'm assuming we all overreacted. Apparently his burns weren't as bad as we first believed. I'm sure the cold compresses made from your petticoat and ice water helped, and he was probably stunned senseless from the force of the explosion."

"What happened anyway?" Ralph asked. He still looked a little dazed, and nobody had answered his question earlier.

"A firecracker went off in your hands," Mr. Gay explained. "If the casings aren't packed so that the pyrotechnic compound is thoroughly compressed, the cavity left in the mixture malfunctions at the time of ignition."

"I do remember lighting the fuse," Ralph said, "but then after that I don't remember anything until I came to and found Grimalkin staring at me."

"Grimalkin?" Isabel looked around the nearly empty space.

"I've got him," Cooper said, bending to scoop the big black

tom into his arms. He stroked the cat's head, and Grimalkin's eyes slitted in pleasure.

Isabel moved to stand closer. "I thought you abhorred cats."

"Not anymore," he answered. "I'll be eternally grateful to this one."

"Neooow, neooow."

"Always," Cooper said.

Everyone laughed.

"I don't know about the rest of you, but I'm tuckered out." Ralph draped his arm around Dora's shoulder. "What say you, shall we head home?"

The five of them left the shadow of the fort behind, along with the littered reminders of the day's near tragedy, and headed toward the road. Tomorrow would be soon enough to put things right again. Leaving Isabel and Grimalkin at the gate, Mr. Gay, Dora, and Ralph continued on down the street toward their respective destinations.

Once inside the walled courtyard, Isabel closed the gate, and Cooper sat Grimalkin back on the ground. The cat immediately bounded toward the "love" tree and jumped up to his favorite perch where the two trees, palm and oak, joined.

Cooper took Isabel's hand, and, leading her toward the tree, he said, "Tell me about the legend."

"Legend? I seem to recall you saying you didn't believe in fairy tales and legends."

"I've said a lot of things since coming to this town that I'm sorry for. One of those was tonight, and when we first met, I scorned your profession."

Her eyes grew large, round, and she would have spoken, but he silenced her with his finger against her lips. "You were very much the professional this evening when you attended Ralph. A trained doctor couldn't have done better." He stopped himself. "Let me say, the trained doctor didn't do any better."

"Then you no longer think me a quack? A snake-oil salesman?"

"No. I think you're a very smart, intelligent woman who can probably teach me a few things about herbs and healing. What your salve did for that young man was nothing short of a miracle."

"A miracle? Oh, no. It was nothing like that. I think everyone there overreacted, and that Ralph wasn't as seriously injured as we first believed. The cool compresses helped, and so did the aloe—"

"And so did Grimalkin."

She jerked her gaze to his. "How—"

"I'm not blind, Isabel. I saw those wounds. They were serious. And I saw what happened to Marcella. Now that I think about it, odd things happen when that cat purrs like a pigeon and rubs against a person's legs."

"A coincidence," she said. "My *padre* claimed Grimalkin was magic, but I believe my *madre*'s theory. She said, 'The only magic that rascally old cat is capable of is disappearing when he's scolded.'"

Cooper laughed. "I can see that as true, but those other things."

"Trust me," she said, "he's nothing but an old cat." Isabel didn't have to tell him how old.

"The legend," Cooper said.

"The legend," Isabel began. She related to Cooper the story of the two lovers, the Indian princess and her Spanish warrior, who met secretly beneath this very tree and fell in love.

"Like us," Cooper said. He looked deep into her eyes. "We did fall in love here, or I did. What about you, Isabel?"

"Yes," she whispered, glad at last that her secret was out. "Yes," she said, louder. When Cooper opened his arms, she flew into them.

He kissed her, she kissed him back, their breathing quickened, and he held her away. "I want to know the rest."

Isabel went on to tell him about how the couple met their death at the hand of the princess's brothers, how the lovers had died in each other's arms. She paused and looked up at the two trees. "That is why this oak and palm grow together from the same root. They are a symbol of the young couple's love."

She wouldn't tell him all the legend; the part about the cat would remain her secret. Isabel stole a look at the faithful Grimalkin still perched in the tree. His fur was the same as the leaping cat's, and the same color as the legendary couple's hair. His cat's eyes were the same orange-yellow as the amber crucifix that was placed on the lover's bodies. Isabel knew without a doubt that Grimalkin was the magic cat Felis, who once lived in the sky as a mystical constellation.

She leaned closer to Cooper. It was magic that he loved her back.

She continued, "According to my *madre,* if a couple decides to marry and the man asks for his lady's hand beneath this tree that grows as one, their marriage will be a lasting one filled with much happiness."

"I like that part of the legend." Cooper kissed her playfully on the nose. "Will you marry me, Isabel? And fill my life with more happiness than you already have?"

"Yes, yes," she answered. He pulled her into his arms and sealed his proposal with a kiss.

Breathless, Cooper pulled away. "I want to make love to you, Isabel. What does the legend say about that?"

Unbeknownst to the two, Cooper's last statement made Grimalkin's eyes pop open. If they had looked at him, which they didn't, they would have seen those amber-gold orbs glowing against his black fur like some distant bright stars.

"I think," Isabel said, standing away from him, "that from now on, you and I will make our own legend."

She turned and flew toward her house with Cooper in hot pursuit.

He ran after her and noted as he did so that she had left him a trail to follow. Not that he needed it; he had made this trek numerous times in his mind. First a red petticoat, then a red dress. At the top of the stairs, he stepped over a couple of shoes. Then there was a camisole, and a pair of drawers. He froze as the light from a lantern on the bedside table flared into life.

Isabel faced him, her hair hanging loose and flowing. She looked no different tonight than she had that night he had watched her air bathing, except tonight all of her would belong to him. A dusky nipple peeked through a strand of golden hair that fell over her creamy shoulders. Cooper allowed his gaze to drink her in, and at that moment he knew the truth of the words that a person's body was a temple. He would worship in hers tonight.

She moved toward him without a show of timidity. When she met him, she helped him remove his shirt, his trousers, his shoes, and his inhibitions. No longer were there any suppressed feelings to hide from this woman; this woman he had coveted from the first day he met her wearing men's britches by the river.

Cooper had fallen in love with her then.

Isabel's heart fluttered against her ribs. She smiled at him when at last they both stood naked. "Aren't you afraid you'll grow warts?" she asked.

"Oh, you can make things grow, my Isabel, but it sure ain't warts."

He placed her hand against his erection. "Oh," she said, "I've always been good at growing things."

He laughed, and they fell back on the bed together, nearly pulling the mosquito netting from around the bed, until Isabel saved it.

"Without this," she said, holding up a hunk of the net in her hand so he could climb under, "we'll be eaten alive."

"I'm sure there will be a lot of that going on, with or without the net."

Whatever did he mean?

His hand slid lower and touched her at the golden nest of curls at the apex of her thighs.

He thought he would tease her. "Same rules for this *privy* as the one outside."

"Rules?"

"I'm not to abuse the privy."

She laughed then. That same throaty laugh that had curled his toes and straightened other parts from the first time he heard it. "Depends on your definition of abuse."

He kissed her, and she kissed him back. Sweaty limbs touched, entwined. When he thought she was ready to take him inside her body, he paused and looked down into her beautiful face.

"This will hurt the first time," he said.

"Is this the abuse?" she asked.

"Yes," he responded.

"Then let's have it and get it over with."

When he thrust inside her, he felt her muscles flinch, and heard her mumble the word "Abuse."

After a moment, they began to move together in the dance that was as old as time itself. He led, she followed, and soon they were twirling out of control. Afterward, they lay in each other's arms, sated.

"Now I know what Consuela meant."

"Consuela?" Cooper kissed her on the shoulder. "Who is Consuela? Another one of your legendary characters?"

"A fairy godmother of a sort."

"That's nice," he said sleepily. "What did this Consuela say that you now understand?"

"She said, 'De louts are put in dis world for only one purpose and dat is to pleasure us women de only way a man can.' "

Cooper lifted up his head and looked at her. "Nice fairy godmother?"

Isabel laughed softly, then began trailing little kisses over his forehead.

"She was nice all right. Nicer than you'll ever know. . . ."

A wind sighed through the trees, setting the many wind-bells into motion, filling the night with the sound of the tinkling, magical music. A perfect accompaniment to the mating dance taking place inside.

Outside, in the branches of the "love" tree, Grimalkin lounged, serving as household god and protective spirit.

"Meow, meow."

Author's Note

~

Unknown to some, the city of St. Augustine, Florida, founded by Spaniards under Don Pedro Menendez de Aviles on September 8, 1565, is the first permanent settlement, oldest city, and cradle of Christianity in North America.

Growing up in north Florida, I had the privilege of visiting the city both as a child and as a young adult, but it wasn't until much later when I became interested in writing, and in history, that I learned what a true treasure the ancient town is.

This book was born of the town with its narrow streets lined with oaks and palms, the seawall, the Castillo de San Marcos, the Spanish houses with covered balconies, the gardens with yard walls, and lastly, Henry Flagler's grand hotels, the Ponce De León and the Alcazar.

Several sojourns to the city led me to tour the oldest drugstore, where the seed of my idea took root. For purposes of my story, I moved the building to St. George Street, but the same vernacular structure with jigsawn decorative features is located on Orange Street and still stands today. From 1887 until 1960 it operated as Speissegger Drug Store.

There actually is a tree that is both oak and palm, and is known by locals as the "love" tree. The lore attached to this tree is vague, so I took poetic license and made up my legend from bits and pieces I heard about the tree.

The Ponce de León and Alcazar Hotels were built in the Spanish Renaissance style. When the Ponce was completed in 1887, it was the first major structure in the United States constructed of poured concrete. Mr. Flagler opened seven studios in the rear of the Ponce De León Hotel in 1889 and were occupied by a group of talented New England landscape painters whose canvases help make Florida landscapes familiar throughout the United States.

Grimalkin was born from my love of cats, and I patterned his behavior after both of my feline-fatales. I hope that Isabel, Cooper, and Grimalkin's story will leave you believing in the power of magic. That magic we call love.

I love to hear from my readers. You can write to me c/o The Berkley Publishing Group, 375 Hudson Street, New York, New York 10014, or E-Mail me at ccotten@mindspring.com.

DO YOU BELIEVE IN MAGIC?
MAGICAL LOVE
The enchanting new series from Jove will make you a believer!

With a sprinkling of faerie dust and the wave of a wand, magical things can happen—but nothing is more magical than the power of love.

☐ *SEA SPELL* by Tess Farraday   0-515-12289-0/$5.99

A mysterious man from the sea haunts a woman's dreams—and desires...

☐ *ONCE UPON A KISS* by Claire Cross

0-515-12300-5/$5.99

A businessman learns there's only one way to awaken a slumbering beauty...

☐ *A FAERIE TALE* by Ginny Reyes   0-515-12338-2/$5.99

A faerie and a leprechaun play matchmaker—to a mismatched pair of mortals...

☐ *ONE WISH* by C.J. Card   0-515-12354-4/$5.99

For years a beautiful bottle lay concealed in a forgotten trunk—holding a powerful spirit, waiting for someone to come along and make one wish...

VISIT PENGUIN PUTNAM ONLINE ON THE INTERNET:
http://www.penguinputnam.com

ices slightly higher in Canada

yable in U.S. funds only. No cash/COD accepted. Postage & handling: U.S./CAN. $2.75 for one
ok, $1.00 for each additional, not to exceed $6.75; Int'l $5.00 for one book, $1.00 each addition-
We accept Visa, Amex, MC ($10.00 min.), checks ($15.00 fee for returned checks) and money
ers. Call 800-788-6262 or 201-933-9292, fax 201-896-8569; refer to ad # 789 (10/99)

nguin Putnam Inc.	Bill my: ☐ Visa ☐ MasterCard ☐ Amex _____(expires)
. Box 12289, Dept. B	Card#
wark, NJ 07101-5289	Signature

ase allow 4-6 weeks for delivery.
ign and Canadian delivery 6-8 weeks.

to:	
ne _____	
dress _____	City _____
te/ZIP _____	Daytime Phone # _____

a to:	
ne _____	Book Total $ _____
dress _____	Applicable Sales Tax $ _____
_____	Postage & Handling $ _____
te/ZIP _____	Total Amount Due $ _____

This offer subject to change without notice.

FRIENDS ROMANCE

Can a man come between friends?

❏ **A TASTE OF HONEY**

by DeWanna Pace   0-515-12387-0

❏ **WHERE THE HEART IS**

by Sheridon Smythe   0-515-12412-5

❏ **LONG WAY HOME**

by Wendy Corsi Staub   0-515-12440-0

All books $5.99

TIME PASSAGES